SHADOWLARK

SHADOWLARK

MEAGAN SPOONER

carolrhoda LAB

MINNEAPOLIS

Carolrhoda Lab™
An imprint of Carolrhoda Books
A division of Lerner Publishing Group, Inc.
241 First Avenue North
Minneapolis, MN 55401 U.S.A.

Website address: www.lernerbooks.com

Cover and interior photographs: © iStockphoto.com/Jacek Sopotnicki
(tunnel); © iStockphoto.com/Yekaterina Rashap (copper pieces);
© iStockphoto.com/Stanislav Rishnyak (sunburst circles).

Main body text set in Janson Text 11/15.
Typeface provided by Linotype AG.

Library of Congress Cataloging-in-Publication Data

Spooner, Meagan.
        Shadowlark / by Meagan Spooner.
            pages   cm. — (Skylark trilogy)
        Summary: "In this second book, Lark finally manages to find her
    brother. Against all odds, he's alive—but the reality and implications of his
    survival are too horrible for Lark to comprehend, if she lives long enough
    to think about it." —Provided by publisher.
        ISBN 978-0-7613-8866-1 (trade hard cover : alk. paper)
        ISBN 978-1-4677-1664-2 (eBook)
        [1. Fantasy. 2. Survival—Fiction. 3. Magic—Fiction. 4. Brothers and
    sisters—Fiction.] I. Title.
    PZ7.S7642Sh 2013
    [Fic]—dc23   2012047643

Manufactured in the United States of America
1 – BP – 7/15/13

For Jeanne Cavelos: You told me
I could do this—and I listened.

And for my friends from
Odyssey, who taught me how
much I still have yet to learn.

PART I

CHAPTER 1

The clockwork dawn is loudest in the old sewers. The sound of the machines pushing the sun across its track in the sky echoes through the tunnels, shaking the ground beneath my feet. Mortar crumbles from the ceiling and falls like snow-flakes, surrounding me in a column of white.

"Don't worry," I say, reaching out for Tansy's hand. "This happens every day. It's safe."

She shrinks back from me, standing just beyond arm's reach, twisting her hands together. "Where do we go?"

I turn in place, peering through the flakes of mortar. For a moment I'm disoriented, trying to make sense of the route I've known since childhood. There: a tunnel gapes black through the haze. "This way."

Tansy can read the trees and the sky and the breeze, but this is my domain. This is the world I know. My path is certain—and where I falter, my brother's ghost leads the way. It's as though Basil's just ahead, waiting for me to catch up.

I crawl into the sewer pipe and hear Tansy follow after. Her breathing grows sharp and heavy behind me, the air thick with magic and fear. She's not used to confined spaces. In the clammy dampness of the sewers, her power shines in my second sight like a beacon, golden and warm despite the tunnel's cold.

When we emerge into a junction, Tansy stumbles into the muck on her hands and knees. I reach out to help her to her feet, but she backs away, scrambling up on her own.

"Do you hear that?" she gasps.

I close my eyes, concentrating. There's wind blowing somewhere, whistling through the tunnels, and in the distance I can hear the rustling of leaves. But beyond that there's something out of place, a sound that doesn't belong. Pixies? No. Splashing, like footsteps. Kids, then. Rivals, trying to beat us to our destination. Other students come to break into the school.

"Come on, let's move faster." I can feel Basil's ghost moving further away, slipping out of my senses. "Hurry, and we can beat them there."

"Wait, Lark." She takes a step toward me, then stops, turning her head, trying to pinpoint the source of the sound. "Listen. They're dangerous."

I close my eyes again, and this time I can hear their snarling. My foot slips in the muck, splashing loudly, and the snarls change to howls. They've heard us. In my mind, I can see their hungry white eyes, their sickly grey skin, their ravenous mouths.

Tansy reaches for her bow, but she's not wearing it. Her hand closes on empty space. "What if we run into them in the tunnels? There's no room to fight in there."

"Fight?" My stomach twists, sickening. "You can't fight them, they're just children. They're just like me."

"That's your problem," Tansy protests. "You're too soft. Too trusting. They'll take advantage of that." She takes a deep breath, trying to calm herself. "Fine. If you won't fight, then we need to run. What about this way?" She sticks her head into a pipe leading east.

I know that route. I used it when I was younger. But something halts me, the hairs lifting on the back of my neck. Basil didn't go that way. I can't sense him anymore—and that alone is enough to trigger the alarm bells in my mind. Basil is everywhere down here. It's the only place I know he still exists, the only place where I have more than just a folded paper bird to remember him by.

"No," I whisper. "No. Not that way."

"Lark, we have to go! Now, or they'll find us!"

"That way's wrong, it's too small. I'm too old now to pass that way." Around us the snow is hissing into the water, melting against our skin. Tansy's hair is a halo of white.

"I don't want to die here, underground, so far from the sky." She starts trying to force herself into the pipe, stopped first by her shoulders and then, when she tries to go feet-first, by her hips.

I move away from her, eyes scanning the junction. It looks familiar. I've been here before, although it's different now. Vines have grown through the cracks in the bricks, swarming up the walls, reclaiming these sewers for nature. In the spring it will all be moss and flowers and earth, like there was never a city here at all.

A snowflake lands on my cheek, and I look up. Beyond the swirling white sky I can see a hatch.

"We have to go up."

"What? Are you insane?"

"We're underneath the Institute now. We can go there instead of the school. They'll have the Harvest list there, too—we just have to get into the Administrator's office."

Tansy pries herself back out of the pipe and comes toward me, peering up through the snow. "We'll never make it. There's no ladder. I have no rope. We aren't wearing climbing gear . . . " Her voice fades into the background, still listing the things we'd need to climb up into the white sky.

In the distance, far above us, I can hear a bird singing. My brother speaks to me, as he often does down here in the old sewers, down here where I'm closest to him. I ask him, *How did you do that?*

He smiles. *Magic.*

"Tansy." She stops abruptly, mid-word, turning toward me. I reach out. "Take my hand."

She shrinks away, fearful. "I can't."

"You have to trust me." I take a deep breath. "I promise, I'll keep you safe."

The howls have grown to the point where I can no longer hear the birdsong, but I know it's still there.

Tansy hesitates a moment longer and then reaches out, her palm meeting mine with a jolt that sends the snow swirling away from us, thrashing against the walls of the sewers.

We rise, and the snow rises with us, up into the sky. The hatch bangs open and we go soaring through it to land on the other side. The snow streams through after us, and it takes us both pushing with all our weight to close the hatch against the storm behind us. It slams shut, the sound echoing through the vastness of the space.

We're standing in the rotunda of the Institute, with its domed sky inlaid with gold and precious stones in a mosaic meant to imitate the world beyond. The sun and moon dance across the interior of the dome in tracks much like the one in the Wall outside.

Tansy is silent now, not looking at me, arms wrapped around herself as she crouches on the marble floor. I can't see the halo of power around her anymore—but there's no time, and I haul her to her feet. She pushes my hands away, but at least she's moving again.

Together we hurry across the floor towards a door on the far side marked "Harvest and Resource Administrator" and, below that, a plaque bearing the name "Gloriette." Even though I know she won't be inside—she'll be preparing for the Harvest Day ceremonies where she officiates—my heart still pounds as we approach.

I press my ear to the door, but it's made of iron, and I can hear nothing on the other side of it. But even if the other students don't catch up to us, there are pixies everywhere, and we have no time to waste. I twist the handle, take a deep breath, and shove.

We stumble through, and the door bangs shut behind us. We're standing in Dorian's house, exactly as it was the day I left the Iron Wood. His bed is neatly made in the corner, the dresser stands covered in curios, and the map still hangs above it. I squint, trying to make out the city where my brother was headed, but the lines and words blur before my eyes, impossible to read.

A flicker of city magic, twisted and unnatural, touches my senses. Pixies.

"Come on, Tansy—we have to find the list of names for the harvest."

I start rummaging through Dorian's kitchen. My heart has risen into my throat, choking me, making my mouth taste like bile. Even though it will change nothing if I find the list, I have to *know*. Either my name is on it or it isn't, but at least I can find out if all of this has been worth it—if this time, finally, I'll be where I belong.

The discordant clang of city magic rises all at once, and something metallic and heavy bangs against the shutters. I slam shut the cupboard I'm searching and back away, scanning the room for a place to hide.

Tansy leaps forward before I can stop her. "Enough," she

cries, breaking her uncharacteristically long silence. "We have to fight."

She throws open the shutters.

I gather my own magic, ready to smash the pixies into oblivion—but it's not the city's spies. It's Nix, and it makes straight toward me, wearing its favorite bee form.

"They're coming for you." Its voice is urgent, clipped. *"We have to go, now."*

Who's coming? The other students in the tunnels? The city's pixies? Gloriette and her machines? The Iron Wood scouts? The shadows? It doesn't even matter. "I need to see that list," I hiss.

As I drop to my knees to search under Dorian's bed, Tansy heads for the door. "I'll just go keep watch."

Nix, hovering behind me, watches her go. *"Is that wise?"*

The space under the bed is empty. I sit up, turning to look at the pixie. "Is what wise?"

"Letting her out of your sight. What makes you think you can trust her?"

My stomach twists sickeningly. The pixie drops down to perch on Dorian's dresser amidst the curios—on top of a leather folder. Somehow I'd missed it when I first scanned the room.

"Nix," I breathe. "That's it."

I scramble to my feet. My hands are shaking as they reach for the folder, the one that will contain the list of names for this year's harvest. Finally I can know whether I'll be safe. Whether I can stop running.

From the doorway, a flash of light drags my eyes away from the desk. It's Tansy, glowing with magic—and yet she's not Tansy anymore. She's a figure in white, light shining from every pore, pinprick pupils almost lost in white irises. *Follow the birds*, she says, and I look back down at the folder in my hands.

I pry it open. It's empty, save for a single object—my brother's bird, folded out of old, yellowing paper. As I watch, the edges begin to turn black, as if burned by invisible fire. The scorch marks race inward until the entire bird is consumed. It flaps its wings once, its song more a scream than music. I reach out to try to take it, save it, and it gives way to my touch.

In seconds the bird crumbles away to nothing—nothing except the shadow staining my fingertips.

CHAPTER 2

I jerked awake, a ragged sound tearing out of my throat. The world was dark and white, and for a moment I was back in the sewer tunnel, watching the mortar hiss into the dank water below. Then I blinked, and reality reasserted itself. Snow was falling all around me, frigid ice water rolling down my neck as the flakes melted against my cheeks.

"Are you all right?"

Nix. It hovered a few feet away, the whirring of its clockwork mechanisms sluggish and sleepy.

"What?" My voice was hoarse, like I'd been screaming. "No. Yes, I'm fine."

"You were dreaming."

I grabbed for my blanket to scrub away the water on my face. "So? What do you know about dreams?" It was barely predawn, only the faintest hint of light to the east to tell of morning's approach. What had woken me? The dream? Or something else?

Nix dropped down onto the end of the blanket by my feet. *"She's out scouting the city."*

"Who is?"

"That other one."

I glanced across the embers of the fire at the empty tangle of snow-covered blankets there. Closing my eyes, I tried to make my mind work through the cold and the exhaustion and the remnants of my dream.

The snow had begun a week after I left the Iron Wood, and Tansy had caught up with me only a few days after that. I'd sensed something out there following me, but only sporadically. The fact that her magic only worked in the rain and humidity meant that here, in this dry, frigid air, most of it was buried deep.

I thought I knew who—or what—was following me. I'd stopped and waited, knowing that if it was him, he'd catch up to me. Better to meet him on my terms, find out if he was human or shadow—if he was the boy who'd kissed me or the animal who would've tried to kill me but for the bars of his cage.

I wasn't ready for the stab of disappointment that jolted through me when I saw Tansy's face emerging from the gloom.

"The truth," she'd said, "is that I couldn't stop thinking what trouble you could get into. No magic, no weapons. Alone except for that thing." She jerked her chin at Nix, who crouched sullenly on the opposite side of the fire, watching Tansy in unblinking, frosty silence.

She had followed me at a distance, respecting my desire to travel alone, but after the snow started she was worried I didn't know how to handle myself in the cold, and came in to check on me.

I knew she was worried about him. I wasn't the only one certain I'd be followed as I headed north, away from the safety of the Iron Wood. "He would've fooled anyone," she said, mistaking my silence for shame when she brought it up. "And you didn't know that They turn human when exposed to magic. It's not your fault. If he ever shows his face again, he'll pay."

I thought of the boy in the threadbare shirt, whose pale blue eyes could be so fierce and so soft. I thought of him swimming in the summer lake, and the utter contentment on his face after he'd finished eating dinner in the clearing with the bees. I thought of that last piercing look before we parted, and I held my tongue.

We kept following the ruins of the highway marked on the map in Dorian's house, and we came upon a ridge overlooking the city the next day. A once-vast city that now lay entirely in ruins.

Tansy wanted to head into the remnants of the city immediately, but I decided we'd make camp on the ridge and wait. If there was anyone living there, we'd be able to see the signs of it—smoke rising from chimneys, people moving around the streets. I was sick of flying headlong into situations I knew nothing about. We agreed to stay a couple of days—which, I realized, sleep-muddled mind slow to comprehend, had passed. Unless Tansy had found anything, we'd be heading down into the city today.

I shivered, though I could not be sure if it was because I was cold or because I was frightened. I shoved a hand deep into my pocket until my fingers found the blunt, creased contours of my brother's bird.

I disentangled myself from my blanket and shoved on my boots. Wrapping my heavy coat around my shoulders, I stepped out past our muddy campsite in the shelter of a ruined restaurant and into the freshly fallen snow. I could see the remnants of Tansy's tracks, half-covered, leading away toward the city. She was always going off on her own, impatient—old habits died hard, she said, and she was used to scouting.

I took a deep breath, trying to shake the uneasiness that lingered in the wake of my dream. There was no reason not to trust Tansy's motives for following me. It was only my subconscious reacting to one too many betrayals, looking for the next blow before it landed.

Something was wrong. My instincts caught on before I did, and I turned in a slow circle, keeping myself from shivering in the cold with a monumental effort. There was something in the air, still though it was. My nose picked up leather. Wind. And, impossible over the snow, the green tang of grass.

I knew that scent.

No. NO.

The snow had almost completely covered the tracks we'd made last night. Searching the ground outside our shelter, I found half-filled hollows to indicate Tansy's footprints and mine, the area I'd trampled looking for firewood, a somewhat more recent path to some trees where Tansy must have relieved herself in the middle of the night. I tried to calm my breathing—it sounded harsh and alarm-loud in the still dawn air.

It was my imagination. I'd thought of him, and my mind was producing whatever evidence it could to make it seem like he was here. He'd have to be a shadow again by now—if he'd found us he would have attacked.

As I turned back toward the shelter and the warmth of my blanket, something caught my eye. I would've missed it except that the light to the east was growing, and the snow was beginning to shine as well with an eerie, violet-orange glow.

Footprints.

Not mine or Tansy's—too large. And too widely spaced. My heart in my throat, I followed them as silently as I could. They led to the ground floor of the structure, to the part of the floor that served as roof to our cellar campsite. There the tracks vanished into noise, as though someone had paced back and forth, churning up the snow. The tracks were fresh— fresher than Tansy's leaving to scout the city.

Though I searched, I could not find tracks leading away—and yet there was no one there and no place to hide.

By the time Tansy returned I had erased the tracks, tramping through the snow and disturbing it to the point where it was impossible to tell anyone but me had passed there. She found me kicking and kicking at the snow, my breath steaming the air, soaked to the knee.

Firewood, I told her, showing her a few branches I'd picked up just before she crested our ridge. To make a hot breakfast. To warm us before we set out for the day.

But despite the hot mash of water and grains, and the roar of the flames, and Nix's fire-heated metal body nestled in the hollow of my neck, I couldn't stop shivering.

I had no proof it was him, and yet I knew. It was as though I could feel him out there, somewhere, as though our time spent sharing the same magic, the same sustaining power, had linked us.

Oren. The boy who taught me how to live out here, who saved my life, whose life I saved. The boy who told me he'd follow me anywhere no matter how he tried to stop himself.

The boy I'd learned was a monster.

And I hadn't forgotten what I'd promised him before he left.

If I find you—and if I'm not me—promise me that you'll kill me, Lark.

. . .

I'd thought my home city was big. When I lived there, it was the only city in the world, as far as most inside the Wall knew. It held the last remnants of humanity. The Wall was the edge of the world.

But it was nothing compared to the sprawling monster that filled the valley. The snow had stopped, and from the ridge we could see all the way to the sea, little more than a grey expanse in the distance. My mind half-dismissed the sight of it, unable to digest how big the ocean must be in comparison—instead it focused on the city, something it could almost comprehend.

The city lay in ruins. Even from a distance we could see that the buildings were crumbling, asymmetrical, falling apart. The tallest structures were metal skeletons of buildings that must have once been so tall they would've dwarfed the Institute in my city. Where my city was laid out artistically, aesthetically, with broad streets and well-designed blocks, this city was crowded and sprawling and slapdash, like it had just grown together over the years, and people had just kept adding taller and taller buildings to make more room. I couldn't even imagine how many people must've lived in it before the wars. The tallest spire at the center of the city had something gleaming, reflective, at its top—blinding to look at even from this distance.

As we drew nearer, though, we could see just how dilapidated the buildings were. I fought down a surge of disappointment. Maybe I'd expected a Wall keeping it safe, like the Wall around my own city. Without that shielding against the magicless void in this wasteland, how was anyone but a Renewable meant to survive? Surely the city had to be abandoned—and to judge from the state of the ruins, it would've had to have been abandoned for decades, if not more.

Which meant that there were no experiments going on to do with restoring magic to the wasteland—and no experiments concerning curing my brother and me of what the Institute had done to us. Which meant that there was no reason for my brother to still be here.

Tansy kept up a running commentary as we headed down from the ridge toward the crumbling buildings.

"There are definitely people down there," she continued. "But not many, and they keep themselves hidden pretty well. There's nothing that I can see that stops the shadows from coming in—no Wall like in your city, no scouts like in mine. So maybe the people just stay inside as much as they can."

"We have to find someone willing to talk to us." I scanned the long street ahead of us, littered with debris and heaps of garbage made unidentifiable by age. "Dorian said Basil was headed here. I can't imagine he stayed—this isn't what he was looking for, that's for certain. This place looks like it fell decades ago."

Tansy readjusted the bow on her shoulder, fingering the string idly. "Maybe, if he talked to anyone here, they might know where he headed next."

I didn't answer. The thought of having to make yet another weeks-long journey, this time through even more snow and bitter cold, with my dwindling supplies, was intolerable. Basil was supposed to be here. He was the only other person who survived what the Institute had done to me—he was the only person who would know how to deal with it. I just had to find him before I lost control with Tansy, and everything would be okay.

Even now, despite the dry air, I could sense her power just a few steps in front of me. And I wanted it. Now that I knew I could absorb the innate magic of other people, I could barely restrain myself. It was like my actions in the Iron Wood had opened a floodgate that I didn't have the strength to close.

I kept my eyes on the street. Even though I could still feel Tansy's magic, at least I didn't have to see it with my second sight, glittering and glinting every now and then, as if shining in invisible sunlight.

Nix alighted on my shoulder, the whirring of its mechanisms oddly comforting in the quiet. Despite my desire to travel alone, I was glad for Nix's company—and for Tansy's too. Though when Tansy was near and chattering away, Nix was always silent. I sensed that the machine had something to say, and so I slowed my steps a little, let Tansy get out ahead of me.

Eventually, the pixie ruffled its wings and spoke. "*Smart.*"

"What is?" I kept my voice to a whisper.

"*Letting her walk in front of you. That way if she turns on you, you'll see it coming.*"

Ice trickled down my spine, and the pixie's words in my dream came back to me, clear as day. *Is it wise, letting her out of your sight?*

Nix's mistrust of Tansy had penetrated even my dreams.

"Don't be absurd," I replied. "Tansy's a friend. She's here to look out for me."

"*That other one was your friend too. Where is he now?*" I looked down at it on my shoulder, and it gave the strangest imitation of a human shrug.

The machine had no reason to lie. In fact, it had proven more than once that it was incapable of lying. I watched Tansy's ponytail bobbing with each step and gritted my teeth. I didn't want to be someone who could only trust a pile of magical circuitry, and never another human, flesh and blood like me.

"*Anyway, that's not what I wanted to say.*"

"Well, maybe I don't particularly want to know what you were going to say."

"*Yes, you do.*" Nix was as calm and unemotional as ever.

I stayed silent, counting each of my weary steps in my head.

"*The people living here are watching you.*"

CHAPTER 3

I stopped dead. Tansy was still moving up the street, oblivious to whatever Nix was sensing.

"How do you know they're watching us?" I whispered, arching my back until it popped, turning my head this way and that. If anyone were watching me they'd see a weary traveler stretching—not inspecting the surrounding buildings for watching eyes.

"Watch the windows."

I shifted my attention forward, toward the dark hollows in the buildings. I saw nothing—no faces or movement. I was about to say so when something did move. Subtle, quick. Just a shutter closing in a building on the next block.

Tansy had stopped, and I caught up with her in a few strides.

"I'm pretty sure there's—" I began, keeping my voice low.

"I see them," she breathed back. "Can't tell if they're a threat."

I sensed nothing, no matter how I strained. I couldn't tell if it was due to the inconsistency of this new ability to sense the world around me or the fact that iron made up the skeletons of these buildings, potentially muffling anything inside.

Nix spoke up, its voice even quieter than Tansy's. *"They do not appear threatening. In fact, they appear to be more frightened of us."*

A shutter cracked open nearby, no more than an inch. I could see nothing beyond it but darkness compared to the pale winter sunlight outside.

I took a deep breath. "Hello!" I shouted. "We're not here to cause trouble or harm to anyone. We're travelers, seeking a man named Basil Ainsley."

Only silence answered me. We kept walking, eyes drawn to every quick movement at the windows, ears tuned for each light click or thud of a shutter closing or door locking. The temperature was dropping fast, and we knocked cautiously on a few doors, hoping for shelter. But we got no response, and when, in growing desperation, we tried a few handles, they were all shut tight.

We'd gotten about a mile into the downtown part of the city when a noise made us jump back. The clang of one of the ancient garbage cans lining the streets.

The people here were afraid of something—I couldn't help but think of the most terrifying thing in this wilderness. Shadows. I reached out with everything I had but felt nothing. I tried to make myself move toward the sound but found my feet rooted to the crumbling street.

Tansy slipped her bow from her shoulder in one smooth movement, dropping into a low stance, ready for action. She nocked an arrow to the string and crept toward the sound, slow. I ached to tell her to be careful, but bit my lip, watching.

Just before she reached the cans, a small figure burst out with a frightened yell, darting past Tansy—and straight at me. We collided with a thud, sending me sprawling and my assailant dropping on top of me with a groan of pain.

It was a kid, no more than seven or eight. Dirty in that little-boy way, but in relatively clean clothes. No blood around his mouth. No signs that he was anything other than a little boy. More than anything else, he felt human. He lacked the golden magic glow Tansy and all the Renewables had, but there was no dark void, hungry for magic, as there was with Oren. He felt like nothing—like walking into a room at exactly room temperature.

"Let me go!" he shouted, scrambling backward, eyes darting this way and that. To my astonishment he started to cry as he scuttled sideways into the shadow of a nearby stoop.

Just then a pair of people burst out of the building across the street. A man and a woman, both brandishing weapons. The man, about Tansy's height and thickly bearded, wielded a knife. Much smaller than Oren's knife, and clearly designed as a tool, not as a weapon. The woman, whose expression was even more frantic than the man's, carried a club fashioned from what looked like a piece of a bedpost.

"Get away from my son!" the woman screamed, voice ragged with fear.

Tansy lowered her bow instantly, straightening out of her hunting stance and lifting her hands. I picked myself up off the ground where the boy had knocked me, stumbling backward a few paces.

"We aren't going to hurt him," I said hoarsely, trying to get air back into my lungs. "It's okay."

As soon as I backed up enough that I wasn't between them and the boy, the woman ran past the man to kneel in front of the kid, who was still leaking tears, frightened as much by his mother's fear as anything else. As his mother ran her hands over him, looking for injuries, and mumbled reassurances, the father stepped forward, fingers white-knuckled around the handle of his knife.

"You'd better keep moving," he said, expression largely hidden by his black facial hair.

Tansy moved over to my side, returning her bow to her shoulder, uncertain how to proceed. I knew how she felt.

"Please," I tried again. "I'm just looking for a man named Basil Ainsley. Do you know him? Did he pass through maybe a couple of years ago?"

The man's eyes narrowed, darting to the side as his wife picked up their child, then back to me again. "Why are you searching for this man?"

My throat was so dry my voice came out like sandpaper. "He's my brother."

The man considered this, watching me suspiciously, then shook his head. "I've never heard of him," he said gruffly. "You may have noticed, we're not looking for company. This place isn't for you, you'd better go."

The woman crossed back behind the man again, carrying the boy. I saw a flash of red and realized he'd skinned his knee when we collided. The blood was dripping down his shin.

I took a step forward, and the man reacted instantly, the point of the knife swinging toward me.

"Wait!" I said, freezing. "I just want to—here." I took off my pack, very slowly, and crouched so I could put it on the ground and go through it. Somewhere in there was a pot of salve from Tansy's mother, an herbalist.

As soon as I opened it I saw Nix, who must have darted inside during the commotion. It looked up at me, flicking its wings silently in recognition—and in warning. I knew why it was hiding; without knowing these people's history, it was impossible to know how they'd react when confronted with a machine, the very symbol of the extravagance and wanton use of magic that led to the wars in the first place.

I took out the bag that held my last few apples and tore a

few strips from it, then located the pot and straightened. Both mother and father were watching my every move, wide-eyed, fearful. What had happened to these people that they lived in such fear?

"It's medicine," I said, trying to keep my voice steady and calm. "For his knee, so it heals faster and doesn't get infected."

The mother cradled the boy's head against her, eyes flicking toward the father, who was just noticing the skinned knee for the first time.

"Can I?" I asked, taking a slow step toward them.

The man and woman exchanged glances, as though speaking privately, without words. The woman broke first, taking a step toward me and nodding. "You may."

I couldn't help a little smile at that—she sounded like my own mother, correcting my grammar. Even if she was broken-hearted from losing Basil, even if she largely ignored me in favor of my other brother, Caesar, I missed my mother.

I moved forward, and the woman crouched so that the boy could lean against her while I tended to his knee. He'd stopped crying and was more interested in examining my face and watching what I was doing. Though he grimaced when I mopped up the blood and spread a thin layer of the salve over his scrape, he didn't cry again. I noticed that he had freckles, something no one in my enclosed city had. How strange to see just an ordinary human—not a Renewable, not a shadow—living out here. I wondered how it was possible, but I knew enough that now wasn't the time to ask.

I wrapped the last of the strips around his knee, tying the tightest knot I could. I knew from having two brothers that boys never stayed still long.

"Thank you," his mother murmured as I straightened. "Sean, what do you say?"

"'anks," the boy mumbled before squirming out of his

mother's grasp and making a beeline for the building his parents had emerged from.

"Okay." The man still had his knife between himself and me. "Get going then."

"Brandon," the woman said, chiding. "Be civil."

He shook his head, still watching me, still suspicious. "Don't trust anyone from the outside. We don't know who they are. *What* they are."

The woman looked up, shading her eyes. I followed her gaze to the bright reflective object on top of the spire. It was dimmer now as the sun made its way down the sky. I still couldn't make out its shape, but I thought it might be some kind of crystal, refracting the light into a million different beams across the city. The way the woman gazed at it reminded me of the way people in my city checked the time by the sun disc. Maybe it was a kind of clock.

"It'll be just as dangerous for them out here in a few hours," the woman said, speaking as though Tansy and I weren't there. "She helped our Sean. They're not here to hurt us."

The man's eyes went from me to Tansy and back again. His beard moved as he grimaced beneath it, uncertainty twisting his features.

"Fine," he said eventually, defeated. "One night only. And that one leaves her weapon outside." He seemed more suspicious of Tansy than of me, his black eyes narrowing at her.

Tansy opened her mouth as if considering protesting. I didn't blame her—if they'd tried to take Oren's knife from me, I would've felt naked. I felt a little guilty not volunteering the information that I was armed, too, but I knew it was smarter to keep it on me. I nodded at Tansy and she nodded back, slipping off the bow and her quiver of arrows and giving it to the man. He left them on the stoop as he led us through a revolving door, into the building.

• • •

Once inside, the man retreated to a comfortable-looking stuffed chair in the corner to work on something wooden with his knife. Sean plunked himself down to play with what seemed to be a set of polished round rocks, bouncing them off each other at random, and the woman closed the doors behind us.

They'd made a home in what looked like the lobby of some other building. The marble floors were covered with a slapdash assortment of colorful, overlapping rugs, and the large reception area had been divided into rooms by wooden screens. The revolving door opened directly into what I could only assume was the kitchen and dining area, dominated by a huge fireplace built into the floor and a chimney that descended from the ceiling to hover above it. It must have been a gorgeous piece of art and design back when the building was new, but now it only held a small cooking fire. The flames had an odd green edge to them, and my nose detected the acrid smell of chemicals. When I looked closer I saw that the wood they were burning seemed to be pieces of old furniture. I realized with a jolt that they wouldn't really have access to firewood here in this forest of buildings. They must have been raiding the other ruins—or the rest of the building, which seemed unused—for wood to burn.

The rest of the furniture in the home was an odd mix of ancient-looking pieces, no doubt liberated from the ruins, and rough but solidly made pieces that looked relatively new. Overhead the ceiling was painted with a faded fresco of winged babies and clouds and swirling ribbons, encircled by intricately molded trim.

"I'm Trina," the woman said as I turned in place, inspecting the odd mix of grandeur and hominess. "And you've already met Sean. My husband is Brandon, ignore him. Are you girls hungry?"

I glanced at Tansy, who seemed uneasy, out of place. If even I, who had been raised in a city with buildings like the Institute, felt overwhelmed, she must feel like she'd stepped into another world. And she looked positively naked without her bow at her side.

I smiled at her, trying to look reassuring, and then nodded at Trina. "Extremely," I answered.

Trina laughed and went to the fireplace, lifting the lid of the pot suspended over the flames. The smell of something delicious and savory wafted toward us, and it was all I could do not to drool.

"I'll just add some more water, there'll be plenty for all of us. Come, sit."

"Thank you," I said awkwardly as Tansy and I made for the fireplace, beginning to strip off our outer layers. My nose and my fingertips began to burn and itch as they thawed in the warmth of the room. I kept my pack close so that Nix could stay near me. I could hear nothing and knew it was probably on the verge of hibernation, doing its best to stay silent.

As I looked around the room, something shadowy darted from right to left. All I could see was a blur of feet under the screen. I tensed, staring. While I watched, a pair of black eyes appeared around the edge of one of the screens, gleaming.

Trina noticed my sudden shift and smiled. "Relax. That's just Molly. Don't mind her, she's shy."

There was a faint squeal of protest and a giggle, and the dark eyes vanished again.

Dinner was a stew made of grains and winter vegetables. I was worried about there being meat in it, but Trina assured me that meat was a rare commodity in the city and that they only ate it when they got lucky—and even then, most people didn't have much of a taste for it. Most of their food came from farms outside the city limits, tended by the whole community. When the harvest was good they all ate like kings all winter, and when it was sparse, they all scraped by somehow together.

Afterward Trina made a weak but fragrant tea out of dried flowers, and we sat by the fire, sipping it. Even Molly emerged for this, bare feet tucked up under her skirt and huge round eyes always watching me and Tansy. She looked no more than four or five years old.

"How many of you are there?" I asked, thinking of row upon row of buildings with shutters that closed as we passed.

"Only about two hundred of us now," Trina replied.

"And fewer every week," Brandon added grimly.

Tansy looked up from her tea. "Fewer? Why?"

Brandon leaned back in his chair with a creak. The fabric was worn and faded, and it sagged in the middle where he sat. He shook his head, setting his mug off to one side and retrieving his carving. It seemed to be a rough approximation of a horse, something I'd seen only seen pictures of in my city.

Trina spoke up instead. "It's not a safe place to be, this city. There are . . . things here. Dark things."

Tansy and I exchanged glances, and I knew I had been right. Shadow people. I leaned forward, forgetting my tea. "Maybe Tansy and I can help. Tansy's from a place that's so good at fighting off the shadow people that they're afraid to even go near it. And I—" I thought of the shadow child I'd killed and its cry as its fell. "I've had a little experience."

Tansy leaned forward, eager. "She's being modest. She survived for weeks on her own with a shadow person right on her heels the whole time. Lark's amazing."

I felt my cheeks redden. I hoped they'd read it as modesty, and not as shame.

"Shadow people?" Both Trina and Brandon were looking at us, curious.

"Monsters that eat people," Tansy supplied. "We always just used the word *Them* where I come from, but Lark's word for them is pretty accurate. Isn't that what's attacking your people?"

They exchanged glances, and Trina nodded slowly. "Maybe. It's hard to know exactly what they are. They only come at night, when the Star fades. And if anyone ever sees them, they don't live to tell the tale. They vanish forever. Gone. Taken."

Eaten, I thought, trying not to shudder. "The Star," I repeated. "That's the thing on top of that tower?"

She nodded. "The Star's how we know when they're coming. Once the sun sets and the light from the crystal dies, it's death to be outdoors. Sometimes they break in, though, when they're too hungry to be turned away by locked doors."

I followed her gaze toward the door, where I saw rows of barricades ready to be shoved against it. Though the window shutters were closed, I could see glimpses of light through the cracks. Not nighttime yet, but close.

"Don't worry," said Trina. I knew she was trying to be comforting, and maybe that confidence was enough to fool her children, but I could hear her fear behind her firm voice. "We're safe in here. Brandon's the best woodsmith in the city—nothing's getting through that door."

"Tell us about yourselves," said Brandon, changing the subject.

Tansy answered first, and I settled back against one of the screens, my feet stretched out toward the fire, content to let her tell our story. I slipped one hand inside my pack and felt the cool metal of Nix's body bump up against my fingers. Sill there, still hiding.

I knew I'd never get used to the way Tansy talked about me, like I was some sort of hero or saint. I never heard her sound anything less than sincere, but I couldn't understand her faith in me. Maybe to her, and her people, I was some kind of hero. I'd stopped the army of machines from my city from overrunning the Iron Wood and enslaving the Renewables hiding there.

But my city also never would have known where the Iron Wood was if it weren't for me. And Tansy didn't know about the child I killed. Didn't know how all I wanted to do was find my brother and a place to be safe. That when I saw shadows, I didn't fight—I ran away.

I was so lost in my thoughts that I didn't notice Molly creeping closer to me until a pair of small, warm hands reached for my arm to move it aside. I shifted without thinking, and the little girl crawled into my lap. I froze, glancing up at her parents. Brandon was intent on Tansy's story, but Trina was watching me and Molly with a smile. I could tell by her faint surprise that this was unusual behavior for her daughter, but that she was happy to see her overcoming her shyness. There probably wasn't much opportunity in a life as brutal and ruled by fear as this one.

I was the youngest of my family and never had any little kids around to take care of. Molly was small enough that I had no idea what I was supposed to do with her. Uncomfortable, I shifted my weight, half-hoping the girl would go away if I did. But no. All she did was turn enough so she could crane her head around and look up at me.

"Can I tell you a secret?" she whispered as Tansy continued chattering on. She wrapped her hands around locks of my brown hair, giving a firm tug.

I nodded and let her pull me down so she could whisper in my ear.

"I like your friend."

Of course. Tansy was the social one, after all. The one with the good stories and the rich voice. I smiled at Molly.

"Why don't you go sit in her lap?"

The girl shook her head, impatient, and tugged at my hair for me to lean down again. "No, your secret friend."

I looked down and saw that Nix had half-crawled onto my hand, its jeweled eyes visible on this side of the pack only. It gave a tiny, startled buzz and dropped back into darkness.

Molly laughed and leaned back against me.

What a bizarre child. Way too observant for someone her age. But then, I'd always been quiet, too. Unusual, out of place. Bemused, I put my arms around her.

The atmosphere inside was so congenial and warm that I began to grow drowsy, and I forgot it was only afternoon, not night. But eventually Brandon stood, setting aside his carving and stretching.

"Time for lock-up," he announced. When I looked, I saw that the light coming through the cracks was almost invisible now, no brighter than the firelight inside.

Tansy and I helped move all the barricades into place, taking over from Trina, who usually helped her husband secure the building. The huge wooden structures were far too heavy for one person—I was surprised they were even able to do it normally with just two. *How afraid they must be*, I realized, feeling a little sick. I wished there was something I could do to help them.

Brandon checked and double-checked all the shutters and then sent the children off to bed. I expected Trina to go tuck them in, but it was Brandon's voice I heard murmuring to the children from the room on the other side of the screen from the fire. The warmest room, no doubt.

Trina smiled at us as she finished wiping the bowls and mugs clean. "I'm afraid we don't have beds for you girls, but it sounds like you're used to sleeping on the ground."

I found myself smiling back. "A dry, clean floor next to a

real fire is far more than we were expecting," I promised. "But it's only just dusk now, isn't it?"

Trina nodded, her smile fading a little. "We usually try to sleep after lock-up. It's just easier that way, rather than lying awake in the dark, listening for every sound. The truth is that if they come for us, we'll hear it. Nothing can get through that barrier without making a racket. It's easier for the children, too. No child should have to grow up knowing that the monsters they dream of in the night are real."

My heart constricted. Suddenly the Institute's methods didn't seem quite so monstrous. After all, what would I give to feel safe again every day, to know nothing could get me, that my family could sleep safely? How much would I sacrifice?

My own safety? My life?

My freedom?

CHAPTER 4

After Trina and Brandon had gone to bed, I stayed awake, pacing. As the fire died down the air had grown cooler, but I could still feel sweat pooling in the small of my back.

I'd been given the opportunity to provide my own people with that kind of safety, and I'd run away. Of course, I wasn't a real Renewable—but at the time, the Institute had fooled me into thinking I was. I believed I had that choice, and I chose to abandon my people. Did it matter that the Institute had planned all along for me to run, so they could follow me? I still made a decision.

I wished I knew what had prompted Basil to abandon his task. All I knew was that Basil had volunteered to try to find the Iron Wood, and that at some point in his journey, he'd destroyed his pixie and vanished. Had he made the same choice I did?

I didn't know whether that made me feel better or worse.

A glint at one of the shutters caught my eye, and I backtracked a pace, putting my eye to the crack. I could just see the Star, dim enough now that I could make out its shape. It truly was like a star, or a snowflake—jagged and uneven crystal spires radiating out from its glowing heart. Though the street outside lay in shadow, the Star was high enough up that it was still catching the last remnants of the sunlight.

The buildings in this city were so destroyed that it was hard to believe only time had worn them down. Some distance down the street, one of the structures was so reduced to rubble that I couldn't even tell what it had once been. With a jolt, I realized that this city must have been attacked during the wars. That some power-hungry Renewable had targeted it for unknown reasons.

I wondered if that Renewable had created the Star, fading in the dying light. As I watched, the light dimmed, like magic in a dying machine's crystal heart. Then it winked out, leaving the city in darkness.

"Can't sleep?" It was barely more than a whisper.

I turned. Tansy was sitting by the fire, arms curled around her knees. Nix was nearby, on the other side of the fireplace, wings half-extended as if soaking up the warmth.

I wondered how long they'd been watching me pace. I moved away from the window and joined them, sitting in the empty space between them.

"Just thinking," I whispered back, conscious of the fact that only wooden screens separated the bedrooms from the kitchen where we were.

"I wish we could do something for them," Tansy said with a sigh.

I found my gaze going to the shutters again. "Why do you suppose the shadow people only come at night?"

Tansy shrugged. "Easier to get people alone? The upper hand when it comes to hunting?"

I chewed at my lower lip, troubled. "That crystal—the Star—it's strange. Dorian said that this city once conducted experiments concerned with restoring magic to the wilderness. Do you think maybe the beacon wards them off, somehow, when it's lit?"

Nix's wings fluttered, a tiny sound in the stillness. I knew it wanted to comment, but we couldn't take a five-year-old's delight as a sign that the family wouldn't mind Nix's presence.

"Maybe," Tansy said, slowly. "But who put it there? Surely not these people."

She didn't need to say it, but I knew what she meant. These people were hovering on the brink of survival, living harvest to harvest. And none of them, as far as I could tell, had a shred of magic beyond what sustained them. How could any of them have had the resources to erect such a structure?

I was about to answer when I saw a flicker of a shadow under one of the screens. When a tiny form emerged from behind it, hovering in the darkness just beyond the edge of the firelight, I straightened.

"Molly?" I whispered. "Can't you sleep?"

She didn't answer, swaying slightly side to side, her night-gown swishing softly against the tops of her feet. Tansy glanced over, then grinned at me, returning to her study of the flames.

"Why don't you come sit with us? You can play with my secret friend if you want."

She took a step forward, just the edges of her toes cross-ing the ring of firelight. I could see only the faintest outline of her face, her wispy hair, the flash of firelight in her eyes. Why didn't she come?

My mouth went dry. I don't know how I knew—it had nothing to do with my abilities, my sensitivities. She made no telling sound, no movement; even the swish of her nightgown had stopped. The steady gleam of her eyes was fixed on my face.

But I knew.

"Tansy," I whispered, not taking my gaze from the figure

in the shadows. Slowly, I reached for the strap of my pack to bring it closer.

I heard Tansy shift, straightening, recognizing the urgency in my voice if not the reason for it.

The girl heard it too. Like a predator scents its prey's fear, she knew. She took another step forward, and I saw the dark grey tracery of veins on her tiny foot. Her teeth gleamed in the firelight, even and white except for a gap where she'd lost a baby tooth.

Shadow.

And then all I saw was teeth and dead, grey skin and desperate, hungry white eyes. She was on me faster than I could register movement, the pain of her fingernails scratching at my skin jolting me into action. I struggled, the shadow girl's screaming and snarling mingling with Tansy's shouts of confusion and Nix's furious buzzing. I heard other howls rising, the scrape of footsteps, the crackle of hungry voices.

The little girl's nails dug into the fleshy parts of my shoulders, clinging to me with unnatural strength, her teeth snapping inches from my nose. A string of saliva ran from her lips to my face. I held her away with one hand pressed against her throat—she didn't even notice, as though she didn't need to breathe. With my other hand I groped for Oren's knife, the one I'd kept hidden in my pack.

Not again. The words flashed through my mind, bright, searing. *Not again. I can't kill another child.*

My strength was giving out. Her teeth caught my earlobe and tore, sending pain like burning needles scattering down my neck and across my face. I heard a scream, not even recognizing the sound as my own voice until I had to gasp for air and the sound ended.

I struck out with the blunt handle of the knife and felt it connect with a dull thud, sending her reeling back with a piercing howl of pain and confusion. I lurched to my feet, a wave of dizziness rushing through me as I swung my pack onto my back. Droplets of blood scattered across the floor as I stumbled, colliding with something warm. I shrieked, only to feel fingers wind through mine and hold tight.

Tansy.

"Tansy—we've got to—"

She hauled me backward toward the door. "My bow's outside," she gasped. One of her eyes was half-shut and streaming tears, and her other arm hung oddly. Before us was the family, silhouetted by the fire behind them, pacing and watching us, looking for their moment. The pale bandage around Sean's knee looked strange and out of place, surrounded by the sickly grey flesh of a shadow person. None of them—not even Molly, who had regained her balance—looked like they'd be slowed down by the meager injuries we'd managed to inflict.

They were waiting. Waiting to see what we'd do, waiting for one of us to make even the tiniest movement.

I stepped backward and hit wood. The door. I groped with my free hand for the handle, only to find rough wood, exposed nails.

The barricades. We'd locked ourselves in with monsters.

"Your arm," I said in a low voice, trying to keep it from shaking. Trying my hardest to keep the creatures from sensing my terror and striking. "Can you help me move this?"

Tansy shook her head, not taking her eyes off of the shadow people. "No," she gasped. "And we'd never get them all moved in time—they'll attack if we try."

My eyes went to the screens, and beyond them, the lobby that stretched back toward a wide staircase. Past that I could see only darkness, my night vision ruined by the fireplace in between.

Tansy swallowed audibly. The sound prompted a gurgle of anticipation from Brandon, his grey face and white eyes sunken behind the black beard. "We'll never get past them."

I knew she was right. Molly, the tiniest of them, had leaped on me before I'd even realized she meant to move. There was no way.

A mad whine cut through the low growls and snapping jaws, and we looked in time to see a copper blur zip across the room, directly at Trina. She howled and reeled back, clawing at her face. The blur slowed enough for me to recognize Nix, shifted into a tiny ball of spikes, zipping from shadow to shadow and screaming all the while. They pawed and clawed at the air, but Nix was too fast for them.

I was frozen, staring—but Tansy didn't hesitate. She surged forward, dragging me with her by our joined hands, making for the back of the lobby. Once I was moving she let go of my hand, stretching her longer legs and putting on a burst of speed. She reached the doors at the back—a pair of them. She ran to one first, jerking at the handle, then skidded to the other. She pulled, pushed, clawed at the wood—but it didn't budge.

"No good!" she shouted. "The stairs!"

I spun, my shoes squealing against the marble floor, and made for the broad stone staircase. I heard the boy give an outraged scream, and then the solid clink of metal striking stone.

Nix. My heart seized, and I almost stopped.

"Don't let it be in vain," gasped Tansy, surging past me for the stairs.

I gasped for breath, the air sobbing in and out of me. Blood was seeping down my neck from my ear and into my shirt, sticky and wet. I fought another surge of dizziness and turned back for the main room. I couldn't leave Nix now.

But just then I heard the familiar whine of madly whirring wings and a voice that only became distinct as it went zipping past me in a flash of copper and sapphire: "*Gogogogogogogogogooo . . .*"

I saw a shadow, indistinct, clawing its way around one of the screens. I bolted up the two flights of stairs, my pack bouncing heavily against my spine.

I found Tansy sprinting down a carpeted corridor on the third floor and I followed, gasping for air. There were doors on either side of the hallway, but though we tugged and pounded on each one, they were all sealed up tightly. The hallway ended in a broad window overlooking an alley below. Only part of the glass remained around the edges, jagged and splintered.

Nix's momentum carried it out the window several feet before it turned and zoomed back in, hovering, clockwork grinding and twitching as it tried to keep flying despite the damage it had taken. Tansy took only a moment to gasp for air and then spun around, ready to try the other direction—but the shadows were there, indistinct in the dark, coming faster and faster.

I looked at Tansy, who looked back at me. Time stopped for a moment and we stood there, her one eye nearly swollen shut, the other wide with terror. She'd only ever fought the shadows at a distance. She'd never seen them up close, seen their white eyes, heard their unearthly screams. A small amount of light came in through the window, and I saw a droplet of sweat roll down her temple, silvery with moonlight.

Sweat. *Water.*

I yanked off my pack and used it to knock out the rest of the glass on the bottom of the window frame before slipping it back on. I grabbed at Tansy's hand, jerking her toward the window. The alley, three floors down, looked a long way away.

She resisted. "Are you insane?" Her voice shook. "We'll break our legs. We'll break our necks. I don't—I don't want to die that way—"

"Do you want to die *that* way?" I gasped back, thrusting an arm out toward the oncoming shadow monsters. "Trust me."

"I can't—" She twisted away from the window, pressing herself into the corner, eyes rolling toward the shadows as they raced toward us. Only a few seconds now before they reached us.

"Tansy." I jerked her arm, turning her toward me. "*Trust me.*"

She stared at me, and then before my eyes the frightened girl turned back into the scout that had so awed me when we first met. She straightened and reached for my hand, her sweaty palm pressing against mine.

We took a few steps and then leaped out into empty space.

I glimpsed her for an instant, the silver moonlight and the golden energy of her power mingling in my vision. I closed my eyes, opening myself and letting the hunger wash over me, and did what I'd wanted to do from the first moment Tansy had caught up to me.

As her power surged into me I turned my face towards the ground racing toward us. I wrenched at the spot inside me where the magic pooled, and with a blinding flash, the alley went white-gold.

We struck something invisible and yielding and bounced off before landing on the cracked ground below—bruised, but whole.

I lay dazed, my head spinning and vision sparking. The rush of warmth and life that enveloped me had wiped away the terror of the last few minutes. I'd saved myself this way once before, in my own city, but that was before I'd gained the second sight. I'd never seen what it looked like to do this magic before. I floated, light-headed and giddy, for what felt like hours, watching the sparks wheel and dance overhead.

It wasn't until Tansy moaned beside me that I came back to myself and realized only seconds had passed. My ear throbbed where the shadow girl had bit me, my neck sticky with blood. Though I could feel the remnants of Tansy's magic still sparking inside me, I already wanted more. But she was starting to shake, and when I reached out to touch her shoulder she rolled away from me, curling up into a fetal position. She had nothing left to give me.

I heard a wretched howl and looked up, the golden light vanishing instantly. One of the shadows—I couldn't even tell which one—was climbing out the window. It came skittering down the wall, leading the way for the other three. Their fingers found purchase on the tiniest of cracks in the brickwork, sliding down the surface as if it weren't a vertical wall.

"Tansy! Come on, we've got to *move*."

I leaped to my feet, buoyed by my pilfered magic, and dragged her with me. She gave a confused cry, but after a few moments she got her feet working again and managed to stumble with me toward the mouth of the alley. We were both looking back over our shoulders at the shadows as they reached the ground when a guttural sound stopped us dead.

A fifth shadow stood before us in the mouth of the alley, framed in the moonlight. I could only see its white eyes glittering, fixed on us, burning with hunger.

Tansy and I lurched back and to the side until our backs hit the brick wall of the building. The fifth shadow advanced on us, its harsh breathing labored and thick with wanting.

The shadow family caught up, the largest stepping up to corner us. *Brandon*, I tried to remind myself, my brain clinging desperately to the knowledge that just an hour ago these had been people, kind and decent, and oblivious to what they really were.

The other three members of the family sent up a low, sighing wail, and I turned my face away, willing my stolen magic to change them back before one of them pounced on me or Tansy.

The Brandon-shadow growled low, the sound building—I knew he was about to snarl and leap.

When it came, I shoved back against the wall, instinct trying to find a way to escape.

But where I'd expected pain and blood and the crunch of my own bones, I heard only an answering snarl of rage.

I opened my eyes. The Brandon-shadow had leaped not for me, but for the fifth shadow. They were no more than a tangle of teeth and muscle and sinew, feral screams. Blood splashed onto the pavement, inky-black in the moonlight. The Brandon-shadow broke away with a cry of pain.

No longer silhouetted, the fifth shadow was easier to see.

I stopped breathing. *No. It can't be him.* My mind refused to believe what my eyes were telling me.

The other shadows jumped on him, the children and mother together, and my eyes blurred with tears of shock and confusion and focus as I tried to concentrate. Tansy slumped to the ground, overwhelmed, still shaking violently from the aftereffects of being harvested.

The knife was still in my hand. My fingers tightened around it, but the fight was moving so quickly I couldn't track who was where, only that it was still going, that the fifth shadow was still fighting. One of the smaller shadows was flung free, stumbling against the opposite wall of the alley.

The Brandon-shadow barked a short command, wordless and wild, and the remaining two shadows broke away and backed up, limping and snarling their rage. After a few more wails and whimpers, the family turned and loped away, vanishing down the other end of the alley.

The fifth shadow turned toward us, its breathing harsh and irregular. I heard Tansy gasping for breath at my side, trying to rise despite the way her legs and arms shook. I put a hand on her shoulder, my own fingers trembling.

Though she could not have understood, Tansy slumped back, too weary to try again.

I summoned every ounce of courage and stepped forward. The shadow snarled a warning, half-fury, half-anticipation. The hunger in its voice was unmistakable.

I swallowed, licked my lips.

"Oren?"

He didn't react, his white eyes fixed on my face, his teeth bared and bloody from the wounds he'd inflicted and received. His hands clenched and unclenched, the muscles in his legs quivering as he stood there, struggling with himself. He twitched forward only to jerk back, the tendons standing out on his forearms, in his neck.

I started to lift my hand and too late remembered that it was the one holding the knife.

The shadow leaped forward, raging, grasping at my shirt and jerking me in close so that I felt the heat of his breath, smelled the grass and the wind and the metallic tang of blood. He growled a low, desperate, drawn-out sound.

The growl turned to a gasping groan, the breath shuddering in and out of him. He stumbled forward, his body heavy against me. Suddenly the hand twisted in the fabric of my shirt wasn't holding me close—it was holding him up, and my knees sagged with his weight.

He coughed and reached out with his other hand for me, trying to keep himself from falling. He lifted his eyes, anguished—for the briefest instant I saw them flicker from white to palest blue.

Then his grip failed and he dropped like a stone, unconscious before he hit the ground.

CHAPTER 5

He looked exactly as he had the day he left. I'd memorized every contour and feature of his face in that moment when he'd looked back over his shoulder at me. I traced them now, my fingertips shaking. His skin was clear again, all signs of the dark grey veins and semitranslucent flesh gone. Long, fair eyelashes, stubborn jaw, sandy hair that fell wildly over his forehead.

Despite the evidence of my eyes five minutes ago, it was nearly impossible to believe he was a monster, looking at him now. I tried to remind myself that no matter how human he seemed when he was feeding off my magic, he was a shadow and always would be. The moment he left my side, he'd become mindless, dark, and hungry. The moment I ran out of magic to keep him human, I'd be dead.

My mind was blank. I'd thought I would never see this boy again. Or, at the very least, if I did, he'd kill me before I had a chance to figure out what I thought of him.

I'll find you. His last words to me hung so vividly in the air that for a moment, I thought he'd woken up and spoken. *Even in the dark, you shine.*

"My pack."

I jerked away from my inspection of Oren's face and turned to see Tansy, half-propped awkwardly against the wall, one eye swollen shut and her arm still dangling uselessly at her side.

"My pack," she moaned again. "I need my pack. I need my pack."

I left Oren's side and crouched, fumbling with the straps of my own pack in my haste to take it off. I knew what she needed. To regenerate magic required energy, and that required food.

"Your pack's in the house, Tansy. But I have food here. See, look—cheese. Take it."

But she shoved my hands away, trying to stand. "No—my pack. I need it."

"Tansy!" I hissed, trying not to shout and alert any other shadows who might be nearby. "We can't go back. We have to leave it. Even if the shadows didn't return there, we can't get past those barricades and we can't climb up to that window to get back inside." I reached out and took her good shoulder, giving her a squeeze. "It's gone. Accept that. We have to keep moving, we can't stay here."

She'd started to shiver, and I realized I had too. Neither of us had had time to grab our jackets before fleeing the building. If we didn't find shelter, and soon, then Tansy's shock was going to be the least of our worries.

I heard a familiar sound and straightened, letting Tansy slump back again. A weight lifted, letting me take my first full breath since the Molly-shadow had lunged for me. Nix came winging fitfully up the alley, the grind of its gears harsh and irregular. I moved toward it and held out my hands. It shifted midair, spiky form reverting to that of a bee, and dropped gratefully into my palms.

"*I followed them*," it said, voice unusually tinny. "*They're gone, they didn't turn around to come back. That one scared them off.*" Its blue eyes turned to the motionless form lying unconscious in the middle of the alley.

"And you?" I whispered, lifting my hands so I could try and inspect the pixie in the meager moonlight. "Are you okay?"

"*I will require some time to repair myself, but I will soon be fully functional.*" Already I saw it shifting, tiny needlelike arms emerging to begin bending damaged panels and pieces back into the correct shapes.

"Thank you." Carefully I transferred the little machine to my shoulder. "You saved us."

It clicked with irritation as it inspected my torn earlobe. "*Keep Lark alive,*" it said absently, dismissively, in its programmer's voice. Kris's voice. I tried to ignore the surge of hurt and confusion that sound brought and turned back for Tansy.

"We can't stay here, Tansy. Can you walk? Did you eat?"

She took a bite of the cheese, uninterested but following orders. Only after she swallowed did a little spark return to her eyes as she discovered her appetite. She finished the rest ravenously and licked her fingertips.

"Your arm?"

"I think my shoulder's dislocated," Tansy said with a grimace, picking herself up with some difficulty, but managing to get to her feet on her own power. I was never so functional after my own experiences with having my power harvested from me.

"What do we do?"

"Pop it back in." Though the grin she flashed at me was nearly feral with exhaustion and pain, it was still Tansy's grin, and a second wave of relief washed over me. We could do this. Recover. Survive. Find a way out of this cursed city.

"Tell me what to do."

By the time it was done, I was the one who had to stagger away and put my head between my knees, sweating and trying not to throw up. I could still feel the scrape and pop of bone under my hands radiating through me like the scratch of nails on a schoolroom chalkboard.

When I felt more sure I wasn't about to lose the dinner I'd eaten not two hours before, I helped Tansy make a sling for her arm. She'd regained a little color in her face, but it was clear her arm wasn't going to be useful for some time.

"My bow is outside the house," Tansy said, remembering. "Not inside. They made me leave it. We can go back for it."

"No. You can't draw it like that," I said, nodding at her arm. "It'd be useless."

"But—it's my bow." She was staring at me like I'd suggested she leave one of her legs behind.

"I know. But Tansy—it's just a thing. If we go back that way we risk the family finding us again. What if the entire city is full of people who turn into shadows at night? That whole street will be full of shadows trying to break through their own doors to get to us."

She shook her head, closing her eyes.

"Your bow, your pack—they're just things. You're what's important. You can make another bow, another pack. But there's only one you, and I need you."

"Would you be saying that if it were your pack? If it was Oren's knife, or your brother's bird, back there?"

I bit my lip, but nodded. "Yes. I would leave them behind."

Tansy swallowed, the fingers of her good hand twisted so tightly together that the knuckles gleamed white in the moonlight.

"We need to move," I whispered, taking that for agreement. "We have to wake Oren."

Tansy's jaw tightened, and her eyes moved past me. I knew

she was looking at Oren's unconscious form in the middle of the alley.

"Leave it," she said, coldly. "It's just a monster."

I fought the urge to clench my own jaw. "Tansy, you saw those people in there. They didn't *know*. None of them know. Oren may be the first self-aware shadow ever, and only because I told him. When they're human, they're *human*. You sat at their hearth, ate their food, told them stories."

"And they betrayed us." Tansy's lips pressed together in pain and determination, confusion and fear.

"It's not betrayal when you don't know," I insisted, moving so that I'd be in her line of sight, force her to meet my gaze. "They knew something happened at night. They thought we would be safest indoors. They were doing their best."

"There's no forgiveness for betrayal," muttered Tansy, looking away.

I groaned. "We don't have time for this. Help me get him up."

"No."

I sucked in a deep breath. "If you want to come with me, then he comes too. It's that simple."

Tansy's eyes flicked from me to the unconscious Oren and back again. After a long pause, she sniffed briskly and nodded. "All right. Wake him up."

She got to her feet as I crossed back to Oren and gave him a shake. He didn't move—not even a groan. I called his name, shook him some more, pinched the skin on his arm, and—in desperation—slapped him across the cheek. Nothing.

"Lark," Tansy breathed.

"I know what you're going to say. I can't leave him. He saved us."

"No—Lark—" She reached down and touched her fingertips to my shoulder.

Something about her touch triggered an alarm at the back of my mind, and I tore my gaze away from Oren's long eyelashes.

A trio of dark figures stood at the mouth of the alley.

They weren't shadows—I could see that right away. They stood watching us with deliberation and poise, lacking the animal eagerness and focus of the shadow people. They were thick and bulky forms, and their heads were bulbous.

I couldn't do it. I was spent. One companion unconscious, the other wounded and despairing, and me—I was just me, what could I do against this new breed of monster?

And then my focus snapped into place and I realized they were men, wearing suits and helmets. Protection against the void. I could hear the sounds of their breathing, harsh and artificial. One took a step forward, and his tinny voice came through some filter in his helmet.

"You three, get moving. You're coming with us."

. . .

They bound my hands behind my back with rough, scratchy rope. Tansy they left unbound after verifying that her right arm truly was useless. Though they tied Oren's hands as well, they were forced to half-drag him along. At times he seemed to regain some level of consciousness, managing to walk a little, but the few times I saw his eyes open they were staring and vague, unfocused. He didn't know what was happening.

I hadn't seen Nix, but I no longer felt it on my shoulder. I hoped the pixie had fled or hidden itself in my pack.

They asked no questions and marched us along in silence. Trina's words came back to me, what she'd said before the sun had set and everything had changed. *They come at night. And if anyone ever sees them, they don't live to tell the tale. They vanish forever. Gone.*

Taken.

We had assumed they meant the shadow people. But they were shadows themselves. What could be so horrible that even the shadow people feared it?

Our captors led us to a round iron disc in the ground. One of them pulled out something that looked a little like a crowbar and inserted it into a hole in the disc, prying it up and open enough for a man to pass through. The smallest of the three figures dropped down into the blackness below, and then they dropped Oren down afterward. I heard him land with a sickening *thud*—no one had caught him. They shoved Tansy forward and she stumbled down, landing only slightly more gracefully than Oren.

The man holding me pushed me to the hole's edge. "Down you go," came his tinny voice.

I wished my arms were unbound so I could use them for balance. But one glance at the impassive, reflective surface of the helmet and I knew there was no point in even asking. So I stepped forward and dropped through, striking the ground and rolling as I hit.

We were in some sort of sewer system beneath the city. The close air pressed in, strangling and dank. The other suited men dropped in and closed the hole over our heads. The tiny bit of moonlight vanished, leaving us in darkness more complete than any I'd known before.

Somehow, the suited men knew exactly where they were going, missing every bit of broken stone and exposed pipe as though they could see in the dark. I heard Tansy stumbling and cursing almost as much as I was—her natural grace and coordination were no use when she couldn't see and was being forced to march along quickly. I couldn't hear Oren, but had to assume from the dragging sounds behind me that they were still bringing him.

Eventually we stopped, the hand that had been propelling me forward now shifting to grab the collar of my shirt and haul me back. I still couldn't see anything, but I heard footsteps moving forward, followed by the grating shriek of rusty metal. I heard Tansy give a grunt of pain as one of them brushed past her, jarring her shoulder.

A weight stumbled against me, a familiar smell on the air. I fought the urge to jerk away, instinct warring with what I knew to be true.

"Oren?" I whispered. "Are you awake?"

For long moments, there was only the shriek of metal and the sound of his breathing. Then, voice so hoarse I almost couldn't understand him: "Lark?"

And then hands were shoving us forward again, into what felt like an even smaller space. The hinges shrieked once more, and a door clanged shut behind us.

A fog descended over my thoughts. Muffling iron surrounded us on all sides, the metal insulating my senses. I was worse than blind. Devoid of every sense, cut off, everything silent and still as death. I gasped, trying to force air into my lungs, and could only breathe the smell of metal, sharp and cold.

Dimly I heard Tansy say something, and then the answering bark of one of the men. A light came on, dazzling my eyes. Our captors stripped off their suits, revealing ordinary people underneath. Their clothes were worn, but nowhere near as ragged as ours—but for the sweat and grime of wearing the suits, they seemed normal. Another door opposite opened and we were shoved through. I couldn't see right, couldn't hear. All around was iron, worse than the Iron Wood, worse than my cell in the Institute.

I went where they shoved me, kept my feet only because falling would mean touching the iron beneath me. Even

Oren felt like metal when his body brushed against mine—I couldn't feel the familiar tingle of energy between us, sensing only death and stillness.

After an eternity they shoved us forward and then clanged a barred door behind us. I ricocheted off the back wall of the room. No, not a room. A cage. Bars on all sides. Trapped. I scuttled to its center, as far from the four iron walls as I could. We were all together, Oren sprawled on the ground and Tansy leaning against the side wall, glaring through her one good eye.

A key turned in a lock.

"Wait," I gasped, as hoarse as if my lungs were on fire. "Who are you? What are you going to do with us?"

Two of our three captors kept walking, but one hung back. I realized it was a woman, now that she'd taken off her suit.

"You'll stay here until he asks for you. If he decides you die, you die. If he has a use for you, you live."

"He," I echoed, starting to shiver as shock settled in. "Who?"

"Prometheus."

CHAPTER 6

They'd left a light on, just enough for us to see by. It glowed a steady white-gold—*magic*, I thought, but I couldn't sense it. The iron bars, the iron in the walls and the floors and the ceilings, kept me from sensing anything properly. The air was thick and close, warmer than outside but still clammy and cold.

Though my head still rang with the silence of iron, my other senses were beginning to return and try to compensate. I hadn't realized how much I'd gotten used to being able to feel the magic around me, and how much there was to sense even in a magicless void.

I dropped to my knees where Oren was slumped on the ground, ignoring the way my instincts told me to get as far away from him as possible. "Are you okay?"

He pressed his palms against the stone floor and shoved himself upright. His face was haggard, making him look older. The blue eyes were distant, confused. Though there was no sign of the monster in his gaze, I could still see the ferocity— that belonged to Oren as well. Not just to the beast.

"What're you doing here, Lark? Why aren't you—" His gaze swung past the bars, the whites of his eyes showing his panic at being closed in. "Where are we?"

I glanced at Tansy, who was watching us with clenched jaw. She shook her head, and I turned back to Oren. "I don't know. Underneath the ruins of a city. You were—" I stopped, unable to say it.

Oren swallowed, gazing at my bleeding ear before turning so that he could see Tansy, taking in her injuries as well. "Did I—"

"No," I said quickly, interrupting him. "You saved us."

He grimaced, brows drawing inward. "That doesn't sound right," he muttered, lifting a shaking hand to rub at his eyes.

"Nevertheless." Steeling myself, I reached out to touch his hand. Despite the insulation all around us I felt a tiny tingle, a buzz where our skin touched. I jerked my hand away and cradled it against my chest.

He looked up, meeting my gaze for the first time as I tried to swallow my fear, my disgust. His eyes sharpened a little, blue even in the dim light. He was searching my face for something, his own expression haunted—but whether he found what he was looking for or not, he pulled away, turning his back, using the bars to drag himself to his feet.

I shouldn't have touched him. He was a monster—a cannibal. How many people had he killed in his short lifetime? Tansy was right, I should have left him there in that alley. The current that flowed between us was only magic—nothing more. Maybe if I thought it often enough, it would be true. He was a *monster*.

And yet, he saved us.

I wanted to curl up there on the floor, pull away from the bars as far as I could, and hoard what little magic I had left from what I'd stolen from Tansy.

"They didn't take my pack away," I said. "But we'd better try to keep it hidden in case it was a mistake. And I've got my knife—maybe we can pick the lock."

Tansy glanced at me dully. "Just use *your* magic to do it." The emphasis was bitter. As if hearing it, and regretting it, she closed her eyes and leaned her head back against the wall.

I understood the bitterness. I could still feel the white-hot agony as the Institute's machines drained my own magic, replacing it with something false and twisted. How could she ever look at me as anyone other than the person who'd done that to her? I swallowed, trying to ignore the surge of guilt. If I hadn't taken her magic and broken our fall, we would've died. I wasn't sure we were much better off now, but at least we hadn't been eaten. Yet. And she'd recover. She was a Renewable. In time, her magic would return.

"I don't think I can use magic," I said finally. "There's so much iron here—I feel like I can barely breathe."

I searched in my pack, hoping to see a telltale flash of copper, but there was nothing. Nix wasn't there. I hoped that it had escaped unseen, that it was outside somewhere. The thought of the pixie trapped in these tunnels made me feel sick.

"Tansy, eat the rest of the apples," I said, fishing the last couple of fruits from the Iron Wood out of the bottom of my bag. They were bruised and a little shriveled, and no doubt mealy-tasting, but still edible. "You need it most. It'll help you recover."

She took them dubiously but began to eat anyway. I crossed over to the door, ignoring the way my skin crawled at the proximity of the iron. Despite crouching to get a better look at it, I couldn't see anything no matter how hard I pressed my face against the bars. I explored it by feel, my arm pressed awkwardly through the bars and wrist twisted back so I could get at the lock. The point of the knife wasn't quite long enough and narrow enough to reach inside, but I tried anyway, wriggling it around inside the keyhole, hoping to hear the telltale click of tumblers.

After a while, Tansy finished the apples and came to my side, dropping to one knee to ostensibly look at the lock with me. But I could tell she had something to say, the tension radiating from her. I braced myself and kept my attention on what I was doing.

"I'm—sorry," she said eventually, surprising me.

I lowered the knife and withdrew my arms, letting my hands rest on my thighs. They ached from the awkward angle, showing bands of red where my skin had been pressing so hard against the bars.

"You saved our lives. I can't—I shouldn't resent you for that."

I tried a smile, though it didn't feel quite right. "It's okay. It's awful. Believe me, I know."

Tansy smiled back, the expression coming more easily to her, though she looked as tired as I felt.

"Can you rest?" I asked Tansy before glancing up at Oren, who had leaned forward and was resting his face against the bars, eyes closed. "I can keep trying for a while if you can sleep."

"I think I could sleep standing up in the middle of a forest fire right now," Tansy admitted. "Wake me up in an hour or two, if those guys haven't come back by then."

She retreated to the back of the cage, as far from Oren as she could get. She settled down and propped herself up in a corner, then closed her eyes.

I kept at the lock for a while, though I knew how pointless it was. The knife simply wouldn't reach. Oren stayed silent, motionless. Eventually I conceded that all I was doing was blunting the tip of the knife, and stopped.

"I remember a light."

Oren's voice cut through the gloom, soft and quick. There was a tremor in it. I looked up—he still hadn't moved, forehead pressed against the bars.

"I remember darkness and fog and a terrible hunger. And that I was supposed to be looking for something. And then, suddenly, there was a light. And I knew where to go."

Tansy's magic, I realized. *In the alley.* I kept silent, remembering how good it had felt to strip her magic away from her, take it for my own, let it pool warm and golden inside me. I tried to block out the sound of his voice, fixing my eyes on the lock again.

Oren pushed away from the bars and turned, sliding down to sit on the ground. He let his head drop forward, hair falling into his face. "Why is it that I always end up caged when I'm around you?"

I gritted my teeth. It'd be easier to keep him at a distance if he'd stay confused, only half-himself. It'd be easier if he'd never come at all. Then he could stay a monster, someone who betrayed me. Someone I never wanted to see again.

I held out the knife, gripping the blade and offering him the handle. "This is yours," I said shortly.

His gaze lingered on it for a moment, then lifted to meet mine. I jerked my eyes away, but not before he would've seen the hurt there.

After a silence, he retreated back against the bars. "It was a gift," he said quietly. "It's yours." He fixed his eyes on the back wall, not looking at me. "Besides, you may need it."

"If I run out of magic and you try to kill us both, you mean?" There was still a little of Tansy's magic left—I could feel it, tingling, singing through my veins. Tansy herself had fallen asleep as soon as she stopped moving. I could hear the soft sounds of her steady breathing coming from the back corner of our cell.

"You had the chance to get rid of me," Oren said. "I *asked* you to kill me."

"Just because I'm not capable of cutting your throat doesn't mean I want you here." The words were out before I can stop them. Anything to keep him at arm's length.

"Lark—"

"We're not a team, Oren." I glanced at Tansy, who stirred in reaction to the sharpness of my voice but didn't wake. "It's not like it was. It can't ever be again. You know that, right? You shouldn't be here."

"I didn't want to be here," he hissed back. "I don't control it, when it takes over. I can't tell it to leave you alone. It—that thing—isn't me."

Except it is. Because I could see the ferocity of the monster even now, the brilliant gleam in his eye, the strength in his shoulders and in the grip of his hands as he balled them into fists.

"You're not even human." I turned away.

"And you are?"

The words hit me like a blow. The silence drew out between us, tense like wire. Then my lungs remembered how to work again. "I'm human. I'm—I'm me, all the time. I make my choices. This power, this is something that was done *to* me."

I could feel Oren's eyes on me. Only, where they'd once made my spine tingle and my stomach tighten, now they made the hairs on the back of my neck rise. He didn't move, but it was like I could hear him anyway. I could feel the shape of the air around him. I knew exactly where he was, though I kept my eyes away.

"Just as this was something done to me." His voice remained quiet, pitched low so as not to wake Tansy. "By the wild. Knowing it doesn't change who I am, only what I am."

The buildup of betrayal was less now. It was still there, simmering quietly, but not fighting to get out—as though by venting it, I'd released some of the pressure. I swallowed, closing my eyes. "I wish I didn't know."

For a long time, it seemed like Oren wasn't going to answer. The tension in the wire pulled between us was less, but I could still feel it tugging at me, making me fight to stay away. Then I felt him draw breath to speak.

"Then I guess that makes two of us."

The silence stretched out again. Oren was watching the back wall as though he could see anything but shadow there, beyond the pool of light cast by the spherical glow by the door. He looked thinner than the last time I'd seen him. Older, despite it only having been a couple of weeks. I fought the impulse to reach out for him, to feel that telltale tingle that spoke of the flow of magic between us.

"Does it help to talk about it?" I asked, watching him. I'd intended it to sound sympathetic. Instead it sounded hurt.

"No." Briefly the muscles in his jaw stood out, and he turned his head. For a quick moment, he caught my gaze, searching.

Then it was back to the wall again. I could see the struggle of emotions on his face as clearly as if they were my own. I realized he'd never really lived among people as an adult, had never learned to hide the things he felt and saw. Though he spoke little, he said volumes.

"It's like an unbearable ache," he said, softly. "Hunger—except that it's not something that food can solve. We eat because it's the only way we know to consume what we really need. It's incompletion, being severed, half of a whole. It's needing something you can never get, not completely."

He closed his eyes, letting his head back to rest on the bars. "And it feels as though if you could only fill that void a little, the tiniest bit, you could come back to yourself. And you'd do anything to feel that way again."

I barely managed to suppress a shudder. The more he spoke, the more I recognized the things he was saying. The hunger, the need to feel whole—the *need* to take what's yours. How quickly and thoroughly I'd consumed Tansy's power. And how quickly I'd wanted more.

"And when you make the kill," he whispered, "in that instant you know it'll never be enough. That you have to keep hunting. Keep searching. Keep killing."

I couldn't speak. Couldn't look at him. He glanced at me, and I could sense his shame and self-hatred, his fear that I loathed him too. How could I tell him that the revulsion he could see on my face was for myself?

"Lark," he said softly. "Say something."

I knew what he wanted me to say. He wanted me to forgive him, to tell him it wasn't his fault, that he couldn't help what he was. Out of the corner of my eye I saw the warm light washing over his face, glimmering in his hair, softening the angles of his face. He wanted me to absolve him.

I wished I could turn into that light, let it touch my face too, wash the both of us in its golden glow. Part of me wanted to comfort him as I had the night he was caged in the Iron Wood, distract him from his claustrophobia. But my tongue felt like lead, my throat choked with fear. I just kept staring straight ahead, my eyes on the shadows at the back of our cage. I couldn't even deal with my own fear; I had no way now of helping him with his.

Eventually he turned away to curl up on his side on the stone and close his eyes. I stayed awake, shivering, hand clenched around the handle of his knife. I wanted to tell him how true his words had rung for me. I wanted to tell him I didn't despise him.

But I knew he despised what he was, and I couldn't bear the thought of him hating me too. Perhaps I was no more than a shadow myself. Was that what my city had done to me in their experimental Machine, tearing out my magic and then synthesizing it again? A shadow killer more perfect than any monster in the wilds—they could only destroy and eat and hunt, never truly sated. I could harvest what I needed from someone with a single thought.

I could feel the tiny trickle of power that flowed from me to Oren even without touching him. I knew I was all that was keeping him human, and yet a part of me wished I could sever that connection, hoard the power for myself, hold onto this feeling as long as I could. Because even if I didn't feel whole, even if I didn't feel perfect, it was better than the hunger.

Surrounded by stone and iron, we were wrapped in silence. I closed my eyes, trying to think past my horror and revulsion. But it was hard to see the point.

I knew my brother wasn't here. Our city had done to him what it had done to me, turned him into the same thing I was now—and I was falling apart. Perhaps my brother had made it this far, and perhaps he hadn't. Perhaps he was one of the cursed townsfolk, oblivious, fearful of the dark.

Perhaps he was nothing but a shadow himself.

· · ·

When Tansy woke again, rousing Oren and me as well, she spent some time trying to get at the lock with the knife. When finally she threw the knife down with a clang, I jumped, heart racing.

She glanced at me apologetically and stooped to pick it up again, offering it back to me. I put it back in my pack. My brother's paper bird looked at me from among my supplies, but I just shut the pack again, ignoring it.

"Well, seems like we're going to be here for a while," Tansy said, flashing me a weak smile. "And I'd rather not be trapped in here with a monster."

She glanced at Oren, who straightened, eyes flicking from her to me. Before I could protest, Tansy held out a hand to me. "Well?" she said. "Take what you need."

I stared at her outstretched hand, uncomprehending. "What I need?"

"To keep him human. I know it's you, your magic, whatever makes you unique. I saw it back in the Iron Wood, and I saw it when you saved us in the alley."

"He saved us," I corrected her, still not taking her offered hand.

"Whoever saved who, he's looking a bit grey around the ears, and I don't want to wait and find out how long it takes him to turn back."

Alarmed, I looked over at Oren. I knew it didn't work like that—you were either shadow or not, no in between—but I couldn't help but inspect him closely. He rolled his eyes, crossing his arms over his chest.

"So," Tansy interrupted my thoughts. "Let's get this over with. Just—not so much this time?"

I swallowed. In the alley, I'd torn what magic she had in one instant, ruthless and quick. Taking a deep breath, I reached out for her hand. Her palm was sweating—she was nervous. But her hand was steady, and she didn't pull away.

"Are you sure?" I asked, glancing at her.

She nodded. "It's necessary. And I trust you."

I wanted to scream at her that she shouldn't—that I'd taken more than I needed in the alley, that I could've stripped her and left her for dead. That part of me wanted to do that now. But she was right. I didn't have much left from what I'd taken that first time, and without it, Oren would revert back to his shadow self. And we'd both die.

I closed my eyes, looking with my second sight for the flicker of magic around her. It was weak, almost invisible despite the dampness of this underground cell. A meager meal of apples was not going to help her regenerate much. But even a little would do.

I let down my guard just a fraction, feeling a little warmth slide into my hand from hers. A few hours and I'd forgotten how good it felt. I opened the channel a little wider, taking a slow breath, basking in it. Tansy's hand felt clammy in mine, but I ignored it, focusing on the magic, the life force. I'd never had the luxury of examining this connection, the intimacy of it, how I could trace it back through our joined hands and up her arm, through her veins and muscles, to her heart, which danced a steady beat through the web of magic inside her. I tugged at a strand of the web and felt Tansy give a strangled gurgle of pain.

I jerked my hand away, gasping, opening my eyes and willing the dark, cold cell to return and banish the lovely warmth of Tansy's magic.

Dizzy with the aftereffects, my vision blurring and dancing, I tried to sit back up, to find Tansy amid the swirling shadows. She was on her back, breathing hard, but otherwise fine, watching me, massaging her hand and grimacing.

"You okay?" she asked.

A sound rather like a laugh escaped me as I tried to put myself back together. "I was going to ask you the same thing."

"I feel a bit like I've fallen out of a tree, but I'll live." Tansy started to struggle up onto her elbows, but Oren left his post by the cage wall and went to her side, offering her his hand. She stared at it for a few moments, gaze flicking from his outstretched hand to his face, and then gingerly let him help her up into a seated position.

"Thank you," he said simply.

I heard Tansy swallow, audible in the muffled quiet of our prison. Her brows drew in, lips pressing together. "Yeah," she replied. "Well, I wasn't doing it for you."

He let go of her hand and retreated again, but I wasn't fooled. I knew Tansy enough to know that a week ago she wouldn't have offered what she'd just offered. She wouldn't have even accepted his hand to help her up.

The bands of tension around my heart eased a little, my mind clearing a fraction as though a fog was starting to thin. Maybe our situation wasn't so hopeless after all. If I could get Tansy and Oren working together, trusting each other as they had each once trusted me, maybe we could get out of this mess.

I started to suggest that we make another pass at the lock but was interrupted by the outer door banging open without warning.

Two men entered, one shutting the door behind them while the other came forward, his hands full. The light was behind him, so it took me a moment to recognize the long, curved shape slung over his shoulder.

Tansy, however, recognized it right away. She sat bolt upright, her eyes on his shoulder. I could sense her tension as though it were my own.

"So we traced you back to where you'd been squatting." The man's lip curled a little, as though we'd been living in a rat-infested dump. "Living with the Empty Ones," he said, and spat through the bars onto the stone floor.

With a start, I realized what he was holding—Tansy's pack. And her bow and quiver, slung over his shoulder. I glanced at her, but she didn't look at me, her wide eyes fixed on the man.

"We were planning on giving this back to you if

Prometheus gave the okay," he said, hefting the pack in one hand, squinting at us through the bars. He wasn't very tall, no taller than Tansy, but he was a burly man, strong. "Which one of you does this belong to?"

I expected Tansy to leap at the opportunity to get her pack back, after her panic in the alley at having lost it. But she remained silent, lips pressed together, muscles tense. I stared at her, confused—and the man saw me looking.

"Ahh," he said. "The rest of you, back against the wall. You—" and he crooked a finger at Tansy, "come here."

Tansy got to her feet, jaw squared, breathing in and out through her nose. She crossed toward the door of the cage, standing just out of arm's reach of the man with her pack.

"We expected the usual stuff, dried fruit, knife, feathers for arrows." The man tossed a couple things out of the pack, whatever had been on top, and then dug his hand back into the bottom of the bag. "Imagine our surprise when we found it was full of these."

His hand emerged, holding a small copper sphere. I'd never seen anything like it before, but I saw Tansy flinch. She certainly recognized it. Her eyes flicked toward me, hidden and guilty. Something tickled at the back of my mind, some instinct that blared alarm.

"Courier pigeons. Now, what reason would an innocent traveler like yourself have for carting a bag full of pigeons around? They're Renewable messengers. And you're not a Renewable, are you?"

Tansy didn't answer, jaw squared.

The man thrust out his hand through the bars, bringing the sphere close to Tansy's face. Her head jerked back, but she stood her ground. So near to her, the sphere unfolded, its surface rippling, extending wings and a faint glow that responded to the aura of magic surrounding her.

A machine.

The man laughed unpleasantly, withdrawing his hand. The sphere shut up tight again, and he dropped it back into the pack. "So what messages were you sending back to your leader, hmm? The location of our city? The number of people here? Our defenses?"

Tansy said nothing. This time she didn't look at me, but I knew. A burning cold spread through my body, an icy weight settling in the pit of my stomach.

The man tossed the bag aside and reached for a key on his belt, unlocking the door. "Prometheus wants a word with you. We've got a great many uses for someone with your . . . talents."

As he grabbed for Tansy's arm, she jerked it away, whirling to look at me. Her eyes were anguished, hot with guilt.

"Lark, please—please, it's not what you think."

I could only stand there, pinned to the stone with shock. "You were—spying on me." The bag of messenger machines lay forgotten on the floor behind the men. Suddenly I remembered her scouting forays, how she'd race through her meals so she could go off alone. To signal Dorian our location. Now I understood her desperation when her pack was lost.

"No!" She struggled as the man grabbed her more firmly this time and dragged her back. "The barrier you made, it's starting to fall apart, and Dorian asked me to—I can't refuse him, no one can refuse him. I really was worried about you."

I swallowed, trying to push the bile back down where it was threatening to rise in my throat. Dorian was no better than Gloriette or the other architects in my city. All anyone saw in me was something unique to be studied. To be used.

"Lark, I'm sorry. Please." The man was dragging her away—the cell door slammed shut, and she wound her fingers in the bars, trying to stay long enough to make me understand. "I never would've let him do anything, he only wanted to know where you were going."

Her eyes met mine. I felt sick, nauseous, barely able to stand. Her fingers were white-knuckled, clutching at the bars. I didn't know who Prometheus was or what these people wanted with Tansy, but the only uses I knew for a Renewable were tantamount to torture. I thought of the captive Renewable powering my own city, in perpetual agony, constantly harvested of her magic, again and again.

Tansy was crying. "Lark, forgive me."

All I could think of was her bitterness in the alley at having been fooled by the shadow family, the anger I recognized now for shame. I said the only words I could think of. "There's no forgiveness for betrayal."

CHAPTER 7

When the outer door slammed closed, it was all I could do not to drop to the ground like a stone. I couldn't think through the roaring in my ears, couldn't begin to pull myself together with my stomach knotting itself over and over.

Kris, Dorian, Tansy, Nix, even Oren himself—I was tired of the people around me taking advantage of this awful power I didn't even want. Tired of them taking advantage of *me*.

Out of the corner of my eye I could see Oren stalking from one edge of the cell to the other, long strides eating up the distance and pale gaze sweeping the shadows beyond the bars. More than ever he reminded me of an animal, some untamed beast raging at its captivity. For a long time there was no sound but the scrape of his shoes on the stone and his harsh breathing.

Then he abruptly whirled toward me with a snarl. "We're running out of time, Lark. You have to do it." There was a faint sheen of sweat on his brow.

"Do what?"

"Kill me." He indicated the knife in my hand with a jerk of his chin.

I took a step back, staring. "What?"

"You couldn't do it at the Iron Wood, fine. You could shove me off into the wilderness and forget me. Here you don't have that luxury. It's now, or it's later when I come at you in your sleep."

I gritted my teeth. "It wasn't like that. I wasn't trying to forget anything."

"But you wouldn't have to watch me fall," he hissed. "You said to me—before, you told me that we weren't a team anymore. Fine, we're not. But Tansy's gone now, and you've got no source of power. When you run out, that's it. I'm a shadow again, and you're dead."

I could see the betrayal in his gaze—but why was it such a crime not to want him *dead?* "You're afraid," I retorted. "Because we're in here, because you don't like not being under the sky."

"Yes," he agreed. "So? That doesn't change the facts."

I shook my head, shoving the knife back into its sheath in my waistband. "Panicking won't help. We'll figure something out."

"By standing there sulking about Tansy?" Oren started pacing again, making two circuits of the cell before halting again and turning toward me slowly. "You'll have to defend yourself."

I met his gaze, watching as his eyes narrowed and he took a few steps to the side, circling me. "*If* you change."

"*When* I change. So I might as well speed up the process. Make you defend yourself now."

I could feel my heart starting to race, wondered whether he could hear it, whether any of his shadow-self traits lingered when he was in human form. "Don't be ridiculous."

The tension drew out between us as he circled, and I could feel it stretching thin. Without warning he feinted a lunge at me, making me fight to hold my ground.

"You don't want to hurt me," I said, forcing my voice to stay even. If Oren decided to take matters into his own hands, I wasn't sure I could hold my own.

"That's right," he burst out. "That's why—" He let out his breath, dropping out of that deadly hunter's stance. "That's why I need you to act. I can't do it. I've tried."

My blood roared in my ears. "What do you mean?" I whispered.

"I mean I tried. After I found out, after you sent me away." Oren turned to look through the bars of the cell, so all I could see was his profile, the tension in his body. "Animals don't kill themselves, and I couldn't—I couldn't do it. Every instinct fought against it, and I wasn't strong enough. I'm not stronger than the thing inside me."

For a moment my mind tried to picture it, tried to imagine what awful thing Oren tried to do to himself, to rid the world of one more shadow.

"Not killing yourself isn't weakness," I said finally. "It's not cowardice."

Oren just shook his head, moving forward until he could press his forehead against the bars, a plaintive gesture. His long fingers wound around the iron. "It's certainly not bravery."

I had no answer to that. Not when I didn't know what I was myself—perhaps we were both no more than things, echoes of who we once were. Maybe we both deserved death. The silence thickened the air.

"That girl," Oren said finally, still gazing out at the darkness beyond our cell. "She was your friend?"

"I thought she was." The words tasted sour, and I swallowed hard. "I can't forgive what she did."

"You thought I was your friend, too, and look where we are now."

"You only follow me because you can't help it, the monster can't let me go. You said yourself that I shine in the darkness."

With a weary groan, Oren straightened and turned so he could look at me again. He tilted his head back, looking up at the ceiling. "You're the only thing that keeps me human," he said after a silence. "But if I woke tomorrow completely cured and whole, I would still follow you anywhere."

My throat closed. I couldn't look at Oren, couldn't listen to his voice, without my mind replaying the night we parted. The sweet softness of his mouth cut by the metallic tang of blood, the wave of longing mixed with revulsion. The hopelessness in his eyes when I told him not to touch me. His bitterness now as I kept him at arm's length, too confused to know what to do with him.

He was so careful not to come near, to stay away as I'd demanded that night—and yet now he stepped forward and lightly brushed the back of my hand with his knuckles. Just enough so that I could feel the electric sizzle of power passing from me to him, pulled away by the dark void of shadow inside him.

"Sometimes we can't help the things we do."

Every impulse in my body wanted to turn toward him, to slide my hand into his and let our fingers wind together. To smell grass and wind all around me, a light in the deep, dank darkness of this prison. Instead I just stood there, remembering the taste of shadow, waiting for something I knew wasn't coming.

I cleared my throat and sucked in a ragged breath. "I'm not going to just sit here and wait to die."

Oren stepped back, letting me move around him and head for the door of the cage. I crouched by the lock, running my hand over it, but I knew I didn't have enough magic left to open it. When I'd freed Oren from his cage in the Iron Wood, I'd been surrounded by Renewables, and though I hadn't known it then, I'd been able to draw on them all to bend the laws of magic and iron and open the lock with my mind.

Here there was only me. And I couldn't magic iron on my own.

My eyes fell on Tansy's pack. It was still lying where the man had dropped it, well out of arm's reach even when I lay down on my stomach and stretched my arm as far as I could through the bars. Even Oren's long arms wouldn't be able to reach it.

There may not have been Renewables around, but that pack was full of machines. And inside them, somewhere, were tiny hearts full of the magic that powered their clockwork mechanisms.

I closed my eyes, trying to reach past the muffling field cast by the iron bars between me and the pack. I tapped into the tiny, dwindling reserve of energy inside myself and concentrated on my arm, still stretched out past the bars. All I needed was a tiny nudge. A spark. One little touch to get one of the copper spheres to roll my way.

I felt the power spark and pop inside me, my head spinning, but I forced myself to keep reaching, keep trying to nudge one of the machines my way. I opened my eyes a fraction, squinting through the haze of golden sparks and threads.

The bag moved, bulging as something inside it shifted. I groaned, head dropping as the magic flowed from my outstretched fingertips.

Something rolled out of the mouth of the pack, and I dropped like a leaden weight, collapsing down onto the stone. I'd thought magic under ordinary circumstances was tiring—working through so much iron was like trying to run uphill wearing a coat lined with rocks.

Blearily, I lifted my head, forcing my dazzled eyes to focus.

One of the spheres had rolled toward me, but when I reached out, my hand still fell short. My heart sank.

A tiny whir of clockwork jolted me out of my daze. A panel separated itself from the smooth surface of the sphere, followed by another, a slow unfolding with a groaning protest of gears, like muscles gone stiff from the cold. A tiny flash of sapphire within the depths of the sphere winked back at me.

"Are they gone?"

I gasped, lightheaded and dizzy from the magic, and unwilling to trust my own eyes. "Nix?" I breathed, staring.

Oren came to my side as I spoke, and together we watched as the sphere painstakingly unfolded itself. It had none of the ease of the courier pigeon the man had shown Tansy—I could tell this form was difficult for the shape-shifting pixie. Nix stopped halfway back to bee-form, gears stirring feebly as it lay on the stone floor. I imagined it panting and sweating, trying to catch its breath.

I reached out my hand as far as it would go, and the pixie crawled onto my palm. "How—I thought maybe you'd escaped when we were taken. Did you double back inside the building?"

"I hid in that antechamber where they keep their suits," the pixie said. *"They never even noticed. When they went out to search the area where you were found, they saw the other one's bag and the machines inside. I flew in when they weren't looking."* With an obvious effort it finished its transformation back into its favorite bee form and then cast its crystal-blue eyes over the cell. *"Where is that other one?"*

"Gone." I tried to keep the anger out of my voice, but even I could hear the way it quivered.

The multifaceted sapphires swung toward me. *"So she turned on you. Correct me if I am mistaken, but I believe someone tried to warn you about that."*

I closed my eyes. Already part of me regretted what I'd said to Tansy as they dragged her away. I'd probably never see her again. "Not now, Nix. Please."

The pixie shook itself and turned, its little legs like dull needles against my palm as it scanned our surroundings. *"I see this one is still with us, though,"* it said flatly, watching Oren unblinkingly.

"The feeling is mutual," Oren muttered, turning away and shoving a hand through his hair.

"I couldn't see or hear anything all balled up like that." Nix lifted off of my hand for a few seconds, testing its wings now that it wasn't stuck imitating one of the dormant courier pigeons. *"This does not appear to be the optimal place to recover and regroup, however. Why are we wasting time in here?"*

"We're locked in," I said, trying to remember that I was glad to see Nix. Even if it was infuriating beyond all belief.

"That ought to be no problem for you."

"Too much iron," I replied. "Not enough magic. I was trying to reach the pack, thinking I could steal some from the machines in there." My breath caught. "Nix—can you fly out there and nudge them closer? If I can just get my hands on one, I think I could do it."

"I can do better."

Nix launched itself off my hand and buzzed out through the bars to land on the outside of the lock. Spidery little legs unfolded out of its body, the way they did when it was damaged and needed repairing. This time, however, they went skittering over the surface of the lock, darting inside, exploring, thorough. Nix's round head disappeared inside the lock as well, and for a while the only sounds were the clicking of its spindly legs and the gears that made them move.

But then came a solid *thunk*. My heart leaped into my throat.

Nix backed out of the lock, half-stuck, tripping into the air. It staggered a bit, struggling to fly while managing far too many legs—but it finally succeeded in folding the extra legs away and zipped back to land on my shoulder.

Hand shaking, I reached out to touch the door.

It swung open.

. . .

The tunnels under the city were a maze as complex as the sewer system in my own city—but I hadn't learned this system as a child at my brother's side, didn't know where each turning led. It was like being inside my dream again, only I didn't know where to go, and I couldn't feel my brother leading me through.

The place was lit at random intervals by tiny shards of magic contained in glass spheres, connected by glass filaments as finely crafted as any I'd seen in the Institute back home. The advanced craftsmanship was more than a little out of place in a sewer underneath the ruins of a cursed city.

Oren was sweating despite the chill. I knew he was suppressing the panic of being underground by sheer force of will—I couldn't ask him to try and help me find our way out. He had been semiconscious at best when we were brought to the cell anyway. Nix had been even more blind and deaf. I'd been struck temporarily senseless by the presence of so much iron. The only one who would've had any chance of retracing our steps was Tansy—and she was gone.

Even in the quiet of my own thoughts, the word made me feel sick. *Gone.*

I kept my hand in my pocket, fingers wrapped around my brother's paper bird, as if somehow through it I could summon his competence and confidence. I chose paths at random, listening for the sounds of wind or the smell of fresh air, but instead the air grew more still, more quiet. I sensed we were moving downward, not upward, and the further we went, the warmer the air grew.

Despite my uncertainty, despite the fact that we were utterly lost, I felt myself breathing easier and standing straighter with every step. I was growing used to the iron supports in the stone around us. I'd stopped long enough to absorb some magic from the machines in Tansy's pack, and I felt the power shimmering inside me like sunlight, intangible but no less real.

Twice we encountered people coming the opposite direction, but we were able to duck down a side tunnel and avoid being seen. The third time, however, came when we were walking down a long corridor without any branching tunnels. A man and a woman came around the corner unexpectedly, chatting. Oren hissed and I jumped, turning and treading on his feet as I tried to escape backward down a route that didn't exist. He put his hands on my shoulders, steadying me, as Nix zipped inside the collar of my shirt.

I reached inside me for the bits of power I had left, ready to use it against them if I had to. *I've been in a prison twice now. I'm not going back.*

I took quick, shallow, steadying breaths, every nerve alive, every muscle tensed. I felt Oren's hands grow rigid on my shoulders as they approached.

They walked straight past us without even looking.

I stared ahead at the spot where they'd been, too shocked to even turn and track their progress away from us, down the corridor we'd come from.

". . . not like we can tend them ourselves," the man was saying, voices echoing back to us through the tunnel. "Or grow anything down here."

"True, but self-sufficiency is the first rule. Prometheus

insists on it. How can we justify—" And they turned a corner, voices fading into unintelligible murmuring.

Oren let out a long breath, the air stirring my hair. I shivered, pulling away abruptly. He just shrugged, looking as confused as I felt.

Nix peeked out from my collar. *"They don't recognize you as escaped prisoners,"* he noted.

"But surely they know we're strangers? That we don't belong here?"

Nix considered this, emerging the rest of the way from my collar and dropping into the air so that he could look us over. *"Unless there are so many of them living here that they don't all know each other."*

We kept walking, silent, shaken. Just how many people could be down here? I wished that I could see the outside, see what time of day it was. Were these people about to turn into ravenous shadows at any moment as well?

It was then that I realized Oren was siphoning less power from me than he had been. What had been a steady stream was now a trickle. Either he was somehow needing less magic to sustain his human form, or—

My eyes caught a glimmer of violet light as we turned a corner, and it hit me. No wonder I'd been feeling better, stronger, brighter. There was magic in the air. Iron all around, still, but it was containing the magic, holding it in. Like the Wall in my home city.

We stopped long enough to share a meal, dividing up the last of the cheese from my pack. It would've been a meager meal for one—between the two of us, it barely seemed like anything at all. My ear had stopped bleeding, and I rubbed the dried blood off my neck. I couldn't do anything about the stain on my shirt, but at least I could minimize how warlike and battered I must look.

When we started moving again, a few more people passed us by, none of them giving us so much as a second glance. This time we knew to act as though we belonged there, but nevertheless my skin prickled. I instinctively reached for my power every time, ready to fight.

It was Oren's idea to follow the people.

"When you're hungry and snares aren't working," he said, keeping his eyes down, trying not to look at the stone ceiling and walls surrounding us, "you follow animals to find their dens. You can follow a bird back to its nest for the eggs."

The people had to be going to and from something, he pointed out. There had to be a base somewhere. Storage for supplies or weapons. Places to sleep and eat.

So the next time we heard the sound of footsteps, we went towards them, ending up at a T-junction. As a trio of tunnel-dwellers approached, we fell into step behind them, trailing enough that they wouldn't try to talk to us, but close enough that we could see where they were headed.

Eventually we ended up in a hallway that was rectangular instead of the round, squat tunnels we'd been in since the prison cell. At the end of it was a huge iron door. Oren put a hand out, touching my elbow, and we slowed, watching the trio carefully. I knew what he was warning me about—if the base was behind that door, then the people who had captured us could very well be on the other side of it. And they would surely recognize us, even if the others didn't.

One of the tunnel-dwellers, a man with thick salt-and-pepper stubble spreading across his jaw, reached out for a leverlike handle and hauled back on it. The doors slid open to either side, vanishing into the walls. Inside was a grate, which he slid open as well. He and the other two stepped into what appeared to be an empty room and turned around as one. It looked hauntingly familiar. The man who'd opened the doors reached out as if to close them and then spotted Oren and me.

"Well?" he said, one hand on the grate.

"E-Excuse me?" I stammered.

"Are you going down?"

Oren's hand tightened on my elbow as he took a step back. Suddenly, my memory clicked into place. I knew what this was—I'd been in one before.

"Yes," I blurted, reaching out for Oren's hand and then heading for the box. For the elevator.

I could hear Oren gasp a quick, anguished breath as we squeezed into the elevator. For someone who didn't like being underground, this must be torture. I wound my fingers through his, putting my body between him and the elevator's other occupants. Though my mind recoiled at his touch, knowing what he really was under the veneer of humanity, the rest of me tingled, goose bumps rising along my arms despite the warm air. I turned my head away, not looking at Oren's face.

The grate screeched as the man with the stubble slammed it closed behind us. Then he opened the lid of a box that stood on a post in one corner and banged his fist into a round, flat button. The elevator gave a lurch—Oren's fingers went rigid in mine—and then with a surge of magic that sang through my head, the whole thing went dropping down.

I was glad it had been so long since the last time I'd eaten a proper meal. My stomach felt like it climbed into my throat, and my feet tingled, desperate to make it known that they were still in contact with the floor.

I looked up and saw that Oren's eyes were closed and his face almost serene, far calmer than I'd ever seen him. Only the tightness of his grip and the glint of sweat in the hair at his temples betrayed his terror. Here he was no monster—he was just a boy trying to trust that I knew what I was doing. I leaned against him and felt the tension in his body relax just a fraction.

For a moment, it was like none of the past few weeks had happened. It was just me and Oren—there was no sickening tang of blood in the air or hunger inside me. The walls between us vanished for a few precious seconds.

Then the box stopped with a shudder and a screech of protesting gears, and I stepped away. I took a deep, quiet breath. We had to act like we made this trip all the time. I kept an eye on the man with the stubble, watching everything he did in case we needed to get back up the same way we'd come down. All we needed was to figure out the quickest way out of this place.

The man shut the lid on the box with the button and then reached for the grate, shoving it aside. I tensed, waiting to see what was on the other side of the outer doors. A base, holding the people who'd captured us; more tunnels, as endless and confusing as the last; even the outdoors. I was so turned around that I couldn't dismiss that as a possibility, though it was now so warm that I could feel sweat starting to form between my shoulder blades.

The stubble man jerked at the handle, sending the outer doors sliding open with a rusty screech. He and the others got out, and Oren went stumbling after them, eager to leave the confines of the box. His hand was still clenched around mine, and he tugged me with him. I staggered, trying to catch my feet, eyes on the ground. We were on some sort of ledge overlooking a space so vast I could feel it sucking at me.

Then I looked up, and stared.

This was no base—it was a city.

Metal buildings of every imaginable shape and design grew out of the rock like mushrooms, roofed with rusty-red iron and corroded copper green. Some were polished, gleaming turrets and towers. Others were rough and pock-marked by time and abuse, looking no better than debris from the ruined city above. Even here there were signs of the wars, as though people simply grabbed what they could and went underground. The buildings were connected by an insane network of stairs and walkways, cobbled together from pieces of salvage—I saw the leg of a giant mechanical walker stretched between two balconies and bolted into place, and just below us, a roof made out of a series of overlapping gears hammered thin and broad.

High above, fog shrouded the ceiling where the warm, moist underground air hit the cold stone overhead. Water dripped in a constant but sparse drizzle. The cavern was so large that there was even a breeze, fitful and changeable, stirred by the convection of the hot air below and the cold above. Overall the air was thick and humid, vastly different from the wintry cold outside.

Above the fog, the ceiling was studded with a series of what looked like the same glass and crystal lights we'd seen in the corridors, but on a far grander scale. They scattered the white-gold light of magic through the fog, which caught it and sent it dancing into a thousand colors that lit the city. It was as though the sky was paved with rainbows.

We stood on a ledge overlooking most of the city, although some of the walkways led upward to buildings higher than us. These were smaller, less rusted, clearly newer. At the very bottom of the huge cavern, on the floor, was a building in the shape of a semicircle, parabolic. In the courtyard before it were multicolored squares of fabric and a throng of people moving around and beneath them.

The size of the place was staggering. There were people everywhere—hundreds, thousands more inside the buildings maybe, more than I could count or guess. In circumference the cavern was not much bigger than my own city, but it went down and down and down, enough to fit my city many times over, stacked on top of itself. The far side was lost in the haze of distance, fitful rain, and fog.

Hope sputtered to life inside me. Perhaps my brother had made it here after all. Maybe they'd captured him the way they'd captured us. Maybe even now this Prometheus was using him the way he—or she, for that matter—was using Tansy.

A memory of the Machine the Institute had used to experiment on me bubbled up in my mind, and I tried to push it away. Tansy made her choice.

"We should go," Oren whispered, although there was no one around and the cavern was alive with the sounds of people and machines, a distant roar of life and chaos. "Try our luck with the tunnels."

"But someone here might be able to tell us how to get out."

"And how would we ask them without giving away that we're outsiders? I'd rather be lost in the tunnels than back in that cage."

"We'll find a way. We could wander in those tunnels up there for a week and never find our way out." I looked at him, his squared jaw and fierce scowl, and added gently, "We don't have that long."

Oren sucked in a deep breath through his nose. I could see him trying to scent the fitful breeze, make sense of it, orient himself in the chaos of light and sound and people. His blue eyes darted this way and that, tracking a dozen different movements, the muscles in his jaw working. Out of his element, he was every inch the animal I'd thought he was when we first met. Cornered. Anxious. Poised to fight or flee.

He turned away from me, but I knew him well enough to sense his fear. Fear of losing himself, fear of hurting me. Fear of dying underground, away from the sun, breathing recycled air.

He was right to say we should go. Part of me knew it. But my feet wouldn't move, rooted to the stone beneath them. My eyes followed the people going about their business below, oblivious to the two strangers watching it all from above.

How could we hope to infiltrate this city as complete outsiders without being caught? And all just to ask for directions?

I sucked in a deep breath, for in that moment I realized that wasn't why I had to stay.

Somehow, as it often did, Nix knew what I was going to say before I said it. *"Don't,"* it buzzed softly, for my ears only. *"She betrayed you."*

I shook my head and then lifted Oren's hand, pressing it between both of mine. "I'll come with you back to the tunnels, keep you human as long as I can, until we reach the surface."

He looked up, eyes fixing on mine, but the relief that flashed through his features vanished the moment he saw my face.

"But then I'll be coming back alone. I have to find Tansy."

Oren turned his head, showing me his profile as his eyes scanned the city before us. His face was as sharply sculpted as ever, the dirty sandy hair falling over his brow, jaw clenched. He'd seen mountains and oceans, and yet I could still see him struggling with the scale of this underground city, with its iron and copper palaces, so large it had wind and clouds and rain.

We still hadn't talked about what happened the night he fled the Iron Wood. How he'd asked me to come with him—how I'd refused. The warmth of his arms. Of his lips. My revulsion at the taste of blood.

It was like an iron forest stood between us, and I couldn't sense his heart any better than I had been able to sense the world beyond the iron bars of our prison cell. Even with our hands still locked together, he was worlds away.

His face didn't change, no intake of breath—my only warning that he was about to speak was that he pulled his hand from mine abruptly.

"Where do we start looking?"

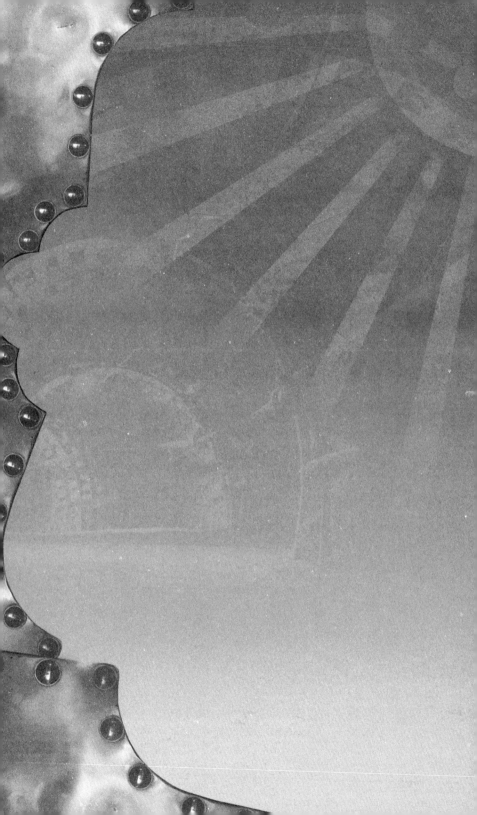

PART II

CHAPTER 8

In the city where I was born, everything ran like clockwork. Workers left their homes at the same time every day, fulfilled their jobs adequately and no more, and returned home again, satisfied by their contribution. The streets were broad, and the mechanized carriages ran without congestion or delay. Children learned and grew, and then were harvested of their magic and sent into adulthood. Anyone who failed to live up to expectations or felt no joy in fitting into the larger machine was Adjusted. Escorted beyond the Wall by friends and family, removed from the machine, left to rust alone. Even the sun crossed the sky in a clockwork track, regular and comforting. Orderly. Neat.

This place could not have been more different. What had seemed a pleasant jumble of people and machines from above was deafening, blinding chaos once we descended the path from the elevator to the main streets and walkways.

I'd been worried we'd stand out for our clothes, the grime of travel. I had only the clothes in which I'd left the Iron Wood, and they were dirty and travel-stained, worn and torn in places during my struggle with the shadow family. Oren was in a far worse state, his multicolored patched pants dirty and full of holes, his once-white shirt grey with age and grime, his hands a full shade darker than the rest of him with ingrained dirt.

But men and women of every shade, shape, and attire walked the paths. Some were dressed far more richly than anyone I'd seen—wealth, in my city, was for the architects alone. Here, people wearing heavy, embroidered fabrics and elaborate hairstyles walked side by side with others wearing whatever they could cobble together. There was no rhyme or reason to it, no hierarchy or division apparent between the classes.

We headed into the thick of it, listening for anything helpful in the snatches of conversation we could hear. My ears strained for the sound of Tansy's name, for news of captives, for any reference to a Renewable. But the noise and tumult of the crowd was too baffling, too chaotic, to get any sense of a pattern. Never had I so longed for the quiet calm of my own city, everyone doing exactly as instructed, living their lives by the quiet rhythm of the sun disc slipping second by meticulous second across the dome of the Wall.

There were machines here, too, far more than existed in my city or in the Iron Wood. Nix had overcome its misgivings and was now darting around my head as we walked, zipping here and there to investigate other machines but always returning to touch down on my shoulder, briefly, regrouping for its next foray. Oren stayed half a step behind me, tense. I imagined that descending into this chaos was like being surrounded by iron for me—in the noise and jumble he was as blind and deaf as I had been.

The muggy air was smothering, and I could feel sweat rolling down the small of my back even after I took off my coat and tied it around my waist. I knew we were going to need a place to rest—sleep was a distant memory for me, and neither of us were used to such an overwhelming riot of color and movement. We needed to pause, to regroup. None of this was what we'd expected.

We turned onto a bridge made of ropes and planks, the whole thing creaking damply under our feet. My hands shook as I moved along the bridge, gripping the handrails. Our steps were far too slow—we hadn't gotten halfway across before someone behind us cleared his throat loudly.

It was a short, stocky man with thinning hair and a brilliant blue waistcoat covered in some kind of iridescent green-brown eye pattern. He stared at me for a moment, eyes meeting mine and narrowing. But before I could react, he raised his alarmingly bushy eyebrows at us, and I realized he was waiting for us to keep moving. There was only room on the bridge for people to proceed single file. Oren and I hurried across, trying to ignore the swaying of the bridge, and got out of the man's way.

He brushed past us without another glance, vanishing into the crowd. I could feel Oren bristling, annoyance at the man's behavior combining with his general unease at being underground, and I took his arm. My arm tingled, but I kept hold of him, ready to march him past the group before he could do anything rash. Something about the man's gaze had unsettled me, and I wanted to find some alley or corner to wedge ourselves into and find our bearings.

I spotted a gap in the crowd, but before I could change course, a voice rang over the tumult.

"Stop! By order of Prometheus, on suspicion of Renewable activity, you are commanded to surrender."

I froze. Oren's arm went rigid under my hand, and I could imagine his already overwhelmed senses jangling. There were too many people between us and the alleyway I'd spotted, and even if we could make it there, I had no way of knowing where it led, or if it was a dead end.

I turned slowly, expecting to see the looming face of one of the guards who'd captured us. Instead, I realized that the crowd had formed a circle around someone some distance away.

A woman's voice split the air in a desperate cry. Through the press of bodies, I could only tell that some sort of scuffle was taking place. I hesitated, then let go of Oren's arm. "Stay here," I whispered. Dragging him into the thick of the crowd would not have been particularly wise.

I carefully wormed my way through the crowd, mumbling apologies here and curses there when appropriate, until I could see what was going on. A pair of men stood there wearing matching charcoal-and-red uniforms. Copper badges emblazoned with some kind of bird of prey adorned their chests. Though they looked nothing like the Regulators in my home city, I recognized them nonetheless. Cops. They were standing over the prone body of a woman, holding weapons—curved, wicked machines I couldn't identify, but clearly aimed with menace.

"You're wrong," the woman sobbed, curled around something. "He's no Renewable—he's not, he's not." Something moved in the circle of her arms, and a white face appeared over her shoulder. She was shielding someone, a child.

"Resisting an Eagle's order is a punishable offense," one of the two guards said, voice harsh. "Harboring a Renewable is another. You'll get banished for that one. Turn him over, ma'am, before we're forced to take action."

But the woman kept repeating, over and over, that the boy was no Renewable. With a sick kind of certainty, I knew that there was no way out of the standoff that didn't involve the weapons.

Then a commotion on the other side of the circle drew my attention, and after a moment someone else entered the circle, pushing through the onlookers. It was the man in the blue-and-green coat.

"The hell is going on here?" he snapped. "It's my day off, don't make me get involved." Though he wore no uniform, the two guards—Eagles, one of them had called himself—snapped to attention.

"We've had reports that the boy's a Renewable, sir."

The man in the coat glanced down at the huddled woman, gaze dismissive. "So? Take him down to Central Processing."

The Eagle shifted uncomfortably. "His mother won't give him up."

The man in the coat gave a long-suffering sigh. "So shoot her," he retorted with exasperation. "You've got talons, use them." But before either Eagle could act, he crouched down at the woman's side.

"Ma'am," he said gently. "Ma'am, you're going to have to let them take your son in."

"He's not a Renewable," she whimpered. It was as if being a Renewable was the worst possible crime. The way they spoke the word, they might as well have been saying "murderer."

"If he's not, then he'll be back before the end of the day." The man in the coat reached out and squeezed her shoulder. "You have my word."

As he continued to murmur to her, I scanned the faces of the onlookers. They were silent now, pale. Afraid. When the woman straightened a little, I could see that the boy in question was no more than eleven or twelve. But when he lifted his head, at least half the spectators drew back, a murmur running through the crowd.

These people were terrified by the mere thought that he could be a Renewable.

I felt a dull anger flicker through me. I'd been that kid before. The dud, the strange one. Any excuse to make someone different, to keep them from fitting in. Even here, a hundred miles away from the city where I was born. Even if they let him go, he'd never be the same again.

The man in the coat was slowly easing the woman away from her child. "We can't take the chance that it's true, Marsa—you did say Marsa, right? Marsa, it was Renewables that caused the cataclysm, forced us to live down here like this. We can't let that happen again—where would we run to now?"

The woman choked back another sob, but before she could speak, the boy interrupted. "I'll go," he said, his voice shaking. "Leave my mother alone. I'll go."

"No!" The mother jerked away from the man in the coat.

"Mom, it's fine." The kid's face was white, but he nodded reassuringly at her. His voice hadn't changed yet, and it sounded high and scared. "I'll be fine."

The man in the coat gave the woman's arm a dismissive pat, then straightened to usher the boy into the Eagles' custody. "Good lad," he said with false cheer. They all turned, passing close to me as the crowd parted to let them through.

"Throw him with the others," said the man in the coat in a low voice to the Eagles. "And put together a compensation package for the mother. If he's a Renewable, we'll have to act quickly."

The Eagles led the kid away, after he shot one last look over his shoulder at his mother, still huddled on the walkway. The man in the coat watched them go, then turned to the crowd. "Well?" he boomed, voice projecting easily over the stunned silence. "We're done here."

As the crowd dispersed, the man's eyes fell on me again—and stayed there. My throat constricted, and I whirled to push back through the crowd. Oren was waiting for me, agitated, asking questions—but I wanted to put as much distance as I could between myself and the man in the blue-and-green coat.

Eventually I spotted an opening and darted out of the flow of traffic into an alcove, evidently disused due to the way the constant drizzle from the rainbow ceiling pooled and collected there.

"What was that?" Oren hissed. "I couldn't see."

"They arrested a kid for being a suspected Renewable," I replied, my breathing harsh and unsteady from our headlong dash.

"So?"

"They were afraid of him—like he was some kind of monster."

Oren gave a small, bitter laugh. "Better him than us."

I shook my head, replaying the scene, trying to understand. "I don't know. It doesn't match up with what we were always taught."

"Taught where?"

I swallowed, trying to catch my breath while keeping an eye on the mouth of the alley. I halfway expected the man in the coat to appear, but all I could see was the ebb and flow of foot traffic returning to normal.

"In my city, the Institute taught us that a huge war destroyed the land beyond the Wall. Here, they mentioned a cataclysm, some event caused by the Renewables."

"You've seen the ruins, what the world was like before. Something had to happen to change all of that."

"But the stories don't line up." I could tell that Oren didn't understand my fixation. The Institute had lied to me about so many things, but for some reason I'd never questioned what little they told us of history. That was fact, something inviolate, as permanent and unchanging as the Wall itself.

"We can't stay here," Oren said finally. "We still don't know where to look for your friend." He kept his eyes on the traffic, both man and machine, bustling by in both directions.

His expression still had that pinched, tense look to it—he wasn't finding the crowds any easier to adjust to than I had found the sky.

"They mentioned something called Central Processing, where they were taking that boy. Maybe that's a place to start."

"You think it's some sort of prison?"

"I don't know," I replied, "but I know the tone of voice they used. That's exactly the way people spoke about the Institute in my city. Whatever Central Processing is, it's important, and there'll be someone there who knows where Tansy is. Maybe even this Prometheus himself."

Oren's jaw clenched, his eyes narrowing as one passerby came alarmingly close to us in order to give way to a large, spiderlike machine skittering urgently down the walkway. "I'll never understand the need you people have to be governed. You all flock to these cities, to places like the Iron Wood, just so someone can tell you what to do."

I looked past him toward the great expanse of hodgepodge buildings, at the streets lined with people, young and old alike. "When people come together like this, they become stronger. They don't have to live in fear the way you do outside. We allow ourselves to be governed because it keeps us safe."

Oren's lip curled a little. Then he ducked his head, hiding his expression until he had it under control again. "If the shadows breached these defenses, if the government fell—if anything at all went wrong, most of these people would be helpless. They've all forgotten how to survive."

For a long moment, I didn't have an answer for him. He was right. I'd been helpless when I left my city. The image of the red-coated architects in the Institute fending for themselves in the woods was ludicrous.

"I guess," I said slowly, "that surviving isn't the same thing as living."

A group of guys about my age came running up the pathway, laughing and shouting, and Oren jumped back, his nerve breaking. His hand flew to his boot, but he no longer had his knife there. So his fist curled around nothing as the boys continued past. He closed his eyes, nostrils flaring as he tried to take a deep breath.

I wondered when he had last truly slept, aside from dozing in the corner of our cell. Did the shadows sleep? Did he ever close those white eyes when the monster inside him came out? He looked so weary, so close to the ragged edge.

But then, so was I. I hadn't slept well since Tansy joined me—and we hadn't slept last night at all.

I couldn't afford to feel sorry for him. All I had to do was keep him moving. I reached out and laid a hand on Oren's arm, ignoring the way he flinched at my touch. Energy buzzed between us, and the hunger coiling in the pit of my being reared up, protesting the slow drain on my reserves.

"It's okay." I carefully kept my voice soft. "It's like me and the sky. Just keep putting one foot in front of the other and it'll slowly get easier."

"It'd be easier if we had any idea of where we were going," Oren replied, his words clipped. "This Central Processing place could be in any of these buildings. Even if I can put one foot in front of the other, we're certainly going to be caught before you can search them all."

I let my hand fall away from his arm and stepped back out into the traffic. "That part's easy." I waited until Oren had steeled himself, then led the way to the edge of the walkway that overlooked the lower city.

"This whole city is pointed down. All the paths spiral inward. There." I pointed.

Oren leaned close to follow the line of sight along my out-stretched hand, and I was reminded eerily of a similar moment when he'd pointed out the Iron Wood in the distance. Before I knew that my city had meant for me to find it—before I knew what Oren really was.

"All the paths lead toward that building," I continued, forcing myself not to look over at him. The building below was the one I'd seen when we first arrived, the one shaped like a semicircle at the very bottom of the city. "That's where we're headed."

CHAPTER 9

From above, the courtyard of the Central Processing building looked as though it was carpeted with big pieces of fabric. When we first started down the winding walkways toward it, my mind turned to Basil. It was like the area was littered with brightly colored squares of paper, all waiting to be turned into animals or shapes or people with a few deft folds and creases. He always said that every piece of paper had a creature waiting inside it.

Tansy's words, when I'd told her she had to leave her belongings behind, came flooding back to me. *Would you be saying that if it were your pack? If it was Oren's knife, or your brother's bird, back there?* I slipped my hand into my pocket, feeling the worn edges and folds of the paper bird Basil had made for me before he disappeared.

Oren's eyes flicked toward me, noting the movement of my hand, but he said nothing. A cloud of flying machines zipped past, and as though they called to it in some undetectable, irresistible way, Nix launched itself from my shoulder and raced after them. Despite the size of the city, though, the pixie always seemed to find its way back to me. I watched it until I could no longer distinguish the glint of its body from the rest and then turned to keep walking.

When we got closer, I realized that the courtyard of the building was a huge marketplace, with tents and stalls scattered around at random. When we reached the bottom of the city it was like descending into a blizzard, only instead of white snow, colors of every shade swirled around us, and instead of the howling wind, voices surrounded us in a cocoon of sound. Vendors hawked their wares, each trying to out-shout their neighbors, while buyers vied for prime spots at the more popular stalls, elbowing each other out of the way. Children and machines were underfoot everywhere. Despite the haphazard placement of the stalls and tents, there was a strangely rhythmic flow to the crowd.

My eyes had trouble tracking everything. I bumped into a knee-high crawling machine that gave such a human-like squawk of disapproval that I stepped back, apologizing automatically.

"Newcomers to Lethe?" a loud, cheery voice called right by my ear.

I jumped back, colliding with Oren. He grunted in surprise and pain, hands coming up to grab my shoulders and steady me.

A middle-aged woman was leaning out over the edge of her stall's counter, watching us. I guessed that she was in her mid-forties by the lines around her eyes and her mouth and the grey that shot through her dark hair. Her eyes were a dark grey-blue, small and bright. Focused. Though her face was smiling and easygoing and her body language relaxed, her gaze was sharp. Assessing.

She was waiting for me to reply, but my mind went blank. In the chaos, I couldn't even remember what she'd asked. "Excuse me?"

"Lethe. You two new here, yeah?" Her voice had a strange, drawling accent, something I'd never heard before.

Lethe. The name of the city? I didn't recognize it, though something about the name seemed familiar. Oren's hands were still around my shoulders, the flow of magic between us slightly muffled by fabric. His touch was warm, steadying.

In my city, the idea of a newcomer was impossible—in my city, the inside of the Wall was all there was. Not so here? I cleared my throat, ignoring the stabbing of my heart. "Yes."

"Travelers?" She gave the word an odd weight, like it was a title.

I fought the urge to glance at Oren and nodded. "Yes, travelers."

She frowned. "If you Travelers, where your rocks?"

"Rocks?" I felt like the ground was slipping away under my feet.

"Yeah, your crystals."

Of course. In the wilderness, non-Renewable people would have to carry some sort of power source with them if they traveled from place to place. Crystals stored magical energy. If they could be somehow rigged to dispense that energy at regular intervals, they'd keep a regular person whole for a time. Keep them from becoming a shadow.

"They're—we, uh, left them at the—"

"They with the rest of your stuff at immigration?"

I nodded wordlessly, grateful that she was all too willing to carry on both sides of the conversation.

The woman's frown cleared, turning into a broad smile. "Well, why you ain't said so?" she exclaimed. "Travelers, my bread and butter. You bring anything shiny? Need trade? Give you good price for first pick."

For a moment I could only stare blankly at her. Then the contents of her booth caught my eye. From the ramshackle wooden frame holding up the lavender fabric hung ropes of chains and pendants, some artistically carved from wood and stone, others fashioned out of bits of old machines. There were stands like miniature trees, branches were coated with rings of all sizes, bearing semiprecious stones and crystals. Carpeting the counter were more pendants, earrings, pins. One pendant fashioned out of old glass circuitry still sparkled faintly with magic to my second sight.

Travelers were some kind of merchant. For a long moment I couldn't answer, my mind spinning. This meant that there had to be far more cities out there than I'd realized. The woman waited patiently as I struggled to grasp just how wrong about the outside world my city's architects were. "Shiny," I echoed. "Um. No. No, we were—"

"Can point you to the right place, tell me what you trade." The woman was eager. No doubt she'd expect some kind of payment or tip for the information.

"No, we were bringing—" My eyes shifted this way and that, looking for something, anything. Something that wasn't at one of these stalls. Some place she couldn't direct us.

Just then Nix flew back in, its flight path wildly erratic from excitement—or alarm.

"Pixies!" I blurted with relief. "We brought pixies, and other machines." But when Nix drew closer and then dove out of sight into my collar, I realized I'd made a mistake.

"Huh." The woman grunted her disappointment and straightened. "Been through CeePo?"

"CeePo." Had I dodged one difficult question only to be caught be another? It was like dancing in the bog, each step pulling me down deeper.

"Central Processing. Everyone goes. Especially when you bring in contraband."

Ice gripped my heart, sudden and shocking. *Contraband.* But there were machines everywhere! How could bringing them in be against the law? Nix settled on my shoulder, buzzing alarm.

The woman watched me, mild-faced but sharp-eyed. She didn't smile, but I could see she knew she'd won.

Oren's fingers tightened, ready to pull me away. It was always fight or flee with him. I could feel his muscles shifting just from the contact of his hands against my shoulders, and my mind conjured a flash of him fighting his way through these people, these soft city people, as he thought of them. The sheer numbers meant we'd never make it, but it'd be a bloodbath before anyone stopped him.

He took a step back—one hand shifted. I felt it slide down my shoulder blade and down my ribs, and I stiffened—but then his knuckles grazed the skin above the waistband of my pants, and I realized what he was doing. That was where I kept his knife sheathed. My body was between him and the stall owner—she couldn't see him reaching for a weapon.

"We intended no offense to your laws!" I blurted. Oren's hand froze, and my mind raced. "We brought them as tribute. A tribute for Prometheus. We've only just arrived, we're trying to get to CeePo."

The woman pursed her lips. She jutted her chin out, scratching at it idly as she watched us. Then, grudgingly, she nodded. "Best hope nobody reports you before you get there."

It sounded like a dismissal, and yet her expression was expectant, waiting for something.

I knew what she wanted. While I'd never been on the receiving end of it, kids in my district practiced that look all the time for when they got harvested and assigned their jobs. Most of them would become laborers, but some would become carriage drivers whose livelihoods depended on their ability to wheedle tips from their architect customers.

But I had nothing to give.

"Why don't you take this?" Oren's voice, low and bitter in my ear, would've made me jump again if he didn't still have one hand on my shoulder.

When I looked, he'd stopped reaching for the knife and was instead holding out one of the courier pigeon machines I'd drained back in the prison. I hadn't even seen him pick it up.

The women jerked back, giving a quick and furtive shake of her head. "Can't have that in here. Not without being scrubbed. Could be carrying anything."

"It's dead," Oren replied shortly. He rapped the metal sphere against one of the wooden tent supports to show it had no response. "You want it or not?"

The woman's eyes flicked back toward me. I shook my head. "We've got nothing else."

She leaned out, looking this way and that, as if she could somehow see through the throng of people whether there was anyone watching us. Then she snatched the pigeon from Oren's fingers and retreated into the back of her booth, beginning to dismantle the machine with surprising deftness. More raw materials for jewelry, I guessed.

We hurried off before she could change her mind. As soon as I could gather my wits, I blurted, "Where'd *that* come from?"

"The prison." Oren's words were still clipped, as if spoken with great effort.

"I know that, I mean—how'd you know how to get rid of her?"

"Dominance." Oren was watching the crowd, eyes darting around, seeking the path of least resistance. "She just wanted to know she'd won, gotten the better of us. Animals do it all the time. A dominant wolf will let a lesser male eat from his kill when he's done, if the inferior animal shows the proper submissiveness. She didn't care about letting us go or not, she just wanted to win."

I stared at him as he moved aside for a cart laden with some kind of textile. My mind raced with questions—*what's a wolf?*—but I had no breath to ask. He led the way to the edge of the market, where we dodged behind a stall that had been closed down and abandoned.

The to and fro of the shoppers and vendors continued, but Oren had managed to find the one out-of-the-way pocket in the entire place. I leaned against the rusting wall at my back and tried to catch my breath.

Nix crawled back out of my collar. *"I see you have discovered the same information I did."*

"No pixies."

"No pixies," Nix agreed. *"More kinds of machines than exist in the Institute, but it seems pixies are illegal."*

"Well, that won't be a problem for you." My eyes were on Oren, who was crouched behind the counter of the stall, searching underneath it for anything the previous tenant might have left. "You can just change shape to look like some other machine."

"Perhaps." The doubt in the machine's voice dragged my attention away from Oren. *"But the number and variety of machines here suggests a facility and ease with technology above average, beyond even most architects. Anyone with that level of familiarity with machines will recognize me for what I am no matter the form I wear."*

I bit my lip. "When we gave her the pigeon, the woman mentioned 'scrubbing.' And it didn't sound like a simple polish. You'll have to stay hidden as much as you can."

Nix clicked its wings irritably but said nothing. I chose to take it as agreement.

"What're you looking for?"

Oren let the curtain fall where he was searching the under-counter storage of the stall. "Something to eat." He shrugged and straightened, narrowed eyes fixed on the crowd bustling back and forth.

As if reminded of how meager its last meal had been, my stomach gave a desperate lurch. I ignored it. I'd been hungrier than this before. Tansy and I had eaten well before we'd been caught off guard by the shadow people in the city above. I could go a little while longer before I'd really start to falter.

But what about Oren? Aside from the cheese in the tunnel an hour or two ago, when was the last time he ate? He wouldn't even know himself. I tried not to think about what his last meal as a shadow might have been.

At least that dulled my appetite a bit.

"We need to go to Central Processing." My voice sounded more certain than I was, enough to get Oren's attention, and Nix's too. The pixie's mechanisms slowed, quieting so it could listen to me.

"We'll need to have our stories straight, though," I continued. "Clearly we can't say we're Travelers bringing pixies for trade. And if we say anything else, they'll want to see our goods. Which we don't have."

"*You could acquire goods.*"

"With what?" Oren broke in, turning away from the crowd to pace restlessly. "We've got nothing to trade."

"*That stall owner will be busy for some time dismantling that other machine. I don't think she's paying much attention to her wares.*"

I stared at the pixie. "You want us to steal? How could we possibly get enough to look like traders in our own right without getting caught?"

"*That one is nimble,*" Nix said, the glowing blue eyes swiveling toward Oren. Its voice was calm as ever, despite my agitation. "*You are clever. And I can make a reasonable distraction.*"

In the blink of an eye, Nix changed from its bee form into its speedy dragonfly shape, and from there into something like a bird, eyes flashing all the while.

Oren was watching Nix as it changed back into its default pixie form, his gaze thoughtful. Considering. For perhaps the first time ever, he and the machine seemed to be in agreement.

"What? No." I shook my head, jaw clenching. "It's far too risky. We'll be caught. And as soon as they look at us, they're going to figure out we're the prisoners who escaped."

"This is why cities make you weak," Oren cut in, crouching down next to me and sifting through a handful of the dust and pebbles littering the floor. "Out there, you see an opportunity, you take it. They eat, or you do."

"You gave me food once upon a time," I pointed out.

His expression darkened, but he didn't look up at me. "And you're saying that wasn't a mistake?"

I just stood there for a moment, mouth still open. I was so floored that I didn't notice how the shadows around us changed until Oren lifted his head—and, focusing on something past my shoulder, tensed.

"Told you, told you." It was the woman from the jewelry stall, her thin lips stretched in a broad, smug smile. "Smugglers. Unregistered. Maybe even Renewables, you don't know. And they got a pixie."

Flanking her were two people wearing the uniform of the Eagles: dark grey pants and shirts under vests made of a dark, smoldering red-orange fabric. Their bearing as government enforcers was unmistakable. The taller of the two could've very well been Caesar himself, standing there in the moment he betrayed me to the Institute.

"Thank you, ma'am," said the shorter one, handing the woman something that flashed briefly in the light.

The taller one, the one who reminded me eerily of my oldest brother, reached out for me. Oren snarled, causing the officer to release my shoulder and turn, hand creeping toward something holstered at his waist.

"You, come with us immediately. And bring that monstrosity."

For a wild moment of panic, I thought he knew Oren's secret. But then I followed the cop's gaze and realized that his narrowed eyes were resting on Nix. The pixie. The contraband.

CHAPTER 10

Oren caught my eye, and I shook my head sharply. Fighting wasn't going to get us out of this. His jaw clenched as he looked away, jerking his shoulder out of the grip of the taller uniformed officer. He moved forward, though, as the uniformed man directed. The crowd parted in front of the officers like a stream around a boulder. People ran to avoid even brushing their sleeves against theirs. I shivered.

It was my fault Oren was in this position. And in it for the second time in as many days. I should have gotten him to the surface before turning back for Tansy—why break him out of our cell only to lead him straight into the arms of our captors? *Why free him in the Iron Wood, if only to live a life as a monster?*

Nix flew in close, pressing itself against my neck as the two officers escorted us out of the stall and made their way toward the huge, crescent-shaped building at the far end of the courtyard. My first thought was that it was frightened, but the ever-present calm in its voice when it spoke reminded me that it was a machine.

Machines don't feel.

"We have a few moments in which to devise a plan. I will hear no matter how softly you speak."

"You have to run." I breathed the words.

"And leave you?"

My mouth felt dry, like I'd been chewing on cotton. "Altruism, Nix?"

"I require proximity to you in order to remain functional." There was no punctuating flutter of its wings to simulate tone or emotion.

"You heard that woman. They're going to scrub you, whatever that means. For all we know, it means they'll take you apart, like she did to that courier pigeon. I think first and foremost you require all your parts to remain functional."

"Quiet," snapped the officer at my elbow, directing a glare down his nose at me. On a larger man, his build would have been imposing—but he was only a little taller than me, and instead he just looked stocky. He had thick, meaty hands that made my arm ache as he gave it a jerk.

Nix gave an irritated little buzz of its wings, and I had to fight a weary smile. Kris had programmed it well—all protectiveness and simulated outrage on my behalf.

The machine didn't reply right away, but I knew it was considering what I'd said. Tucked so close to me, the whirring and clicking of its mechanisms sounded like explosions. I could feel it thinking where its body pressed against the hollow below my ear.

Finally, it pulled away from my neck. *"Very well."*

And without further warning, it launched itself from my shoulder, shifted forms in midair, and sped straight upward.

"Hey!" My captor dropped my arm, fumbling for a pouch at his waist. I was as dumbfounded as he was, staggering back. He retrieved something from a pocket and threw it after Nix. My dazzled eyes struggled to follow it as it unfolded into a flat, winglike blade, wobbled once as if orienting itself, and then sped after the pixie. The second officer followed suit, and for a while I could just make out the two knifelike flyers in pursuit of what was now only a copper gleam.

I shielded my eyes with both hands against the dazzling rainbow sky, but in seconds I'd lost all sign of them. The sky was filled with machines, and though my eyes strained for some telltale sign of Nix, it was like the pixie—and its pursuers—had simply melted into the sky.

"Summon it back this instant," a voice snarled.

I blinked, staggering back, refocusing my eyes on the man beside me. "How?" I glanced from him to the machine-filled air above us. "It does whatever it wants; I don't control it."

The man's eyes bulged, his heavy hands coming down on my shoulders and giving me a shake that rattled my teeth. "Bad enough you brought a pixie in, but it's *rogue*?"

"Hey." Oren's voice was quiet, but it cut through the man's bluster like a knife. "Don't touch her."

The officer rolled his eyes toward Oren. He was standing an arm's length away from us. The taller officer who was supposed to be in charge of him was still scanning the sky, trying to catch a glimpse of Nix and the flying blades. Oren's expression was blank, but I knew him well enough to recognize the fury in his ice-blue eyes.

"You're not in a position to make demands, Outsider," said the short man, his hand drifting toward that holster on his belt. "Keep moving, or I'll do more than grab her shoulder."

Where I was standing, I couldn't see the man's expression. But he leaned close enough that I felt hot breath on my ear, and he must have done something to demonstrate what he meant by "do more," because Oren gave an inarticulate growl and lunged for him.

The taller man whirled, cursing, but Oren was already beyond his reach. Oren slammed into my captor, whose hand tore away from my shoulder as the collision drove him down into the ground. He grunted painfully at the impact, gasping for breath.

Oren pinned him there with a knee against his chest and slammed the heel of his hand into the man's face. Something cracked wetly, and blood spattered the dusty ground. Dimly, through the rushing in my ears, I heard a scream—the crowd had gathered around us at a safe distance, surrounding us in a ring of staring, horrified faces.

"Stop—Oren, *stop!*" I tried to grab at his arm, pull him away, but he shook me off.

I caught a glimpse of his face, transformed—violence was what he knew, how he coped. He was a creature of the wind and the sky and the rain, and each moment he stayed underground was a torment. It was all written on his face and in the strangely elegant lines of his body as he transformed the man's face into something unrecognizable.

"You're going to *kill* him!" I started toward him again, but somehow a tiny movement in the background caught my eye instead.

The taller of the two officers had drawn one of those curved machines they called talons out of a holster at his waist and was sighting down the length of it at Oren. I didn't have to know what it did to recognize it as a weapon.

I shouted something unintelligible—time slowed to a trickle. The air suddenly split, rent in two by a torrent of magic. My knees buckled as my body tried to remember which way was up. On the other side of Oren I saw someone in the crowd reel back with a scream and fall, twitching for a horribly long moment before lying still.

I wrenched my gaze back to the officer with the weapon

and saw him lining up another shot. I saw his finger tightening on the trigger as though each movement was an individual picture flashing before my eyes. My second sight snapped into focus, outlining everyone with a faint halo of golden light. They weren't Renewables—the only magic here was the barest needed to keep them alive.

But it was enough for me.

Time rushed back in with a roar, sweeping me up and shoving me at Oren, who was still pounding on the prone form of the officer. I threw myself at him with all my strength, colliding with him and rolling him off of the bloodied man. I grabbed at the officer's face, ignoring the hot, sticky flow of blood, and yanked at the magic I could feel flickering inside him.

The shadowy pit inside me leaped up, snapping at the energy, gleeful. This was no gentle, careful bloodletting the way I'd used Tansy's power in the cell—I tore the man's magic away so fast that my dazzled eyes could see the ragged edges of it flapping around the gaping black hole I'd left in his soul.

I curled my body around Oren, who was still thrashing, trying to shake me loose, but I wrapped the man's power around us both like a blanket, like a shield. I heard the air tear apart again, and this time something hot and metallic swept over us, rolling off the blanket like beads of water on a hot pan.

Oren stopped struggling, though I could feel his chest heaving for breath. My cheek was pressed against it, my arms gripping tight around his body. I braced myself, trying to hold the ragged clumps of stolen power together for another attack. My head spun, my vision blurring—I knew I wasn't going to last much longer.

"What the *hell* is going on here?"

A voice boomed across the courtyard, resonant enough that it penetrated even the muffling blanket of magic I held around us.

"Holster your weapon, you idiot!" The voice snapped with fury. "Firing in a crowd like this; you could have hit—"

Holding the shield together was an agony. I hadn't had the time to absorb the man's magic properly, and the hungry pit within me was sucking at the shields, trying to digest them. My body was on fire, and I could no longer hear what was going on beyond the screaming of my heartbeat and the frantic echo of Oren's. But there was no third blast, and after a few interminable moments I gave in, letting the darkness consume everything I'd taken.

. . .

It seemed I lay there for hours, but in reality I think only a few seconds passed before a hand touched my shoulder. I gasped for a breath, lifting my head. A new face swam into focus above mine—a middle-aged man, balding, familiar somehow.

He threw himself down at the side of the motionless man, bending over him. I saw him check for breath, his cheek close to the man's lips. He pressed his mouth to the bloodstained lips, and I saw the uniformed chest rise and fall as the balding man tried to breathe for him. After a few breaths he stopped and thumped the injured man on the chest, over his heart. I'd never seen anything like it before—in my city, when someone stopped breathing, they were just dead.

Finally, he jerked upright. "He's breathing," he gasped. I felt my own breath falter with relief. I hadn't killed him.

The taller officer was staring, mumbling something, his weapon dangling from one hand.

"You call a medic," the balding man snapped, getting to

his feet and then reaching for my wrist to haul me upright. "I'll take them from here."

The tall man said something else—I couldn't hear properly, as though something had exploded right by my ear.

"No, he isn't dead," the man in charge said, his tone frosty. "But if you don't get him to a medic, he will be. And make sure they take a look at the unlucky bastard you just shot."

The middle-aged man ushered me and Oren along, sending the crowd scattering back away from us with muffled cries and gasps. "Quick now," he said, his resonant voice pitched low.

I looked up at him, trying to force my eyes to work properly. I knew I'd seen him before. I glanced over my shoulder, at the still form lying within the ring of silent onlookers. I couldn't tell if he was alive or dead. Our unlikely rescuer had implied that he was still alive, but I knew how quickly and ruthlessly I'd acted.

All I could see, over and over again, was the gaping black hole I'd left there when I ripped the life force from him.

I stumbled, too shattered to keep up the pace this man was demanding from us.

"Not yet. The Eagles will be watching. Keep moving—fall apart later."

He managed to get us out of the courtyard, but I couldn't tell where we were headed. When we stopped we were in some kind of alley, a space between two rusting metal buildings. Oren dropped to his knees when the man let him go. Mine buckled, but the man kept hold of me, pushing me against the alley wall to keep me upright.

His face swam into focus, and suddenly I realized how I knew him. He had changed clothes—though he didn't wear the badge with the bird on it, he was dressed like they were, in charcoal grey and smoldering red-orange. But I recognized him anyway—he was the man from before, the one who'd caught my eye after the boy was taken away as a Renewable. The man in the brilliant blue coat.

"I know what you are," he said, his face not far from mine. "And we need you."

CHAPTER 11

The man refused to answer any of my questions, pulling us back out of the alley again and marching us through the square towards the Central Processing building. When I glanced at Oren, he was moving along blank-eyed. The knuckles of his right hand were bleeding, the blood sliding down his finger-tips and spattering the ground every time he took a step. He didn't return my gaze.

There was no sign of Nix. Every time I heard the buzz of wings or the click of a mechanism turning over, my heart leaped. But it was always a courier pigeon on its way to deliver a message, or occasionally one of those bladelike flying machines the officers had worn.

We stumbled up the steps, as if he was leading us into CeePo itself. But then he let go of my arm and nodded to one of the officers standing guard outside the massive copper doors.

"Just taking these prisoners around the back, to interrogation."

The guard nodded, and then we were moving again, this time following the arc of the building, marching in a giant parabola. When we reached the end of the crescent, however, instead of continuing around behind the building, he pulled us off to the side. We headed behind a huge metal support for a building above, something that must have once been a giant walker leg. There, concealed in the shadows, was a door.

It was barely visible, made of the same rusting metal as the wall, so that it melted into the background. It was only when I leaned close that I realized the rust was painted on. It was so skillfully done that it looked three-dimensional, indistinguishable from its surroundings.

Our rescuer leaned against it, spreading his palm against the surface for a few moments. My skin tingled, and I realized I could feel a slight stirring of magic. It was tiny, so deftly and quietly done that I would've missed it had I not been standing a few feet away. But this close, it was unmistakable.

A Renewable.

Before I had time to process what that meant, there was a solid clunk somewhere inside the door and the slow, steady clanking of a mechanism turning over inside. Part of the rust-painted exterior slid aside, revealing a long dark slot into which the man inserted his arm, feeling around inside the door.

Then all at once the door swung inward, so abruptly that the balding man staggered. Standing on the other side was a young woman crowned with a wild halo of curly blonde hair. Her eyes went from the man to Oren and his battle scars—and then fell on me, where they stayed, widening. As if I was the shock and not Oren, who was dripping blood and staring all around with fierce, wary eyes.

"You got her," she said, letting out a long sigh. "Damage?"

"Bystander," the man replied. "Not one of ours. And they brought down an Eagle, don't know if he's going to make it. I'm meant to be taking them to the cells under CeePo."

She nodded. She had a youthful face and a sweet voice, but something about the way she stood made me think she was older than she appeared. She kept watching me for a few moments, her gaze troubled. Then she turned back toward the man.

"Ready?" she asked.

"Just a second." The man turned toward us, glancing first at Oren and then turning to me. "Olivia's going to take you from here on in. Try not to kill anyone, okay? We're trying to help you."

"But—I don't understand." My head was still spinning, my eyesight sparking with magic. For some reason the man looked as though he was surrounded by pinpoints of gold and violet light, even though a second ago he'd looked completely normal. *The aftereffects of the magic I stole and used,* I realized. The effect was dizzying, but I held myself upright, refusing to lose control around people I didn't know.

"We'll explain later. Just trust us for a little while."

His face was so earnest, his eyes so piercing, and yet I felt the bottom dropping out of my stomach. How many times had I been asked to trust someone over the past months? I felt my muscles tensing, my mouth going dry. And then a hand touched mine, a tingle of magic thrumming between us.

For once, Oren was the one keeping me grounded.

The man was watching me, waiting for my response. I nodded, and he breathed out in a rush, as if he'd been holding his breath. He straightened and started backing up, putting some distance between him and the hidden doorway.

"Okay, Vee. Make it count this time. Just don't break my nose again."

The blonde girl laughed and flexed her hand—which I noticed, suddenly, was wrapped up in strips of tape. "I'll do my best." She followed him, stretching and flexing her fingers.

"Confidence-inspiring," he muttered and then closed his mouth, dropping his shoulders.

Without further warning, Olivia bounced up onto the balls of her feet, leaned back, and then threw her whole shoulder forward into a punch that knocked the man flat before he could utter another word.

I lurched back into Oren, who cursed, staggering as well. But we were in a corner formed by the wall and the old walker leg, and the blonde girl was between us and escape. My mind just quit, going absolutely blank. There'd been too much running, too much thinking—now it was like it had just given up.

The blonde girl advanced on us, shaking out her fist, wrinkling her nose. "Guess it's better to be me than him, but goddamn, that hurts." She must have seen my face. The chagrined, amused smile vanished, her brows drawing inward, lips pursing in concern. "Oh, hell, Wesley didn't tell you guys anything, did he?"

It didn't look like she was about to turn her fists on us. I tried to speak, but my dry throat made the words come out in a croak. "Not so much."

Olivia sighed, rolling her eyes. The expression seemed bizarrely out of place on her angelic features, like it had been painted on a doll's face. "Of course he'd leave it all on me. Asshole." She ran her hand through her hair, setting the curls to disarray.

"Well, for starters, I'm Olivia. And you two just fought your way free from one of the Eagles' deployment officers." She inclined her head toward the prone form of the man she'd called Wesley. "When they find him, he'll wake up and tell them all about it. But you'll be long gone."

I stared at her. She'd hit him hard enough to knock him out—and all for show?

Olivia winked. "Welcome to the resistance."

. . .

The door in the wall led to a walkway that was half tunnel, half disused alley. At times I could see narrow snatches of the rainbow sky overhead, between the tall buildings on either side. Others, we had to stoop to fit through ventilation chambers and crawl spaces. We went up ladders and down staircases, and on one occasion climbed down a crumbling brick wall, using spots where the mortar had fallen away as handholds.

It seemed that earlier in the city's history these were occupied buildings. But the other buildings had been built right on top of the old, half-crushing some, leaving others empty and abandoned, forming a strange undercity.

Cities under cities under cities—I thought of the people above, of Trina and Brandon and their children. They had no idea what existed beneath their feet.

It was like being in the tunnels under my home city again. Basil would have loved this. For the first time since the little girl had turned into a shadow, I felt as though I was able to take a deep breath. Sometimes it seemed as though the world was made of walls—I just hoped I'd come out on the right side of this one.

Olivia gestured for quiet the first few times I started to ask questions, glancing at the walls of the alley, the open air, the vents in the corridors. I could only assume we were passing between and below and above houses, or even government buildings. Eventually, however, we emerged into a broader corridor. We passed people occasionally now, and they'd nod at Olivia, eye Oren and I curiously. When one of them used the same name as Wesley had used, Vee, I asked about it. This time she didn't shush me.

"Most of us don't go by our real names. I guess it started as a way to stay anonymous, back when everyone was living double lives in the city. But now even most lifers, like me, have other names."

"Lifers?"

"People who live entirely inside the walls. People Prometheus would have locked up, if he could find them."

Oren made a small sound in his throat. When I looked at him, his face was stony, unreadable. But I could tell from the tension in his shoulders that he was ill at ease. One of us claustrophobic, the other afraid of the sky—there was no place where both of us could be.

"Will that man—Wesley—will he be okay?" The last I'd seen him, he wasn't moving, lying in a heap on the ground.

"Oh, don't worry about him. If prisoners disappeared on his watch all the time, they'd suspect him of being one of us right away. Make it look like he simply got overwhelmed, and knocked about in the process, and it's much harder to point fingers at him."

"Earlier, he was working with the Eagles—he sent someone away, just a kid."

Olivia nodded. "He told us. Don't worry, he wasn't a Renewable. They get half a dozen reports like that a month. A neighbor misinterprets something, or just plain doesn't like someone, or something turns up missing, and bam. Renewable sightings everywhere."

"What's going to happen to him? The kid they took?"

"They'll run some tests on him and find out he's not a Renewable, and he'll be free in a day or two."

"And what if he had been a Renewable?"

Olivia didn't speak, but I saw the answer in the way her face tightened and smile vanished.

"Why go to all this trouble for us?" Oren didn't bother to hide the suspicion in his voice.

"No offense," Olivia replied. "But we don't give a damn about you. It's her we want. You just happened to get here with her."

My chest tightened again. So much for being able to breathe here. I'd been here only a few hours, and already people wanted to use me. At least Olivia was being up front about it.

"Why me?" I sounded as suspicious as Oren.

"We're not—we're not sure." Her voice was slightly troubled. "If nothing else, though, we could always use another Renewable."

Oren glanced at me, blue eyes piercing. Though he didn't speak, I knew what had prompted the look. These people thought I was a Renewable. I shook my head a fraction.

Let's keep it quiet for now.

Wait until they told us what they wanted from me—and what would happen to me if I couldn't help them.

I should change the subject, ask something else, but curiosity got the better of me. "How did you know what I was?"

"Wesley," Olivia replied. "He's Sighted. Most Renewables are, but he's sharper than anyone. Usually his position within the Eagles makes him perfect for spotting new Renewables when they come through CeePo, but you just happened to catch him on his day off."

It was strange that I hadn't been able to tell Wesley was a Renewable until he'd opened the door with magic. Even then, the feel of magic nearby was faint, easy to miss. In the Iron Wood, everyone was surrounded by a warm, golden light when I used my second sight. But then, everyone there was a Renewable. There was no need to learn to hide it. Here, being a Renewable was grounds for being locked up.

Olivia turned and caught me staring hard at her, trying to see if she carried any telltale sparkles of hidden magic. She laughed. "You can stop squinting like that, I'm no Renewable."

"Why do Renewables have to go through Central Processing?"

"Well, everyone does. But Renewables especially. Most people still hate them, so even if someone tries to hide, they're usually ratted out by their neighbors."

Deciding to redirect the conversation back to Olivia, I asked, "So if you're not a Renewable, how do you know so much about them? About—us?"

Her reply was quiet. "I'm not a Renewable, but my twin brother was."

I fell silent.

We reached another door, this one round and squat with a wheel on it. There was a small glass window in the top of the door, but it was so grimy that I could only see that there was light on the other side of it. The door was unlocked—Olivia just reached forward and heaved at the wheel, swinging the door open with a screech of hinges. Beyond it was a low-ceilinged room dominated by a long table covered in papers and half-dismantled machines. A few people stood around it, and heads turned towards us as we followed Olivia inside.

"Hey, guys," she said as everyone's eyes fell on me. "This is her. Lark Ainsley."

I never told her my name. It was like someone had thrown a vat of ice water over me. Beside me, Oren tensed, drawing nearer to me.

Part of me knew I should just run. Wrench away some magic—because more than one of the men around the table was a Renewable—and cast some sort of barrier, and use the confusion to get myself and Oren out of here.

But I was tired of being batted around from prison to prison, from one group of people using me to the next. Enough.

"How do you know who I am?" My voice was tight, stiff—iron-cold.

One of the men around the table straightened, breaking the tableau. He was a tall man in his forties, with well-worn clothing and a thick stubble spreading down his neck. He was staring at me as though looking at a long-lost friend, like someone he'd seen once in a dream.

"You *are* her," he murmured. His eyes were wide, wondering.

I braced myself, slipping into my second sight, picking my targets. Part of me recoiled at how easy this was becoming. Where was the girl who'd once had nightmares of a shadow child's scream as it fell down a cliff face?

"Parker." Olivia's voice was low, warning. Though she wasn't a Renewable, she could clearly tell I was bracing for something. I saw her move, place herself between me and the door.

He swallowed, wrenching himself out of his stupor. "Yes, I see. Lark—Miss Ainsley. Please, stand down. You have to understand what a huge moment this is for us. You're her— you're really her."

"I don't see it." That was one of the other men, a younger one, his voice full of skepticism.

Parker shook his head, though he never took his eyes from my face. "Trust me. This is Lark Ainsley. Imagine her five or six years younger—it's her. The girl in the journal."

CHAPTER 12

It had been so long since I'd seen my own reflection that at first, the girl in the journal seemed utterly unrecognizable. Familiar, like I'd known her once, long ago—but there was no moment of instant recognition. Until I started flipping pages backward.

They'd given me and Oren each a room to stay in. Though they were barely bigger than closets, they had enough room for a bed. Oren was eating and showering—who knew when he was last clean? But I'd refused to do anything until they brought me the journal.

It was really more of a sketchbook. After the first few pages, which were covered in handwriting, the rest of the pages were filled with drawings and only the occasional caption or paragraph of text. Schematics for machines, mostly, with numeric notations and little else to contextualize them. Some I recognized from the machines I'd seen walking around the city outside, and others were wholly unrecognizable. I couldn't even tell whether some drawings were of machines or simply geometric patterns, nonsensical.

But here and there, tucked into margins and occasionally dominating half a page, were sketches of a girl.

Me.

At first, early on, the drawings were clumsy, inexpert. Drawn by someone with the ability to create technical drawings but for whom faces weren't easy. But the artist had gotten better. Gradually, as the pages went on, the lines smoothed out. The eyes were more confidently placed, the hair following much more graceful lines. The drawings changed from something almost childlike to something admirable.

Even so, it was the early faces that seemed most like me. It was as if the artist had known me long ago and was drawing me from memory—but even as their talent at drawing increased, the specific details of my face had started to slip away. The last entry in the journal was just my face, a pencil sketch. Artistic, sweet. The mouth didn't seem quite right— the cheeks were too round, the chin a bit too long. But the eyes were mine, and they stared back at me from the page, as though the child I'd once been had caught up to me. Below it was my name, *Lark Ainsley*.

When I flipped all the way back to the first page, my fingers froze.

Written there, in the neat, perfect lines of machine-formed lettering, were the words:

Property of the Institute of Magic and Natural Philosophy

The journal was from my home city. And then, in that instant, I knew whose it was.

I bolted off of my bed and shoved the door open so hard that it slammed into the wall. Retracing my steps wasn't easy—so many of the corridors looked alike. But after a few wrong turns, my heart slamming in my ribcage, I found the War Room, as Olivia had affectionately called it.

"Whose is this?" I gasped, brandishing the tattered journal.

My eyes scanning startled faces. Olivia wasn't there

anymore, but the man who'd recognized me—Parker—was. He looked from my face to the journal and then back again.

"Lark—" he began slowly.

I knew that tone. It didn't mean anything good. "Tell me!" I could hear my voice cracking and didn't care. I was so close. "Where is the man who owns this journal? Tell me, or I swear I'll walk right out there and find Prometheus and tell him where—"

"If I could tell you, I would!" Parker shouted over me. His voice rasped uncomfortably; he was clearly not a man used to raising his voice. When I had to stop for lack of breath, he spoke more quietly. "We don't know whose it is. It was here before we were."

My stomach roiled. The jolt of recognition, of adrenaline as I ran through the corridors, receded, leaving me nauseous. "What do you mean, before you were here?"

"We've only been living in the walls for three, four years. It was after Prometheus took over and named our city Lethe. That's when it became unsafe for Renewables to live openly. The earliest rebels against Prometheus are all gone now; it's not exactly a healthy life choice to go off-grid. But the story goes that when the very first Renewables went on the run from Prometheus, they only found this place because someone else did first. Someone else made the door, the ladders."

Someone skilled at moving underground, unseen. Someone at home in the tunnels under the world. My eyes stung, and I willed them to stay dry. I still didn't know what these people wanted from me—I refused to let them see me weak.

Parker was still watching me, the others in the room silent. "We keep the journal close at hand. To study it. He or she had made it their job to study the machines here, figure out how Prometheus's walkers and blades and ornithopters operated. And there are machines here Prometheus has never even dreamed of that we're trying to build, to get the upper hand. It's our only real weapon against him."

I shook my head, trying to make sense of what he was saying. "This person—where is he now?"

Parker shook his head. His expression was wary—he hadn't forgotten how ready I was to use magic against them earlier. But there was a sympathy there too, in his brown eyes, that made me look away. "He was long gone before we found this place. We always assumed . . ." He hesitated, and I could feel his eyes on my face. "We always assumed that he made a move on Prometheus and failed."

Failed. I stared at the wall, numb. Maybe it wasn't him. Maybe it was all a coincidence.

Parker took a step back. "But we do have the other things he left behind."

I couldn't speak—my mouth was too dry, my throat too tight. But Parker must've seen my face, because he turned and went to one of the many chests lining the room. He lifted out a few papers, glancing at them and then setting them aside. Eventually he found what he was looking for.

It was a small box, no bigger than a backpack. He hadn't left much behind. I sat down on the floor, ignoring the way the stares of everyone in the room burned holes in my back. There were a few commonplace objects in there. A lighter, a canteen, a roll of bandages and a tube of ointment. A flashlight. A pocket encyclopedia, a couple of other small books. A few parts from unidentifiable machines.

And a paper bird.

My fingers stopped a hair's breadth from the crumpled, grubby paper object in the bottom of the box. Eyesight blurring, blood roaring in my ears, I almost missed Parker's question. But only almost.

"Do you know who wrote the journal?"

"My brother." I swallowed, but it didn't help. My voice still sounded strange, like it didn't belong to me and never had. "The journal belonged to my brother, Basil Ainsley."

CHAPTER 13

Oren came to my room that night after I'd managed to swallow a few bites of dinner.

I had eaten apart from the others on Parker's advice, both to let myself have some time, and to let the others come to terms with my existence. Apparently, the "girl in the journal" was almost like a religious figure among the resistance movement. I was the only name associated with the person who'd unwittingly founded their anti-Prometheus movement. There were those who thought that Lark Ainsley was the one who'd written the journal. A few even thought I'd come back to finish what I started and take down Prometheus once and for all.

I'd taken the box of Basil's belongings with me when I left the War Room and spent the time sitting on the cot in my tiny room, searching each item for answers. I couldn't quite bring myself to read my brother's journal, not yet—it was too much like reading his last words, bidding him farewell.

After I'd answered his knock, Oren stood in the open doorway, characteristically quiet. His eyes rested on the objects strewn across my blanket, didn't lift to look at me. He was looking better—less like he felt the need to pummel the nearest bystander, at least. I'd gotten used to the sky after a few days, so maybe he was slowly getting used to being underground.

"They don't know what I am," he said eventually, surprising me. I'd expected him to say something about my brother—no doubt he would've heard any number of things at dinner.

Part of me resented the fact that Oren, the monster, could move freely amongst these people, with no one staring at him or whispering his name. But I saw how much more settled he looked, how his shoulders had dropped and his barely scabbed-over hands had relaxed, and I couldn't keep the resentment burning.

"I think there's enough magic in the air here that you'd be fine, even if I wasn't around." I dropped my eyes back to the blanket. The paper bird my brother had carried with him lay next to mine. But for the fact that his was dirty, more crumpled, and torn, it could've been the twin of the one that had rested in my pocket since the day I fled my home.

Oren made a noncommittal sound, still lingering in the doorway. It wasn't a big room, but I wished he'd decide whether he wanted to come in or leave. Abruptly, I remembered the chill in his voice when he said that saving my life in the woods by giving me food was a mistake.

"You could stay here, you know." I kept my eyes on the birds, the identical folds and creases. "You wouldn't have to risk hurting anyone else."

"Are you going to stay?"

The question caught me off guard, despite the fact that it'd been lurking at the back of my thoughts for hours. How could I stay in a city ruled by the man who killed my brother? And yet—where else could I go?

"I don't know yet."

I heard him shift, the metal doorframe creaking a little

as he leaned on it. "Parker says that Prometheus is one of the best manipulators of magic anyone's ever seen. He's responsible for almost all the machines here, and for the magic in the air. The lights, the air filters, everything."

"But he does it using Renewables as slaves. And he's a murderer."

"Maybe."

I looked up to find Oren watching me, his usually clear, fierce eyes troubled.

"But they say he's been studying the—the shadows, as you call them." His lips twitched around the word "me," but he didn't say it aloud. Our hallway was hardly private. "I'd be interested in finding out more about his research."

I knew what Oren was after. If he was cured, he could live anywhere and never have to worry about the monster inside him ever again.

Despite the way he leaned against the doorframe, he seemed taller, more assured. He wasn't sweating anymore, and he'd gotten a change of clothes from someone. Gone were the patched pants, the transparently thin shirt. He'd washed the Eagle's blood from his face and hands. But for a few bruises, he could've fit in anywhere.

For a strange, confusing moment, I missed his ferocity. In my mind that was who Oren was—all action and quick thinking, instincts honed for survival. Strong, uncompromising. Even when he was afraid in the outside city, it was the fear of a caged animal waiting to be set free.

But now he had purpose.

"Then you should definitely stay," I said, forcing myself to look down at my blanket.

The doorframe creaked again as Oren stopped leaning against it. He didn't speak right away. I tried to imagine him hesitant, uncertain, but I could only see his new sense of purpose, changing him.

Eventually, he just said, "Good night, Lark."

When I lifted my head again, he was gone.

I stared at the empty doorway for a few moments, then got up to shut the door with a screech of rusty hinges.

Why wasn't I more excited for Oren? If Prometheus had information that could help him, it would change his life. The life I'd ruined by revealing his secret, the one he didn't even know he had. If I'd never come along, Oren would never have known what he really was.

But if he were cured—it would change everything. He wouldn't have to hate me for what I'd done to him. I wouldn't have to feel that same disgust, imagining the things he's done, every time he touched me. I'd be able to kiss him and not taste blood.

And yet. If he were cured, there'd be nothing tying him to me. He'd no longer be forced to stay close to me, leeching my magic to stay human.

I tried to shove thoughts of Oren aside and sat back down on the bed. I piled everything Basil had left behind back into its box, but for the books and the journal. Leaning back against the wall behind the cot, I sorted through the tiny pile. There was an encyclopedia of plants, languages, animals, geography, and basic science—everything a city boy would need to survive beyond the Wall. It was marked with the same line of ownership as the journal. The other books, however, had no seals of ownership. Either he'd gotten them later, elsewhere, or he'd stolen them from the Institute and not given them a chance to claim them. One, a heavily worn paperback, was a handbook on aerodynamics. Another was a small, thick book on magical theory—it was ancient, nearly falling apart. Probably from before the Renewable wars. And the third—I stopped and reached for it, frowning. The last one was a book of stories. Basil had never shown much interest in stories beyond those he made up to tell me as a child when I had nightmares. At home, he was never that interested in reading at all unless the books were about machines and magic, because he dreamed of becoming one of the vitrarii, the glassworkers who created the circuitry to carry magic.

I opened the book to its title page. *Myths and Legends from Long Ago*, it read. Collected and presented by one Tiberius L. Minton. I skimmed some of the pages, which were filled with odd tales of imaginary creatures, supernatural powers, and pantheons of petty gods and goddesses. It wasn't until I started flipping through the rest of the book that it fell open, and I realized that one of the pages had been dog-eared and marked.

My heart skipped as I saw the name printed there in the title of this particular story: *"Prometheus and the Fire of the Gods."*

For a wild moment, I considered the idea that the leader of the city was some kind of legendary being. Then sense reasserted itself, and I realized that he must have taken his name from this story. And that Basil had been trying to figure out why.

I kicked the blankets away from my legs, trying to keep cool, and started to read.

Prometheus was a figure in the stories from a culture I'd never heard of, an ancient race called the Hellenes. It seemed that in their time, Renewables were considered to be divine, descended from a pantheon of gods and goddesses that lived on high and dabbled in mortal affairs for their own amusement. Prometheus predated this all, part of a group called the Titans, from whom the Hellenes' gods were descended.

According to the Hellenes, the time before Renewables was lost in a terrible darkness. Men were cold, hungry, and—I swallowed, sick to my stomach—cannibalistic. Mankind knew no better because there was no fire in their lives. There was a footnote there, but most of it was worn away at the bottom of the page. Something about literal versus figurative translation, but beyond that I couldn't read.

Prometheus saw mankind struggling and destroying one another and felt sorry for them. And so he stole the fire of the gods and delivered it to them. And after that, mankind was enlightened and could lead normal lives. The phrase "fire of the gods" had been underlined, but there were no notes to explain why. I reread the passage, searching for some kind of clue as to why the city's leader would choose this figure as his namesake. From the description, it sounded as though fire was a metaphor for magic. Without it, men became savage shadows. But this city was here long before Prometheus came to power, according to Olivia and Parker. So it wasn't as though he had saved them from being shadows, or created this haven in the midst of the darkness outside.

I turned the page to see a gruesome woodcut depiction of a man—Prometheus, according to the caption—sprawled on a rock, having his stomach torn apart by a bird of prey. The same bird, I realized, that figured on the badges of the officers. Eagles.

I kept reading and found out that the gods were infuriated by Prometheus's intervention. They punished him by chaining him to a rock for all eternity and sending a giant eagle to peck out his liver every day. And every night he'd regrow it, so he could suffer the same torture the next day.

I shuddered, shutting the book with a dull thud. What kind of man would ever want to model himself on that? And why name his personal police force after the creature that tortured his namesake?

The kind of man who uses Renewables as batteries. The kind who killed my brother.

Part of me just wanted to flee, get out of this city while I still could, but an even larger part of me wanted to unravel the mystery of it, take it apart, see what made it all tick.

On a whim, I opened the book again. There was an index in the back listing all the entries alphabetically. I slid my finger down the columns until I found the one I'd been looking for: *Lethe.*

I flipped back to the right page. It was a story about a girl named Persephone in the Underworld, but I wasn't interested in her. I scanned the sentences until the word popped up. "*. . . the river Lethe, whose waters allowed the dead to forget their earthly lives and cares.*"

I pushed the books away, head spinning. Had my brother found something in these stories that I'd missed? They were about a mythological figure, not the real man in power. If only Basil were here to explain. Trying to retrace his steps was like trying to assemble a puzzle where most of the pieces are missing.

If only Basil were here.

. . .

Sleep was impossible. Though I knew that my door wasn't locked, that I could leave whenever I wanted, it felt so much like my room in the Institute that my eyes wouldn't stay closed. I found myself longing for the outside, for fresh air and the open sky. Here the air was too warm, too humid. Too close. I'd become used to tracking the sun, to letting nature dictate when I woke and when I slept. Here I just flipped a switch, and the world changed from day to night.

For another thing, I couldn't stop thinking about Basil and Prometheus and what had transpired between them.

There wasn't much in my tiny room, just a chest for clothes I didn't own and the box containing Basil's belongings.

I half-expected to open the clothes chest and find sets of tunics and trousers made for children, like in the Institute. I could feel the weight of expectation bearing down on me like the low ceiling—these people weren't all that different from the architects. They needed me for their plans.

Eventually I gave up, throwing back my blankets, which were clammy with perspiration. I pulled my shoes on and pushed open my door as carefully as I could, every creak and cry of the hinges sounding like an alarm in my ears. They hadn't told me I had to stay in my room, but creeping down the empty corridor, I still felt like an intruder.

I hadn't had enough time to make a mental map of the place. From what the others had said, the spaces in the walls existed everywhere, throughout the city. Around it, beneath it, inside it. But I could at least explore my immediate surroundings, so long as I kept track of how to get back.

There were dim lights spaced at intervals along the corridor, just barely enough to see by. Creating a false night, I supposed. I traced the wall with my fingertips as I walked, listening to the dull echoes of my own footsteps.

I saw a brighter light in the distance. When I got closer, I realized that it was a light from someone's room, shining through their open door. I hesitated, remembering what Parker had said about giving the rebels a chance to get used to Lark Ainsley being a flesh-and-blood girl. Moving as silently as I could, I crept up to the wedge of light. Stopping at its edge, I peered inside.

Olivia was sitting on an overturned packing crate, unwrapping her hands. The skin beneath the tape was red, irritated, but otherwise undamaged. I could see her in profile, her head bowed, the light from her lamp catching in her golden hair. She gave no sign that she saw me, focused on her task.

When she'd pulled off all the tape, she flexed her hands, grimacing a little. I'd never thought about the fact that it might hurt the puncher as much as the punched—and Olivia was hardly a large person. A little taller than me, but nowhere near as big as the man she'd decked earlier with one blow.

"Can't sleep?" Olivia's voice made me jump. She turned her head a little, looking at me out of the corner of one eye with a faint smile.

I cleared my throat, feeling my cheeks beginning to burn. "I'm sorry. I was exploring. I didn't mean to—"

She gave a dismissive wave of her hand and got to her feet. Massaging her knuckles, she turned toward me. "What's the matter?"

I opened my mouth, but nothing came out. It wasn't that I didn't know, but the opposite: there were so many things the matter that I didn't know where to start. But none of these things make their way out of my mouth. Instead, I muttered, "I'm not used to there being no nighttime."

Olivia blinked at me, surprised. "Is that all? You must have arrived in the morning, Lethe time."

"Lethe time?"

"As opposed to the time Above, in the ruins outside. When it's day here, it's night there. Here, I'll show you."

"I don't mean to keep you up," I protested. It'd been hours since the halls had gone quiet, and everyone else—I'd assumed—had gone to sleep.

She shook her head, lips curving in something a little sadder than a smile. "It's okay. I don't sleep too well these days, anyway. I'm not used to sleeping alone."

Olivia had mentioned losing a brother, but she hadn't mentioned losing anyone else. A husband? It was hard to tell how old she was, but she didn't seem that much older than me. Maybe her boyfriend? But she was already past me, leading the way down the corridor. If she didn't want to volunteer, I wasn't going to ask.

I soon lost track of all the turns, but Olivia moved with absolute certainty. She knew this place like the back of her hand. She'd called herself a lifer—I tried to imagine spending all my time inside the walls, always living on the edges of the real city.

If I stay, I realized, *this will be my life too.*

This was how Basil had lived, before he vanished. Before he challenged Prometheus and lost, or before Prometheus found him. I tried to imagine his presence here, the way I always could in the sewer tunnels at home, but I couldn't.

Eventually Olivia and I reached the end of a particular narrow tunnel that terminated in a metal door. She unlocked it with a twist of its handle. I braced for the shriek of rusty hinges, but this one opened as silently as a sigh. And as soon as it swung open, I realized why.

The door opened onto a wide, slightly rounded platform that was open to the outer city. If the hinges made noise, it'd give away this entrance to the walls. They must keep them carefully oiled.

And Olivia was right—outside, Lethe was shrouded in night.

The sky above, which during the day was lit by thousands of magic lights fractured into rainbows by the mist, was dark. The only hints of light up above were nebulas of pale blue and green, so faint I wasn't sure my eyes weren't playing tricks on me. The effect was like nothing I'd ever seen before—nothing like the stars or the moon, or the faint violet sheen of my home city's Wall when the sun disc set.

Olivia led the way out onto the platform, which I soon realized was the roof of a building. Though the surface was rounded, giving the unsettling impression that I could slide off at any moment, it was actually broad enough that it was as easy to walk on as the flat ground.

She took a seat on the roof, stretching her legs out and leaning back on her hands.

"This is incredible," I said, staring.

She quickly raised a hand to stop me, then held a finger to her lips. When she spoke, her voice was merely a murmur. "Most people are asleep right now, but on the off chance someone nearby's awake, we try to keep quiet up here. The door's pretty well hidden, but we don't want anyone getting curious about voices coming from up here."

I bit my lip. But she patted the ground beside her in a clear invitation, so I sat down cross-legged next to her.

"What happened to all the lights?" I whispered.

"They're still there," Olivia replied. "They're just not shining. At night there's no magic coming through to light them up. That glow is just from the fungus that grows on the cavern ceiling. Phosphorescence, completely natural and magic-free."

I thought of Oren, my pulse quickening a little. "What about all the people who aren't Renewables, who can't survive without the magic?"

"Enough comes through during the day to keep us going at night." Olivia tilted her head back, eyes on the ceiling. "Those lights are designed that way. They're imperfect vessels—they leak. The magic comes into the air through the mist formed when the hot air down here hits the colder air up near the surface."

"Designed? By whom?"

"Prometheus. He saved us."

"But—I thought you were all fighting him, that he was the bad guy."

Olivia sighed. "It's not really that simple. For a long time, since the Renewable wars, this place was a haven. Huge reserves of magic kept the city running, kept its people human despite the chaos above. The idea was always that by keeping one bastion of sanity in the chaos, at whatever cost, people could survive the fallout from the wars and find a way to restore the land."

"Dorian—that is, a man I met while traveling—mentioned that this place was experimenting with fixing what the Renewables broke."

Olivia nodded. "The Star—the giant crystal tower, you would've seen it in the ruins Above—was one of those experiments. But it was put up so long ago that by the time the energy reserves in the city began to run out, no one was alive who knew how to shut it down. It takes a huge amount of magic to light that Star and keep the land around it saturated with magic. There's no insulation there, just open air that lets all the power just dissipate out into nothing."

"So people moved down here." I remembered the muffling doors and airlocks and rooms lined with iron that we'd passed through in order to enter the city below.

"Exactly. It lets us keep the magic in. But even that wasn't enough. The city was dying, bit by bit. They shut down all the machines except the ones that bring us air and water. People were leaving in droves. That was when Prometheus showed up."

"Who was he? Where did he come from?"

Olivia shrugged. "No one knows. He just walked into the courtyard one day and started talking, and people listened. He laid out an entire framework for how to save the city. He recruited teams to help him, and together they built the crystal lights on the cavern ceiling. So by day Above, the Star keeps the shadows there human. But by night, Prometheus's inventions siphon the Star's magic into the lights, and we have our daytime down here. And we have enough magic to live by."

"He stole fire from the gods," I murmured, staring at the ceiling, where the crystals lay dormant, waiting for magic.

"What's that?"

"Nothing. Something I read." I swallowed. "So why not funnel all the magic down here? Aren't you still losing a lot of power by letting the Star shine during the day?"

"If you haven't noticed," Olivia said wryly, "there's not a lot of room down here to grow crops. We need the Empty Ones above to work the farms."

Horror crept over me. "You—keep them human long enough to grow you food? And let them turn into monsters at night?"

Olivia didn't look at me, gazing out toward the far wall of the cavern, lost in the darkness. "They only think they're human," she said softly. "It's an illusion brought by the presence of magic. Without them, we'd all starve. Would you rather they stay Empty all the time, without even the echo of the people they once were?"

I had no answer for that. But I felt sure Oren would.

"Not everyone agrees with Prometheus. But after he saved us, he became the uncontested leader of the city. Renamed it Lethe, citing something about a new start." Olivia eased back until she was lying on the roof, her blonde curls splayed out against the rusty surface. "Most of us have lived here long enough to know what life was like before Prometheus showed up five years ago. We know we'd all be dead without him, later if not sooner."

"It sounds like he's a savior," I said bitterly, trying not to think of Basil. "Why fight him? Why the resistance?"

Olivia hesitated. "Because in some things, he's wrong. We know he's wrong."

"Like locking up Renewables."

She nodded. "They're given a choice. They can volunteer to help Prometheus, or they can be forced. Sometimes the Renewables who volunteer seem to be totally fine. Sometimes they just vanish. But whenever he finds an unregistered Renewable, someone who didn't volunteer—" Her voice gave out for a moment before she got herself under control again. "They're gone forever."

Like Basil. Like Olivia's brother, too.

I pressed my palms against the roof under me. They were sweaty, and the metal was cool and smooth against them.

"So that's why you took me?"

Olivia's head turned toward me. "What do you mean?"

"You think I have the answers, somehow. That I can decode my brother's journal, figure out what he was planning for Prometheus. How to take Prometheus down, or at least force him to treat Renewables fairly without sacrificing the city itself."

"That's the hope." But her voice was anything but hopeful.

"Everywhere I go." My whisper is barely more than a breath.

Olivia sat up, face turned toward me in the darkness. "Lark?"

I shook my head. "Everywhere I go people want me for things. They arrest me, take me captive, pull me this way or that."

Olivia paused, then reached out to cover my hand with hers. It was strange to touch someone again who was neither shadow nor Renewable—to not sense the shadowy pit that was Oren or feel the bright warmth that was Tansy.

I could still sense the life force in her, the barest magic that even non-Renewables had. The memory of what I'd done to the Eagle still lingered in my mind, but despite the prickle of fear, I didn't pull away. I could control this.

Olivia took a deep breath. "You're not a captive here, Lark. Yes, we want your help, but we're not going to force you to help us. We'd be no better than Prometheus. If you wanted to leave right now, this second, I'd show you the way to the surface myself. Well, if I knew how."

"If you knew?"

Olivia tilted her head back, eyes on the ceiling. "We don't have a way out," she said softly. "There are a few known routes to the surface, but Prometheus's Eagles patrol them all. We'd have to fight our way out, and even if we made it out alive, there'd be nowhere for the non-Renewables among us to go. We can't even get to the surface to gather food, or to patrol for other Renewable survivors that might be out there."

"You're trapped here."

Olivia nodded. "Most of us wouldn't want to leave, but we don't even have that choice. Those among us who are Renewables live every day in fear that they'll be discovered. And that's nothing to what our undercover operatives face—Renewables living in plain sight, hiding what they are."

Her voice was quiet, her face tight and hard. I think of her brother, and that only makes me think of my own. I keep trying to imagine him in this place. Had he ever sat here on this roof, looking up at the ceiling, figuring out what Prometheus had done to the Star? Had he struggled with his conscience, trying to figure out if the city's safety was worth the mistreatment of a few people unlucky enough to be born Renewables?

"I'd like to stay."

I heard Olivia's breath catch—her surprise was almost as tangible as my own. Until I'd spoken the words, I hadn't known what I wanted.

"My brother died for this," I continue. "I don't know any-where near as much about engineering or magic as he does, but if there's anything I can do, anything I can read in his journal that you can't, I'll do it."

Olivia's fingers closed around mine, squeezing tight.

"Good," she said. "Because we've got nothing else."

CHAPTER 14

In the morning, I discovered that someone had left a fresh set of clothes on the chest for me. It was so like the moment when I discovered the architects had left me clothes at the Institute that I hesitated. Olivia's words came back to me: *You're not a captive here.* Somehow, by the artificial light of day, they seemed less reassuring. Still, I couldn't turn down clothes that didn't smell like weeks of travel, so I changed gingerly. I poked my head into the room next door, but Oren was gone. His room looked untouched, all his clothes tucked away, the bed neatly made. It seemed his fastidiousness in erasing his campsites in the wild extended to sleeping in civilization, too.

I followed the distant sounds of conversation until I wound up in what had once been a building. The place was half-crushed by the weight of the newer buildings constructed on top, but someone had shored up the walls with metal beams. A motley assortment of mismatched tables and chairs occupied the floor space, the seats about half-full of resistance members. A door to one side was propped open, allowing the smells of something spicy and sweet to float through.

I'd located breakfast. And to judge from the sudden wave of hunger that swept through me, it was just in time. I scanned the room and saw Oren sitting across from Parker, the man who'd recognized me from the journal.

"Wesley's our highest operative," Parker was saying to Oren as I moved across the join them. "But even he hasn't seen all of CeePo."

Oren looked up as I approached and slid down to make room for me on the bench beside him. That was all the greeting I got, though, because he turned his attention back to his bowl, which contained some sort of porridge.

"Good morning, Miss Ainsley," said Parker. He had a quiet, kind voice. He reminded me, oddly, of my father. I swallowed the pang of homesickness and sat.

"Lark," I corrected him. "Please. The only people who call me Miss Ainsley want something."

He smiled, rueful. "Well, if what Vee tells us is true, you're well aware that we want something from you." He raised his gaze a moment, signaling to someone behind me who brought me a bowl of the porridge.

I lifted a spoonful, giving it a cautious sniff. Some kind of grain, sweetened and spiced with something I'd never smelled before.

"If your cause was good enough for my brother, then it is for me too," I replied, lowering the spoon again.

Parker took a deep breath, looking relieved. "Then Vee was right. You are staying."

"At least for now." I tried a bite of the porridge, pleasantly surprised to find that the spicy smell made it taste strangely fragrant, the sweetener counteracting the slight bitterness of the spice. "What were you saying about CeePo?"

Parker glanced at Oren. "Your friend was asking about the complex, and I was explaining that we don't actually know too much about it. Prometheus is careful. No one except him gets full access everywhere. Wesley—you met him yesterday—is one of the deployment officers and has free rein in the Eagles' dormitories, training facilities, and so forth. But he's not allowed, for example, into the records room, or into the machine workshops. And whatever else is down there."

"Down?" The building covered a large area, but it had only looked two or three stories tall at the most.

"The building goes on down, underground. We don't know how far. Which is why we don't know how much there is that we don't know about."

I glanced at Oren, who was staring at the remains of his porridge, moving clumps of it around with his spoon. I took another bite of my breakfast, willing my stomach to register that I was feeding it and stop grumbling. It had been long enough since I'd stolen the Eagle's magic that I was beginning to feel another type of hunger altogether. I could see, scattered here and there throughout the meal room, glints and glimmers of shielded Renewables.

I dropped my gaze and ignored the fact that I could still feel them, like little flames radiating heat.

"You, at least, we can register with CeePo," Parker continued, looking at Oren. "And we can get that done today. You're not a Renewable, so there's no risk that they'll catch you. If you're a registered citizen, you'll have a lot more freedom of movement. And be a lot more useful to us."

Oren set his spoon down. "Registered?" His expression was wary.

"You have to be registered before you can do business here or get a job. If you've got any special skills, aptitudes for science or organization, you might even be able to work in the CeePo complex."

I stared at Parker, uncertain whether to be horrified or amused. The idea of Oren working behind a desk in the government building, or doing scientific experiments, was absolutely ludicrous. But then, Parker know where Oren had come from.

I glanced out of the corner of my eye at Oren. But instead of snarling his disgust at the small-minded pettiness of city life, he just sat there, face set in a thoughtful scowl, hand clenched around the spoon. Like he was actually considering it.

A commotion outside the mess hall saved me from having to speak. Raised voices caused heads to turn all across the room. Suddenly, a man in a familiar blue waistcoat burst into the mess hall, trailed by a couple of rebels I didn't recognize.

"You two!" Wesley, sporting the most magnificent black eye I'd ever seen, jabbed a finger at me and Oren. "Come with me. Parker, you too."

Parker was on his feet before Wesley had finished turning and walking out. It took me a moment to scramble to my feet without getting tangled up in the bench. Wesley didn't sound angry so much as agitated.

With Oren following silently half a step behind me, I headed after Parker and Wesley. We ended up in the War Room again, and though I'm not sure I could have found it on my own, the corridors were already starting to look more familiar. I was good at finding my way underground.

Thank you, Basil, I thought as I slipped inside the room, skirting the large table that dominated it.

Parker and Wesley were there, along with a few other people I didn't know but recognized from yesterday, when I first arrived. Wesley paced to the far end of the room, lifting a hand to rub it over his balding scalp.

"Who blew their cover?" Parker's voice was quiet, but full of dread. "Spider? Hawk? Oh—not Nina?"

Wesley shook his head. "No, they're fine. Nina's fine." His eyes swiveled toward us, flicking between Oren and me.

"Did you figure out if it was true?"

Parker's gaze followed Wesley's. "It's her," he confirmed. "Lark. The girl in the journal. But she says it's her brother's journal, not hers."

Wesley grimaced, still watching me, his gaze troubled. A sick feeling began to rise in my throat, though I couldn't have explained what it was. Just some instinct telling me something was wrong.

"And that one?" He turned to Oren.

"He's normal. Name's Oren, we were going to take him through registration today."

Wesley straightened, resting his hands on the back of a chair. "No, you're not."

Parker frowned. "But—"

"The Eagle, the one this kid pummeled, didn't make it. Just died this morning, a little before lights-on."

It was like a blow to the stomach. I glanced at Oren, who was staring fixedly at the far wall. It was only once Parker replied, saying something I couldn't hear over the roaring in my ears, that he glanced at me out of the corner of his eye.

I knew why. That man was still alive after Oren was done with him. He'd had a broken nose and probably other, more significant injuries, but he wasn't in danger of dying from them. But then I tore the life force from him to shield myself and Oren from his partner. I'd ripped the life out of him, and I'd seen the gaping hole in his soul where that magic should have been.

Oren hadn't killed that man—I had.

". . . with a warrant out on his head," Wesley was saying. "They've got a picture of him. Don't know how, one of the spy-wings, maybe."

Parker turned away to pace, unconsciously echoing Wesley. "Okay. Okay, we can handle it. We've dealt with manhunts before. We put Renewables on every door to put up illusions, keep Oren inside at all times. Cut back on our missions, lay low. They didn't get a picture of Lark, so we can still use her. Use the time to study the journal. She can look for anything useful, any blueprints or insights we missed, any way to decode his maps . . ."

Wesley nodded as Parker and the other people around the table made plans. Though the atmosphere was tense, it wasn't panicked—this had clearly happened before. As the discussion grew more intense, Wesley's gaze drifted.

Toward me.

I realized he was watching me again, the grey eyes piercing. When he saw me looking back at him, those eyes narrowed. Thoughtful, calculating.

My heart began to beat harder as I realized—he knew. He knew Oren hadn't killed the Eagle. I didn't know how, but I knew it as certain as I knew my own name. Which meant that he knew what I was—and what I could do. Though I could see nothing in his gaze beyond cool, thoughtful speculation, my mind conjured up the image of the Eagle, of his still body, of the ragged remnants of the magic that kept his heart beating.

"I'm going to be sick," I whispered, bile rising swiftly in my throat. I whirled for the door, pressing my hand to my mouth, and sprinted away. Anywhere but here. Anywhere that didn't have Wesley's knowing eyes forcing me face-to-face with what I'd done.

I'd consumed the man's life. I was no better than a shadow—I was worse. They were hungry, mindlessly desperate because they could never truly consume what they sought, what they needed. They were imperfect monsters. But not me. Because I didn't just eat his flesh, tear him apart.

I devoured his soul.

. . .

I knelt, shivering, on the washroom floor. I tried not to look as the water carried away the mess I'd made, unable to find a bathroom, forced to vomit over a rusty drain in the floor. From the muddy boots and tools and buckets strewn about, I'd guessed this was a room to clean gear worn in tunnels that weren't as tidy as the ones housing the resistance. At least I hadn't stumbled into someone's bedroom.

The sound of the water covered up the harshness of my breathing as I tried to calm myself, tried to find reason and logic amidst my panic. I had thought I'd escaped the Institute, outlasted whatever they'd done to me. But the girl I had been wasn't a murderer. She wasn't someone who'd do what I had just done.

The Institute had carved away every last scrap of magic I had and filled the cavity with their synthetic power. Enough to get me to the Iron Wood, lead Nix to a magic-rich haven ripe for the taking. But not enough to keep on living. They'd told me I'd die, but what did they know? Only two people had ever survived the process. Me—and Basil. And he vanished before ever reaching the Iron Wood.

A normal person, left alone in the magicless void outside, would slowly have their life, their soul, drained away. Until they became a shadow, permanently, forever. Magic would turn them back temporarily, cover up the madness of the empty pit inside them. But only for a little while. It wasn't real.

Maybe I hadn't escaped after all. Perhaps I was nothing more than a shadow, given the semblance of humanity by the magic the Institute had installed inside me.

Self-defense. Killing that man was self-defense. Just as it had been self-defense when I killed the shadow child attacking Oren, back on the ridge by the summer lake. And Tomas's death—I'd killed him, but it was a mercy. I'd only ended his pain.

All explainable. Not my fault.

Except I enjoyed it.

I closed my eyes, shuddering. Even now I could feel the remnants of that man's magic, warm and fluttering inside me like bottled sunlight. There was so little of it left—the part of me that didn't care about anything else just wanted more.

"Feeling better now?"

I jumped, stumbling over a bucket and ending up in a sort of crouch. It was Wesley, standing just inside the doorway, hands folded across the expanse of his waistcoat. The green and brown eyelike pattern was muted in the low light, shining here and there.

He saw me looking and grinned. "Peacock feathers," he explained with pride. "They're a type of colorful chicken. Some farm off to the west raises them, and traders bring the feathers through once in a while. Coat costs more than some people make in a year."

I swallowed. My mouth tasted sour, my throat so raw it burned. "Why wear it?" I croaked.

"It's expected. Prometheus pays his lackeys well."

Prometheus again. I wondered what would happen if I just walked up to Central Processing and said, *Here I am. I'm a monster. Lock me up.* Maybe they'd experiment on me, like the Institute. Maybe they'd just toss me up to work on the farms like the shadows Above. Maybe at least I'd find out what happened to my brother.

"Oh, for the love of—snap out of it." Wesley strode forward until he could look down at my face. "So you hurt someone. We've all done it. Vee punches me in the face on a regular basis, and she still sleeps at night."

I gaped at him.

"No, I'm not a mind reader. I just recognize the signs." Wesley smiled, one corner of his mouth twitching. "Your face is pretty expressive, you know."

I sucked in a deep breath through my nose. "How come you know what I did? And no one else does?"

"I was there," he pointed out. "And I've got the sharpest Sight of anyone in the city. You're not exactly subtle when you're ripping the magic out of someone. It also helps that what you did should've been impossible, so it won't be the first conclusion people jump to."

I was suddenly glad my stomach was already empty.

"It's different from what Vee does," I said, swallowing. "For one thing, you planned it. For another, she didn't kill you."

"But she's killed others," he replied, to my surprise. I tried to picture Olivia, all golden hair and smiles, murdering someone the way I had, and couldn't. Wesley shook his head. "Life is short, Lark. Sometimes we die and sometimes they do. It'd be nice if it didn't have to happen, but life here is just as brutal as life out there in the wilderness."

"And that makes it okay?"

"No." Wesley moved toward me, nudging the fallen bucket aside with the toe of his boot. "I'm saying it doesn't make you special. Whether a man dies because he's been stabbed with a knife or because he's had the magic ripped out of him, he's still dead."

"But someone wielding a knife can choose to put it down. They can stop themselves."

"Tell me something." Wesley dropped into a crouch in front of me. "Could you kill me? Here, now?"

I stared at him. *He's insane.* Except that he seemed merely curious, not frightened or even alarmed. He didn't recoil, but examined me with interest. Cautiously, I let my other senses come out, letting the golden and violet sparks of his shielded magic overlay themselves over my normal vision.

Slowly, I nodded. "I think so."

"Fascinating," he murmured. "And why don't you?"

My mouth fell open. "What? I—because there's no reason to. I mean, you helped us."

"So if you're not a murderous psychopath on a rampage, why are you so afraid of what you are?"

"Because—it feels good. When I take someone's magic. A part of me wants it, all the time."

"But you're controlling yourself."

I grimaced. "I didn't exactly control myself out there, with that Eagle."

"To be fair," Wesley pointed out, "they were shooting at you and your boyfriend."

My head snapped up as I tried to formulate a protest. Wesley waved a hand. "Whatever. The point is that you didn't have time to think. You had to operate on instinct, so you did what your instincts told you. Survive, at whatever cost. It's hardwired into us—doesn't make us monsters. Even the shadows up there"—and he flicked his gaze toward the ceiling—"are only doing what they're programmed by nature and magic to do."

"But if my instincts are to kill to save myself—"

"Then you learn to control them." Wesley straightened and offered me his hand. "And I think I can help you with that. That is," he added, raising an eyebrow at me, "if you want to stay, and finish what your brother started."

Somehow, the simple knowledge that someone else knew my secret, knew my fears about myself, and hadn't cast me out made it feel as though the weight of the world had been lifted from my shoulders. I took his hand, all too aware of the supernatural warmth of it, my traitorous senses telling me he had magic ripe for the taking.

"Good," he said, hauling me to my feet. "Now, you'd better put something back in your stomach, because before today's done, you're probably going to wish you were dead."

CHAPTER 15

After a shower and a second attempt at breakfast, I felt better. I would've thought having someone know my secret would be panic-inducing, but instead, it was just a relief to have it known. Wesley had promised he wouldn't share the truth of what I was with the others. "For one thing," he'd said, "I don't even know what you are, so how can I explain it to them?" But I knew that the instant I became a danger to anyone within the walls, all of that would change.

And so I agreed—I needed help. I needed training. I expected Wesley to leave Oren behind, but instead he led the both of us down into a vast cavern. It was, he said, one of the few "rooms" that wasn't left behind from a previous incarnation of the city. The training room was a natural cave, undiscovered until my brother had explored these hidden passageways and found it.

Most of the people working in the training room were children barely old enough to have been harvested in my home city. There were half a dozen of them, all working with older mentors. And every one was a Renewable.

I averted my eyes, jaw clenched. Control.

"So, I'm up, huh?" The cheery voice belonged to Olivia,

who sauntered in after us. Her eyes were on Oren, thoughtful, speculative.

"Morning, Vee," Wesley said, fiddling with a rack of machines against one wall of the cavern. "Be nice."

"I'm always nice," she replied, eyes still resting on Oren as she smiled. She looked none the worse for having been awake much of the night, talking to me—whereas I felt like I'd been run over by a carriage. Her hair was as bright and curly as ever, her eyes gleaming, cheeks and lips flushed. And she was *still* looking at Oren.

His eyes darted from her to Wesley. "Why am I here?" His voice was quiet enough that it didn't echo in the cavern. "I'm no Renewable."

"Ah, but is it true you killed an Eagle by pummeling him to death?" Olivia put her hands on her hips, circling Oren and making a show of examining him.

Oren glanced at me, fleeting and quick. I felt Wesley watching me as well and kept my eyes on Olivia as she moved. "I didn't mean to kill him," Oren said finally, warily.

"Of course you didn't," she replied. "Accidents happen. We're going to try to help you learn not to make those same mistakes again. But first I'm going to need to see what you're made of."

And then, without warning, Olivia feinted in one direction and then leaped at Oren, swinging low and aiming for his ribs. Oren danced away, turning as he did and dropping into a half-crouch, lips curling in surprise and anger.

"Oh, this is gonna be fun," said Olivia, delighted. "You're not going to balk at the idea of hitting a girl, are you?"

Oren frowned, anger and wariness replaced by obvious confusion. "Why would I do that?"

Olivia laughed. "*Finally.*"

A hand on my shoulder jerked me away. I pulled my eyes

from Olivia and Oren sparring to find Wesley there with a rueful smile. "Do I need to ask them to find another place to play, or are you going to be able to focus?"

I opened my mouth but was interrupted by a cry of surprise and pain from Olivia, followed by a peal of laughter, albeit a bit breathless.

Gritting my teeth, I said shortly, "I can focus just fine."

• • •

Wesley wanted to teach me control so I could masquerade as a Renewable. Though I knew I needed help, a tiny part of me kept asking, *Why is he helping you? What does he want?* If I could control this power, I'd be the perfect spy—or the perfect assassin. I half-expected him to lead me through a series of deadly drills and lessons.

But it didn't take long for me—and Wesley as well—to realize I knew nothing about magic beyond the instinctual level. To my humiliation, he led me over to a group of preteen children and then sat back in a chair, watching *them* teach me. It was like being in my home city again—too old, stuck with children who knew I was different. Only this time, instead of being a magical dud, I was just the opposite.

All morning they walked me through meditation exercises that were supposed to help me get to know my power. The magic was part of us, sustaining the machines that were our bodies, pumping the heart, expanding the lungs, sparking from neuron to neuron in our brains. First and foremost, we had to turn our attention inward and learn every pathway and reservoir the magic filled.

The exercises were far from peaceful and relaxing, though. An hour in, I was sweating, my concentration slipping in and out, my head pounding. The kids' energy seemed unflagging, whereas I felt like I'd been locked in some sort of endless purgatory. I wanted to *do* something, not sit here and think about my heartbeat. Seeing Wesley sitting on the sidelines, watching with amusement the entire time, didn't help. Neither did Oren and Olivia, who were now going through a slowed-down series of combat moves, him copying her with flawless grace.

By the time a middle-aged woman—a Renewable as well, to judge from the warm glow all around her that she wasn't bothering to hide—came to send the kids off to their midday meal, I wanted to scream. Seeing my face, Wesley got up out of his chair with a laugh.

I felt my face warming with embarrassment, but I kept my mouth shut, chin lifting.

"Stand down, girl," he said, still chuckling. "Matthias, stay back a moment, will you?"

One of the kids, a lanky boy of maybe ten or twelve, peeled off from the rest of the group as they all headed out of the cavern. "Yes, sir?"

"Lark's wondering what the point is."

"The point, sir, is that we must know how to control our magic before we can use it without hurting ourselves. We have to know our limits, and we have to know the source of our power before we can tap into it."

"All true. Can you give Lark a demonstration of what happens when we overextend?"

For the first time, the lanky boy hesitated. "Really?" I couldn't tell if he was excited or afraid, but whatever Wesley was asking, it was significant.

"Really. Quick now, so you don't miss lunch."

Matthias sat down on the mat cross-legged, laying his hands on his knees and beginning a series of deep, slow breaths. Wesley moved up next to me and murmured, "Watch."

"He's not doing anything," I whispered back, confused.

"Not like that," Wesley said. "Watch with your other sight."

With a jolt, I narrowed my eyes, stretching out with my senses until the boy's golden aura came into focus.

"Look closely," Wesley said. "See if you can follow what he's doing."

The dark hunger inside me flared up, the longing so intense I nearly took a step toward the boy. But Wesley reached out, his own magic carefully shielded, and took my shoulder. I swallowed and forced myself to look closer.

I'd never had time to examine these auras before. Regular humans didn't have them, possessing only the tiny sparks of magic that kept their bodies running. But Wesley was right—there was more to a Renewable's aura than a simple golden glow. I couldn't tell whether it was more like fine particles of dust or like dye swirling in water, but there were patterns to it. And as I watched the boy's expression shift minutely, echoing the shifts in the magic surrounding him, I realized that he was controlling it.

Gradually, the flow of magic began to slow. At first there was as much inside him as swirling around him, but as the seconds stretched on, it seemed like more and more of the power was leaving his body. The boy was forcing it out.

With my second sight, I could actually see inside him—to where his heartbeat was growing slower, slower . . . His head sagged forward as his muscles stopped getting magic and oxygen. His lungs weren't moving anymore. He'd stopped breathing. And then, as I watched, horror leaping up in my own chest—his heart stopped.

"Wesley!" I broke away from him and leaped for the kid, gathering my own remaining magic without thinking.

I caught Matthias as he began to fall forward, but as suddenly as his heart had stopped, it started again. He sucked in a lungful of air and sat up, eyes unfocused. He blinked a few times and then saw me and smiled ruefully. His lips were a little blue, but already growing rosy again.

"It sucks being the best one in the class at doing that," he complained, getting unsteadily to his feet, as if he hadn't been technically dead five seconds ago.

"Thank you, Matthias," Wesley said. "You can go catch up now."

The lanky boy wandered off, leaving me kneeling on the mat, bewildered. Wesley watched him go, thoughtful. I waited for him to tell me what I had just witnessed, but he seemed content with silence. Eventually, I couldn't stand it anymore.

"What was *that?*" I burst out, lurching to my feet. "You teach kids how to kill themselves?"

Wesley turned toward me, feigning surprise. "It's perfectly safe. It takes great focus and concentration to shift all the magic away from the basic functions of the body."

"But—his heart stopped."

"And then as soon as it did, and he started to lose consciousness, he was no longer concentrating on draining his magic away. And it all came back again."

I stared at Wesley, still shaken by what I'd seen. "Why teach them this?"

"In these controlled situations," Wesley answered me, "the magic isn't gone. The kids are just moving it around, manipulating its flow. It's still there, ready to be tapped the second the mind fails and instinct kicks back in. But if Matthias were to use all his power on something—powering a machine, moving something large, tapping into the elements—it would be gone. He'd have to wait for it to regenerate on its own, but that's a slow process. If he drained himself to the point of death, there'd be no magic to jump-start his body again. We do this so that they know what it feels like, how to recognize it. So they know how much they have before they start tapping into what keeps them alive."

I closed my eyes, trying to summon the awareness that had been so infuriatingly fleeting during the morning's meditation exercises. I tried to see how the magic flowed through me, but I could only sense it pooled within me. There was no connection to my heart, to my brain. But then, my magic wasn't *mine*. It was the Eagle's.

"I didn't show you this so you could get in touch with your own life force." Wesley's voice interrupted me. "Although that's exactly how a Renewable would begin her studies, too. But you're not like them."

"Then why?"

He didn't answer, but instead turned and began to lead the way toward the exit. The room was quickly emptying, and I realized with a pang that Oren and Olivia were nowhere to be seen. I turned to follow him, suddenly realizing, now that the children were gone, that I was ravenous.

But Wesley wasn't done yet.

"I showed you," he said as I trailed after him, "because now you know exactly what you did to that man who died. You know *how* you killed him."

I stopped short. He kept walking, the eyes on his feathered coat watching me with a hundred unblinking stares.

"And now you know how to keep yourself from doing it again."

· · ·

I saw very little of Oren over the next several days. Wesley moved my training into a private room, citing secrecy, but I knew it was at least in part because I couldn't focus when Oren and Olivia spent half the time I was trying to concentrate rolling around on a sparring mat. Whenever I did see him, at mealtimes, he'd be sitting with her. They'd always ask me to join them when they saw me—but sometimes they didn't even notice when I came in.

In the mornings I trained with Wesley, and in the afternoons I learned about magical theory from Parker. I struggled to get along with Wesley most days, rubbed raw by his unfailingly blunt attitude. But Parker was different. He was quiet, thoughtful, hugely knowledgeable. Though my father knew nothing about magic theory, Parker still reminded me of him. Something about the comfortable silences and insightful questions, maybe. The golden glow of his Renewable power was gentle, warm. It was easier to control the shadowy hunger within me around him.

I learned that the very first people to make a science out of studying magic were the Hellenes, the same people whose myths had inspired Prometheus. They existed thousands of years ago in a land across the ocean. It all boiled down to what their philosophers poetically called the music of the machine. In their eyes, all of nature was a machine, from the vastness of the world, with its weather and intricate ecosystems, down to the tiniest plant. A seedling machine needed magic to draw water up through its roots, just as the human machine needed it to have a heartbeat. There was magic in everything, and therefore everything could be manipulated by magic.

And it was the Hellenes who first used magic to power a manmade machine, though their attempts, while aesthetically impressive, were so inefficient as to be useless.

Parker clearly loved studying these people, his gaze lighting up when he spoke of them. He had a habit of wandering from the subject, branching off onto tangents that I could barely even follow, much less apply to my own experiences.

"Many scholars think that the music of the machines

theory was fundamentally flawed, as no one has been able to reconcile the concept that magic is in everything, to a lesser or greater extent, with the truth that iron repels magic. The Hellenes had no scientific explanation for this, but I believe it's simply because we don't understand it yet. The theory is so simple, so elegant, that to abandon it for one loophole seems ludicrous."

I remained silent, letting him continue. Wesley had stayed true to his word and not shared my secret with anyone—and even he didn't know that I had magicked iron, first on the lock on Oren's cage, and then again on a huge scale, turning the Iron Wood into a living forest again.

Parker—and the Hellenes—were right. There was magic in everything, even in iron, because I'd tapped into it.

Though I was exhausted by the end of each day, I still felt the nagging, irritating desire for action. Somewhere out there, Nix needed my help. The pixie was linked to me and could find me anywhere, and the fact that it hadn't returned yet had to mean it was in trouble. And of course there was Tansy. Being forced to sit there meditating and learning about archaic theories made me want to scream. But even if we could manage to get inside and rescue her without being caught or killed, where could we go?

There was no way out.

• • •

In the evenings, after I'd forced myself to eat dinner and dragged myself back to my tiny room, I read Basil's journal. My brother was not skilled at writing—none of us were, really. There was no reason for us to learn to express ourselves that way, living behind the Wall. Still, I found myself dragged into the brief glimpses of his journey marked down on the pages. I combed the entire thing, searching for mentions of alternate routes to the surface, anything that might help these people, but found nothing.

I kept hoping—and dreading—to see my name somewhere, to see him write that he missed me. But he wrote nothing of his feelings, noting only observations of the world around him. The evidence that he missed me was in the way my face peeped out of the margins every few pages. The drawings were the real window into Basil's heart.

I paused, sitting up on my bed. *Of course.* It was late on the fourth day since we'd arrived at the underground city, the fourth day of training and studying. I'd been so focused on trying to find clues in Basil's ramblings that I'd been ignoring the pictures, most of which were sketches of faces or plants, or else technical diagrams of half-imagined machines. Most— but not all.

Flipping the pages back, I found what I was looking for. To the casual observer, the page was filled with a nonsensical pattern of little lines, some slashing through others, some ending in meaningless symbols. But they weren't meaningless—I knew what they were. The memory was distant, but not gone. Now that I knew what the rebels here needed so badly, the memory came flooding back.

When we were children, Basil would sometimes let me come with him when he snuck into the school and other architect-run buildings by navigating the long-unused sewers. He knew every turn and hatch, but I—I was little and knew nothing about it, and I didn't know my way. Afraid of getting separated and leaving his little sister alone in the tunnels beneath the city, Basil had made me diagrams of the tunnels that I had to memorize so I could always find my way home, no matter where I was. He'd come up with a code, so that anyone who stumbled across our maps wouldn't realize what they were and give away our escapades.

I stared down at the page in the journal, my fingers smoothing over ink and paper. This wasn't nonsense. This was a map. It was a way out of Lethe for the Renewables—it was an escape route.

An idea began to form in my mind, and even though it was new and only half-formed, my mind tingled with excitement. But before I could approach anyone about it, I had to ask the one person on whom my plan hinged. It'd be dangerous—too dangerous, if I let myself think about it.

So don't think, for once. Just go.

I pushed myself up off my bed and headed for the door, which I'd left open to try to let the air circulate. I plucked at my shirt, which felt damp and sticky against my skin, and wished my complexion was a bit more forgiving in this heat. I knew my face would be bright red, my hair lank, nothing like the bouncy curls Olivia sported.

I turned for Oren's room next to mine, only to find the door ajar and the lights off. I whispered his name and pushed the door open a little further, but there was no response. He was gone. I had no idea what time it was, but I was pretty sure it had been hours since most of the rebels had gone to bed.

With a sinking feeling, I made for the corridor where Olivia's room was located. Even though I knew the layout of this place now, at least the section that we inhabited, I still felt like an outsider after nightfall. The silent corridors echoed my footsteps back to me, broken only by the dripping water here and there and the occasional banging of a pipe.

I stopped a few paces away from Olivia's door, which was closed. I couldn't hear anything from this distance and refused to put my ear to the door like an eavesdropper. *Just wait until tomorrow*, I told myself. *Are you really going to storm in there like some jealous girlfriend?* I swallowed. I had rejected Oren, not the other way around. Who was I to say he couldn't fall for someone else, someone far better suited to him?

And yet I couldn't turn away. I told myself it was because I had to know if he'd help me, but it felt weak, even in the privacy of my own thoughts. Clenching my jaw, hating myself, I reached out and banged on the metal door with the heel of my hand.

Nothing.

I waited, my heart pounding painfully, then tried again. There was still no response, and I was about to try a third time when the door next to Olivia's opened a crack and a sleepy, disgruntled face peeked out. I recognized Copper, a skinny, black-haired boy about my age who specialized in tinkering with machines and often helped Parker as he tried to unlock Basil's journal's secrets.

"The hell, Lark?" he muttered, staring blearily at me. "A little late for a romantic rendezvous, isn't it?"

"Sorry." Why would I show up at Olivia's door for romance? Unless he'd just heard the clanging and mistook it for his own door. At least I could blame the heat as the reason my cheeks were red. "Do you know where Olivia is?"

"Not here!" Copper replied shortly. Then he rubbed a hand over his face, groaning. "Try the training grounds, or the roof. She doesn't sleep a lot these days."

I took a deep breath. "Thanks, Copper. Sorry I woke you!"

He rolled his eyes. "Yeah, yeah. Not all of us can run on magic, might think about that next time you decide to wake up the whole hallway." But his tone was, at least, a little bit mollified.

I headed toward the training cavern, unsure of what I meant to do when I got there. All I knew was that I couldn't spend another day here doing nothing but waiting.

The cavern was dark except for a few lights over the sparring mats. Olivia and Oren were the only people there, and they showed no signs of fatigue. Oren was as much of a night person as Olivia was. They were circling each other, their eyes locked, every shift and movement deliberate. When Olivia feinted to the right, Oren slid smoothly sideways. When he darted forward, she twisted neatly away. They looked like dancers, graceful and strong, always moving. The pool of illumination in the dark cave was like a spotlight, setting each mote of dust ablaze to twirl after them as their movements caused eddies and currents in the air.

Neither of them spoke—the only sounds were the occasional swift gasp of breath or murmur of effort.

And then, a shift. Olivia stumbled and Oren leaped forward, ready to take advantage of her mistake. But in his eagerness he moved too far, and Olivia miraculously found her feet and ducked under his arm. Quick to capitalize on the success of her ruse, she grabbed his wrist as he passed, and twisted. With a grunt of effort and a cry of surprise from Oren, she slammed him down into the mat. He started to twist free, stopping only when she pressed her knee to his throat. For a moment the only sound was their harsh breathing as they stared at each other, expressions mirror images of fierceness and exertion. And then Oren laughed.

It was only a chuckle, barely more than a quick exhalation. But my heart stopped, and I couldn't take my eyes off of him as Olivia helped him to his feet, laughing as well. I'd never seen Oren laugh—I'd barely ever seen him smile. He was always serious, focused on the next task. Focused on surviving, on winning, on keeping us safe.

I struggled for breath, backing up a pace. I couldn't ask him to come with me. For the first time since I'd met him, and maybe for the first time ever, Oren was happy. How could I ask him to risk all of it for my own personal vendetta?

I had turned for the door, trying to rethink my plan, when Olivia suddenly called in surprise, "Lark!"

I grimaced, briefly considering pretending I hadn't heard her and finishing my awkward exit. The moment they'd just shared had been so beautiful, so graceful—my presence felt like an intrusion. But when I turned, Olivia was smiling, jogging toward me.

"What're you doing up?" she asked, breathless, cheeks perfectly pink. Behind her I saw Oren stretching, one arm folded up behind his head.

"I was—I couldn't sleep." I jerked my gaze from Oren, focusing on Olivia.

"What, again?" She grinned. "We're going to have to start drugging you to get you to rest."

"You're one to talk." I smiled back, but it felt weak. I wanted to slap myself—*Pull yourself together, Lark.* I took a deep breath, lifting my chin. "I heard you guys as I passed in the hallway outside. I didn't mean to interrupt your training. You looked amazing," I added, sounding less hesitant. Because that much, at least, was true.

"Thanks." Olivia smiled at me, clearly loving the praise. She took a couple steps closer and added, "But it's okay, we were just finishing up."

Before I could reply, Olivia strode on past me, turning to walk backwards for a moment and call out, "Later, Oren! See you tomorrow." Then, more quietly, "'Night, Lark. I hope you find some rest."

And then she was gone, leaving me and Oren alone. It was the first time we'd been alone for more than a few seconds since the first night we came here and we spoke in my room. I toyed with the idea of leaving—I had a plan to rethink. But Oren was watching me as he stretched, clearly waiting to see if I'd speak first. Never had I wished more that the gulf that had sprung up between us was gone.

I made my way toward the mats, my racing heart at war with my roiling stomach. More than ever, I knew I couldn't ask Oren what I'd planned on asking him. I scanned his features for a few seconds before looking away, focusing on the equipment lining the edge of the cavern.

"Hey," said Oren, after a breath.

"Hey." I searched for something else to say. "That was pretty incredible to watch. It looks like you two are pretty evenly matched."

He nodded, pulling off a pair of gloves that no doubt afforded his hands some protection while he was fighting. "I suppose so. If I had a knife, she wouldn't stand a chance. But I'm not used to fighting unarmed, so it's good practice."

That made me smile in spite of myself. At least the arrogant side of him hadn't gone anywhere. "It's good you get along outside the training, too. At least that way it's not awkward when one of you pummels the other."

"Get along?" I looked up to find Oren watching me blankly.

"You're spending a lot of time together. You know, meals and so on."

Oren considered that, then nodded. "I think she likes me because I'm not afraid to hit her back. Apparently that's a thing here. Guys aren't supposed to hit girls."

I knew by "here" he meant "cities" in general. He managed to say it without that disgusted curl of his lip, though. "It's generally frowned upon," I replied.

Oren shrugged, depositing the gloves in a bin at the edge of the mats. "You ask me, if someone's trying to kill you, you'd better try and kill them first, whether they're a girl or not."

I took a step back. "Well, I ought to—"

"Did you come looking for me?" Oren turned back from

169

the bin again, watching me through the sandy-brown hair that fell across his eyes.

"What? No. No, I was just going for a walk."

Oren made no move to leave. "You just had that look, that's all."

"What look?"

His lips twitched—it might've been a trick of the low light, but it looked almost like a tiny smile. "You scowl when you're thinking. You get a little line, just here." He lifted his hand to touch a fingertip to his own forehead, just between his eyebrows. "You weren't scowling at Olivia, so I can only assume it's me you're after."

There was no reply to that. I'd had no idea Oren could read me so well. He read the tracks of animals and the patterns of the weather, but where had he learned to understand people?

I sighed, shaking my head. "I *was* looking for you," I admitted. "But I changed my mind. It's something I have to figure out on my own."

Oren flexed his fingers and rotated his wrists for a few moments, then put his hands in his pockets. "Something to do with your new teacher?"

His voice made me pause. His face was blank, even cool, his pale eyes lingering on mine. But there was a darker edge to his tone, so subtle I would've missed it if I hadn't gotten so used to scanning him when we first started traveling together for the slightest hints of what was going on inside his head.

Could he be as thrown by our sudden separation as I was? Even if—and I refused to acknowledge the way my throat closed—even if he was happy working so closely with Olivia, it didn't mean he'd completely forgotten I existed.

Suddenly I found myself saying, "I think I know a way of getting to the surface; it's in Basil's journal. I think if I can do that, the people here will trust me enough to let me lead a rescue mission, too. Because I had an idea about getting into CeePo—about finding Tansy, and Nix too if they've got it."

Oren's expression flickered as he gave a little grunt. "You're sure you want to go after them? A girl who betrayed you and a machine built by the people who used you?"

I had to smile at that, albeit wearily. "Nix defied its programming to help me. And I believe Tansy genuinely wanted to do the right thing, even if she wasn't being honest about it. I can't let whatever happened to my brother happen to her."

Oren lifted a shoulder in another shrug. "If you say so. Where do I come in?"

I hesitated. It wasn't Oren's fight. I'd already uprooted his life, made him the only self-aware monster in existence, made it so this underground prison was the only place he'd be safe. And now I was asking him to risk losing that too.

"Tell me." He moved closer to me, his voice quiet and calm.

"I could find a way to do it without you," I said slowly. "I think." I kept trying to push down my uneasiness, to trust that Oren could say no if he wanted to. *I'd follow you anywhere,* he told me. I wasn't sure it was fair to ask this of him.

But he nodded, urging me on, so I took a deep breath and said, "You're Lethe's most wanted criminal right now. Don't you think Prometheus himself would want a look at you?"

Oren was silent, his eyes on mine. I could almost see him thinking, his gaze searching, his lips pressed together. Then, very slowly, he nodded. "We're going to need Wesley."

I let out a breath I hadn't even realized I was holding. *We.* Relief was like a cool breeze stirring the still, humid air. I felt the muscles in my shoulders relaxing by degrees. No matter what was happening between him and Olivia, Oren was still my ally. Still my friend.

"We can go to him in the morning," I suggested. "I'll work out the details tonight."

"I'll help," Oren said firmly. He started to move past me, leading the way out of the training cavern.

I had turned to follow when a thought struck me. "Oren— why do this? You could live here. You could be happy here."

"Why do this?" Oren echoed. He paused, looking over his shoulder. "You're asking me to."

My throat closed, stomach lurching oddly.

"Besides," he continued with a shrug. "I may not be your scout friend's biggest fan, but I owe that little demon bug."

I blinked. "Owe Nix? For what?"

Oren looked mildly surprised, his tone suggesting I should have guessed his answer. "It saved your life."

CHAPTER 16

"This is absurd. She's been here less than a week—why are we even listening to her?" Marco, the young man who had doubted me when I first arrived, slammed his hand down on the table in the War Room. "She's going to get herself and her friend grabbed, and she'll blow Wesley's cover to boot. If she wants to throw her life away, that's her business. But we need Wesley."

I held my breath and hoped Oren would restrain himself. But I couldn't spare him a glance, couldn't afford to show signs of uncertainty or weakness. I was just a sixteen year-old girl facing down a room full of people older, smarter, and savvier than I was.

I expected Parker to defend me in his quiet way, remind Marco that I was the girl in the journal, the sister of the only boy who'd ever gotten close to Prometheus. But instead he was silent, expression troubled behind his beard. My heart started to sink even as my thoughts kicked into overdrive, trying to think of some new way to explain the idea, some way to convince them it was the right thing to do.

Instead, to my surprise, it was Wesley who spoke.

"I believe we ought to consider her proposal," he said

slowly. "She may not have been here long, but she and this young man survived alone in the wilderness for weeks. This one faced down a horde of Empty Ones with only a knife, and Lark turned away an entire army of machines."

Parker spoke up, his expression still conflicted. "But the journal," he protested. "We need her."

"And this is what she's gotten from it. That's what you wanted, right? Some new information only she could decode? Parker, do you really think we can afford to ignore the strongest weapon we've found since the journal was discovered because we don't have the guts to go through with anything?"

My mouth was dry, as though it had been stuffed with cotton. Being described as a weapon made me feel sick, lightheaded. But Wesley was the only one speaking out in favor of my plan, and I couldn't afford to correct him. Besides, we needed him. I could hardly believe what I was hearing—if we failed, he stood the most to lose.

Wesley's statement had silenced the room. The rest of them hadn't heard more than the vaguest details about my escape from my city and what had happened at the Iron Wood. I'd only told Wesley because he demanded the full account to better understand my abilities. That I'd faced down an army and won was news to them. Even Marco went quiet, glancing at me and then dropping his gaze.

I cleared my throat, the sound harsh in the silence. "If it doesn't work, you're under no obligation to respond. If we can't reach Prometheus, if Oren and I get caught, then we won't expect you to come in after us. Wesley's reputation will remain intact because he'll have been the one who brought us in."

"And what do you expect to do if you come face-to-face with Prometheus?" That was Parker, his expression still troubled.

I glanced at Wesley, who was inspecting the sleeve of his fantastical coat and plucking off bits of imaginary lint. Only he knew the real answer to that question: if there were no other options, then I would kill Prometheus.

Out loud I said only, "That's where Oren comes into play. If you can neutralize his Eagles, according to Wesley, Prometheus's protections are entirely magical. Oren will be armed, and the Eagles will have to contend with him and me together. Prometheus may be able to stop a Renewable like me from getting past his shields, but he won't have anything to stop an iron knife. We can threaten him with that, force him to step down."

Marco was breathing quickly through his nose. "He'll have half a dozen Eagles at least around him at all times," he said flatly. "You really think your pet savage can take on that many guards at once?"

I waited for Oren to explode, but instead he merely shifted his weight, hands in his pockets. "Would you like to try me and see?"

Marco swallowed, gaze shifting from Oren to Wesley, who shrugged as if to say, *You got yourself into this, you're on your own.*

"Look," he said finally, looking down at the table, "there's a difference between being able to take me out and being able to take out all the Eagles plus Prometheus at once."

"I can handle myself," Oren said quietly.

"Then why do you need to go at all, Lark?" Parker asked, his eyes on me. "There's still so much to learn from the journal, so much you could help us with."

"I'm not my brother," I said helplessly. "I don't know machines the way he does. I've told you all I can. But I have to go. If they lock Oren up, he'll need me to get him out. They won't know I'm a Renewable, and they won't necessarily take precautions."

I avoided holding my breath just barely. This was the important part—they had to believe I could pass for normal the way Oren was. It didn't matter that I had no intention of hiding that I had magic once I was inside the CeePo compound.

"They'll figure it out quickly enough," protested Parker. "All they'd need to do was use iron to disrupt your shields, your concentration, and—"

"Enough," said Wesley, cutting through the rest of Parker's words. "Lark, we've heard your plan, and unless you have anything you'd like to add . . . ?"

He raised an eyebrow at me. I knew he suspected that I was keeping something back. He'd spent enough time with me over the past few days to know that I didn't always volunteer important information without being prompted. But if they knew I intended to go in blazing with my stolen magic like the worst-trained Renewable on the planet, they'd never allow it.

I shook my head.

Wesley waited half a breath longer, then nodded. "Then if you and Oren will leave us for a while, we'll discuss this. Why don't you go get something to eat?" he added. "Build up your reserves."

He knew as well as I did that food no longer had any effect on my magic. When I needed power, I stole it. But no one else knew that, so I nodded, and Oren and I hurried out.

We headed for the mess hall and found it mostly empty. There were a few people there finishing off their breakfasts, and a few more cleaning tables, but we were able to secure a corner of the room for ourselves.

I picked at the peeling paint on the table we'd chosen, grimacing when it splintered and jabbed me under my fingernail.

"It'll work," Oren said, watching me.

I flicked the bit of paint away. "I know. But the question is, do they know that?"

"They all seem to listen to Wesley."

That wasn't necessarily a comfort. "I wish I knew why he's behind this."

Oren put his elbows on the table and hunched forward. "Why wouldn't he be?"

I hesitated. Oren knew what I could do—he'd seen me open the lock on his cage, for one, and he was there when I'd killed the Eagle in the square. But we'd never really talked about it. He didn't talk much about his inner demons, and he didn't ask about mine.

"He's the only one here who knows I'm . . . not really what the rest of them think I am." Though the other people in the room were out of earshot, habit lowered my voice.

"So?" Oren asked bluntly. "That should make him more willing to give it a shot, not less."

"What? Why?"

His mouth twitched in the barest hint of a smile, his blue eyes holding mine. "If I was headed into the viper's den, I'd want someone with me who could rip the life out of my enemies."

I felt my muscles tensing, and I looked away, sick.

"Lark, it's not—this power of yours. It's not evil." He reached forward and took my hand, shocking me into looking back at him. But instead of curling his fingers around mine, he turned it palm-up, toward the ceiling.

"It's a tool. See your hand, here?" He carefully curled each of my fingers over until my hand was a fist. "It can be a weapon. But only when you want it to be. How you choose to use it is up to you."

The tingle of magic where his hand cupped mine caused an answering tingle that ran down my spine. I swallowed, keeping my eyes on our hands.

"The magic doesn't give you a weapon," he said softly. "It gives you choice." His hands curled around mine, my fist enclosed within both of his.

"Olivia's taught you more than fighting, hasn't she?" What was wrong with me? I couldn't even hide the bitterness in my own voice. I just hoped he didn't hear it.

With my eyes on our hands, I felt him react more than anything else. His muscles tensed, and then he released my hands. "She doesn't know the whole truth, but she knows I've done things I regret."

"Would she still tell you all of this if she knew you were a shadow?" I cursed myself as soon as the words left my mouth. I wish I could just *tell* Oren what I was afraid of. That I was like him, only worse.

But for once Oren didn't back away, go silent, close down. He didn't answer immediately, and when I looked up, he was watching me. Slowly, he leaned across the table and reached out toward my face. His fingers brushed my earlobe where the Molly-shadow had torn it, sending a spark through me. Magic or something else, I couldn't tell.

"It's healing," he said softly.

I had to hunt for my voice. "One of the Renewable kids brought disinfectant for me."

Oren's eyes were on my ear, brow lightly furrowed with concentration. "You never gave me a straight answer. Did I do this to you?"

My heart ached. "No. Oren, you didn't. I promise you."

He smoothed some of my hair away from my face, his fingers tracing the curve of my ear as he pushed the strands back. "I'll never know if you're lying to me," he murmured, speaking almost as if to himself.

I couldn't pull my eyes away. His face seemed so sad, the long, fair eyelashes lowered, veiling his blue eyes. My palms, pressed against the tabletop, felt damp, and my words stuck in my throat. When he moved his hand toward my cheek, I couldn't help but tip my head into his touch.

Just then the mess hall door clanged open. We both jumped, and Oren jerked back with a clatter of the bench he was sitting on. His hand dropped to the table, clenching into a fist, and when I glanced at his face, it was as closed and unreadable as ever.

It was Wesley, come to find us. If he had any comment on the scene he'd interrupted, he didn't share it. Instead, he glanced at Oren almost dismissively before his gaze landed on me.

"They can't agree on your plan for CeePo until they know whether your info about the journal is true," he said. "You're going to lead an expedition of other Renewables to try to find the surface. If you can do that, then they'll let you confront Prometheus and finish what your brother started."

I drew in a shaky breath. I wasn't sure I could lead anyone, even just myself, to the surface. But I had to trust Basil.

"You've got two days including today to get ready," he said. "Morning of the third day, it's showtime."

CHAPTER 17

I expected the two days to drag and leave me itching with impatience. Two days could make all the difference to Tansy or Nix, and part of me chafed at having to wait. But there was so much to do that the time passed in a flurry of preparations. We memorized maps of the known tunnels, studied the latest reports about patrol patterns of Prometheus's Eagles. We learned the names and functions of all the known machines they used. Oren trained harder than ever with Olivia, while I learned to absorb magic faster, more efficiently, with greater control.

Olivia would stay behind—she wasn't a Renewable, and if we did find a way to the surface, it'd be dangerous for her in an atmosphere without magic. The outside air would drain away the little magic she did have, and if we got stuck outside, she wouldn't last more than a day or two without becoming a shadow. Wesley wasn't coming either. He was considered too valuable to risk losing on what Marco described as a "little girl's fancy."

But the worst part was that Oren was staying behind, too. For the others, it was simply because, like Olivia, it was risky for a normal person without magic to spare to be out in the open long. But I knew it was even riskier than that—without the magical atmosphere down here, if my magic ran out up there, Oren, already a shadow inside, would become a monster instantly.

I still saw him as the rest of us trained and planned, usually from across the training ground, where he worked constantly with Olivia. The distance between us felt greater than ever. It seemed one of us was always leaving the other behind.

The plan was for me to set out on my own and meet a handful of Renewables hidden undercover throughout the city. While most of them lived in secret, off the grid, there were a few who were good enough at hiding what they were to live among the citizens. My head ached at the idea of living each day with such deception—hiding my nature from an entire city, every day for the rest of my life, was unthinkable.

Parker would be there, because he had spent the most time studying my brother's journal. His inclusion went a long way to calming my nerves. His manner was so gentle and reassuring, and he reminded me so strongly of my father. Unfortunately, Marco would be going as well. I protested this choice—in private—to Wesley, but he countered by saying Marco was one of the strongest Renewables he had. He also told me that while Marco had protested this mission, once it was decided upon, he'd been the first one to volunteer.

And then there was Nina, a woman a few years older than me who'd been living undercover her entire life to avoid the fear and hatred of normal people, even before Prometheus had come to power. Despite being the youngest of the three, she'd be the leader of our little mission, at least, when it came to the combat decisions—if it came to that. I'd be making the calls on where we went.

Marco and Parker, who were "lifers" as Olivia called them and therefore not free to roam the city at large, would leave ahead of me, going the long way around through the alleys. They'd go ahead and find Nina, tell her about the mission, and meet me at the far edge of the city, where there was an entrance to the tunnels not far from where they guessed Basil's map began.

I'd memorized the plan and my route through the city backward and forward, had copied out Basil's map and memorized that too. By the time we all headed to bed the night before the mission, it seemed as though we'd planned for every potential eventuality. But instead of feeling calmer, I just felt more nervous. For everything we had planned, there had to be a dozen possibilities we couldn't foresee.

I lay on my bed, the humidity making me lethargic and restless at the same time. The room smelled musty and damp, reminding me unpleasantly of the mildewed tunnels below my home city. My brother's paper bird sat on the chest at the foot of the bed, side by side with the one he'd made me before he left. When did he make its twin? Did he carry it with him through the wilderness, as I had, or did he make it when he was living here, researching Prometheus?

I reached for the journal he'd left behind, even though I knew its every page, even the nonsense I didn't understand. It was full of machines and schematics, inventions to use as weapons and as shields, ways to channel magic through clockwork that I'd never even dreamed of. But what it didn't have was a reason why my brother had chosen this battle.

He'd come here looking for answers about what he was and how to cure what our city had done to him. That much Dorian had told me in the Iron Wood. But when he got here to find that the city had fallen apart, he must have lost hope that anyone here would know enough to help him. And then a man named Prometheus had taken over and made Renewables all but criminals in this city—and people like me and my brother could never hope to live normal lives here. At least not for long.

So why did he stay? Why not pack up and leave, find another city, another chance at survival?

I left the journal on my bed and headed over to the wall my room shared with Oren's. I pressed my ear to the metal, but I could hear nothing except a distant vibration caused by some machine. I ducked out into the corridor and paused by Oren's door, unable to stop myself from thinking of his face as he looked at my healing ear, as he touched my hair. But his room was dark and quiet, and if he was asleep I didn't want to wake him. At least one of us could get some rest.

I knew I should go back into my room and sleep. But instead I put my back to Oren's door and slid down to the ground with a bump. I missed the journey. I missed making a new camp each night and starting fresh the next day. No plans except surviving, no pressure. I'd been terrified, exhausted, half-starving—but it was just Oren and me, and Nix, and no one counting on us but ourselves.

I ducked my head, letting my hands dangle between my knees. Morning was coming all too soon.

· · ·

The sounds of people stirring roused me, and I sat up, stifling a groan at my stiff neck. I was still sitting outside Oren's room, but I must have drifted off. Dragging myself to my feet, I slipped back into my own room and changed.

They'd found new clothes for me—well, not new, but new to me. Black pants of a thin canvaslike material, strong and durable but flexible. A light top made of breathable fabric, good for the humidity. A jacket made of some kind of leather—my skin crawled a little as I put it on, the idea of wearing animal skins almost as abhorrent as the idea of eating meat.

But Olivia had assured me that it'd help protect me if the route we were following was unstable, if there were environmental dangers along the way. They all fit perfectly—someone must have tailored them for me.

After days of wearing ill-fitting, borrowed clothing, it was a relief to have something that was just right. I couldn't remember ever having clothes that fit me so well. Even in my home city, everything I wore was a hand-me-down from some other child who came before me.

The idea was to go during the day, Lethe-time, when the city's machinery siphoned power away from the Star above. That way, if we made it to the surface, we'd get there during their nighttime. At first I protested, remembering the Mollyshadow and the rest of her family, but Wesley assured me that only dusk and dawn were dangerous Above, that the shadows left the city for most of the night to roam the countryside, looking for prey. We'd be safer then than we would be if we emerged in broad daylight, easily seen by the people living Above or—even worse—by patrolling Eagles.

I ate a quiet breakfast on my own, avoiding the whispers and furtive looks from the other people gathered for their morning meal. Officially my mission to find a route out of Lethe was secret, but the people here were no better than the kids I went to school with. There were rumors flying everywhere, and they all knew it had something to do with me.

I expected the others to be waiting there, and I braced myself for a tense send-off I didn't want. This mission could mean everything for these people living on the fringes of the city—it could mean a way out. Freedom. The pressure was monumental, and I knew that seeing all those expectant faces would only make it worse.

When I got to the door, though, there was only Wesley. No sign of Marco or Parker or Olivia—and no sign either of

Oren. I tried to ignore the unexpected stab of disappointment at that. Popular opinion among those in on the plan was that I was not coming back from this. I was relieved not to have to deal with anyone else, but Oren hadn't even come to say goodbye.

Wesley smiled at me as I approached, but it was a grim sort of smile. "Ready, Lark?"

I nodded, searching for my voice. The last thing I wanted was to sound as frightened as I was. "Ready," I replied firmly.

"I thought you might prefer to slip out quietly," Wesley said drily. "Everyone else thinks you're leaving in an hour."

That made me smile. Wesley had gotten to know me pretty well through our training sessions. Because it *was* a relief, especially now that I knew the reason Oren wasn't there. I drew in a deep breath. "Thank you for everything," I said awkwardly.

Wesley waved a hand. "No need for that. We'll be the ones thanking you if you can get this done."

"If I can find a way to the surface, do you think the Renewables will all leave? What will happen then to the rebels without magic, like Olivia?" *Like Oren.*

Wesley shifted his weight from foot to foot, turning his gaze on the door leading out into the city. "I can't speak for anyone else," he said finally, resting his hand on the crude but effective mechanism locking the door from the inside. "I know what my choice would be, though."

I glanced from his hand to his face, which showed a strange kind of pride as he gazed at the place the rebels had built. The place my brother had built.

"What if I hurt someone?" The words came out in a rush, easier to say here in the quiet and the gloom. "What if I kill someone again?"

Wesley let his hand fall and turned to face me. "Then you kill someone," he said shortly. "But you're strong. And stronger now than you were when you first came here. You know how much power a person needs to keep breathing, to keep his heart beating. It's in you to kill, but it's also in you to preserve life."

I swallowed. I didn't feel any different, and I certainly didn't feel any stronger. All that had changed was that I'd gained an intimate understanding of just how I killed that man. Then it had been instinctive. Now I knew how it worked.

Wesley reached for my hand. I tried to jerk it back as I felt the familiar hunger rise at his touch, felt the warm tingle of power trying to flow from him to me—but he held on, his grip tight. "What I've taught you won't prevent you from killing anyone, Lark. All I've done is teach you enough that it becomes a choice. What you choose is up to you."

His eyes met mine for a long moment as I struggled against the urge to siphon away some of his magic.

Surely a little wouldn't hurt him. Just a tiny bit, he wouldn't even notice . . .

"You can go ahead, if you want." Wesley's voice was low, and abruptly I realized that avoiding a scene might not have been his only reason for making his farewell in private. "I trust you to stop before you hurt me."

I gazed at him, my vision blurring as I fought the hunger. It made sense to refill my reservoir of magic before I left, in case I needed it on the journey. It made sense to try it here, now, when there was help close at hand if something went wrong. It was the logical thing to do.

But I could feel the hunger, too dark and too deep—and this time when I yanked my hand away, Wesley let me go. His expression flickered briefly, and though I might have imagined it, he looked almost disappointed. I'd failed his test.

"No," I gasped, rubbing my palm against my shirt as if trying to scrub away the intensity of the hunger. "I can't, not yet."

Wesley waited, scanning my features, but ultimately nodded. He turned for the door again, this time to send a pulse of magic through the mechanism to set it clanking and whirring, unbarring the door.

"Good luck, then, Lark," said Wesley, running the hand that had been holding mine over his balding scalp. I couldn't help but wonder what it felt like for him, on the other end of my hungry power. I imagined it was like standing on the edge of some dark, shadowy abyss.

I nodded again, not trusting myself to speak, and stepped through the doorway. It was the same entrance we'd come through that first day, letting me out into the city alongside Central Processing. I could hear the calls of the merchants hawking their wares in the marketplace just around the corner, and when I lifted my face, the fine mist raining down from the ceiling sprinkled my cheeks.

A familiar voice cried out, echoing in the tunnels. "Lark! Lark, wait—"

It was Oren. I whirled in time to see the door slam closed, the locking mechanism clanking back into place. Then there was a loud clang—I winced. It was the sound of Oren's body hitting the inside of the door. I could still hear him shouting, though the sound was muffled now by the layers of bronze and iron between us.

"Lark—damn it, Wesley, open the door! I'm not letting her go without—*open this door.*"

Wesley's reply was too quiet and muffled for me to hear it, but whatever it was, the door stayed locked. I heard Oren bang on it once, twice—I could hear him tearing at the mechanism, trying to figure out how to open it without magic.

"Lark—can you hear me? Are you there?"

Part of me wanted to shout back, to tell him I was all right and that I could do this alone, that I didn't need him. But if I shouted here, someone in the marketplace, or in CeePo, might hear me. I couldn't attract any attention to the door.

I pressed my palm against its surface, silently willing Oren to just let me go.

Another clang, softer this time. I imagined his fist hitting metal. "Be careful," came his voice. He wasn't shouting anymore, but I could still hear him—he must've been speaking directly into the metal. "Come back safe."

I stepped away from the door and out toward the marketplace and the city, breathing deep. I was alone.

CHAPTER 18

Despite the city folk all around, it was the first time I'd been alone—truly alone—since I'd first crossed the Wall, back when I left my home city. That girl would've hardly recognized me now. Though my heart was pounding and my every sense on the alert for anyone paying me more attention than they should, my steps felt surer than they had for a long time. There was no turning back. This was my mission, and no one had manipulated me into it.

I did my best to avoid eye contact with anyone in a uniform. There was still a chance someone might recognize me as Oren's companion.

I picked up my pace, aiming for one of the many ramps leading up into the city stacked on itself. The entrance into the tunnels that I was looking for was, officially, just a drain for runoff from the constant drizzle overhead. I hiked upward until I reached the top of the ramp, following Marco's instructions, until I heard running water. The source of the sound was a trough running along a corroded metal roof. I followed it, ducking and weaving between the traffic of city dwellers and the ever-present machines, until it gushed out of a drainpipe and into a gutter that led down a different ramp.

The city was like a three-dimensional maze—here and there I had to leave the gutter to follow another path, sometimes heading up in order to ultimately find another path down. It took me the better part of an hour, but finally I ended up splashing into the gutter as it flowed into an alley between two dwellings. I glanced over my shoulder to make sure no one had seen me vanish into the shadows and then dropped to my knees in the rushing water.

The drain was covered by bars, each about a hand's width apart—too small to fit through. But Marco had prepared me for this, too. I pulled out Oren's knife and dug at the top of the bars with its tip. The "mortar" there was nothing more than wet clay, high enough out of the water that it wouldn't get washed away, but damp enough that it could never truly dry. I pulled several of the bars free until there was a gap wide enough to fit my shoulders, and then I wriggled through.

Even as my lungs constricted, an automatic response to the close quarters, the rest of me had to suppress a thrill. This was exactly the kind of thing my brother would've done. More than ever, I knew we were on the right track.

Inside the drainpipe there was enough room to get up on my hands and knees, and I took enough time to put the bars back, replacing the clay and wedging them in until I felt confident they'd stay put. Then I crawled forward, my sleeves and trousers soaked from the water. The tunnel branched—Marco had said nothing about this. One tunnel was significantly smaller than the other, but I was used to tight spaces. It was too dark to see anything, but from the way my labored breathing echoed, I could sense a larger space somewhere ahead down the smaller path. I made my way toward it.

Just as I spilled out of the pipe and into what felt like a broad cavern, a pair of hands grabbed me and threw me against the wall. Instantly my senses knew it was a Renewable, but the power signature was so muted and well hidden that it kept slithering out of my grasp. I opened my mouth to shout, hoping that Marco and Parker were close enough to hear me, but before I could get out a sound a hand clamped over my mouth.

"Hush!" It was a woman's voice, strangely accented. "Don't scream. I'm going to let you go—slowly—and when I do you'll tell me your name and what you're doing here."

Her grip over the bottom half of my face eased and then pulled away. I could still sense her close, though, ready to silence me if I screamed. Her other hand still pressed me back against the wall.

"My name's Lark," I whispered. "I—I got lost."

Her other hand loosened, and a quiet chuckle echoed over the chamber. "Like hell you're lost," my captor said. "You're *almost* exactly where you're meant to be. My name's Nina. Marco and Parker are at the other end, where you were supposed to come out."

I tugged my shirt straight as I got back on my feet again. I squinted in the darkness but could make out no more than a dim outline of someone a few feet away. "You could've just asked me without smashing me into the wall," I pointed out.

"Well, you could've actually come out where you were supposed to," she responded, sounding unfazed.

I heard a tiny trickle of magic, and then a flame flickered to life. It was nestled in the palm of Nina's hand, and she cupped it to the end of a torch.

"Is that a good idea? Wasting magic?" I spoke to cover the wave of wanting that coursed through my other, darker half at the display.

"The torches are too wet to light any other way." Sure enough, the torch hissed and popped loudly as the water evaporated—and finally came to life.

We were in a stone room, different from the tunnels the rebels inhabited, which were formed by alleys and forgotten buildings. This must've been part of the original city that now lay in ruins overhead. A sewer system, perhaps, not unlike the one my brother and I explored beneath our home city.

Nina was about my height but several years older. The torchlight revealed the barest hint of crows' feet at the corners of her eyes, but she didn't look more than twenty-five. She had dark hair and skin, though in the tricky firelight it was hard to tell exactly what shade. She smiled, her teeth white, and jerked her head toward a corridor that led off away from the drainpipe.

"We'll grab Marco and Parker, and then it'll be up to you to take us where we're going."

When we reached the others, Parker greeted me warmly while Marco stood off to the side, arms crossed over his chest, his every movement radiating dubiousness as he watched me. We were in an intersection of tunnels, three paths in addition to the one we'd arrived through.

Parker had brought the journal, after a long debate about whether it was worth risking such a priceless artifact. But both Parker and I had argued that there might be clues in the journal that wouldn't translate into a copy, and because we were going on the mission, we ultimately won out. He pulled the journal out of his coat lining and handed it to me.

"As best I can tell, this here is the cistern where Nina was waiting," Parker said, stabbing his finger at a rounded star shape at one edge of Basil's diagram. "It's the only thing I know that's shaped like that, and it's the only distinctive mark on this map."

"If it even is a map," Marco interjected.

"Oh, shut up, Marco." Nina dismissed him with a roll of her eyes. "You haven't changed a bit."

"Nice to see you too," Marco muttered in reply. Despite the banter, there was an obvious affection between them, and I wondered how long Nina usually went undercover without direct contact with her fellow rebels. Her life must be an exceedingly lonely one.

I took the journal from Parker, my eyes on the mark for the cistern. A series of crosshatches led in different directions, but I could see a rectangle leading off from the cistern—Basil's symbol for a pipe—and I knew which way we must have come. I traced the path to an intersection—the symbol was like an asterisk, but with five branches. I looked up, scanning the other tunnels. There were only four in total.

Where was the fifth?

I handed the journal back to Parker absently and headed for the far wall, where the fifth branch would've been. It was stable, even—the stones looked undisturbed, no sign that there had been a rockfall or a recent change to brick up the tunnel. I frowned, running my hands over the stones.

"What's she doing?" Marco's voice echoed.

"Shush," said Nina. "Let her work." She lifted the torch, giving me more light to see by.

I could feel their eyes on me, all expecting me to pull some kind of miracle out of the shadows. How badly they must need this exit, to allow this wild goose chase on the word of a girl they barely knew. Forcing them to the back of my mind, I concentrated on the stones.

I could see nothing out of place, but my fingertips felt something different, a ridge where there shouldn't be one. I dropped to my knees until I was eye-level with the stone. It was covered in algae and mildew, and I scraped my fingernails along it, clearing some of the gunk away. There was a design scratched into the stone, the barest of indentations. It was shaped a little like a V, only the lines were curved.

"Did you find something?" Nina came to kneel next to me, the torch flickering.

"I've seen this somewhere before," I murmured. "Parker, can I see the journal?"

He handed it to me, still open to the page with the map. But that wasn't what I was interested in. I flipped back toward the beginning until I found one of Basil's sketches of the landscape. I scanned it, then stabbed my finger at a cluster of markings over one of the mountains.

"There."

When I'd first seen the drawing, which was subtly and artistically done, I hadn't even noticed what was there that shouldn't have been: birds. They were distant in the picture, lacking detail—nothing more than lines, curved V's to give the impression of flight. But there were no birds out there; at least, none that I'd seen outside of the Iron Wood. And I noticed, now that I stared at them, that the shade of ink they were drawn in was subtly different. As though they'd been added to the picture much later.

"Shit, she's right." That was Marco, who'd given up being doubtful and was leaning in over my shoulder.

I handed the journal back and reached for the stone, giving it a sharp shove. It was loose, and it gave a little with a teeth-aching screech of stone on stone. I pushed again, and this time it slid all the way through, clattering down onto the stone on the other side.

I'd been expecting some sort of secret panel to open and tried to conceal the stab of nervous disappointment as I leaned down to put my eye to the hole. There was nothing to see there except darkness, and the hole was too narrow to fit the torch through.

"Now what?" Nina asked.

I couldn't afford to look like I was as lost as they were—they were counting on me to know my brother, to think the way he thought. I dropped down onto my side and put my hand through the hole.

"Lark—wait!" Parker's voice rang out. "Don't just stick your arm in there, you don't know what's . . . it could be a trap, you could hurt yourself."

I shook my head. "Basil wouldn't put a trap here. He left this trail to be followed." I hoped I sounded more sure than I felt.

I kept easing my arm through until I was shoulder-deep in the hole. It was a little wider than my arm was—which made sense, because Basil's arm would've been thicker than mine. I groped around blind, my hands encountering slimy stone and little else. My skin crawled as my hand passed through a cobweb and something large and skittery dropped onto my hand—I stifled a gasp and gave my arm an abrupt shake, and whatever it was flew off.

Nina must've noticed my flinching, and she silently put a hand on my arm. Her touch was warm, steadying. She was not a large woman, and not strong like Olivia, but there was strength in her reassurance regardless. I took a deep breath and kept feeling around for some clue to what to do next.

It wasn't until I bent my elbow up and started groping at the wall itself that my scrabbling fingers encountered something different. Metal, not stone. A long, rough spar about as big around as my finger. I wrapped my fingers around it, ignoring the way rust flaked off at my touch, and gave it a downward yank.

For a long, heart-pounding moment, nothing happened. Then there was a solid *thunk*, and then the clanking of an invisible gear somewhere under the stone floor. The wall itself shifted with a shower of dust and mortar, making me choke. A pair of hands dragged me backward abruptly, and I was grateful for the leather jacket—my arm would've been shredded without it. Nina hauled me to my feet as the wall—the entire wall—swung a foot inward.

Marco thumped me on the back while I stood there hacking and coughing up dust and then strode cheerfully past me. "Now that's more like it."

. . .

We pressed on, into the dark. Every now and then we could hear voices and knew we were passing within earshot of the known tunnels honeycombing the underground. We kept mostly silent, whispering only when we hit intersections and other doors, searching for the telltale marks that would lead the way. The further we got, the more my heart sang—it really was my brother's passageway. I could almost feel him here, like I could feel his ghost in the unused sewer system of my own city. It was as close as I was ever going to get to him again.

I was almost disappointed when Parker pointed out that we were heading upward, suggesting that we really were heading for the surface. The tunnel floor was set at a barely imperceptible slant—so mild that it was only the slow burning in our calves that alerted us to the fact that we were walking uphill.

The air grew fresher as we walked, and drier—and colder. The leather jacket was good protection against cuts and scrapes, but it didn't offer much warmth. We picked up our pace, as much to warm ourselves as to hurry toward the destination.

Eventually we reached another of Basil's hidden doors, but when Nina knelt down beside me to offer more light, the torch flickered abruptly, the flames licking backward.

"There's air coming through here," she murmured,

nudging me aside so she could press her cheek to the nearly invisible seam in the stone. "Dry air. Outside air."

The surface.

Our eyes met briefly, and then she jerked her head to the side and moved away so I could get at the latch to open the door. This time when the door swung open, it opened on the cold night air of the outside. A rush of wind howled past, throwing our hair back and plastering our clothes to our bodies.

"You've done it," shouted Parker over the air, stepping forward and gripping my shoulder.

"We should shut the door again," I shouted back. "This air is going somewhere—if it starts howling out of the pipe, someone's going to notice and come looking for this exit."

"Let's go," Marco said, pushing past us.

"Wait—we don't know what's up there—"

He put his face close to mine so I could hear better. "We've got to know where this comes out before we send people up here. We've got to scout."

I thought of the hungry shadows that could be waiting up here—and of Wesley's assurances that they'd all be out hunting and not in the city. I gritted my teeth and nodded.

We stepped forward, pushing against the door until the air pressure sucked it back against the rock with a slam. It was going to take all our strength, on the return trip, to pry it open against the force of the wind.

Gasping, lungs protesting the sudden shift in air temperature, I turned and got my first look at where we'd ended up. We were in the skeleton of a ruined building, something that had been hit far harder than the abandoned hotel where Trina and Brandon lived with their children. The windows were all gone, open to the outside, and parts of the wall had caved into rubble as well. We'd emerged from some sort of cellar entrance, half-sunk into the floor of the building.

The others climbed the few steps up to ground level, looking around, clapping each other on the shoulders. It must've been years since any of them had seen the outside, if they'd ever even come from the outside. Nina had an accent, and I assumed she must have come from somewhere else—but for all I knew, Parker and Marco had lived underground their whole lives. All three of them were drinking in the moonlight and the crisp wintery air.

I followed them up, saying quietly, "We should go back now. We know this comes out to the surface, we accomplished our mission."

"Are you kidding?" Marco grinned at me. "This is my first jaunt Above since I ended up on the run from Prometheus's goons. I'm staying put for a while."

"We do need to figure out where we are in relation to the farms, the occupied houses," Parker added, more sensibly. "When we send raiding parties up here they're going to need to know exactly where to go to cut down on the potential for incidents."

"You don't know what it's like out here," I whispered back, wishing the others would keep their voices down. I missed Oren—his silence, his caution. Even at his most infuriating, when I first met him, his first consideration was remaining unseen. "This isn't like anything you guys have encountered below."

"We're well-trained," Parker replied, sure and confident. It was easy to trust him, to believe he knew best. He was so like my father, back before the Institute broke him. "We know what we're doing, Lark, I promise." He headed out, the others close behind him.

We spilled out onto the deserted street. It had snowed again while I was in Lethe, and everything was coated in several inches of white powder that glowed in the moonlight. There were tracks everywhere, signs that the shadow people came through this way on their route in and out of the city at dawn and dusk. I scanned the horizons for any sign of light, any hint that we were running out of time before the sun rose, but I could see nothing. We ought to be out of danger.

Nina suggested following the freshest-looking tracks, so we set off toward the western edge of the city. The other three took the lead, but I held back, senses tingling. Though it made sense that the shadows would roam during the night, looking for prey, I wasn't convinced we were alone. Still, all was silent and calm, and I could hear nothing but the crunching of our footsteps and the breathing of my companions. Eventually I was forced to concede that Wesley was right. There was no sign that the shadow people were anywhere nearby.

I picked up my pace so I could walk with the others. We headed down a side street, following the tracks and scanning the buildings for any supplies the shadows might have left behind while in their daytime human forms.

The wind shifted, bringing with it the tang of coming snow. I paused for half a breath to wrap my jacket around me more tightly—and in that instant, my senses jangled abruptly.

"Something's wrong," I whispered to the cold, sharp wind.

Half a second later, before the others could react, a howl split the air. They all jumped, looking around, hands going to weapons and power gathering to strike. But I knew that sound. There was no fighting them, the shadows.

"Back to the door," I whispered sharply, my voice hoarse.

"But—" began Nina. She was the one in charge of combat situations—but this wasn't combat. They had to understand—this was running or dying.

"*Now!*" I cried. "Before they catch up to us. They're downwind of us now—they've caught our scent, that's why they howled! It's going to take time to get that door open again, time we won't have if the shadows are on our heels."

Nina's olive skin paled a little, and she nodded. Before she could speak, though, another sound rent the air, carrying across the snow—a scream. A *human* scream.

I froze, the others streaming past me to retrace our tracks back the way we'd come. "Wait."

"Go back, stay here—make up your damned mind!" Marco hissed at me, skidding to a halt with a spray of snow.

"Someone else is out here—the shadows aren't after us. They're after whoever's screaming."

"So? That's not our business!" Marco gave my arm a sharp tug. "They'll slow the Empty Ones down long enough for us to get away." I could see fear in his eyes, real fear banishing his bravado.

"Marco," Parker snapped. "That's not how we operate, you know that. Whoever's out here—they've got to be Renewable or they'd be shadows themselves. Part of the reason we wanted a route out was so we could recruit."

Marco protested, and while he and Parker argued, I caught Nina's eye. If we stayed, we'd be in a fight for our lives. It was her call.

She gazed at me, brows drawn in concentration. Then, abruptly, she raised her voice and cut through the argument. "We go. We go now, quietly. If there are only a few shadows we'll try to help. Otherwise it's back to the door, as fast as we can."

Decision made, the others were quick to move. Even Marco, whose face had gone white with fear, kept up as surely as the rest of us. We headed toward the sound of the scream, and as we drew closer we could hear snarls and shouts. There was more than one person there—and more than one shadow, too.

The alley we cut through opened up onto a broad avenue. A pack of at least a dozen shadow people were throwing themselves at a heavy metal door and clawing at shuttered windows—the human shouts were coming, muffled, from inside the building, echoing with each impact of the shadowy bodies against the door.

I cast out with my senses, skin crawling as my mind encountered the dark, empty pits of the shadow people. Beyond them, though, I could feel five, six . . . no, there were more further back. At least a dozen warm, glowing beacons in the darkness. Too far away for me to tap into, but close enough that I could tell what they were.

Renewables.

"They're in there," I gasped, eyes blurring with the effort of seeing with both senses—my eyes and my mind. "A dozen, maybe more."

Nina was scanning the scene. We were outnumbered three to one by the shadows—and even though these rebels couldn't know just how savage the shadows were, three-to-one odds in any situation wasn't going to look good.

But there were at least a dozen Renewables on the other side of that door, and if they heard us going into battle for them, maybe they'd come out and help. Alone, neither group stood a chance. But together . . .

I saw Nina's eyes land on the door and knew she was thinking the same thing.

"Marco, Parker, circle left. Lark and I will draw them away from the door, and you'll come in behind them, we'll try to keep them disoriented."

They both nodded, committed as soon as Nina ordered them to fight. I tried to find that certainty, to find the faith that the Renewables behind the door would help. But I knew this world too well—knew how selfish and how cold it was.

Before I could say anything, though, Nina barked a command and the others leaped out of hiding to carry out her plan. I scrambled to follow. I didn't have much magic in my reserves—but I had a little.

The shadows peeled away from the door as our shouts dragged their attention away from the barred door—they bounded toward us, all jaws and grey flesh and white eyes. Behind them I dimly saw Marco and Parker, and then they were on us. I had Oren's knife in one hand—I threw up a wall of magic and knocked a shadow to the ground, bringing the knife down into its arm. I couldn't bring myself to kill it— what if it was Trina behind that shadowy mask?

The world descended into a chaos of shouts, howls, the roaring of the wind and the tangy smell of blood. The snow underfoot churned crimson in places—a shadow person fell, slammed into the earth as Marco stepped on its throat. I saw Parker go down, and I lunged for him, knocking into the shadow person attacking him a half-second before its jaws closed on his throat. I felt sharp nails scrabbling at my body, squeals of animal protest piercing my ears as the shadow person squirmed and tried to get its balance back—and then screamed again and fell still, Parker's blade buried in its eye socket.

I scrambled back, gasping, my eyes scanning the courtyard. Nina was cornered, pinned back against the wall of the building, holding the trio of shadows at bay by swinging her knife in a low, glittering arc. I couldn't even see Marco— Parker leaped forward again, but he wasn't a fighter, I could tell by the way he moved. He was a scholar.

I whirled and banged my fists against the barred door. "Help us!" I screamed, my voice tearing out of my throat. "We're trying to save you—open the door and help us!"

But there was no answer from behind the door. I lifted my fist to bang again, but before I could, claws dug into my thigh and dragged me back. I slipped in the snow, dropping face-first and hitting my chin on the stone. Dazed, dizzy, tasting blood, I struggled. A pair of jaws snapped inches away from my face, and I threw what little magic I had left at it. It snarled, shaking off the blow as if it was nothing more than a nuisance. I saw blood pouring from its arm—it was the monster I'd refused to kill earlier.

I slammed my fist into its face, but it scarcely noticed. The shadows didn't feel pain the way we did—it lunged for my shoulder, tearing the skin and sending lances of agony down through my body. I screamed.

Then something invisible collided with the monster, sending it flying away from me and rolling over and over to lie still against a snow bank. Nina grasped at my uninjured arm, hauling me up by the wrist. She'd saved my life.

"I'm out," she gasped, exhaustion warring with fear and adrenaline on her face. "Nothing left. We've got to run."

I lifted my head, but there were shadows everywhere. There were more now than there had been, drawn no doubt by the sound of combat—and the smell of blood. Our way back was blocked.

I stepped close to Nina so I could shout over the screams and howls raging around us. "We need to get this door down—if it's broken they *have* to help us or they'll die too. You've got to blast it."

She shook her head. "Can't—don't have enough. Can't push more out or I'm going to go down."

I was out, too. Nothing left but the hungry pit inside me. Where Nina's hand gripped me, her skin touching mine just below the sleeve of my jacket, I could feel her power—the tiniest hint of magic left. The image of the boy in the practice room flashed before my eyes—his heart stopping as the power left him.

Out here, if Nina used all her power, there was nothing in the air to sustain her. She'd die.

But if she didn't, we'd all die.

"You have to!" I shouted, kicking out as a badly wounded shadow tried to drag itself over to us. My foot connected with its face with a crunch. "I'll get you back inside—you'll only be out for a few minutes, I swear!"

Nina's face was ashen despite her color. "I can't—Lark, I can't."

How do you will yourself to stop breathing? How do you order your heart to shut down?

I looked up to see Parker on his back, wrestling with a shadow inches away from his face—Marco was still missing, but to judge by the swarm of shadows by the far wall, he was too far to help us. And they were both too far away for me to touch their magic.

My gaze snapped back to Nina. "Forgive me," I whispered to her and then closed my eyes.

I let the hunger flare up, and it snapped greedily at the tiny threads of power I could feel where Nina's body touched mine. The power flowed into me, and I turned toward the door, feeling every bit of stolen energy pushing outward, warming my fingers, my toes, singing through my body. Nina's body stiffened, then sagged, and some part of my mind screamed at me to stop. I had enough—I had to let her go.

Let her go!

I threw her hand away from mine and she slumped down, motionless, in the snow. I turned my attention to the door and threw the magic outward. It met the door with a deafening slam, and the entire thing was ripped from its hinges and sent shattering inward. I caught a fleeting glimpse of terrified faces in the darkness.

"*HELP US*," I screamed at them, then turned to use the last of Nina's magic to throw back a shadow bounding toward her motionless form.

The cowering Renewables inside were slow, far too slow, to react—but once they did they streamed out of the building, meeting the battle without further hesitation. It was all a blur, but I could tell they could fight—we'd taken out enough of the shadows that they could fight back, pushing the line of monsters further and further away.

My head spun with magic as I fought the urge to succumb to the euphoria, the delicious warmth spreading through me. Every time I tasted new magic, the hunger grew. Everyone's was different—Nina's tasted like cinnamon. And I wanted more.

I threw myself down at her side, uncertain even as I moved whether I was going to finish her off or check to see if she was alive. I reached for her, turning her over—her eyes stared blankly skyward.

No. *No.* There was still something there—the tiniest flicker. I could feel it within her, like a dying flame.

I pressed my cheek to her chest and heard nothing but the sounds of battle surging around us, felt nothing but the vibrations of feet running past. I could feel no breath coming from her lips. As I bent over her, the image flashed before me of Wesley, before I knew who he was, breathing for the fallen Eagle until his body remembered how to do it on its own. The Eagle I flattened. He died, yes, but only later—Wesley had managed to find his breath, find his heartbeat again.

Frantic, I bent my head, forcing Nina's mouth open so I could press my lips to hers and force a lungful of air into her. Her chest rose, then fell as I pulled away. I tried again, and again—then felt across her chest for her breast bone, thumping at it the way I'd seen Wesley restart the Eagle's heart.

We're just machines. Parker's voice came over the sounds of battle. *Machines that run on magic.* And machines sometimes needed a jump-start.

I kept at it, some part of my mind realizing that the sounds of battle were waning—there were no more howls, fewer shouts. I could hear the wet, horrible sounds of blades entering flesh, but I recognized them as knives—not claws, not teeth. The tide had turned, the hiding Renewables had made the difference.

But I couldn't spare the time to see, growing lightheaded and dizzy as I kept blowing oxygen into Nina's lungs, willing them to remember how to work.

Please, no. I didn't choose this. I'm never choosing this again.

Dimly I realized that the others were standing around me, watching.

"I saw what she did." It was Marco's voice, hushed and terrified. But that wasn't right—the shadows had been beaten. There was no reason for him to be afraid now. "I saw her—I saw her tear the life out of Nina."

"No." That was Parker. "It can't—it's impossible. She'd have to be . . . she'd have to be empty inside."

She'd have to be no more than a shadow herself.

I gasped for a full breath, the air sobbing in and out of me as I thumped my hand down on Nina's chest again.

This time her body jerked. Her lungs expanded in a rush—on their own—and I half-fell back, staring, uncomprehending. At some point her eyes had rolled up into her head, and now her eyelids were mostly lowered, flickering lightly. She was unconscious—but she was alive.

I groaned, crawling back away from her until I could collapse, my arms shaking, my face pressed into the freezing snow. I felt hands reach down to pull me up, gentle. A voice I didn't know said something in my ear—only I did know it.

It wasn't Marco's, it wasn't Parker's. It was farther away than that. A more distant memory.

I struggled to focus, letting the hands prop me up as a face swam into focus in front of mine.

"It is you," the voice whispered. I saw brown eyes gazing into mine, and for a wild moment my brain tried to make the face become Basil's, and my eyesight warred with memory.

But it wasn't Basil—the eyes were brown, yes, but lighter than Basil's, and he was older than Basil would be now, and his hair a different color. Nevertheless, I knew him.

"Dorian?" I gasped.

The leader of the Iron Wood cupped my face in his hands. "We found you," he whispered, hope and joy on his haggard, bloodstained features. "We're saved. Finally."

CHAPTER 19

"We've been following your trail for weeks." Dorian leaned against the wall, his face looking worn and drawn in the flickering torchlight. "For a while we were following—" He broke off, guilt flashing in his eyes.

"You were following messages from Tansy," I finished for him.

Dorian cleared his throat. "Yes. But the messages stopped abruptly, and we were afraid that you'd either discovered she was sending them and had left her behind, or that something had happened to the both of you. Where is Tansy?"

My eyes fell. "She's gone. Captured. Probably powering Prometheus's machines as we speak." I swallowed, sick to my stomach.

"I see." There was pain, genuine pain, in Dorian's voice. "Lark, I'm sorry for how this has happened."

I turned away from him, unable to look at him any longer. Instead my eyes fell on Nina's motionless form, half-propped up on Marco's lap. She was still breathing but showed no signs of regaining consciousness. Parker was with them—they kept their distance from the Renewables from the Iron Wood. They kept their distance from me. While I watched, Parker glanced up. His eyes met mine, and in them there was no sign of the gentle affection, the warm assurance I'd come to value so much from him. There was nothing of my father there. There was mistrust, and fear, and betrayal—the hurt was so tangible that my throat closed and I sank down to the ground, averting my gaze from him as well.

We had to get Nina back to the resistance hideout, to healers who might be able to help her. This pause was only to light enough torches for everyone, to wrap up our injured, to get ready to make the trek through the tunnels, going the long way back to the other side of the city. There would be no cutting through the open city undetected this time—not bloody and carrying an unconscious body. Not with a dozen Renewables who'd never had to learn to shield themselves from detection.

As Marco and Parker picked up Nina's unconscious body and led the way, Dorian fell into step beside me. I wanted nothing more than for him to leave, to let me think, to make sense of what was happening. My two worlds, my two havens, colliding—the Iron Wood and the rebel fighters of Lethe.

But he spoke, scrambling my thoughts. "Don't you want to know why we had Tansy follow you?"

"I know why," I spat back. "Because you wanted to make sure you knew where I was, in case you ever wanted to use me as a weapon again."

"That's not—" He paused, ducking under a low, protruding stone. "That's not entirely true. Yes, we wanted to know where you are. But only because the barrier you created, the one that kept us safe from the machines and the soldiers your city sent—it's failing."

Torn between Kris's demands that I join with the architects of the Institute again, help to plunder the Iron Wood's power in exchange for my freedom, and Dorian's plans to use me as a weapon to destroy my city's forces, I'd chosen a third option—I'd created a barrier preventing anyone from destroying anyone else. I knew what would happen if that barrier fell. The architects, led by Gloriette herself, would help themselves to the Renewables in the Iron Wood, enslaving them to power their machines.

I clenched my jaw, hardening my heart against the image of the Renewables there cowering behind a faltering shield. "That's not my problem."

"We need your help," he pleaded. "They keep sending scouts every few days to test the barrier. The second it falls, the Iron Wood will be lost. You have to do what you did again—you have to find a way to get rid of your city's people permanently."

"I don't *have* to do anything," I replied, my voice tight.

"Your people are getting desperate." Dorian reached for my arm, dragging me back as the others went on ahead. "The Renewable they have in your city isn't going to last much longer. It's a miracle she's lasted as long as she has."

My footsteps ground to a halt. The air felt thick, hard to breathe. Hard to think. "How do *you* know how long she's been there?" I whispered.

He gazed back at me, haggard features twitching.

I felt cold, far colder than I'd been while standing in the snow outside. "Gloriette, when she was after me—she told me that they'd captured the Renewable they have powering the city. She claimed someone had sent her to spy on the city, and that justified the way the architects treated her."

Grief aged Dorian's features, his eyes closing, the corners of his mouth drawing in. "Would anything justify what they've done to her?"

I could still see the image of the Renewable's face, her silent, eternal scream, the way her white eyes stared as though seeking something, anything, that looked like salvation.

Dorian ran a hand over his features as though he could wipe his grief away. I wondered if he knew the woman who now lived in agony in the bowels of the Institute. I wondered if he'd sent her. "Your city," he said slowly, "is the only one that survived. The Iron Wood, we came there later, after the world burned and the magic twisted it. This place—you saw what the city above looked like. That's what the rest of the world looks like now. Only your city survived. Only they had a barrier up."

"I don't—"

"They had to know it was coming, Lark." He let go of my arm. "They were ready for the cataclysm before it ever happened. These are the people after us. I can't protect my people from them without you."

My head spun with exhaustion—I just wanted to curl up in the muck coating the floor of the tunnel and let Dorian, and Nina, and Wesley and everyone just drift on past.

"I have to do this first." My voice was hoarse, tired. "The resistance movement here will keep you safe for now, especially if you're willing to help them."

"But—"

"Maybe if you help them," I said firmly, "they might be able to help you. They need more Renewables to help fight Prometheus. Talk to me after we've gotten rid of him, Dorian. I'm not doing anything for you until then."

· · ·

I barely had enough energy to see Nina, still unconscious, safely into the rebels' crude infirmary and under the care of their healers. News of her condition spread quickly, and as I limped back out of the room, I heard a voice scream her name, sobbing. The voice was familiar, but in its rawness I couldn't tell who it was. I didn't *want* to know—I was the reason Nina was half-dead, and I couldn't face it, not now. Wesley took charge of the new Renewables, and after a quick nod at me— *good job*, his eyes said—he left me to stagger down to my room. I thought of Oren and knew he'd be at my side as soon as he heard that I was back. Olivia or no, he still cared about my fate. Still, the moment I hit the mattress in my quarters, I was asleep.

. . .

When I woke I had no way of telling how much time had passed, except that I was clear-headed enough to sit up and actually notice my surroundings. I'd slept for hours, at least. And there was no sign of Oren—I was alone, and if he'd come while I slept, he hadn't woken me.

I swung my legs over the side of the bed, my muscles stiff and aching. My shoulder throbbed where I'd been bitten, and when I pulled the edge of my shirt away, I saw that it had been bandaged neatly while I slept. I moved it experimentally and found that the injury wasn't that bad. It ached, but the healers here knew what they were doing. Out on my own, a wound like the one I'd received in the fight would've taken weeks to get better.

Someone had left a plate of food for me on top of the clothes chest at the foot of my bed. Thanking whoever had the foresight to know I wouldn't be up to facing the entirety of the resistance fighters *and* the emissaries from the Iron Wood, I ate sitting cross-legged on my bed. I was still exhausted, in that bone-deep, head-aching way that always followed over-taxing myself with magic. But recovering here, where there was magic in the air, was much quicker than recovering out in the vacuum outside.

The recovery was only superficial, though. I wouldn't

be able to recharge my magic unless I could harvest it from someone.

Then, with a rush, it came back to me—Nina. Parker and Marco had seen me siphon away her magic. They knew what I was, or at least what I was capable of. And by now they could've already told everyone.

I had to find Wesley and figure out a way to minimize the damage—some lie that would convince the resistance that I wasn't dangerous. Either that, or some way for me to get out of here before it was too late. I already knew how these people felt about shadows—how would they feel about me? Whatever I was.

I lurched off the bed and reached for the door latch. I stumbled when it failed to give, my momentum carrying me forward and into the door, where I had expected it to open.

Blankly, I gave the latch another shake. Nothing.

My heart froze. The door was locked from the outside.

· · ·

Though I couldn't be sure without any way to keep track, it felt like several hours before the clank of the lock alerted me to the presence of someone outside. I scrambled to my feet as the door swung open. It was Wesley.

My protests died on my lips when I saw his face. He looked grim and weary. "Come with me," he said shortly. "The others want to talk to you."

"Nina?" I managed, heart pounding.

Wesley paused in the doorway, looking back at me. "She's alive," he said finally, making relief sing through me. "But she won't wake up. Her body's okay, but it's like she's just not in there."

My relief soured, stomach roiling. "What do the healers say?"

"They don't know." Wesley stepped aside, making room for me to slip past him into the hall. "They've never seen anything quite like it. Their best guess is that she's in some sort of coma. There could be damage to her brain because she stopped breathing for a while."

I swallowed as Wesley shut the door again behind me. My feet felt like lead. "Parker and Marco, they're okay?"

He nodded but didn't say anything else, turning to lead the way toward the War Room. He didn't speak again until we were just outside the doors. I could feel Renewables in there— I thought I detected the particular signatures of Parker and Marco, but I was still tired and not completely sure.

"Lark," said Wesley in a low voice, "it's time for you to tell the truth now. I can't lie for you, not when there are witnesses. And if we're being completely honest, I'm not sure I want to lie for you now."

"Were you close to Nina?" I whispered.

His expression flickered briefly, but I couldn't identify the emotion that passed through it. "We're all close to each other here. This is our family. But that's not why. You're dangerous, and it was irresponsible of me to keep that danger from the others. No matter how valuable that power of yours might be."

I kept my eyes on the door, fighting back when my sight started to blur. I wasn't going to cry, even faced with losing one of my only allies. This was, after all, what I deserved. Like Oren, I was a monster hiding in plain sight. But unlike him, I never stopped being myself, even when I killed.

"For what it's worth," Wesley added, softer still, "I think you may have made the right choice. From what I've put together from Parker and Marco, and the leader of the group that you rescued, you'd all have died if you hadn't gotten that door open."

He reached for the handle of the door, but paused before opening it. "And I think they'll probably still want to use you, because even more now, you're the best weapon we've got. I'm just not sure they're ever going to trust you."

Wesley left me swallowing the lump in my throat and pushed the doors open, leading the way into the War Room. I recognized Dorian and a couple of other Renewables from the Iron Wood there, clustered in a group. Parker and Marco were there too, and both of them snapped their heads up when I entered, their gazes dark and unreadable as they fell on me. The others were no different, watching me with wary suspicion.

As if it could smell their fear, the shadow inside me stirred sluggishly. I could feel it flickering as though scenting the air, tasting each golden beacon of power in the gathered Renewables. I shoved it back down with a shudder, drawing my shoulders back and lifting my chin.

Good, then. If they were afraid, well, they *should* be. Wesley was right. It was time to stop hiding what I was. "I'm from a city south of here," I began. "Where there are no Renewables. There isn't anyone with this ability there, either. I think my brother may have been like me, but he's gone now. As far as I know, I'm the only one."

"And what are you?" That was Parker, who hadn't moved from the back of the room. His shoulder blades pressed back against the wall, as if he half-wished he could retreat further.

"I don't know," I replied simply.

I told them about the experiments the architects had run at the Institute and how my brother and I were the only ones to survive the process. How they'd turned us into something that looked, on the surface, like a Renewable, so that we'd be able to survive beyond the Wall. How my brother had made it this far, only to get captured once Prometheus started rounding up Renewables. I told them about the Iron Wood and how it was only when I'd used the last of the power the Institute gave me that I discovered the emptiness inside me and the way it could absorb the power in others.

I didn't tell them about Oren, though. If I was going to be branded a monster, it made no sense for us to both be outcast. As long as Oren stayed below ground, he was safe, and he'd never become a shadow again. He might as well be able to live free.

"I never wanted to hurt Nina, or anyone else." My voice was growing hoarse, and I had to clear my throat several times before I could go on. "If you want me to leave, I'll go. Take the route we found up to the surface and never come back. But not before I find a way into Central Processing to save my friend, and avenge my brother—and get rid of Prometheus. I've been tortured the way he tortures Renewables. I'm not letting it happen to anybody else. I'll go by myself if I have to."

I fell silent. Under the weight of all their stares, I could feel myself starting to sweat in the warm damp that pervaded Lethe. My muscles were still stiff and sore, and my arm arched. I longed to sit in one of the empty chairs at the edge of the table closest to me, but I knew I couldn't.

I'd go alone into Central Processing if I had to, but if I wanted any chance of reaching Prometheus before the Eagles overwhelmed me, I was going to need help. I thought of Oren and the way he always stood when hissing orders at me in the wilderness—strong, tall, sure. Competent. I willed the Renewables in the room to see that in me. My plan was a good one, and that I was something new and different didn't change that. If anything, it gave us the edge we'd need to win.

"Do you have anything else to add?" asked Parker. He sounded tired too. One of his hands was bandaged, but he seemed otherwise unhurt—on the outside, anyway. He was gazing at the table in front of me and not meeting my eyes.

I swallowed. "No."

"Then Marco will escort you back to your quarters, where you will stay until we've made a decision about what to do with you."

I expected Marco to complain, to show his distaste at being given this task—it was his way, the show of petulance that kept him aloof. Instead he went silently, his expression stony, his muscles tense. I could sense power gathered all around him, at the ready, and I was reminded abruptly of what Wesley said—that he was the strongest Renewable they had. They were using their best to keep watch on me.

He walked me back to my room in silence. I strained to listen as we walked away, but I could hear nothing from the War Room. Marco had mistrusted me—or at least doubted my abilities—from the very beginning, but I wasn't reading any smug satisfaction at having been proven right. He walked just ahead of me, jaw clenched.

When we reached my room, he waited outside as I took the last few steps into the tiny space. I expected him to slam the door in my face, but instead he stood there silently for a long moment, his hand on the doorframe, white-knuckled.

Finally, he said shortly, "I volunteered for that mission, you know."

I nodded. Wesley had told me.

"Do you know why?"

"No," I whispered. "Why?"

He sucked in a lungful of air through his nose, bracing. "Because I wanted to believe you. I wanted you to be right, even though most of me was sure you weren't." His voice was tight and strained. "You were the girl in the journal. You were supposed to—you were supposed to be our salvation."

I couldn't speak, the force of his emotion and his disappointment cutting me like a blade.

He struggled with himself for a long moment and then said, quietly, "At least with Prometheus, we know who our enemy is." He grasped the door handle, stepping back. "I don't know *what* you are."

CHAPTER 20

For hours, there was nothing. No word from Wesley or anyone else from the War Room, no food brought. I still hadn't seen Oren or Olivia since coming back from the mission, and even Marco failed to return. I examined the lock as best I could by feel, with my second sight. It was solid iron, and for anyone else it'd be impossible to magic. I had no idea if they knew I could, but either way it made no difference. It'd take a lot more magic than what I had now for me to do anything at all to the iron lock.

Though I'd felt fine in my room just hours before, knowing it was now a prison cell made my skin itch, my mind shudder. I'd been locked up now more times than I could easily count, and I was tired of letting it happen. I wasn't meek little Lark Ainsley anymore, the child who was content to wait for Kris to slip her a key in the Institute. Too much had happened since then for me to let them keep me here.

I ran my hands over the door. The lock might have been iron, but the rest of the door was some sort of copper alloy. The door—and more importantly, the hinges—were as susceptible to magic as anything else. If I wrenched the hinges free, the rest of the door would give way.

I could get out on my own, if I had to. If they decided I was too dangerous to have fighting alongside them, then I could fight my way through them.

I was resting my forehead against the door, exploring its structure with my mind and searching for invisible stress fractures in the metal, when something in the air beyond it shifted. The shadow in me recognized it before my thoughts did. The darkness was getting stronger. It recognized its own kind.

Oren.

The lock clanked open and the door swung inward. Oren looked as exhausted as I felt, but his head lifted a little as he saw me. He stepped inside and let the door thud closed after him.

"Are you okay?" he asked, his voice rough. His eyes raked over me, taking in the bandage visible at the collar of my shirt. I must've looked pretty ragged, because his face tightened.

"For now."

"You didn't tell them about me." It wasn't a question, though his voice sounded uncertain.

I smiled a little, sinking down on the edge of my bed. "No point in us both being locked up."

He leaned against the wall in front of me, stepping finally into the light so I could get a good look at him. There were a number of new bruises visible on his arm below his sleeve, and on his jaw—and a cut on his cheekbone where a blow had split the skin.

"What happened to you?" I breathed, my heart tightening.

He blinked, then lifted a hand to his face as though he'd forgotten about his injuries. "Oh. Olivia happened."

Olivia did this? To Oren?

"I thought you said she couldn't take you," I said slowly.

"She's—upset." He glanced away from me, eyes flicking

from the wall behind me to the door. "She and Nina are close." There was something soft, painful, in his voice. Her pain was hurting him. Oren cared for her.

There was no end to the damage I'd done in that one, fleeting moment. A tiny part of me almost wished I'd just let the shadows overrun us all. I swallowed down the sick feeling in my stomach. "She's taking it out on the wrong person."

Oren shook his head. "She just needed an outlet. She met Nina when her brother was taken by Prometheus—Nina was the one who helped her through it."

I remembered the quiet warmth in Nina's touch, and understood. "I wish I could talk to her. Apologize, somehow. But I doubt they'd let me out of here."

"That's actually why I came," Oren said, gaze finding mine again. I was struck anew with how much he'd changed since we'd been in Lethe. It was like the animal side of him had been . . . not tamed, exactly. Harnessed. He was still strength and confidence and sharp intelligence, but he was in control of himself. He didn't jump anymore at sudden noises or tense whenever anyone new walked into the room.

Distracted, I almost missed what he said next.

"They're going ahead with the mission."

My breath caught and my hands curled around the edge of the mattress, my muscles suddenly going tense. "My mission?"

He nodded. "They asked me what I thought, since I'd be the one facing a death sentence if something goes wrong—for the Eagle's murder. I told them it was a good plan."

I listened in silence, caught between the way my heart swelled at Oren's confidence and the way my own uncertainty flared, knowing that lives would be at stake because of me. Again.

"I think Wesley argued for it, too. And Dorian told them what you did for the Iron Wood. At any rate, they're going to go through with it, but they're all going to be armed with these."

He pulled something small and round out of his pocket and tossed it to me. I caught it and felt an odd tug at the ever-present web of magic in the air. It looked like a crude iron sphere with no distinguishing characteristics. I glanced up at Oren dubiously.

"Parker rigged them up using the Eagles' talons. You throw them at the ground, and if it's enough of an impact, they go off like an explosion. But instead they banish all the inorganic magic within a certain radius."

I recognized Parker's turn of phrase and knew Oren was repeating him word for word. Another time, I would've smiled to hear him using words like *inorganic* and *radius*. Instead, I asked, "So what's the point of them?"

"Parker's theory is that you're like a machine, and that the magic in you is like the magic in the machines. Stolen, not generated. The idea is that these won't have any effect on a real Renewable. But they'll knock out any machines in the area. And—"

I breathed out slowly. "And they'll take me out, too."

Oren nodded. "I'm supposed to be carrying that one. But I think you should have it, for tomorrow."

It wasn't much use to him—he was safe from me. The shadow in me didn't want anything from him. There was no hunger to steal what little magic he had inside, keeping him human. But why give it to me? When I started to ask the question aloud, he just pushed away from the wall and folded my fingers gently around the sphere, holding my hands between his.

"If there was a way to switch me off when the darkness comes," he said softly, "I'd never go anywhere without it."

His face was close, his eyes meeting mine. For the first time, I realized that it wasn't about hating him the way I hated myself, for being what we were. For the first time, I realized that Oren understood me. He was the only one in the world who could. He was giving me a way to take myself out, rather than let the hunger take over again.

Oren let go of me and stepped back, shoving his hands into his pockets. "So, you'll get your chance to face Prometheus. And if Tansy and Nix are in there, you'll get your chance to find them, too."

I took a deep breath, feeling dizzy.

"But—here's the thing. They're going tomorrow."

"Tomorrow?" I burst out, staring. "So soon?"

Oren shrugged. "They didn't tell me why, but I suspect it's to do with you. The less time you're here, the less opportunity there is for you to . . ."

He trailed off, but I knew what he meant. "Less opportunity for me to hurt someone."

Oren grimaced. "They don't know you, Lark."

I shook my head. "No. The problem is they *do* know me now. The real me."

Oren was silent for a long moment, gazing at me with those pale, unreadable eyes. I knew was he was thinking about, knew with utter certainty that at any moment he'd give me another speech about strength and power and only being a weapon when I choose to be. Just as surely, I knew I couldn't stand to hear it, not now. Not while Nina still lay unconscious, while Tansy might be being tortured at that very moment, while Olivia was pounding the life out of anyone who came near.

So instead I stood abruptly. "Is that all?"

Oren opened his mouth, but stopped, hesitating.

"Try to get some sleep," he suggested, his voice rough. Then he turned his back, and was gone.

I let myself sink back down with a creak of the mattress.

I knew I should do as he said—that I should do as I was ordered by the Renewables here. But I was buzzing with nerves, and with energy, and I knew I wasn't going to sleep. There was a good chance I wasn't coming back from the mission tomorrow. I paced the confines of my room, fingers tracing the curves of the blackout device in my pocket. What do you do when it might be your last night alive?

. . .

I waited in the muggy heat of my shut-in room, letting the hours tick by, until the sounds of feet moving past and machines being used and switched off again faded. I'd come to know the rhythms of this place, and I could tell as the world grew quieter that the rebels were all settling down to sleep, that they weren't plagued by the same restlessness as I was, the night before we faced Prometheus.

I pressed my cheek to the door. Oren hadn't locked it on his way out. If it were anyone else, I would think they had simply forgotten, but Oren didn't miss details like that. He left it unlocked on purpose, giving me the option to escape. He was worried about me.

Beyond the door, I could sense the telltale glow of the guard's energy. A Renewable—they weren't taking any chances with me. I didn't recognize the signature, but whoever it was, I didn't want him or her tagging along when I went to find Olivia. I didn't even know what I was going to say to her, but I knew I didn't want an audience.

Burying the thread of guilt warning me against what I was doing, I reached out with agonizing slowness until I could just tap into the edge of the man's aura. I didn't need to take a lot of his power, just enough to make him drowsy. The darkness inside me stirred sluggishly, and I fought to keep it down. If I let it wake, there was no telling what it might do.

You don't have to do anything, whispered my guilt. *Just do as you're told and wait.*

But I kept at it, knowing that if I paced inside my room all night, I'd go mad. Gradually, I could feel the man's consciousness waning, his power flickering and dulling all around him. I eased the door open as silently as I could and found him leaning back against the wall. He twitched as one of the door hinges squealed, but didn't wake.

I slipped down the hallway in the opposite direction from the guard, my senses buzzing and tingling with the extra magic in my system. The air was only slightly cooler out here than in my tiny room. Though there were giant air-circulation vents all over the place, the air was still close and warm. It made me long for wind, the same wind that had so frightened me the first time I'd heard it howling through the ruins. Still, the farther I got from my tiny room, the better I felt.

I'd been to the infirmary only once, right after the mission. But I remembered where it was, and my feet brought me there without hesitation. There were no guards on that door—after all, they believed the monster was contained, safe in her room. I let my mind trickle out carefully, enough to sense one presence in the room. Nina? Had they left her alone?

But when I eased the door open a fraction, I saw a healer sitting at the foot of one of the beds, head drooping onto his chest. His was the life force I'd sensed. There was a form in the bed, but I felt nothing from it. My throat closed. Nina's body was as inert to my senses as the bed she rested in.

They had connected her to a number of machines, one of which I could tell from here was trying to artificially restore her magic. I could hear their mechanisms whirring and clicking, a gentle cacophony echoing through the silent night. Though the healer seemed to be asleep, I stayed where I was.

I told myself that it was because I couldn't risk waking the healer watching over Nina, but I knew the truth. From here, I could just glimpse Nina's face, ashy and drawn. I didn't want to see more.

I stood there on the threshold for what felt like an hour, unable to enter, unable to leave. My handiwork, lying there at the edge of life.

When I finally turned away, I knew where I was going. I had a good idea of where Olivia would be if she wasn't in the infirmary with her friend. I headed for the roof, pausing at the door that opened up onto the nighttime Lethe air. I couldn't sense anything beyond it, but Olivia wasn't a Renewable. She had the same magic all normal people did, untapped—but it was quiet and hard to detect this far away. I took a deep breath and swung the door silently outward.

She was there, sitting on the edge of the roof, legs dangling over empty space. She didn't look back as I entered, but I saw her stiffen and I knew she'd guessed it was me. I hesitated, hanging onto the edge of the door, unwilling to let it swing closed. Now that I was here, I had no idea what I wanted to say. I wanted to confess, but she already knew what I'd done. I wanted to take it back somehow, but it was impossible.

"Olivia—" I began, my voice emerging as a whisper. "I'm so sorr—"

"Don't." Her voice was quiet but sharp, cutting through mine like a knife. No bubbly enthusiasm, no friendly warmth. She sounded tired. Angry. "If what Oren tells me is true, then you didn't mean to hurt anyone, and you have nothing to apologize for. And if he's wrong, and you did it on purpose— then I don't want to hear you lie about feeling regret."

I took a step back, half-intending to leave her alone. But before I could act on the impulse, she turned, glancing over her shoulder me. "You're thinking about tomorrow, aren't you?" she asked. "About the fact that you might not come back."

I nodded, and she tilted her head to the side. A silent summons.

When I settled down beside her, she leaned forward with her elbows on her knees. "I always come up here the night before a mission. I don't know why, but it helps."

The ground was a dizzying distance below us, but Olivia seemed unconcerned. I tried to ignore the drop, focusing instead on the city and the phosphorescent glow of the fungus on the cavern walls. For a while we sat in silence, me staring upward and Olivia looking down at her feet as she swung them gently side to side.

I wanted to speak, but I had nothing to say. At least, nothing I could put into words. She was the closest thing I'd made to a friend here, but now it was like we didn't even know each other. Maybe I was just torturing myself, sitting beside this walking, talking reminder of what I'd done to Nina, the people I'd hurt by hurting her.

Because the truth was that I liked Olivia. No matter how much I wished I could hate her for how close she'd grown to Oren, she hadn't done anything wrong. She was helping him, giving him training—and friendship—he desperately needed.

I found myself saying, "Tell me about your brother."

Her head snapped up, and I hurried to add, "I'm sorry— you don't have to answer. Oren mentioned him, and I thought—it's fine."

"No," she said slowly. "No, I don't mind. You've lost a brother too. Maybe talking about it would help."

She sucked in a long breath through her nose, letting it out in an audible sigh. "We were . . . close. That seems like such an inadequate way to say it. We were twins. Two halves of a whole. From childhood we were like opposites—he had black hair, I had blonde. He was quiet and thoughtful and I was anything but. He was born a Renewable, and I definitely wasn't. But we worked that way.

"Things weren't great for Renewables even before Prometheus. People fear them, hate them, because of what they did all those years ago, causing the cataclysm. Causing all of this. Bran—that was his name, Bran—he'd get teased a lot, bullied by the other kids. I'd beg him to use his magic on them, but he always refused, said it'd just prove them right. That's when I started to learn to fight. If he wouldn't defend himself, then I would."

The thought of Olivia as a child beating up the other kids made me smile. She already looked angelic, sweet, incapable of violence—she must've been an even more improbable warrior as a cherubic little girl.

"Once Prometheus took over, things got worse. Bran moved into the walls early on, while I stayed on the outside as long as I could. I'd do odd jobs for Parker and Wesley, the occasional jaunt inside CeePo. Until one day I was caught. And my brother, my stupid, stupid brother, came to rescue me. I made it out. He didn't."

I waited, but she didn't speak again, her jaw tight as she looked down at the city below us, her eyes resting on the shadowy, semicircular building that housed Prometheus and his government.

"What does Prometheus do to Renewables when he catches them?" I asked softly. It clearly still hurt Olivia to talk about her brother, but whatever happened to Bran might've also happened to Basil.

"They die," she said shortly. But then, before I could absorb it, she added, "Eventually."

Unbidden, the image of the Institute's Machine rose in my mind. I hadn't thought of it in what felt like forever, but as soon as I saw the low, squat chair, I could almost feel the glass shards slicing into my skin and draining away my magic.

Olivia saw the horror on my face. "This is why we fight him, Lark," she said in a low voice. "He's done amazing things for this city, but it all comes at a price we're not willing to pay anymore. Just remember this is why we're doing it. This is why they're carrying out your plan, even though—" She paused. "Even though everything."

I nodded, not trusting myself to speak.

"Usually, the Renewables he does this to die not long after. Bran was in the middle—he lasted a few months before he finally gave up." Olivia was dry-eyed, but the sadness in her voice was overwhelming.

"Olivia," I said, my voice sounding strange, "what's the longest any of Prometheus's Renewables have survived being repeatedly harvested?"

Olivia tilted her head to the side. "I don't know for sure, but I've heard that there are a few that predate Wesley. And he's been there for two years now."

Years. There were Renewables who'd been down there for *years*. And it'd only been four years since the resistance fighters moved in and found my brother's journal. There was a chance, however slim, that if Basil was like me, he could've leeched power from the other captives and survived Prometheus's harvest each time.

I'd assumed Basil was dead. But maybe I was wrong.

We sat in silence for a time, each lost in our own separate thoughts. I could feel Olivia's tension—her easy manner was gone, despite her willingness to talk to me. She had a part to play in tomorrow's mission, too, just as important as mine. She was going to be the distraction, drawing away Prometheus's Eagles to give Oren and me a chance to get close to him.

Though she was usually so open, it was impossible to read Olivia now. There was still grief and anger there, and part of me wondered, if Oren weren't going to be there, if she'd let me run in blind, without the distraction, and get caught.

"Make sure you have no regrets," she murmured, interrupting my increasingly dark thoughts.

"What?"

Her feet had stopped swinging, and she sat motionless, gazing into the middle distance ahead of her. "That's how you go on these missions time after time. You make sure you have no regrets. Just in case."

Something in her voice chilled my heart, and I shivered.

She went on. "You talk to the people you care about, and you make sure there's nothing you wished you'd said."

For a moment, I thought she was talking about me, about the ruins of our seedling friendship. Then I recognized the quiet desperation in her voice, and I realized.

"Have you spoken to Oren yet?" I whispered.

Olivia hesitated, but then I saw her nod out of the corner of my eye. "We spoke a little after we finished training this afternoon. I told him what I'm telling you now."

No regrets. I couldn't argue with Olivia on it, because it made sense. Make sure that you leave things as well as you can, so that you can face what's coming with a clear head.

"I'm glad he found you," I said quietly, quickly, as though my mind might interfere and stop me once it realized what I was saying. "He's had a very lonely life. A terrible one, sometimes. But here, with you—he seems happy. I think my one regret would be leaving him alone, but he won't be alone. And that's a good thing."

Olivia didn't answer, and when I turned to look at her, she was staring at me, her face unreadable. "You think I love him, don't you?"

My heart seized for half a beat, and I fought to catch my breath. "No—I mean, maybe. I know he cares for you. You spend so much time together."

She laughed, but it wasn't a comforting sound. "I promise you, Lark, I don't have the slightest interest in Oren. Not the way you're imagining."

"But—"

"I have somebody," she said simply, dropping her chin onto her knees. "And I haven't given up on her yet."

My thoughts ground to a halt. *Her?*

Then it all clicked. *She and Nina are close*, Oren had told me. Nina took care of her when she lost her brother. Suddenly my heart froze altogether. I'd nearly killed the woman she loved. I might well have killed her yet, if she never woke up.

And this was the woman we were trusting to keep the Eagles off our backs—where one wrong move on her part would leave us with Prometheus's entire army closing in around us.

"What I regret," she went on, softly, "was not getting to see her before the mission. She's undercover most of the time, and comes through so rarely. I wish I'd been able to speak to her one more time."

I looked down to see Olivia gripping the edge of the roof, white-knuckled and tense. I could feel the fury and helplessness in her as if it were magic, visible to my other senses. She didn't look at me, all the intensity of her gaze dissipating into the mist-filled air over the city.

I began to retreat, knowing there was nothing I could say. But as I got to my feet she spoke again, her voice emerging in a mumble.

"Oren told me once that he hurt you."

I swallowed, thinking of my torn earlobe, and of Oren's

refusal to believe that he hadn't done it in his shadow state. "No," I said. "No, he never has."

"Then he's certainly afraid he might. That's why I've been trying to help him. There's a darkness in him that I don't understand, but he's terrified of it. He's afraid it'll make him hurt you, the way you hurt Nina."

Sick with regret, I wished I could reach out to Olivia—but my touch was the last thing she'd want. I had no idea Oren was so afraid of the shadow inside himself down here, when there was more than enough magic to keep him human. But then, wasn't I terrified of the darkness in me?

"Thank you," I whispered.

"I was never doing it for you," Olivia said, her voice as dry as ice. "But he is."

"What?"

"That's why he works so hard. So he won't hurt you."

. . .

I walked back to my room with my thoughts buzzing. About Olivia and her unreadable face. About Nina, the girl she loved, out of touch and in such danger for so long. About Wesley, and how readily he'd agreed to our plan despite the huge personal danger to himself. About Basil, and the tiniest possibility that he could be alive somewhere in Prometheus's cells, suffering the way I had in the Institute. My thoughts circled around and around, meshing together like delicate, intricate cogs in a machine, always spinning back to one thing.

Oren.

I told him what I told you, Olivia had said, as we parted. *That he should talk to the people he cares about before tomorrow.*

I was so lost in my head that I forgot to check for the guard in the hallway and put up an illusion to let myself back in. It was dark, but not so dark that I couldn't see the figure leaning against the wall opposite my door. I skidded to a halt, heart pounding.

It was as if I'd summoned him with my thoughts, as though reality had somehow replaced my guard with the one person I actually wanted to see. Oren lifted his head, raising an eyebrow at me. "So much for not wandering around by yourself like I told you."

"I don't take orders so well anymore." I pressed a hand to my ribcage, where it felt like my lungs were seizing with the sudden jolt of adrenaline. "What're you doing out here?"

"You weren't very good at taking orders to begin with," he pointed out. "I told the guard I'd take over for him for a while. You think I can't sense you in there? And more importantly, when you're not in there?"

I gaped at him. I knew I could feel him with my magic, could sense the dark pit of the shadow inside him. But I had no idea that the connection went both ways.

"Did you find whatever you were looking for?" he asked, straightening.

"I don't know," I admitted. "Maybe. I have no idea."

He didn't ask what I meant, and I didn't offer an explanation. After a long pause, he broke the silence. "It's a good plan." He was repeating himself, his voice low to avoid echoing down the long corridor. "Despite everything that's happened, they believe in you."

I took a breath, a knot of tension uncoiling under the pressure and making me blurt, "That's what scares me."

He shifted, straightening and stepping away from the wall half a pace. "What do you mean?"

My eyes met his, and then it was like the rift between us had never been there. I could almost imagine us back in the forest together, under the stars, where my biggest fear was the vastness of the sky.

"Making these decisions for people," I whispered. "Asking them to give their lives. I'm not supposed to be this person—I was never supposed to be this person. I barely ever made decisions for *myself*." I could feel the fear and doubt rising up, prickling behind my eyes, choking my voice. "The first real decision I ever made was to run away."

I half-expected Oren to reach for me and attempt to comfort me in some way, but he stayed where he was, listening, watching me through the gloom.

"Nina almost died because of me." I wrapped my own arms around myself, a barrier between me and the world. "Tomorrow more people might die, because of *me*."

"Yes." The word was quiet, calm. It brought me up short, made my gaze swing back to Oren's. I could see his pale blue eyes in the dark, startling, fixed on mine. "But they've chosen it, this fight. You haven't forced them to do anything. If we die tomorrow, we die having chosen for ourselves."

We stood on opposite sides of the corridor, staring at each other across the empty space between us. There was so much I wished I could say—that I was glad he'd chosen what he did, that I was glad he was fighting for me, that if we survived tomorrow I wanted us to stay, or to go, or to do anything, as long as it was both of us together.

But the words stuck in my throat. All I could think of was what Olivia had said to me, her words buzzing in my thoughts. *No regrets.*

"Oren, I wanted to tell you—"

"I should get back to bed." Oren spoke almost at the same time I did, drowning out my words. He stopped, blinking. "What?"

My throat felt scratchy, dry as chalk. "Nothing. I'll see you in the morning."

Oren took a few steps back, so that when I reached my

door there was still more space between us than either of us could reach across. He stopped then to nod at me, the pale eyes serious. "In the morning," he echoed. And then he was gone.

CHAPTER 21

A hand shook me awake, scattering my incoherent dreams. I didn't remember falling asleep, but as my eyes focused sluggishly on Marco's face, I knew I must have done so at some point.

"Time to get ready," he said, his voice flat. There was no sign of the emotion I'd glimpsed in him the night before. Now he was all hard angles, giving me nothing. "Get to the War Room when you're done here."

He left me to get dressed. There was no silent gift of new clothes this time, no thoughtful touches. So I pulled on the same clothes I'd worn during the mission with Nina, ignoring the smell of sweat and battle that still clung to them. The hole in the shoulder of the jacket lined up perfectly with the bandage over my healing wound. The rest of it was littered with scratches that hadn't made it through the thick leather, and I realized how close I'd come many times over to being torn to ribbons.

I slid both paper birds into my pocket next to the blackout device, then slipped Oren's knife into a sheath secured to the inside of my boot. The boots were slightly too large for me, but they were better than the ratty shoes that had brought me

Watching his face as he glared at Wesley, I wasn't entirely [sur]e he was playing a part at all.

"And the girl?" one of the officials asked.

Wesley shrugged. "She was with him when I found him. [Sh]e's probably guilty of something, if only by association."

The officials chuckled and waved us on through, saying [so]mething about prisoner processing. Wesley had explained [t]hat all prisoners go through a questioning process. I shud[d]ered to think what they might do to Oren if they guessed he [w]asn't being entirely truthful, but Wesley assured me they'd stick to the protocol laid out for them by Prometheus. Oren just had to stick to his story.

Prisoner processing was two floors down, below the "ground" level of the city. Wesley himself didn't know how far the tunnels and caverns of Central Processing stretched below Lethe. Prometheus kept his lackeys separate, allowing certain jobs access to particular parts of the complex and not others, so that no one person knew the entire layout of the place.

The iron on my wrists was weighing heavily on me, making my head spin and my eyes blur. We traveled corridor after corridor, the faces of the people working in CeePo blurring as we passed. There was an elevator much like the one Oren and I rode when we first arrived at the city, although it moved much more smoothly and efficiently. I was determined to make a mental map, keep track of all the twists and turns so that I could find my way out again when it came time. I forced myself to focus despite my blurring vision.

And then, abruptly, we stopped.

I blinked, looking up from my study of the corridor floor to find a tall, slim man standing in front of us. Wesley was staring at him blankly, but I could see his cheek twitching. He knew this man, and running into him wasn't part of the plan.

here from the Institute. I laced them up and headed out.

The others were waiting in the War Room when I got there, with bowls of porridge for breakfast. Parker, Marco, Wesley, Olivia, Dorian and a couple of Iron Wood Renewables were scattered around the table, and all looked up when I walked in. Oren was seated at the far end of the table and glanced at me before looking back down at his bowl as if surprised to find it there.

"Our leading lady arrives," said Wesley, folding his arms across his peacock-feather coat.

I shifted my weight uncomfortably. "Oren's the one they want," I reminded them. "They don't know about me."

"Of course." He gave me a faint smile, the only hint of warmth in the room for me.

I found a seat in front of an untouched bowl, and the others started running through the plan one last time.

Wesley, undercover, would bring Oren and me to Central Processing, claiming to have caught the fugitive—Oren—and his companion. We'd undergo the questioning and screening processes while Wesley met with Prometheus to tell him we were captured and ensure that he asked to see us personally. Meanwhile Olivia would lead the rest of the rebels, Renewable and non-Renewable alike, to cause a commotion in the courtyard and draw as many of Prometheus's Eagles out of CeePo as they could.

Originally, before Nina, only Wesley had known that I was the one who'd be attacking once we got to Prometheus. The others all thought that Oren, the fighter, was their best bet, and I was just backup. Now everyone fell silent, their eyes shifting toward my end of the table. I picked at my breakfast, feeling their gazes like heavy iron bars.

I glanced at Oren, who would be walking straight into the enemy forces with me. He looked up from his breakfast long enough to meet my gaze, his ice-blue eyes grave. He seemed calm, almost serene, whereas I felt like my stomach was trying to leap out of my throat. Most of my breakfast went untouched.

In terms of supplies, we took very little. We couldn't very well go armed to the teeth when we were supposed to be captured prisoners. Oren had brought no weapons at all, and I had only the knife he'd given me in the Iron Wood, concealed inside my boot. There was also the blackout device that the others all carried as insurance against me—and none of them knew I had one too. It was still only theoretical, anyway, that it even worked. They wouldn't have been able to test it here without risking all their machinery. And me, their best weapon.

"How long until we go?" My voice cut through the chatter. I sounded strained, impatient, and I forced myself to take a breath.

Wesley unfolded his arms and straightened. "If you're ready? We can go right now."

. . .

Every eye in the square was on us as Wesley marched us toward CeePo. We'd taken a long, roundabout route to another point in the city, far from the secret door into the walls we'd entered that first day. Wesley held one of Oren's arms roughly, jangling the chains around his wrists now and then. I was chained as well, but allowed to walk freely. After all, Oren was the murderer.

We'd toyed with the idea of making the chains out of some metal other than iron, but we couldn't get the weight right. "It has to be absolutely real," Wesley had said as he locked the manacles around our wrists. "Otherwise they'll figure out the instant I bring you in that something's not right, and we'll never get to Prometheus."

And so my senses were muffled, the i[r] wrists, a constant reminder of how powerless For a brief, wild moment I wondered if all of could get rid of me—turn me over to Prom[etheus] the threat once and for all. I glanced at Wesley[kind of reassurance, but all I could see was his and cold.

The faces of the crowd blurred as Wesle[y] by. I tried to look out for the woman who'd tu[rned] that first day, but I couldn't even remember [what she looked like, much less focus enough t[o out of the throng. Now and then we'd pass an E[ible despite the crowd with their grey-and-fire u[but they didn't stop us. Wesley was in his plain cl[though plain was a stretch, considering the expense peacock feathers—but it was clear they recognize[d without any difficulty.

The crowd fell back when we reached the steps of [Cen]tral Processing, leaving us out of earshot for a few prec[ious] seconds.

"If you want to change your mind," Wesley whisper[ed not looking at Oren and me as we climbed the steps, "this[your last chance."

I took a deep breath. They weren't betraying me. This was real. I glanced at Oren, who looked back and shook his head. "No," I said. "We're ready."

We were met at the doors by a pair of officials recognizable in any city as bureaucratic lackeys. One reeled back when Wesley announced he'd found Sampson's killer—with a jolt, I realized that it was the first time I'd even heard the name of the man I'd killed. Of course, Wesley jerked Oren forward then and not me. Oren snarled, playing the part of the dangerous, vicious savage beautifully.

"On Prometheus's orders," the slim man said. His voice was soft, resonant, trained as if he were a singer. Not a hair was out of place, his charcoal-and-ember suit fitted perfectly across his chest. "The prisoners are to come with me."

"What do you mean, on his orders?" Wesley was saying, bristling. This man held some kind of authority—he outranked Wesley in Prometheus's organization. I held my breath.

"New evidence has come to light in the case of Sampson's death," said the slim man.

"New evidence?" Wesley scoffed. "Please. The man was beaten to death in front of an entire courtyard full of witnesses. Trust me, I was there. This is the boy."

The slim man smiled a little. "We know, Commander. That has not escaped our notice."

Wesley's hand tightened around the chain holding Oren. The links clicked together like bones, muffled by the flesh of his palm. "This is my arrest. I will see him to prisoner processing myself."

"Be our guest, Commander." The slim man was still smiling, a calm, cool smile. It wasn't a pleasant expression, but I felt certain it wasn't meant to be. "Our interests aren't with him anyway."

Wesley twitched, but managed not to glance at me. A little snaking spark of ice began threading its way down my spine. "What're you talking about?"

"Examination of the body revealed that Sampson did not, in fact, die of the wounds sustained to his face and torso. Therefore it was not this boy who killed him."

"Then who did?"

I held my breath.

Wesley's grip on the chain was white-knuckled. He didn't have to look at me to pass along the message that everything was going wrong, that our carefully laid plan had fallen apart only minutes past the door.

"We're not certain. But as there were only a few people within range of Sampson during the attack, we have only a few suspects. You will report to prisoner processing along with the boy you have in your custody."

Wesley didn't answer, standing stock still in the middle of the corridor, face draining of color.

"And as for our other suspect," said the slim man, turning a few degrees to his right until he faced me, "I will be taking her with me."

That unfroze Wesley, who stammered, "I arrested her— she's still my capture, I still want to be the one to—"

The slim man lifted a hand, cutting Wesley off with one gesture. "You have your orders. Carry them out."

Oren met my eyes, staring over his shoulder as Wesley slowly took him down the hallway away from us. I wanted to scream out for them, run after them, anything. This wasn't how the plan was meant to go.

The slim man turned to me, hands folded politely behind his back. "And now, miss, if you will come with me?"

I swallowed, my throat dry as sand. "Who are you?"

"That doesn't matter right now. If you please?" He held out a hand, gesturing down the corridor in the direction opposite the one Wesley and Oren had taken.

"I'm not going anywhere with you until you tell me your name." I knew I was stalling, and for what purpose? Wesley and Oren were gone. Even if I could overpower this man, there was no assurance I could find them and certainly no way to return to the plan. They didn't know anything—they just knew it wasn't Oren who killed the man. They didn't know who I was. What I was. This could still work.

The man smiled, amusement written clearly on his

features. He knew as well as I did that I was the one chained and not in a position to deliver ultimatums. Still, he indulged me. "Very well. I am Adjutant. If you like, you may think of me as Prometheus's right hand." He inclined his upper body very slightly in something like a bow.

My heartbeat roared in my ears.

"If that answers your question, miss," said Adjutant, "then we shouldn't keep the examination rooms waiting."

My body went cold. The Institute in my city had held me for weeks, poking and prodding me, experimenting on me, strapping me to their harvest chair and noting the results. I would not go back to that again.

Never.

It was time. Reveal I was a Renewable—or something like it—and get taken wherever they keep the noncompliant Renewables. Wherever they might have my brother.

I pulled every last scrap of power I had. I didn't have much—we'd agreed that stocking up with too much power would potentially attract attention from Renewables working with Prometheus. I'd stolen the power from a few unneeded machines, ignoring my inner shadow's protests—machine magic was not as satisfying as live magic. But what I had taken was enough. I gathered it and narrowed it and lashed out with all my strength.

The iron manacles around my wrist vaporized into dust in an instant.

Thank you, Wesley, for your endless drills and training.

I leaped back from Adjutant, ready to strike out at him. Sensing nothing, neither darkness nor the light of the Renewable magic in him, I expected rage, surprise, even fear—because until me, no one could magic iron. Instead, all that marked his features was a mild curiosity. I paused, staring.

"How fascinating," he murmured.

243

And then he drew a small machine out of his pocket, stretched out his hand and aimed it at me, and pulled the trigger.

Pain erupted through my entire body, and I hit the ground with a crash. My arms and legs stopped responding to my brain, every muscle cramping tighter and tighter. I felt as though fire consumed me from the inside out. My skin itched, my body burned—it was somehow familiar, though no less agonizing.

I had only a blurry vision of Adjutant standing over me, looking down, before I blacked out.

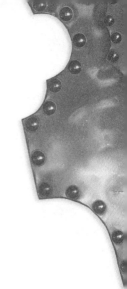

CHAPTER 22

I wasn't out for long. I came to while still being dragged. Dimly I could see Adjutant ahead of me, leading the way—he'd summoned assistance somehow, because I was being dragged by two faceless Eagles. I still couldn't move. Every bump and jostle made my nerves scream in protest. My vision was dazzled—everything was surrounded in violet rainbows, like I was staring at the world through refractive crystals. My skin tingled.

I tried to speak and it came out as an inarticulate moan. Adjutant looked over his shoulder at me. I felt the Eagles' grip falter, and Adjutant said sharply, "She's still overloaded. She can't do anything, so stop acting like children."

Eventually we reached a small room, big enough only for a table and a chair. The room had no windows and only the one door. Suddenly I was reminded of the Machine in the Institute, a room containing only a chair, ringed with darkness.

The Eagles dropped me into the chair, but my muscles still weren't responding to commands from my brain, and I slid out of the chair and onto the ground. I didn't even feel pain when I hit, too dazed and dazzled to do so.

"Thank you," came Adjutant's voice somewhere above me. "You may go."

The Eagles withdrew, shutting the door behind them. I half-expected it to be made of iron and clang shut with awful finality, but instead it was just a regular door. But then again, they knew iron wouldn't stop me. And they knew what would.

With a muffled groan of effort I rolled over enough that I could see Adjutant looking down at me, his face thoughtful. In one hand he was still holding the device that had incapacitated me, tossing it up and down idly.

"What an interesting specimen," he said quietly. "Prometheus will be fascinated."

"What—" I croaked, my mouth cramping as I tried to force it to speak despite the odd convulsion my muscles were locked into. "What'd you—"

Adjutant raised an eyebrow. "This?" He held up the device and examined it. It was small, curved, designed to fit into the palm of his hand—a smaller sibling of the devices Prometheus's enforcers carried. "The Eagles affectionately refer to the process as being 'zapped.' The talon overloads the systems with magic. It works against the normals, but it's particularly effective against Renewables. I'm told it's exceedingly painful."

Overloaded with magic? My teeth ground together, muscles still locked down tight. The magic was overcoming my brain's ability to send signals to my body. The realization was enough that I could begin to fight it, carefully pushing the magic down away from my mind. My vision began to clear a little. I found myself better able to speak.

"Why—me? Haven't done anything."

Adjutant tossed the device onto the table with a metallic clang. "Perhaps not," he agreed. "But you were about to, back there in the corridor, were you not?"

He'd seen me vaporize iron with a single thought, prepared to attack. I swallowed convulsively, finally getting my throat to listen to what I wanted it to do.

"You acted when I mentioned examination." Adjutant stooped into a crouch, bringing his face closer to mine. "It seems you don't like the idea of being a subject."

There was no malice in his expression, no hint that he derived any pleasure from my pain and confusion. There was only detached interest, the regard of someone making observations about some new and interesting phenomenon.

He stretched out his hand and took mine. "If you concentrate, I think you'll find you can move a little. Unless you prefer the floor?"

I let him pull me up and settle me back into the chair. Both the chair and the table were made of some lightweight, silvery metal. The chair was frigid to the touch but soon began to warm to my body heat.

"Tell me," said Adjutant, taking up a position on the opposite side of the table. "Have you been held somewhere as a subject before?"

I stared at him, jaw clenched. It was still an effort to speak—and even if it wasn't, I wasn't going to answer his questions.

"Never mind," he replied. He tapped his fingers against the table. "Your body language is all the answer I need."

My eyes flicked from his drumming fingers to the device lying on the table between us. Could I make my arm, cramped and slow as it was, move quickly enough to grab it before he could stop me?

"We have no plans to mistreat you, young lady," said Adjutant, leaning back far enough that I'd be able to beat him to the device even if I fumbled with the task. "If you'll only just answer a few questions and meet with Prometheus, you'll see that what we're doing here is important, and that we need your help."

I didn't waste any more time. I flung my arm forward, struggling to make it work the way I wanted. My hand fell short of the device and I wrenched it forward again, eyes watering with effort. My clumsy fingers scrabbled against it for a moment before closing around it, drawing it back to myself.

I dragged my eyes up to find Adjutant unmoving, watching me, one corner of his mouth lifted in a small smile.

"These smaller versions are only good for one discharge," he said calmly. "Then they need to be recharged again. Don't worry. I have others fully charged and ready." He patted his pocket gently.

My fist was still wrapped around the device, its metal edges digging into my skin. After working so hard to get my hand to cooperate, I couldn't get it to uncurl again.

"What is your name?" asked Adjutant.

I swallowed. "Margaret." I said the first name that popped into my mind—the name of one of my classmates back in the city where I was born.

"And your place of origin?"

"All over the place," I replied promptly, surprising myself with how easily the lies came. "My parents were Travelers. They were killed by Empty Ones a few years ago."

"How tragic," said Adjutant. "And what is the boy's connection with you?"

"I met him in the ruins above right before the Eagles found us. I'd never met him before that night, I don't even know his name."

"Hmm." Though the Adjutant made no physical notes, I could almost see him mentally filing away my answers, trying to build a picture of who I was. I had no idea if he believed anything I was saying, but I was surprising myself with how easily the lies came. "Were your parents Renewables as well?"

"Yes."

"And the boy?"

"No, I don't think so."

"Can't you tell for sure?"

"I don't have the Sight as strong as others do."

"I see. And how long have you been able to magic iron?"

The question caught me off guard, coming so quickly after the others. I had no ready answer for this one, hadn't rehearsed it beforehand in the planning stages of this operation.

But when I opened my mouth, some instinct took over. "I didn't know I could," I said, widening my eyes, letting fear and confusion into my expression. "That was the first time. I just got so angry."

Adjutant paused, watching me. "I see," he repeated. "I'll leave you now for a little while. The door will be guarded by Eagles, all of whom will be armed." He retrieved the device from my now-lax fist and slipped it into his pocket. "I'll return soon enough, but in the meantime, please consider your story again and think about whether it's the one you wish to present to Prometheus himself."

Even after Adjutant left, it took me a long time to recover from being "zapped," as he called it. Though the worst of the muscle cramps had passed, I was still seeing strange halos around everything, and my skin buzzed. The sensation was hauntingly familiar, but it wasn't until I closed my eyes against the violet double images that I realized why.

The last time I'd felt like this was when I'd stripped all the magic from the Renewables in the Iron Wood.

Overloaded with magic, Adjutant had said. For a regular Renewable, who couldn't absorb the power like I could, it must simply interfere with their abilities, incapacitate them.

But me . . . ? I got to my feet carefully, still not quite trusting my legs. But the more time passed, the better I felt. Buzzing with power. Drunk with magic. Insanely, I felt like laughing—without realizing it, they'd given me all the power I could digest.

But those devices could still take me out for a while, knock me flat. If I wanted to get out of here I was going to have to be careful.

Before I could formulate any plan, however, the door opened again, and Adjutant stepped back through. Hovering above his shoulder was a machine, half-concealed as Adjutant turned to close the door behind him.

"Prometheus is most excited to meet you," Adjutant said. "If you will come with me, we won't waste any more time."

He turned again, and this time I got a good look at the machine. It was a pixie, larger than usual.

Adjutant saw me staring and glanced at the machine hovering next to his face. "Ah, yes. Pixies are not exactly welcome in Prometheus's city, but we keep a few around for specific purposes. There aren't any machines better suited for detecting magic, for example. If you seem to be regaining control over your power more quickly than expected, this device will alert us."

Something dark twisted in my stomach, but it wasn't until the pixie opened its eyes that I figured it out. The eyes glowed white, not blue, and the pixie was staying in one shape, but I knew it well. I knew it better than I knew most people.

Nix.

It hovered there, its blank white eyes on me, unseeing. "Where did you find this one?" I asked, unable to keep my voice from shaking.

Adjutant was watching me carefully—I wonder if he knew this was the pixie that had come with me. If he did, he gave no indication. "Machines occasionally find their way here on their own, attracted by the magic here in Lethe. Sometimes they're brought in illegally by Travelers and confiscated. I believe this one was found on its own, trying to camouflage itself in a scrap heap."

The pixie spoke. "I am PX-148," it said in a shockingly female voice. "My purpose is to assist Prometheus and his servants in any way asked of me." The voice was unrecognizable, bewildering—nothing like Nix's voice. Nix's voice was neither male nor female, a familiar amalgam of other voices: me and Oren, Kris and Tansy, sprinkled with hints of everyone it had ever interacted with.

Nix, wake up. I willed it to shift, to wink at me as it had once, to give me some sign of my unlikely friend. *Nix, help me—please, wake up.*

"Don't be alarmed," continued Adjutant, misreading my distress. "Although we often find these machines malfunctioning and dangerous, we always scrub them well before employing them here."

"Scrub?"

Adjutant opened the door again, gesturing for me to precede him. "Erased," he explained. "Wiped. The only way to ensure no lingering, well-hidden program remains hidden inside is to completely destroy its memory and replace it with entirely new programming."

I let Adjutant propel me down the hallway, too sick with confusion and grief to resist. My eyes blurred, and this time the only halos I saw were from the tears fighting to escape.

It was just a machine, I told myself angrily, trying to pull myself together. *What does it matter? It had no feelings. No soul to destroy. It served its purpose.*

But it didn't help. Every time I glanced up, the thing that had once been Nix was flying steadily, its white eyes staring straight ahead, its wings a monotonous blur. There was no joy in its flight. No curiosity, no engagement. All it did was what it was told to do.

I longed to reach out and touch it, see if somehow giving it a jolt of my power would jar it back to life. But I knew it didn't work like that. Everything that had been Nix was gone—all that was left was its shell, formatted with new orders. But even though it didn't have the brilliant blue eyes, the tendency to shapeshift when startled, the expressive buzzing and clicking of its wings when irritated—it was hard not to see it as *my* Nix.

And yet—why hadn't it alerted Adjutant to the fact that I had possession of my full faculties? I felt certain that if I wanted to, I could have swatted it out of the sky with a second thought. Perhaps it couldn't sense me the way it sensed ordinary Renewables?

Perhaps it had chosen not to alert Adjutant.

I closed my eyes for half a second. Wishful thinking, I knew. *Nix is gone*, I told myself. *Stay focused.* We were going to see Prometheus. I was supposed to be there with Oren and Wesley to back me up, but I had no chance of finding them now, even if I could overpower Adjutant and Nix. *The pixie*, I corrected myself, struggling to change the way I saw it.

So I would have to face Prometheus on my own. Maybe it was better that way. If I ended up needing power and leveling the entire room, then at least Wesley would be spared. I hoped that, wherever they were, they weren't being mistreated. Especially Wesley—if they'd discovered his treachery, there was no telling what might be happening to him.

And if they discovered Oren's secret? There was nothing to stop them from killing him as soon as they found out what he was.

I clenched my jaw. *Focus.* The only way I could help them now was to take out Prometheus himself. If I could manage that much, then someone would be able to rescue them when the resistance took over CeePo. And they'd find Basil too, if he'd defied the odds and managed to survive in Prometheus's holding cells for this long.

I tried to imagine seeing him, but I couldn't think past the confrontation with Prometheus. Surely the instant the Eagles realized I'd done something to their leader, they would kill me. In my mind there was no time after that. Just him, and me, and the confrontation . . . and then nothing.

I tried not to think about what that meant for me. I paid only enough attention to walking as I needed to avoid falling on my face. The rest of my focus I turned inward, running through Wesley's meditation exercises in fits and starts, trying to calm the too-fast beating of my heart. I needed control. I needed deliberation.

Dimly I was aware of riding in the elevator again, although I couldn't tell whether we were going up or down. Adjutant spoke now and then, but didn't press me when I said nothing in reply. More hallways. Always more hallways—whether it was here, or the Institute, or even the world in the walls that had adopted me. It was always corridor after twisted corridor, never the straightest path.

Eventually we reached a pair of intricately carved bronze doors that were swung outwards, framing an archway. Through it was a large cavern with throngs of people inside. The crowd wasn't as dense as the one outside, and it was comprised of much more richly dressed citizens. My dazed eyes picked out Eagles here and there, monitoring the crowd.

The crowd parted as Adjutant half-pushed, half-dragged me forward. Conversations everywhere began to die as heads turned toward us. As the people drew back, giving us more space, I was able to see the room more clearly. It was some sort of audience chamber, culminating in a series of chairs on a raised dais at the far end. Most were simple, but one—the one in the center—stood out like a throne. Although it was not significantly larger or more ornate than the others, it was clearly Prometheus's chair. Made of blown glass and copper, it shone like a beacon.

The moment I saw the glass chair I grew lightheaded, dizzy. There was magic here, more than I had even after the experience with Adjutant's talon.

A number of men stood at the far end of the room, and I turned my dazzled eyes toward them. Although he was facing away from me, I recognized him instantly. All the others arranged around him in a semicircle deferred to him with their body language.

And when I looked at him with the Sight, I nearly lost my balance. He wasn't a Renewable, and he wasn't a shadow. But he wasn't an ordinary human either. I could see a dazzling tracery of violet and gold magic mottling his skin, surging and roiling as though some fiery disease was consuming him.

I stopped short a few yards away, surprising Adjutant into releasing me. His voice buzzed in my ear, but I paid no attention to him. Here was the man I'd come for, standing within easy reach.

I had no way of knowing whether Olivia was carrying out her end of the plan. What if, after everything that had happened with Nina, she decided she'd rather see me captured and killed here? She wouldn't be the first friend to betray me.

If she was true to her word, the Eagles would be leaving here to go deal with the rebel uprising happening outside in the courtyard. If she'd turned back, though, I'd be left on my own in a room full of soldiers with all their weapons trained on me.

"Prometheus," called Adjutant, clearing his throat. "The girl, the one you asked to see."

The man on the dais straightened, saying something to his advisors, dismissing them with a wave of his hand.

Now or never. I reached for the power this place had unwittingly given to me and gathered it to strike.

Prometheus somehow sensed me, and with movements so quick my dazzled eyes struggled to follow, he ducked to the side and leaped for the glass chair. The moment his hand touched it, brilliant power flared all around him. He looked as though he were on fire, blinding me.

I cried out and jerked away from my second sight. And froze.

It was Caesar.

My mind raced. It couldn't be Caesar—I'd left Caesar behind at the foot of our fire escape, broken and bloodied. He was in the city; he couldn't have come after me. He couldn't be here—he couldn't be Prometheus. Prometheus was here years before I ever even left my home.

But there was his nose, his stern jaw, the thick dark stubble that shaded his face when he skipped a shave. There were his brown eyes, hard and cold.

And then Prometheus saw me, too. His expression went from one filled with icy fury to one of confusion. Then recognition flared all across his features—confusion turned to horror. "No," he whispered.

And then I knew who it was. It wasn't Caesar. Of course not—because that was impossible. Caesar was still at home.

It was my other brother. It was Basil.

PART III

CHAPTER 23

My brother and I stared at each other. For an interminable moment the rest of the audience chamber ceased to exist, no more than an animated blur outside the tense corridor of space between us.

Then, abruptly, everything around us came rushing back, and the moment shattered. A pair of Eagles grabbed me, pinning my hands behind my back while Adjutant came between me and Prometheus, wielding another of those talon weapons.

"Is that how you greet your god?" he hissed for my ears alone, eyes snapping. Gone was the polite, almost considerate man from the interrogation room, replaced by an utter madman. Shaking, he stretched out the device, and I braced myself for another dose of overwhelming magic.

"Stop!" My brother's voice was deeper, more resonant than I remembered. And yet I could hear it threatening to crack, held together only by determination. "Stop. Take her—take her away. Put her somewhere."

"But sir," Adjutant said, straightening out of my vision, calm once again. The Eagles were forcing my head down so I couldn't see my brother. "Sir, this is the girl. The one who can magic iron." A murmur rippled through the crowd, shock

and fear and disbelief. "This is the girl you wanted to use."
Adjutant sounded patient, as if he suspected Prometheus—
Basil—simply didn't understand my significance.

"I'm aware of that," said Basil, regaining some control
over himself. "And I asked you to take her away. I'll deal with
her later."

Adjutant hesitated. Even though my shock and confusion I could tell he was not pleased to have been so ordered—
perhaps there was a seed of dissention in Prometheus's rule.
Before I could process the thought, Adjutant gestured to the
Eagles restraining me. If I could have spoken through my
shock, I would have told them no restraint was necessary. All
desire to fight had drained away the moment I recognized my
brother's face. They hoisted me up under my arms and started
to make for the door.

"And Adjutant," said my brother, "don't throw her into
one of your interrogation rooms. She's our guest. Make sure
she's treated like one."

I didn't resist as they took me away. I couldn't see, couldn't
think—the hallways passed in a blur. I had no sense for how
far we traveled or for how long, only that my brother was here,
my brother was alive. My brother was Prometheus.

My brother is the madman . . . my brother.

The world intruded on my horror when the Eagles
dropped me unceremoniously on the floor. I hit carpet, the
thick plush cushioning my fall.

I heard Adjutant clear his throat, and I looked up at him
blearily.

"It seems Prometheus has decided to seek your volun-
tary cooperation," he said calmly. There was no sign of that
fury I'd seen before. Part of me wondered if I'd imagined the
way his face transformed earlier—it seemed so impossible,
coming from this quiet, controlled man. "It wasn't what I

recommended, but I suggest you consider his offer very, very carefully."

And then he was gone with the sound of a door shutting gently behind him.

Reluctantly I lifted my head, staring numbly around at my new surroundings. It was a small room but richly appointed. A full-sized wooden bed with fluffy white bedclothes stood in the corner, with a matching wooden nightstand and a desk opposite. The desk had an ink blotter, paper, and an array of pens. There were no windows, but landscape paintings on the walls gave the illusion of being aboveground.

It was the nicest room I'd been in since the dining hall at the Institute, and yet my mouth tasted of ashes.

How could Basil be Prometheus? Basil was *fighting* Prometheus. And yet . . .

The resistance movement had found a journal full of schematics for Prometheus's machines, Prometheus's plans. They'd assumed it was the very first resistor, the very first person to go off-grid and study Prometheus. They'd found the journal after Prometheus took power—but that didn't mean it was *written* after he took power.

I imagined my brother living in the walls of a dying city, trying to figure out how to save it. Imagined him walking into the square and talking until people listened, until they agreed with him, decided to help him do what he knew would save the city. My brother had always been good with machines, with magic. That Prometheus, the one who swayed a whole city with his words, who figured out how to save it—that Prometheus, I could believe was my brother.

But how could my brother enslave an entire race of people? Even the Institute only held one Renewable. How many did my brother hold captive in the bowels of Central Processing, their life torn out of them, only to regenerate enough to be harvested again?

Sick, I recalled the picture of Prometheus in the book, his liver torn out each night, to regrow each day. He took that name when he first took power. He had to have planned it all then.

I dragged myself to my feet and tried the door. I was unsurprised to find it locked, but surprised when it opened and an Eagle stood there, watching me. "Do you need anything?" he asked politely.

I swallowed. I needed my brother. My real brother, not this monster in his place.

"No, thank you."

The door closed again. Locked again. I scanned the room again, more closely this time, only to discover that the pixie who had been Nix was there too, perched now on the desk chair.

"What're you doing here?" My voice was hoarse, hostile.

"I have been assigned to watch you," replied PX-148. "If there is anything you require I will communicate it to Adjutant."

Exhausted by grief and revulsion, I sank down onto the carpet. To use the bed felt too much like submission, acceptance.

"Nix," I whispered. We were alone for the first time since I'd seen it again, but it hadn't dropped the act. "Please wake up. Talk to me."

"I am PX-148. What do you wish me to say?"

"Anything. Tell me a story." I let my head fall to the carpet, my muscles screaming at me from the abuse of the talon. Exhausted, I felt as though I'd been hiking through the wilderness for weeks, only to end up back where I'd started.

"I am not programmed to entertain. Please issue another command."

I closed my eyes. "Never mind. You're not Nix."

"Correct. I am PX-148."

. . .

Sometime later the door opened with a clang, startling me upright. Adjutant stood in the doorway, looking down at me half-prone on the floor. "Pick yourself up," he said coolly. "Prometheus will see you now."

"I'm not going anywhere for him," I croaked, dragging myself up onto my knees.

"Then you're in luck," replied Adjutant, his eyes cold. "He has come to you." This was clearly a source of dismay for Adjutant—he disapproved. But he would never question Prometheus.

I got slowly to my feet. At least I could face what my brother had become while standing.

Adjutant nodded after a moment and then straightened. "Prometheus," he announced, and then stepped to the side to make way for his master.

My brother walked in.

"You may go now, Adjutant," said Basil, his eyes on me.

Adjutant was good—the shock barely registered on his features. "Sir, you are unarmed. Do you think it's wise to—"

"I said go." His voice was heavy, final.

Adjutant hesitated only half a second longer and then retreated back out the door, closing it gently behind him.

Basil was silent, watching me, his expression dropping slowly into one of disbelief and sadness and confusion. He was wearing an impeccably tailored suit of robes, black and red, the uniform of Prometheus. Fire and ash, light and dark. It made him look taller, grander—nothing like the brother I knew. There were only his eyes, the warm, soft brown that I remembered, to tell me I hadn't gone mad.

"It really is you," he murmured, taking a step toward me. I stayed silent, not trusting myself to speak.

"When they told me they'd found a girl who could magic iron, I thought—here, at last, someone like me. But I never thought—I *never* thought . . ." His face changed suddenly, his sadness mingling with horror. "Does that mean—how are you here? Why aren't you in the city?"

"They did to me what they did to you," I said, choking. "I ran away. I reached the Iron Wood, and Dorian told me you had come here. I came to find you. I came to find Basil."

He shut his red-rimmed eyes for a moment. "I'm here. I'm so sorry, Lark. I never thought they'd—I thought their experiment ended with me." He broke off and came towards me, putting his arms around me.

For a moment he was just Basil again. My eyes burned, my body shaking with the effort of not breaking down. My big brother, the one who always made everything right—I ducked my face against his shoulder, gasping for air.

In that moment, all I wanted to do was let myself go, sob into my brother's shoulder, let him comfort me the way he had always done. I'd found him, finally. We were together.

He squeezed, his own voice choked when he spoke.

"I would never hurt you," my brother said fiercely. "Never, you hear? Ignore Adjutant, ignore everyone."

A sick feeling twisted inside me. *No, not my brother*, I corrected myself. My brother was someone who would never, *ever* become this. My brother was dead. This was Prometheus.

I pulled away, stepping back. "But you'd hurt others?"

Prometheus slowly lowered his arms. "Lark," he said slowly. "You don't understand. It's so much more complex than you—this city needs me. It needed me when I first got here, and it needs me now."

"Why do any of this?" My eyes were still burning. Out of

my peripheral vision I could see PX-148, motionless, the white eyes staring straight ahead.

"Because of you," Prometheus whispered.

I stopped short, jerking my eyes from the pixie to look at the leader of Lethe. "Me?"

"All of it was for you," he said, closing his eyes. "I wanted a place that would be safe for you. I was going to come back and get you when this was all ready. Before the architects could do to you what they did to me."

I felt as though the floor was sliding away from me, making me struggle just to keep my balance. "I never asked for this," I said, horrified.

Prometheus shook his head, standing there just inside the door to my richly decorated cell, looking so much older than I remembered. "It was only supposed to be for a little while. I was going to fix the city and then once it was safe, return for you."

"And they'd just accept their beloved Prometheus living among them with his kid sister?"

He shook his head again, taking a step toward me. "They see the office, Lark. They don't see the man. They recognize the uniform and the power and the command, but they don't know *me*. Only the people who've been with me from the beginning know me at all. Adjutant, a few of my advisors. If I left and came back in ordinary clothes, as an ordinary citizen, no one would ever know it was me. You and I could live normal lives here. Safe lives, away from the Institute, away from the Empty Ones."

"So why didn't you come for me?" I couldn't help but spit the question, anger overcoming my shock. This betrayal, more than any other, burned me to my core. "Why didn't you do what you set out to do?"

"It wasn't that easy," he said softly. "There was always

something more to do. It was never quite enough. Every time I thought things were under control something else would fail—Adjutant would report something else needing power I didn't have, that the city didn't have. It never ends. I'm never done."

His eyes were haunted, tired, riddled with guilt. I had to fight the urge to go to his side, try to comfort this stranger who had once been my brother. But in my mind's eye I saw Tansy, I saw the Institute's enslaved Renewable. I imagined Olivia's brother, and everyone who'd ever fallen to Prometheus.

"All those Renewables," I whispered. "You're no better than the Institute. How could you?"

"So few Renewables actually come through here, and the cost to keep all these people safe is so high. I offer them the chance to help—it's only the ones who refuse, Lark. It's only the people who won't do their part."

He was actually pleading with me, begging me to understand. I shook my head. "You should have found another way."

"There *is* no other way," he snapped before closing his eyes, rubbing at his face with both hands. "You don't think I've tried? We'd need three, four times the Renewables we have, all cooperating, all willing to contribute. We'd need an army of them. I've done the calculations a thousand times, Lark. There's no way I can make it sustainable without using them. And it's only a few people, a very small number. A small sacrifice for the good of the entire city."

"A small sacrifice," I echoed. Nina's face, right before I took her power to save all our lives, flashed in my mind's eye.

Emotions warred inside me—I wanted him to hug me again, I wanted him to tell me stories, I wanted him to tell me what to do next, that everything would be fine. And I wanted to hit him, tear into him, hurt him the way he'd hurt so many people—destroy him for what he'd done.

"Lark—please." He came toward me, hands outstretched. But when I backed away, he stopped short, as though he'd run into an invisible barrier.

I struggled to speak, my voice shaking. I had to keep my eyes on the motionless pixie, not trusting myself to look at my brother. "I looked so hard for you. Everything I've done, I've been looking for you. There was no one on this earth I wanted to find more than you, to be with. And when I thought you were dead, I would have killed Prometheus for you." Swallowing, I forced myself to look at him. Basil. Prometheus. Someone entirely different, who I didn't know anymore. "But now I wish you had been dead. At least then I'd still have the memory of Basil, my brother. Not this—this monster."

Prometheus inhaled shakily, as close to tears as I was. "Lark, you're still my sister. I still—"

"No." I cut him off. "No, I'm not." I dug into my pocket abruptly, my hands closing around the pair of paper birds: one half scorched and crumpled, telling the story of Basil's journey, the other yellowed with water and exposure, squished flat and carefully reconstructed, revealing everything I'd been through. I threw them both at him, watching them ricochet off his face and neck—he flinched, eyes falling on them where they hit the carpet.

"You're not my brother," I said shortly. "I don't know you."

He gazed at me and I stared back, unwilling to crumble first. This world had broken my brother, but I wouldn't let it break me. Basil—Prometheus—swallowed and then, very carefully, knelt and gathered up the paper birds, breaking eye contact. I closed my eyes and kept them closed, even when I heard the door open with a screech and then clang shut again.

It was only after he left that I let myself go, sinking to the floor where I'd stood, too shell-shocked to cry.

"Nix." My own voice sounded alien, as if it belonged to a stranger. "What do I do?"

But the pixie wasn't programmed to deal with such a vague question. It couldn't answer me.

CHAPTER 24

It was impossible to track the passage of time. There were no windows in my room, but even if there had been, I had the nagging suspicion that we were so far underground that it wouldn't have mattered. *Underground*, I thought dully. I'd been underground from the moment I arrived in Lethe—when had I started to think of Lethe itself as the world, rather than underground itself?

I kept replaying what I'd seen in my brother's journal—the drawings of machines, the schematics for altering the flow of magic. My face, here and there. Always on his mind.

How could Basil have fallen so far in the past few years to think that this was what I wanted? That peace and safety, even in this wilderness, was worth these monstrosities?

This landscape twisted things. Took good things and made them something dark.

I sat up, unable to sit still any longer. I tried asking the pixie what time it was, but it didn't understand the question.

"Is it day? Night?"

"The position of the sun is irrelevant here."

"Yes, but is it . . . are people sleeping now? Awake?"

The pixie gave no sign of thinking, none of Nix's little

ticks and tells that showed it was considering the question. Kris told me that they'd programmed Nix to appear more human—to think, to learn, to be sympathetic. Without those little touches, this creature was just a machine. "Without concrete data, it is plausible that some will be awake and some asleep."

I gave up. I crossed the room and spread both palms against the door's cold, metal alloy surface. Grimacing at the chill against my face, I pressed my ear to it. I could hear sound, but warped through the metal it sounded only like clinking and clanking. It could be pipes—it could be footsteps. I had no way of knowing whether there were still guards outside my door, but it seemed likely. And surely Prometheus would be smart enough to post Renewable guards, capable of sensing if I used too much magic.

In all the confusion, they still hadn't searched me thoroughly. I still had Oren's knife in its sheath in my boot. I also still had the blackout device—but after what the talon had done to me, I wasn't quite willing to try it. If it knocked me out the way Parker had theorized, I'd be worse off than before.

Closing my eyes, I let my awareness trickle out through the door. Although it wasn't solid iron, the particular alloy made it difficult to sense what lay beyond it. I could, however, sense the lock. It was risky, if there were guards outside who could sense me, but I had no choice. I refused to sit here quietly, waiting for Prometheus to come back and try some other way of winning my understanding. Besides, somewhere out there was Oren—and Wesley—and they might need my help. Not to mention Olivia and her crew, who had surely been captured by now.

Carefully, I gathered up a thin tendril of magic and sent it through the surface of the door toward the lock. It buzzed in response, making my heart jump—it was responding to the magic. I could do this. Fraction by fraction, quietly.

And then something landed on my shoulder, whirring. I jerked back, flinching away. The pixie, dislodged as I lurched backward, hovered in the air a few inches away. Its eyes were still blank. It said nothing.

"What are you doing?" I gasped, clasping a hand to my chest, willing my heart to stop pounding. "Are you trying to stop me?"

"I am programmed to see to your needs," it replied in that jarring female voice.

"I need you to leave me alone." I tried to shoo it away, but it dodged my hand in a smooth dip to the side.

"Do not attempt to open the lock."

I ground my teeth. "So you *are* programmed to keep me from leaving."

"No."

"But—"

The pixie made an odd sound, a high-pitched whine of gears that I'd never heard before. Then, after a pause, it said, "The lock."

I stared at it. Although it gave no impression of emotion or effort, it seemed as though it was trying to say something. "What about the lock?"

"Do you wish to ask me about the locking mechanisms in CeePo?" The pixie spoke swiftly.

"Yes. Yes, tell me."

"The locks here are wired with explosive energy, rigged to detonate when tampered with."

A chill ran down my spine. The lock had buzzed when I touched it with magic—but I'd thought it was just responsive. What would've happened if I'd pushed harder, tried to open it?

"Why help me?" I asked, searching the blank eyes for some hint of Nix, anything. "You may have saved my life. Did they program you to do that?"

"No."

The pixie just hovered there, motionless but for the blur of its wings through the air, blank eyes fixed on me. I thought of Nix's very first command, given to it by its programmer, Kris: *Keep Lark alive.* If that command was still active, what else was still in there?

"Nix?" I whispered.

"My name is PX-148."

Tears blurred my eyes, and I blinked them away angrily. "Go away. Just—go away!"

Before the pixie could respond to my order, a clunk from the door sent me backing away. Someone was opening the lock. I gathered up my magic. I wasn't sure I could attack my own brother—but if it was a guard, then so help him. I was getting out of here, one way or another.

The door swung open, the entryway filled for a moment by a guard in Eagle uniform. Then I heard a grunt of pain and a crackle of magic, and the guard sagged to the floor. A man stepped over him into the room, head turned to look behind him. He slipped something small and mechanical and crackling with energy into his pocket—then turned to face me.

"Basil!" I stared, hardly recognizing him out of his Prometheus clothes. He was wearing plain pants and a shirt with a hood, pulled over his head to help conceal his features.

"There's a battle raging in the city," he whispered. "I take it that's courtesy of your friends?"

Olivia.

I drew in a shaky breath, trying not to get carried away by the little spark of warmth I felt at that news. "What're you doing here?" I whispered back.

"I'm here for you. Let's go."

"Go?"

His face tightened. "I'm getting you out of here. We're leaving."

I hung back. How could I trust him now? "Why not just order them to let me go?" I asked bitterly. "These people would do anything for you."

He gazed at me from the shadow of the hood. "They'd do anything for Prometheus," he said quietly. "The man who'll stop at nothing to save them. And what do we need more than someone with your abilities? If I let you go—that'd be the end of Prometheus anyway." He shook his head. "Come on."

Basil crossed swiftly to the doorway and stuck his head out, scanning the hall in both directions. He then stepped through, gesturing for me to follow. I hesitated—but what better way to escape than with Prometheus himself helping me? Just because I accepted his help didn't mean I'd have to side with him.

And so I went after him—and the pixie came after me.

Basil's face locked down as soon as he saw it. He pulled the mechanical device out of his pocket and stretched out his hand. I felt him gathering magic and in that instant realized what he meant to do.

"No!" I shoved at his arm, knocking it away and breaking his concentration. "Don't. I think there's still something of Nix in there."

"Nix?" Basil stared at it. "Lark—is that your *tracker* pixie? From the Institute? Are you insane?"

"Yes." I glanced at it, still hovering emotionlessly in the air. "You don't understand—it's changed. It learns, and it can make its own decisions. Maybe yours was different, or you destroyed it too quickly, but this one—this one is my friend."

His gaze had swiveled toward me, eyebrows drawn in. I

could almost see him wondering if his little sister had experienced some complete mental breakdown.

"Your people scrubbed it," I continued, swallowing. "It doesn't recognize me anymore, except—I think there's something there still."

He shook his head. "These models can't be scrubbed. Believe me, I tried—their memories are buried too deeply in their programming. That's why I destroyed mine."

"They did something to it," I insisted, trying to ignore the thread of hope flaring up inside me. Maybe Nix really was in there somewhere. "And I won't leave it here."

"Maybe they just put some sort of programming in on top of the old, bypassing it." Basil glanced at it again. "Fine. Fine, bring it with us. But I'll kill it the second it tries anything."

Basil led the way out into the hall and down the corridor. He was still holding that thing in his hand—I couldn't get a good look at it, but he clutched it in his fist as though it was all that stood between us and certain death.

"Basil," I whispered as we turned a corner. "I can't leave without my friends. I came here with others—I can't leave them here to be tortured or killed by your people."

He stopped, retreating into the alcove of a doorway. "Lark—you're in no position to make requests. I've got to get you out. You don't know what they'll do to you—what I'll be forced to do to you. We don't have time to make stops for others."

I inhaled slowly. This wasn't the brother I knew. The Basil I knew would've stopped at nothing to rescue innocent people. "Then you'll have to watch them torture me, because I'm not leaving without them."

He stared at me, anger and fear clouding his features. I realized that he wasn't used to anybody arguing with him anymore—no one ever debated Prometheus. He leaned back, staring down the corridor again, then turned back to me. Struggling with himself, he shut his eyes, teeth grinding against each other. "Fine. Fine. Okay—we'll find your friends, then we'll go."

"And the rest of the Renewables too."

He took a step back, staring at me. For a moment he was speechless, mouth opening with no sound coming out—then he shook his head. "You don't understand. Those Renewables go free, this city falls within the week. And then everyone will die, or become Empty Ones. I can get your friends out, but we can't let them all go. Lark, we *can't*."

You can, I wanted to scream at him. But for the first time, the tiniest tendrils of doubt came snaking into my thoughts. Could I really demand they all go free, knowing that it was a death sentence for everyone else? Which counted for more, the lives of a handful of Renewables, or the lives of hundreds, if not thousands, of innocent people?

I thought of Nina, lying prone in an infirmary bed. One life for dozens—Marco, Parker, Dorian, and all the Renewables with him were alive because I took that power from her. In the heat of it, I'd made the same decision my brother had.

"Let's go," I said tightly, shoving the question aside—I would deal with it later. I'd have to make my decision when it came to it. I could always free them myself once Basil led me to where they kept the Renewables. "Wesley's a Renewable, I'm assuming he's wherever the rest of them are. Oren's— Oren's not. But I'm hoping he's there too."

"Wesley?" Basil had begun to step out of the alcove but stopped short, eyes widening. "Wesley—no, he was the one who arrested you and the murderer."

I stared back at him. "You didn't know? Adjutant came and ordered him and Oren taken away. I thought . . . I thought you had ordered it."

"Why would I?" Basil was still standing, stricken. "Wesley's one of my closest . . . "

"He's one of us," I said simply. "A member of the resistance. You really didn't know?"

Basil swallowed, his eyes sliding down to the floor. "I didn't know," he confirmed, his gaze troubled. "Adjutant has a certain amount of autonomy—he has to, or else he'd never get anything done. But I thought . . . I thought he'd just arrested you two."

I opened my mouth to respond, but before I could speak, sparks exploded from the archway over Basil's head. He ducked, cursing. Without thinking, I took a step out and looked down the hallway. A pair of Eagles stood there, holding out the same magical weapons that the Eagles in the square had—the same weapon Adjutant had. Talons.

And they didn't even recognize their leader.

CHAPTER 25

The second guard fired as I looked out around the corner. For a moment I could only stand there, frozen, my eyes blinded by the wave of magic flowing toward me. I couldn't think what would happen if it struck—I was already full to capacity after the first time I was zapped.

And then the wave exploded inches from my face. My dazzled eyes barely made out the tiny, metallic form of the pixie dropping to the ground from where it had flown between me and the weapon's bolt. Without thinking I reached out and pulled, dragging enough magic away from the two guards to send them twitching to the floor. Wesley's training stopped me short of taking all they had—but only just.

It felt as though my entire body had turned to mist—I couldn't feel the ground beneath my feet or hear anything going on around me. With their magic added to what I'd already been given, my head was spinning so much I could barely stand. And still, even now, part of me wanted more. I could see the last bits of power lurking inside the guards, the vestiges that kept the machinery of their bodies working—and I wanted it.

This was all a dream . . . who would I be hurting? I reached out dreamily.

Hands wrapped around my shoulders and shook hard, and my second sight fell away. My vision returned, Basil's features wavering in front of my face.

"Snap out of it!" he was hissing, still shaking me. "What did you *do?*"

"I—took their magic," I said with an effort. "You have the same power. It's what the Institute did to us."

He was staring at me like he no longer recognized me. "No," he murmured. "I can't do any of that, Lark. I can pull power from machines, from crystals—anywhere the magic's been removed already and put somewhere else. And I have to be touching them. I can't . . ." He trailed off, eyes slipping past me down the hall to where the guards lay unconscious.

I struggled to focus despite the insane urge to laugh through my grief, despite the giddiness coursing through me. "But—we're the same."

Basil just stared at me, eyes tracking me as I sagged to my knees, reaching for the motionless form of the pixie. "I don't know if it's something intrinsically different about us or if they changed the process since they did it to me," he said slowly. "But we're not the same. I can't do what you just did."

I swallowed, pushing away the flickers of despair that kept trying to edge in. All this time I'd thought that if I could just find Basil, he'd know what was wrong with us. He'd know how to fix me. "That's why the glass chair, up in the throne room," I whispered. "It's connected to Renewables on the other end, so you can pull the life out of them."

I kept my gaze on the pixie, trying to force my eyes to work right. I willed the extraneous magic to flow from me to it, the way it did when it was Nix. I couldn't see Basil, but I heard him shifting his weight from foot to foot.

"To the reserves taken from them, yes." His voice was strained, quiet. "I'm the only one who can do it. Work magic and machine that way. That's why it has to be me, little bird."

"Don't call me that." I took a deep breath. "Just don't. You could've found another way. You were brilliant, Basil. You were—you could have done it."

"I tried. I'm *trying*. I've been designing a machine that'll let an ordinary person do what I do, manipulate this power, but it doesn't work. It's too unstable, it's dangerous for the Renewable and for the user. I've tried everything."

I didn't answer. I couldn't even look at him. Part of me wanted to just get up and walk away, because who could stop me? Not Basil. Not his Eagles. Not Adjutant. Walk away into the wasteland above and never come back.

But Oren was here, and Wesley, who risked everything for us.

"Let's go." My voice sounded cold even to me. I got to my feet, my back to my brother.

"Wait." Basil touched my shoulder, but I felt nothing, no tingle, no pull of shadow, nothing but the weight of his hand. "Let me see." He reached for the lifeless pixie cradled in my hands.

I felt my fingers curl around its body, protective. "It saved me," I mumbled. "Even though it didn't remember me, it flew in front of the blast."

"Lark," Basil said softly in the same voice he'd used when I was a child, when I'd wake from a nightmare. "I'm good with machines. Let me look, please."

What could it hurt? Nix was gone twice over—first its thoughts and memories, now its very life. I let my brother take it gently from my palm.

We made a strange picture, huddling over a tiny machine in a pool of flickering light. The corridor stretched away on both sides, silent and still. The Eagles hadn't even had time to call for assistance. We had time—but how much?

Basil turned the machine over in his hands, inspecting it carefully, lifting it to his ear to listen for any signs of life. Though my ears strained, I heard nothing—and I could tell from Basil's lack of reaction that he didn't either.

Then he reached into his pocket and took out sheath of soft brown leather, which he unrolled on the floor to reveal a set of tiny, delicate tools. Architect's tools. Was this something the Institute gave him before he went, or did he have them made for him here? I didn't ask, gritting my teeth as Basil opened up Nix's tiny body, gazing down at it through a tiny magnifying glass that fit between his brow bone and the top of his cheek when he squinted.

Nix's inner workings were made up of hair-thin wires and pins, and gears so small I couldn't even see their teeth. Behind all of it, nestled amidst the incomprehensible clockwork, was its tiny crystal heart. When I'd half-destroyed Nix when I first encountered it, its heart had pulsed blue as it repaired itself. Now it was quiet, still. Dead.

I leaned away, pressing my back to the wall and forcing myself to breathe. Even when Nix vanished without a trace, I'd never truly believed anything had happened to it. I always assumed it was holed up somewhere, hiding. I always, always thought I'd simply wake up one morning and find it perched on my bedpost, watching me with its unblinking stare and criticizing my laziness. But now it was here, dead, the man I used to call brother poking around in its corpse.

I was about to tell Basil to stop, to close it up, let it be, when my brother let out a soft "Hmm," voice registering surprise. I felt, rather than saw, Basil reach out with his own magic to feel around inside the pixie.

"That explains how they got around its programming," he said, fascinated. "There's some kind of override here. The blast must have overloaded it."

"Override?"

"The Institute built this model like a tank—the programming is so well shielded even I can't get to it. But this—Adjutant must have had them put something here that supersedes that programming, takes over before the incoming data even reaches it."

In spite of myself I felt a flare of familiarity, listening to my brother speaking gibberish as he tinkered with some machine or other. While I sat with him on the couch, in our home. How could he be so like him, and so unlike him, all at the same time? More and more I didn't know how to feel, how to react. There's no one I loved more than my big brother, and yet—and yet.

"I didn't even know we had anyone who could do this," he continued softly, fascination shifting to confusion. "Adjutant handles recruiting, and he never . . ."

"Maybe you let him run too much of your city." My voice was soft too, but bitter. "Maybe it's all getting away from you."

Basil looked up, the magnifying glass falling from his eye into his lap. "Adjutant is absolutely devoted," he replied, a flare of anger in his voice. "He's my oldest supporter, my oldest friend. He's been with me since the beginning—without him, none of this would be here."

"You mean the enslaved Renewables? The all-powerful uniformed guard everywhere? The people forced to live in secret and fight for their freedom? None of that would be here?"

Basil's jaw clenched. "This city wouldn't be here."

Just then, footsteps echoed down the corridor. Basil tore his gaze from mine, glancing down the hall behind me. Then, silently, he pulled me into the alcove of a doorway, pressing me back against the wall and then pulling as far into the corner as he could. We each held our breath as a pair of guards approached the intersection behind us.

If they happened to look to the right, down our hallway, and saw the two bodies lying at its far end, then we'd have to add two more bodies to our count.

We waited, ears straining. But the footsteps soon faded again, the two guards continuing on their patrol, not even noticing that two of their fellow Eagles lay unmoving at the other end of the corridor.

Basil let out his breath. He glanced at me, his brown eyes meeting mine for a brief moment. Then he looked back down at the pixie in his hand and closed his eyes.

"What are you doing now?" I whispered.

"Seeing if I can remove the override."

"I thought you said you didn't know how it was done."

"I said I didn't think anyone else did." Basil sent tendrils of magic out, making the air taste of copper and silk. "I never said I couldn't. Its original programming may well be intact underneath."

I closed my eyes as well, the better to watch as he explored the pixie. His movements were so subtle I could barely follow what he was doing. When I acted using magic it was like swinging a battle-ax. Basil wielded it like a scalpel.

Trying not to hope, I reminded myself that even if he could remove the programming, the pixie was still dead.

I itched for action—the magic buzzing through me demanded an outlet, and I couldn't sit still while I knew that Oren was here somewhere, in danger. I started tapping my fingers against the floor, eyes fixed on the ceiling. Long moments stretched in which I strained to listen for the sound of footsteps or an alarm that would mean they'd discovered I was missing. I wondered if it was nighttime here, if everyone was asleep except for the Eagles on patrol.

And then there was a sound. A tiny screech of metal on metal jerked my eyes back down to the ground where Basil was working on Nix. As I stared, the empty crystal heart flickered once as though it contained a tiny bolt of lightning. Then, like a star winking into existence, the blue glow swelled.

"What did you do?" I gasped, afraid to move for fear of dashing the illusion.

"Removed the override," Basil said, leaning back with a grin. "It was fried by the blast, clogging up its systems. Remove it, and it's back to normal."

As I watched, Nix's spindly little legs came shooting out, busily putting itself back together where Basil had taken it apart. It made a spluttery sound of indignation, as if protesting the state in which it had found itself.

"Nix?" I whispered, my heart pounding.

Its dull eyes flickered a few times and then lit with the same blue glow as its heart. *"That was unpleasant."*

A sound that was half-shriek, half-sob escaped a second before I clapped both hands tightly over my mouth. Nix righted itself, extra repair arms folding away. Buzzing its wings experimentally, it made a click of satisfaction. Then it looked at me, the blue eyes unblinking and so familiar. *"What's wrong with you?"*

"Nothing." My smile forced its way through despite my hands pressed to my mouth. "Nothing." I tore my eyes away from Nix to look at my brother, who was watching, bemused, as the pixie began to groom itself furiously, as though it had been rolled in the mud since the last time it tidied up.

"Thank you," I said softly.

Basil looked up at me, startled. Beads of sweat dotted his brow, his face weary. Still, hesitantly, the corners of his mouth twitched up in a smile. He nodded. It was only fleeting, gone again in moments, replaced by that same desperate sadness. He folded away his tools and shoved them back under his belt, then got to his feet and offered me a hand. "Let's go find your friends," he said quietly.

Nix zipped up onto my shoulder after Basil pulled me to my feet. As my brother led the way down the corridor, Nix flicked its wings in irritation. *"Not another one,"* it murmured in my ear. *"And we only just got rid of the other ones."*

I hid my smile as best I could and followed my brother.

CHAPTER 26

Basil led me down a dizzying maze of corridors and staircases. He avoided the elevators for fear of running into somebody who might ask who we were or what we were doing. We were taking the roundabout way down, he said. Longer, but safer.

I had no option but to trust him. And although my mind knew he was Prometheus, knew he'd done horrible, monstrous things to get to where he was, it was growing harder and harder to keep him away. I wanted to forget everything and just let him be my brother again. He was helping me, after all. He would help me rescue Oren and Wesley. He'd brought Nix back to me.

And he was no better than the architects at the Institute, with their secret, dying Renewable.

We paused at the bottom of a stairwell while Basil fiddled with the lock on the door. "What are you going to do when we get there?" I stood behind him, speaking in a low voice. Basil's hands paused for a few seconds, then resumed their work until the lock opened with a soft click. "I don't know," he said finally.

"You'd better figure it out."

We slipped through the door. Moving more quietly now, Basil led me past patrols and through side corridors to avoid more guards. Nix rode on my shoulder, its weight so familiar, comforting in a way I hadn't noticed before it was gone. Eventually we reached a hall that ended in a thick iron door flanked by guards. We paused around a corner, peeking out at them.

"They'll let me through," Basil said tightly. "I'm their god."

"But you left your costume behind," I pointed out.

"*I believe I can be of assistance,*" Nix said, rustling its wings.

"Oh no you don't." I craned my neck to the side so I could eyeball the pixie. "Last time you made a diversion you were captured, brainwashed, and then killed."

"*Brainwashed is perhaps not the right word.*"

"Let me handle this."

I closed my eyes and started searching for the hungry void inside me, but Basil reached out and touched my arm, interrupting me. "These are loyal men," Basil hissed. "They've done nothing wrong."

Except be complicit in slavery and torture. But I just took a deep breath. "I'm not going to hurt them. Just trust me."

He hesitated, then let his arm fall. I breathed deeply, in through my nose, then blew the air out through my pursed lips, letting it focus me. The reservoir for magic inside me was overfull already. Still, I reached out with my thoughts until I could sense the tiny currents of magic running through the guards' systems.

I'd never tried to harvest magic from two people at once, not since I'd leveled the army sent from my city to enslave the Iron Wood. Then, it had nearly killed me. But I didn't have the same training then, the same awareness of what made my power work—and what made it kill. Silently thanking Wesley for his insistence on learning control, I eased open a channel between myself and the two Eagles at the end of the hall.

For a long moment, nothing happened. I dragged at whatever scraps of magic I could get, and then finally, little by little, the shadow in me stirred and woke. As much power as there was already buzzing through my veins, it still wanted more—and once it caught the scent of the men down the hall, it was all I could do to hold it back.

The guard on the left fell first, dropping so fast that my own heart stuttered as if in sympathy. Dimly, as though from half a mile away, I felt Basil grab my arm. I couldn't pay any attention to him, though, not with the other guard stumbling forward, trying to reach his partner's side. He fell to his knees, clutching at his chest, and then slumped to the floor.

I couldn't move, locked in a struggle against myself. I wanted to finish the job. I wanted to feast. It wasn't until Basil gave my arm a jerk and started hurrying me toward the door that I was jarred free, sending the beast snarling back into my subconscious. Dazed, I watched as Basil stooped to check the two men for signs of life. He said nothing, just glanced at me with his lips pressed together. I knew they were alive, though—if they'd died, I would've felt it. It was always those last scraps of magic that tasted sweetest. And I'd cut myself off before going that far.

Basil wasted no more time, turning his attention to the door. It was locked with one of the same turning wheels that were on some of the forgotten doors inside the walls, and he turned it with a grunt of effort and a sigh of oiled bearings.

We slipped through the door and eased it shut behind us. Then we turned.

Behind the door lay the prison complex for Prometheus's enslaved Renewables. The corridor stretched on into what seemed like infinity, lined on either side by heavy doors. I took a few steps into the room, skin crawling at the presence of so much iron, more than I'd felt in one place since the tunnels between Lethe and the world above. Each door seemed to be made of solid iron, with only a grate maybe a foot square for the prisoners to look out of—or for the guards to look in. There were lights over the doors closest to us, barely more than dim red spots. There were only six of them. Did that mean the rest of the cells stretching onward were empty?

Basil's jaw was tight, his eyes cold, shut down. He didn't look at the cell doors but instead kept his eyes on the endless hallway, standing by the door. "Go look for them," he said shortly.

Nix launched itself from my shoulder to explore as I walked forward, skin crawling with more than iron now. It was as though I could feel the eyes of the Renewables on me as I passed. No wonder Basil didn't like to come here—guilt roiled inside me simply for being free while they were captive. What must it be like to come here when you were *actually* their captor?

I cleared my throat and called softly, "Wesley? Oren?"

For a moment all I could hear was the pounding of my own heart. Then, so rattly and tired that my chest tightened, came Wesley's voice. "About time," he called, his voice coming from the end of the row of lights.

I hurried down and peered in through the grating. He was there, waiting for me. His face didn't show any signs of mistreatment, but I knew the damage would be deeper, harder to see. He smiled at me, though, when my face came into view.

"Does this mean you got him? Got Prometheus?"

I glanced back at my brother, who was still standing just inside the doorway, not looking at us or at anything else.

"We can talk later," I said finally. "Let's get you out of here. Which one is Oren's cell?"

"Which one?" Wesley stuck a hand through the grating, wrapping his fingers around a bar. "Open all of them, get us all out of here."

I closed my eyes, feeling sick. "I can't," I whispered. "For now I can only get you and Oren. Where is he?"

Wesley gazed at me, confusion quickly shifting to wariness in his features. "He's not here," he said quietly. "They're keeping him somewhere else."

My heart sank. For a moment I just wanted to scream at Wesley for letting Oren out of his sight, at Basil for allowing any of this to happen, at myself for not realizing that they wouldn't be keeping a seemingly normal person with the Renewables, even if he came with one. Instead I drew in a shaky breath and said, "Basil, open the door."

"Basil?" Wesley's eyes grew round. "Your brother—the one—"

But he was interrupted by a mechanical whine and a heavy clunk in his door. I grabbed for the indented handle and pulled, and Wesley stepped out into the hallway. His eyes went past me to Basil, whose hand was still on the heavy switch that controlled the lock.

"The boy who wrote the journal," Wesley breathed, staring at Basil the way that Adjutant had stared at Prometheus.

Basil's gaze shifted toward me, but I had no answer either. How to tell Wesley that the journal was written by none other than Prometheus himself, before he came to power? That the one saving him now was the one who'd ordered him captured in the first place? It didn't matter that Adjutant had taken it upon himself to arrest Wesley—he was acting in Prometheus's name.

I turned back toward the cells and called tensely, "Tansy? Tansy, are you in here?"

No answer. My heart pounded in the silence, and I walked

up the row of cells, trying to feel for her familiar power signature. But aside from Wesley, the golden Renewable glows here were faint, flickering and weak. These people had been drained.

"Is someone there?" The voice was tired, weak—and unfamiliar. I turned to see hands curling around the bars in the door, all that could be seen of the prisoner behind it.

Basil took a step backward, away from the panel of door release switches, swallowing hard. He looked sick, even as he squared his jaw. "Let's go," he called softly.

"No." I planted my feet, gazing at him across the prison block. "We take them all, or I stay here and wait for Adjutant. I'm not leaving without them."

Basil's hands curled into fists. "Lark, I can't have this fight with you, not here. We have to go. We have to just—we have to get out of here."

"And then what?" I hissed back. "We just run away and find some new place to live? Some new place to turn into your idea of a utopia?"

"I never said this place was perfect!" Basil fired back. "If you hadn't noticed, the world out there is far from perfect. This is the best we can do. We go, we disappear, we try to live our lives as best we can with what we've got. That's all there is, Lark!"

"Maybe that's true," I whispered, my voice echoing in the chamber. I knew Wesley might overhear, might figure it all out—but I didn't care. "Whether it is or not, I'm not leaving while these people are still enslaved. So you can make your choice."

My brother stared at me across the gulf of space between us, his muscles tense, his gaze unreadable. He looked sad—sadder than he did the day he left me, volunteering for the Institute's top secret mission. He looked tired.

And then he turned and flipped every switch on the wall, causing a cascade of metallic thuds all down the corridor as every door swung open.

Half a dozen captive Renewables streamed out into the hallway, exclaiming, murmuring relief. Wesley hurried toward them, recognizing some as members of the resistance who'd been captured. I didn't care about what he was doing, though—I could only look at my brother. It was like there was a line between us, connecting us again, and even though people crossed through it again and again as they reunited with each other, it stayed unbroken.

I whispered, "What are you going to do?" If Basil was right, then without the Renewables, Lethe would fall.

He was too far away for the sound to carry over the sounds of relief and celebration, but somehow he heard me anyway. "I don't know," his lips said back, the words carrying directly to my heart.

"All right," Wesley said, cutting through the rapidly rising wave of sound from the newly freed Renewables. "We're not free yet. We're going to go find Prometheus and end this once and for all—and Lark's going to need our help."

My eyes were still on Basil's. He shook his head slightly—don't interrupt. If they knew Basil was Prometheus, they'd turn on him right here and now. We'd never find Tansy. And Wesley was right, I was going to be grateful for the help once we reached the harvesting room.

"If any of you are too weak or injured," Wesley continued, "then raise your hands and we'll arrange one group to go back. You two, I don't recognize you—you're welcome to join us in the walls. We live free of Prometheus's grip."

But not a single person raised their hands, not even the man with pale, brittle-looking skin and purple bruises around each eye—the man who had clearly just been harvested.

"Very well," said Wesley. It was a relief to have him back—to have someone else making the decisions again. I felt wrung out, too many horrors and revelations in one day. "Then we all go." But then he turned to me—and waited.

I stared back at him, uncomprehending.

"This is your party," he said, smiling that irritatingly self-assured smile. This time, however, there was a glint of sympathy in his face.

For a long moment I struggled not to beg him to take over, to finish this mission. Take the decisions out of my hands, handle everything. But then Basil stepped up beside me, and I found myself nodding.

"We have to find Tansy. She would've been about my age, taller than me, strong—"

"I know the girl you're talking about," Wesley interrupted. "She's gone. She's not here."

"What do you mean she's not here?"

"They took her." Wesley's face was thin, drawn. Afraid. There was a faint dull gleam of perspiration on his thinning scalp. "They brought one of the men across the way back, empty, and took her. I think she's the one they're draining now."

I remembered the Renewable in the Institute, the one they held captive in secret, in eternal torment as they drained her power away and let it regrow in a never-ending cycle. I remembered the agony of the Machine as they tore my natural magic away and replaced it with dark, twisted city magic.

I turned to Basil, who had walked back toward the door and then stopped. He was watching me, his face calm, his eyes sad. For a long moment we just stood there, at either end of the row of occupied cells, looking at each other.

Then he said quietly, "She'll be in the harvesting room. I'll show you."

CHAPTER 27

Now that we were prepared for the guards, with an army of half a dozen Renewables at our backs, we encountered surprisingly few of them. It turned out one of the freed captives, a resistance member who called himself Curio, was especially adept at using his magic on the human consciousness. Whenever we encountered more than one at a time, Nix dived into the fray, using the venomous stinger the Institute had equipped him with to knock the second Eagle out. We left the few guards we did encounter sleeping peacefully in the hallways behind us.

Basil and I talked quickly as we moved, our voices low. "When this is over," he whispered, "you and I will have to slip out."

"What are you talking about?"

My brother grimaced. He looked so tired, so much older than I would have ever guessed. "Without the Renewables, there's no way to keep Lethe going. Better to get out before it falls."

"The resistance," I whispered. "If they all came forward, volunteered to be harvested—"

"Unless there are fifty, sixty of them hidden away, it won't help. No one would volunteer to spend their lives in that kind of torment."

"You want us to run." I couldn't imagine my brother, my brave, kind older brother, so ready to abandon these people to the darkness. But then, he didn't know about Nina—he'd never believe me capable of making these choices, either.

"You want to stay?" he asked, incredulous.

"You said yourself that Lethe will fall without them." I gestured at the Renewables ranged out behind us, all watching for guards. "I'm the reason they're going free. I have to stay and figure out a way to fix the city. No matter what."

Basil fixed his eyes on the ground ahead of us. "You know that's how I got started, too?"

"I know."

His hand brushed mine, then turned and wrapped around my fingers, the way it used to when I was a child. "You were right to let them go," he said softly. "It's easy to justify a monstrosity in light of the greater good. I don't know whether—I don't know what the answer is. But it was wrong to keep them there."

Before, I would've pulled my hand from his, angry, hurt that he was no longer the brother I knew. But now, listening to the marching footsteps of the freed Renewables, of our tiny, dedicated army, I didn't. It was easy to say what he'd done was wrong when speaking required no answer, no action. Still, the words meant something. And I let him keep hold of my hand.

The harvesting room was not far from the chambers where the Renewables were held. Basil explained that his workshop and the other experimental laboratories were all branches off of the harvesting room, for easy access to the machines when it came to making adjustments.

I tried not to imagine my brother calmly and casually making notes and turning dials and controls while a captive

Renewable hung suspended, screaming silently as his power was torn away. I tried not to imagine him using that stolen power in his work.

But as we walked, hand in hand, I knew that Basil and I would never be as we were. We'd never be big brother and little sister, it would never be simple and trusting again. I didn't know if I could ever love him again.

No, that wasn't true. I still loved him. In spite of everything, despite what I'd said and the things he'd done, he was my brother. And I loved him. I just didn't know if I'd ever trust him again.

Nix thrummed against my neck, nestled close. Trust was hard to come by in this world beyond the Wall, but it could be found, if you looked hard enough. I had Nix; I had Oren. Most of all, I had myself. That was enough.

Basil didn't know where Oren was being kept when I asked, but thought that maybe he'd be with the regular prisoners, the people detained for not having the proper papers or for starting brawls in the streets. I still hadn't told anyone the truth about what Oren was—I was hoping no one had found out, that he was merely being kept with the drunks and the petty thieves. Basil promised to take me to find him once we freed Tansy.

When we reached the harvesting room, we stopped some distance back in the corridor to hold a whispered conference.

"There'll be guards outside," Basil said as the rest of us crowded around. "Probably two, but maybe four. If this is the door," and he drew his finger across the ground, pushing out just enough magic to leave a dimly glowing trail behind, "then the two guards will be here and here. If there are four, the other two will be posted on the opposite wall of the hallway, here and here." The floor was marked now with glowing X's.

"Inside, the Renewable—Tansy—will most likely be in

the harvesting column." Basil drew a large oval on the other side of the door he'd drawn earlier, to indicate the room beyond, then etched a series of lines radiating out from a circle in the oval's center. "The column is here," he said, pointing at the circle. "These are catwalks. The entire thing is suspended over the machinery that powers the harvester, drawing the energy up to—to Prometheus's chair."

"How do you know so much?" Curio was staring at Basil, brows drawn inward suspiciously.

Basil opened his mouth, but Wesley got there first. "This is Basil Ainsley," he said swiftly, watching my brother. "He's the one who wrote the journal. And this is his sister, the girl whose picture is in it. He knows everything there is to know about Prometheus."

Curio's eyebrows lifted, lips parting as his mistrust shifted to awe. He and the others took Wesley's words at face value, but I wasn't so sure. I watched him, trying to find any sign that he'd recognized Basil as the man he'd pretended to serve for the past two years. But Wesley just gazed back, steady and unflinching.

Basil dropped his eyes. "When we get inside there may be some of Prometheus's researchers working there. Let's avoid killing them if we can. And let *me* get Tansy out. Tearing her out of the machinery would be more dangerous than just leaving her in there. The machines are designed to stop before the Renewables are in any danger of dying. It'll hurt her to stay in it, but it won't kill her."

"Right," I said, lifting my eyes to scan the faces of the Renewables around me. "Are we ready?"

. . .

There were only two guards. Curio was able to handle them both, but he was starting to sweat and shake and clearly didn't have much left. I hoped that the other Renewables were half as adept at incapacitating enemies.

The entrance to the harvesting chamber itself had a complicated locking mechanism, but Basil pressed a series of brass knobs with incomprehensible symbols on them, then paused and looked at me. I nodded, and he pressed the last button.

The door hissed open, and we spilled into the room, down the catwalk.

The first thing I saw was a column of pale gold light and a human body suspended in it. The head was thrown back, muscles tense with pain, fingers bent into claws and toes curled in agony. Her features were obscured by the light and the angle, but I knew who it was—I recognized her hair, her height, the clothes she was wearing.

Tansy.

The second thing I saw was a series of machines arranged around the perimeter of the room, banks of levers and knobs and displays, many of them with exposed wires darting this way and that. Staircases led up to a second level and then a third, where there were more machines. Beyond the banks of machinery were sheets of darkened glass, no doubt opening onto individual experiment bays, but closed off when not in use. Chairs were arranged at each station, but they were all empty. No researchers. One station on the ground level was recognizable as Prometheus's—his robes were draped over the back of the chair, somehow duller and smaller now that they weren't being worn.

And the third thing I saw was Adjutant.

I froze, and Basil came to a halt beside me. The entry catwalk wasn't wide enough for more than two, and the other Renewables were forced to stop behind us.

Adjutant strolled toward us, halting beside the column where Tansy hung suspended. "Miss Ainsley," he said, as calm and polite as ever. "I thought as soon as I learned that the Renewables had escaped that you would be coming here. I'm gratified to find I was right."

Seeing my face, he smiled. "Of course I know who you are," he added. "Your brother spoke of you incessantly for the first year he lived here."

Basil stepped forward, fists clenched. "You should have told me, Adjutant," he spat, his voice taut with fury.

Adjutant inclined his torso in a slight bow, spreading one hand in a conciliatory gesture. There was some sort of machine on it, bands of metal around each finger, spreading over the back of his hand like an exoskeleton. "I live to serve you, Prometheus," he said reverently. "My life and my actions have always only been to protect you."

"Prometheus?" It was Curio, his face transformed by confusion and, slowly, loathing. I glanced at Wesley, but instead of seeming surprised, he only stood there, expression unreadable, his gaze on mine. Wesley worked in CeePo every day—perhaps it was stupid of me to have thought that he wouldn't have recognized Prometheus, even out of uniform. The other Renewables behind us were murmuring bewilderment and anger, trying to understand what was happening.

"The rabble are turning on you, Lord." Adjutant lifted his hand, stretching the other out toward the column containing Tansy. "Allow me." That hand had a similar machine on it—as he turned towards the Renewables, I could see that the devices on each hand ran up over his shoulders and connected in a knot of copper and glass at the nape of his neck.

Before I could figure out what he was doing, a jolt of magic flowed from Tansy, into the device, and then out through his other hand. Basil knocked me to the metal catwalk with a clang, his body on top of mine—I felt the heat of the blast through my hair as I fell.

A man screamed—I jerked my head up in time to see the Renewables fall, every last one of them, writhing on the ground. By the time I shoved Basil off of me and dragged myself to my feet, all of them lay still. I could see flickers of magic there—they weren't dead—but they were all incapacitated. Nix was no longer on my shoulder, but I couldn't see it anywhere—whether it was in the pile of bodies or hiding somewhere else, I couldn't tell.

"What did you do?" I screamed, turning back toward Adjutant, who was staring at his hand as though seeing it for the first time.

Basil got to his feet and pulled me back, ignoring my attempts to claw my way past him.

"He's like us," I gasped, holding onto the catwalk railing.

"No." Basil was staring at Adjutant. "The device—the one I made to let others take over where I left off."

"It's perfect," breathed Adjutant, still gazing at the hand that had delivered the blast. "You truly are more than human, Lord."

"It's not ready," Basil said through gritted teeth. I could feel the fury behind his voice—I wondered why he didn't just lash out, didn't just try to get the machine away from Adjutant. "There are still flaws—it's unstable, Adjutant. Dangerous for you; dangerous for her." He jerked his chin toward Tansy, whose mouth I could see opened in a silent scream.

Adjutant lifted his eyes finally, gaze going from me to Basil. "Lord, I never wanted you to find out that Lark Ainsley was here."

"That wasn't your decision to make."

"But it was." Adjutant sounded surprised, slightly wounded. "It's my calling to keep you safe, Prometheus. To keep you from the hard decisions. I thought by presenting her to you after we'd learned the extent of her abilities you'd have no choice but to—"

"To use her?" Basil stepped forward, shoulders tense and eyes hard. "Like we've been using these others?"

Adjutant's eyes widened, and for a moment I could see a hint of the madness he'd showed in the audience chamber. When he'd told me to show respect for my god. "It has always been in the name of the greater good, Lord."

Basil shook his head. "It may have started that way, but it's not that way anymore. It's not about just saving ourselves—we have to be worthy of salvation."

There was silence for a moment while Adjutant struggled to digest this. My mind raced, trying to go over the options. I still had Oren's knife, but there was no chance I'd get close enough to Adjutant to use it. And while Oren might have been able to throw it, my aim was nowhere good enough.

But that wasn't the only weapon I had. The blackout device. In a place like this, the blast would disrupt every machine in the entire room. The one Adjutant was using to imitate Basil's powers—and the ones holding Tansy captive.

I slipped my hand into my pocket. All I had to do was throw it hard enough at the floor for the impact to set it off. But I remembered what Basil had said—jerking Tansy out of this machinery could kill her. Surely cutting power abruptly would do the same.

Adjutant's gaze swung over to me, burning. "This is just proof of what I've known for a long time," he said quietly, his voice low and tight. "You're too soft. Too trusting. Even I can't protect you from every tough decision—and when I try, you . . . disappoint me. You're letting this girl ruin in one night everything we've worked together for years to create."

"She's my sister."

"And I am your Adjutant!" A fleck of spittle lingered on Adjutant's lips as he breathed heavily, struggling with himself. Then he straightened, in control once more. "I didn't want to do this, but you must be shown the truth. Your innocent, kindhearted sister consorts with monsters—her lover is one of the Empty Ones."

Adjutant gestured toward one of the experiment bays across the room, the one I'd guessed was Prometheus's station, and on cue its dark glass cleared and the cell lit up from within.

Oren.

He lifted his head—he hadn't been able to see out either, and evidently the windows were soundproof as well. Shock staggered him backward a pace as he saw me—then he threw himself against the wall of his prison, pounding his fists against the glass. I saw him screaming soundlessly, shouting to be let out, to be allowed to go to my side. His lips formed my name as he met my gaze, and then he launched himself forward. A sound tore its way out of my throat as he threw his entire body against the glass and fell to the ground.

My heart was tearing itself in two as I watched him dragging himself upright again, dazed and bruised, but I'd seen the madness in Adjutant's face. I didn't know what he'd do if I moved from where I stood.

"You see," Adjutant said, moving over toward the banks of machines in front of the glass box that held Oren, "he's a savage even when he's human. There's no room in our new world for monsters like him."

"Let him go," Basil said coldly. "I trust Lark." But I could see the confusion in Basil's face. First I'd asked him to trust a pixie—now he was being asked to trust this.

"You don't understand," said Adjutant. "Let me show you." He reached out and pulled a lever. My head rang with magic as something shifted, sucking the power out of the cell. Then Oren was gone, and in his place was the shadow.

It snarled soundlessly and threw itself against the glass

with ten times the force Oren himself had been able to muster.

I couldn't look at Basil. I couldn't look at Adjutant, either. I could only watch as the thing that had been Oren threw itself at the glass over and over and over, mindless, full of rage and savagery and hunger. All I could hear was the dull thud of Oren's body hitting the glass, his muffled snarls. My eyes burned.

"You see," said Adjutant. "You see what she is. These are the creatures she pities. She wants to see them take over. She wants to ruin everything we've done."

"No," said Basil. I lifted my head with an effort, my eyes streaming. "What we've been doing, you and I, is wrong."

Adjutant let the lever slide back into place, and I felt the ambient magic sliding back into place with it. The Oren-monster dropped to the floor of his cell, sides heaving. "Lord, allow me to remove this girl from your presence. Please, she's infected your—"

"She's done *nothing!*" shouted Basil. This was the voice of Prometheus, the voice of Adjutant's god. "It has nothing to do with her—or this creature. We're the monsters, Adjutant. Look around—this isn't the new world. This isn't right. *This isn't what we set out to do.*"

Adjutant gazed at Basil. Beyond him I could see Oren, himself again, but too dazed and injured by his shadow self's attempts to escape to do more than lie there, gasping.

"You've lost your way, Lord," Adjutant said softly, his hand falling on the robes laid over the chair. "Lost sight of the utopia we're creating here."

"You're the one who's lost his way," Basil replied, fists clenched. I could see tears standing in his eyes and realized that this was costing him as much as it had cost me to stand up to him. *Adjutant has been with me since the beginning,* he'd said.

His oldest—his only—friend.

"I wish you could understand the pain and the sorrow that I feel." Adjutant's voice was soft, sad. "To lose you this way. You were my mentor, my friend, my savior. My beacon. My god."

Basil stood silently, opening and closing his fists, unable to speak.

"But the people must have direction." Adjutant's wide, staring eyes fixed on the wall above us. He reached for the robes on the chair, picking them up slowly, caressing them like something precious and beautiful. "If their god falters, then a new one must rise and take his place."

I stared, drawn in by the insanity in his gaze, the way his eyes were fixed on something none of the rest of us could see—some vision of the twisted paradise he sought.

"Prometheus is dead." Adjutant slowly swung the robes up and settled them over his shoulders. "Long live Prometheus."

And then he reached out for Tansy again, thrusting his hand out toward Basil. A beam of violent purple light shot forth, hitting my brother square in the chest and throwing him back against the far wall with the force of the blast.

"NO!" The word tore from my throat as I lunged for him, but it was too late. The beam stopped, but crackling energy pinned Basil against the wall, several feet off the ground. He struggled, but the magic containing him was so thick I couldn't even sense him behind it.

Adjutant turned to me. I threw up a barrier a millisecond before he turned the same blast on me. The force of it drove me backward until I hit the handrail of the catwalk, and I braced myself against it, throwing everything I had into my shield.

Oren was pressed against the glass, staring, his eyes anguished. Basil was still pinned, unable to speak or move.

Adjutant laughed, shoving his other arm deeper into Tansy's aura of magic.

"No wonder he didn't share this with me," he said, his wild grin only a flash of white teeth behind the violet beam spilling off my shield. "It's glorious. Dare I say it, divine. I'd hoard it for myself as well."

I had no strength to answer, every fiber of my being thrown into the shields. I didn't have enough to do anything but block his attack—no way to enact a countermeasure. And I wasn't going to last much longer.

And then Nix zoomed out of nowhere, its mechanisms screaming bloody murder. It flew directly at Adjutant, stinger extended. Adjutant swept it aside with a flick of his head, and Nix went tumbling through the air, disoriented. Righting itself, Nix hovered for a moment, indecisive. Then, so fast I couldn't track it through the tears of pain and effort streaming from my eyes, it flew over to the bank of machines in front of Oren's cell. It started throwing itself at every button it could find, frantic.

Adjutant laughed again, turning his gaze back on me. "I see you found your way past our reprogramming. Shame, I was hoping we'd be able to use that device. I'll see to it that it's destroyed as soon as we're done here."

He didn't seem to be tiring at all—in fact, he seemed stronger and more insane with every passing second, his very skin alive with magic, crackling. But behind him a series of red lights began to flash.

The machines are designed to cut off before the Renewable runs out of power and dies, Basil had said. I glanced at Tansy, squinting. I couldn't see her well through the layers of magic between us, my second sight interfering with my regular vision. She was rising in the column, arms and legs splayed, eyes turned toward the ceiling. Up to the second tier of machines, and on, and on . . .

A dull pounding grabbed my attention and dragged it back to Nix. Oren was banging on the glass—Nix heard and looked up. Oren gestured frantically, miming, pointing toward some particular dial or button that I couldn't see. Nix launched itself straight down, slamming into the button—and the door of Oren's cage slid open.

Adjutant turned, leveling his arm this time at Oren. Without the force of the beam on my shields I stumbled forward and fell, crying out a ragged warning. But Oren was fast—as fast as Olivia. Faster. He dodged easily, sprinting around to the other side of the circle. Nix went the other way. There were too many targets—Adjutant roared frustration. I started to gather my own power, ready to end this once and for all.

And then he looked at me, teeth bared, his eyes burning violet and gold, magic leaking from his ears and nose and dribbling out of his mouth like flames. "I will not let you destroy paradise," he said in a voice that was no longer his own, hissing and crackling with power.

In one surge he jerked the remaining magic from the harvester—and it exploded, throwing us all outward. My head struck the wall and I slumped to the ground, dazed. I dragged myself up by the handrail, dizzy and nauseous. I looked up in time to see Tansy thrown from the column as it vanished, her body striking the wall and landing on the catwalk three stories up.

Adjutant was stirring feebly, smoke and steam rising from his body as he pulled himself up. I ignored him, sprinting for the nearest staircase. Nix, flight path wobbly and slow as it repaired itself at the same time, cut past me, headed straight for Tansy.

My muscles and lungs burned as though my struggle against Adjutant's magic had been a physical one, but I ignored them. I just had to get to her—give her enough power to keep her heart beating. Repay the gift she'd given me—give her magic back.

I reached the top of the second flight of stairs and ricocheted off the wall as I lurched forward. I threw myself down beside her, ignoring the pain as the metal catwalk stripped several layers of skin from my knees. I pressed both hands to her body, willing my magic to go forth.

Tansy was still moving—her eyes turned toward me as I touched her. But I could see she was empty, that there was nothing left inside her. She was as black and hollow as the man I'd killed in the square. She was bleeding from a number of abrasions from striking the wall, but the blood was seeping gently, slowly. Her heart wasn't beating.

"No, nonono—Tansy, stay with me. Look at me. It's Lark, I'm here, you're going to be fine." I shoved harder, trying to force my magic into the black chasm of her heart.

Her staring gaze fixed on mine. For just a moment, it seemed as though she recognized me—her eyes widened. Her lips moved—they twitched into the tiniest smile as she gazed at my face.

Then she died.

For a moment I couldn't breathe, couldn't think. There was just Tansy's face, her eyes gazing up at me, gazing through me, blood still seeping sluggishly from the gashes on her arms, on her cheek. There was no longer a black emptiness inside her—there wasn't anything. There was no hole where her life used to be because everything that made her Tansy was gone. The thing I was touching, cradling, was a husk and nothing more.

Breath returned to me with a jerk, as violently as if I'd had the wind knocked out of me. It sobbed in and out of me as I got shakily to my feet, staggering to the handrail and looking down.

Adjutant stood there, looking up at me. Burns covered his body in patches, his once-handsome face distorted in a snarl. Sections of his hair were gone, the rest of it sticking out in patches. The robes of Prometheus were charred and soot-stained, unrecognizable. But he still wore Basil's device—and despite the explosion, it was intact.

His eyes on me, he reached out and threw his hand against the banks of machines. Tiny explosions and sparks jumped up everywhere, landing on his skin, on his clothes, but he didn't even flinch. Painfully he dragged the magic out of the machines and into himself, gathering for another strike.

Tansy's death wasn't enough for him.

When it came, I didn't have time to throw up my shields. The blast hit me off-center, in the arm, throwing one shoulder back. Something cracked, sending pain shooting up my arm as it fell to dangle uselessly at my side.

I don't need hands to kill you. I gritted my teeth, sucking air through my nose, trying to focus on Wesley's meditation exercises. *Pain is nothing. Pain's just in my mind.* But as I started to get some focus together another blast came, this one knocking me back against the wall, hitting me squarely in the stomach and dropping me to my knees.

Where were Oren, Nix, Basil? I couldn't see—through the grating, on my hands and knees, I could only see bodies everywhere. The smell of burning flesh and hair and chemicals singed my nostrils, and something dripped down my back—sweat or blood, I couldn't tell.

I was alone. And I had only one more trick to try.

I pulled myself up with my one good arm, choking back a groan of pain as a wave of nausea rolled over me. I tried to reach into my pocket but found that my fingers were burned, too swollen to fit inside it. I couldn't get at the device. Another bolt came at me, hitting the railing of the catwalk instead and blasting it into in a million white-hot shards that stung me all over my face and throat.

I stood up, and my eyes found Oren. He was lying face-down, but as I watched he picked himself up on his arms, his gaze sweeping the catwalk and then resting on me. For a moment I just looked at him, thinking of all the things I should have said before we left.

No regrets, Olivia had said to me. I gazed at Oren, willing him to understand. I took a deep breath.

Somehow Oren sensed what I was about to do a fraction of a second before I moved.

"Lark—NO!"

But I was already running, aiming for the gap in the railing—I jumped—and then I was falling.

One good impact will set it off.

My instincts tried to kick in, tried to form the same sort of magical cushion that had saved me twice before. I fought them tooth and nail, trying desperately to override my body's natural desire to save itself.

And then I hit.

The world exploded. Adjutant screamed, and for a moment there was only a column of fire burning purple and gold, and his screams turned hoarse and raspy and then melted away into silence—and then everything was gone.

CHAPTER 28

"Don't move her—don't touch her!"

"Oh god, is she—please—"

"I don't know. Move back, I said!"

"It's coming this way—I don't think Curio can hold it."

Snarling, screaming, flashes of light and dark.

"You've got to get her up—I can't do it, I have to be touching things and if I get close enough it'll tear me apart."

"Lark." A voice breathed into my ear. "Lark you have to wake up."

No. Leave me alone. I'm dead, let me stay that way.

"Oren's going to kill us all, or we're going to have to kill him. You have to stop him."

Oren? But Oren was safe. Oren was human.

"I know it hurts. I know it hurts more than anything's ever hurt before. But Lark, I know you're in there, and you *have to open your eyes.*"

Suddenly everything *did* hurt. And with that pain came the realization that I wasn't dead—but I wished I was. Agony split me starting from my arm, which I couldn't move, and radiating throughout my body. I couldn't feel my toes, my legs wouldn't respond to my commands. My eyes opened to darkness broken only by flashes of magic. I screamed.

"There's my girl." It was Wesley. "Breathe. Just breathe." His voice was tense with something I couldn't recognize, but his hands were gentle, one resting against my cheek, the other against the shoulder less torn with agony than the other.

"Oren," I groaned. "Oren?"

"The blackout device turned him," said Wesley. "They're trying to hold him off, but he's too fast. The device stripped the magic out of the air and out of everyone else—we need you to stop him."

I tried to find the magic within myself but there was nothing. The blackout device, Parker said, attacked unnatural magic. Magic stolen, magic installed—magic given. That's why Oren had turned into a shadow. That's why everything I had was gone.

"No—can't." I tried to move and screamed again, the sound tearing itself out of me before my overloaded mind could even register the pain. "Nothing left."

As if my scream had summoned him, the monster that was Oren burst free of the Renewables trying to fight him and came at us, snarling. I couldn't even scramble back, my body too broken to listen to my mind's commands. The Oren-shadow snapped its jaws a few inches from my face, hungry and desperate.

I closed my eyes. My only regret was that when this was over, they'd know what he was. They'd make him leave this place that had become home. He'd be alone. I waited for the blow, hoping that he'd kill me quickly, without more pain.

But it never came. I opened my eyes to find the monster inches away, the white eyes locked on mine, teeth bared in a snarl. It growled with each breath in and out as it stared at me, motionless. My good arm twitched and the monster growled—I fell still. No sudden movements.

The only other time I'd been so close to the creature was in the alleyway in the ruins Above, where the monster hesitated. But that was because my magic was working on it, turning it back into Oren. I had no magic now, nothing to bring Oren back into himself.

And yet, I was still alive. And he was still a shadow.

"Take my power." Wesley shifted slowly, achingly slowly, so that both of his hands were touching my skin, one on my face and one on my neck. "Do it. Now."

I wanted to protest, but the dark thing inside me had sensed his magic. It wanted him, the hunger rising so swiftly and violently that it shoved everything else aside, all conscience, all pain. I was the shadow, I was the darkness. And here was my salvation.

I pulled at the magic with all my strength, hungry, feasting. The Oren-monster howled, and I wanted to howl with him—the magic was life and death and everything in between, and it was *mine*.

Dimly I heard Wesley screaming, trying to pull his hands away, but I held him motionless with a single thought. The air stank of fear, and the shadow inside delighted. I felt his heartbeat slow as the magic left him, felt his lungs struggle to rise just one more time. I watched with my true eyesight as the reserve of warm, heady magic inside him dwindled and faded, leaving an increasingly empty, black void.

Like Tansy.

I jerked, shoving Wesley away. The pain as I tried to move my shattered arm knocked me back into myself. I gasped, tasting blood. The lights had gone out while I drained Wesley—but I knew the Oren-monster was still there, snapping at me when I forced myself to sit up. His teeth closed on empty space—it was a warning, not an attack. I reached out with my other sight, feeling for the dark, empty pit in front of me that would be Oren. I eased out with my magic, trying to force it into the air faster. Willing him to change.

Abruptly the snarling stopped. Something moaned in the darkness—Wesley or Oren, I didn't know. And then, silence.

I lay there, gasping, eyesight sparking, trying to make sense of the blackness. I was afraid to look around with my other sight again, for fear the temptation to attack the Renewables would be too strong.

Eventually a dim glow appeared overhead, visible first as a glowing red filament of glass, then brightening until I had to look away. Basil stood by one of the dark, lifeless banks of machines, one hand spread against the controls as he slowly fed power back into the lights. He was bruised, the side of his face swelling where he'd struck the wall, and his clothes were scorched, but he seemed otherwise unharmed. The Renewables were ranged on the opposite side of the room, looking around, finding each other. One was on the ground, bleeding heavily from his shoulder where Oren had scored a hit.

Wesley was half-propped against the monitors, arms wrapped around himself, white-faced and sunken-eyed. I expected him to look away in fear and loathing, but instead he met my eyes. He was shaking, his muscles tight and noncompliant, but with an effort he nodded just a little.

Well done.

One of the Renewables—Curio—helped me lean against the bottom of the catwalk railing. He had a row of parallel scratches across his chest, torn right through his clothing, but they were shallow. He seemed otherwise unscathed. When I looked away from him, trying to ignore the allure of his magic as the newly awakened monster inside me stirred, he retreated.

I closed my eyes. All I wanted was to sleep, to go somewhere my arm wasn't on fire, where I hadn't almost killed

Wesley. I heard a buzz of wings, and a small weight landed on my good shoulder. Nix said nothing, but its tiny metal body was warm from the friction of its mechanisms, and it huddled close against the hollow of my throat.

Then a commotion jerked me awake again.

"Where is she? What did I—oh god, is she—"

Oren was back. They must've dragged his unconscious form away from me, because his voice came from some distance away. I opened my eyes in time to see him shove one of the Renewables aside hard enough for him to bounce off the railing, stunned. He saw me and came sprinting over, his long legs eating up the distance between us hungrily.

He threw himself down at my side, making me wince for the fate of his knees on the metal catwalk. Nix buzzed at him, irritated, and Oren snarled back, knocking the pixie off my shoulder. But he did it gently, I noticed—and the pixie gave an annoyed click of its wings and retreated to the railing, watching.

"Are you okay?" His voice was hoarse. There was blood on his face, on his clothes. When he reached out to touch my face, his fingers were tacky and warm.

"I think my arm is broken," I whispered. "But I'm okay."

"Did I—I remember you, in the darkness, I remember wanting to—" His voice broke, and he felt at my face, at my throat, checking me for injuries.

"You didn't." I wanted to reach for his hand, but my arm wouldn't move right. "You could have, and you stopped yourself."

He stared at me. "How?"

I shook my head. "I don't know. All your training. You controlled it, all on your own."

Oren swallowed, brushing my hair out of my eyes with his fingertips. "When I saw you up there—I knew you were going to jump. How could you be so—" I could tell he wanted to grab me, touch me somehow, demonstrate his frustration with my foolhardiness, but he was afraid to hurt me. Instead he just gazed at me helplessly.

"I didn't realize it would affect you. I'm so sorry, Oren, I didn't—"

"You idiot!" he interrupted. "I meant, how could you be so stupid as to jump off a three-story catwalk? You could have broken your neck."

"I had to stop Adjutant. He would've killed us all. I knew the impact would set off the blackout device and—"

Oren's fingers were exploring my face, and as they reached my lips, my voice stuttered to a halt. I wondered what I must look like—bruised, battered, bleeding in various places. But alive. Alive.

"Just don't ever do that again. Not when you're too far away for me to save you."

"I'll try," I whispered back.

Oren leaned down, brushing my hair aside, his lips touching my forehead for an instant before he broke away with a jerk. As if he'd forgotten himself, overcome—and now, remembering he wasn't supposed to touch me.

It hurt, muscles all over my body screaming a protest, but I leaned up anyway, brushing my lips against his. It wasn't much of a kiss, my arm radiating agony, his weariness evident in his every movement. But when I fell back again, hissing for my broken arm, he gazed at me, the pale blue eyes unreadable except for the surprise there.

"You're bleeding," he whispered, reaching out to trace his finger along my lip, where I'd bitten it in my agony.

I had to laugh, even though it was more of a groan than a laugh. "Now you know what it's like to kiss someone who tastes like blood."

Oren stared at me for a breath, and then, against all odds, he smiled—just for a moment, but it was there, and it was all for me.

CHAPTER 29

There are worse ways to recover from bone-shattering injuries than in a warm room, attended by an entire horde of resistance fighters who think you're a hero. I got so much attention I had to start forcing people to leave me alone just so that I could get some sleep. Olivia came to see me, and while her face was solemn and tired, I knew now that she didn't blame me for what happened to Nina, who'd been showing signs of regaining consciousness. Maybe the budding friendship was gone, but at least she didn't hate me.

There was still fear among the rebels—I was pretty sure none of them would ever fully trust me again. I was, in their eyes, something uncontrollable and dangerous. But I'd faced Prometheus and won. They were free. And every one of them wanted to come and see the girl who'd made it happen. Even when I got everyone else to leave, Nix stayed, perched on the bedframe, watching over me, criticizing me for staying in bed, chastising me when I tried to sit up.

But the healers among the rebels knew what they were doing. The healing sessions were agonizingly painful as they encouraged the bones of my arm, broken in two places, to knit together. But after only a few days I could get up on my own, move around, go to the bathroom by myself. This was of particular relief to Olivia, who was on Lark-can't-take-care-of-herself duty. As she put it, "If I never have to stand there awkwardly while someone pees again, I'll die a happy girl."

With Prometheus "dead" and CeePo under Wesley's interim command, the resistance fighters in deep undercover had come out of the woodwork. Only those of us who'd fought Adjutant knew the truth about what had happened there, about who Basil was. Wesley and the others had decided it would be best if the city knew only that Prometheus had gone mad with power and died. There was no identifying Adjutant's body—it was little more than ash and bone, only the scorched copper emblem of a flame to say that he'd been wearing Prometheus's robes.

Eventually I was able to come out of my room for good, learning to dress myself one-handed, operate doors with my left hand. The splints made moving awkward, but they kept my arm still, which the healers said was critical to my recovery if I wanted to ever have full use of my arm again. The idea of being one-handed like this forever was enough to make me listen.

Four days after the battle for Lethe, as it was coming to be known, the ache in my arm woke me from a nap and sent me restlessly down the corridor. The rest of my injuries had all but healed, the gashes and scrapes treated with bandages and, in a few places, stitches. My splint itched, but I ignored it, channeling the restlessness into movement.

I was looking for Wesley and the others in the War Room, but when I got there, I found only Basil, sitting alone. He'd visited me during my recovery, but only for short periods. And never to speak about anything real—about what he'd done as Prometheus, about what he'd do next, about the bond between us and whether it could be repaired.

I hovered in the doorway, watching him. He was flipping the pages of the journal—his journal. His brow was furrowed, gaze distant. Every so often he'd shift his hand, tracing his fingertips over the lines of a drawing.

When I stepped inside, he spoke without lifting his head. "I really did it all for you," he said softly. "I wanted a place we could be safe."

"I believe you," I said, making my way to one of the chairs so I could sit and rest my splinted arm on the tabletop.

"When you look at it a day at a time, you don't see what's happening. One day you siphon power away from a prisoner wanted for murder, because they'll be banished anyway. Then it's only those people convicted of treason." He turned a page of the journal, eyes falling on the last page, the one with my face on it. "Then it's anyone who opposes you."

My splint itched, but my heart ached more, and I leaned forward. "It's done now."

"And so is Lethe." He closed the journal with a slam, lifting his head and looking at me. His eyes grew even sadder—even four days after the battle, I knew I looked half a step away from death, covered in scratches and bruises. "Everyone's celebrating out there because Prometheus is gone and the Renewables are free, but it's only because they don't realize yet what it means for Lethe. Without the magic from the Renewables, it's over."

"You'll find a way," I told him firmly. "You're brilliant. You've always been brilliant. If anyone can save Lethe, it's you."

He shook his head, expression grim. "No, we're leaving. You and me, as soon as you're well enough to travel. It's over here. It was over the moment I knew I couldn't hurt you even to save Prometheus. Adjutant was right, I can't make those kinds of decisions. I never could."

My pulse quickened, and I fought to keep my voice even. "Basil, you can't leave. This is your city. These are your people now."

"But they don't know that," he snapped, fierce. Desperate. Afraid. Where was my brave, confident big brother? "They'll figure out that I was Prometheus, sooner or later. They'll all figure it out. But until then I'm just Basil Ainsley, and I don't owe anyone anything. You and I can go. We can find some other place, some safer place."

For a moment it was easy to imagine. Me and my big brother, on the road, striking out for territories unknown. We could leave all this uncertainty behind, all the guilt. I'd never see Nina or Olivia again, Basil wouldn't have to watch the long, painful recoveries of the Renewables kept captive in CeePo.

I closed my eyes. "You chose to make Lethe what it is," I said slowly. "That was the hard decision you made. You just didn't know, at the time, how hard it'd turn out to be. Believe me, Basil. I know what it feels like to run away. And you can't do it, not now. You're not going to find a safer place out there."

He dropped his head into his hands, fingers tangling through his thick hair. His face was worn, so much older than I remembered. Even though it had been years, in my mind's eye Basil was always still a child, still the age he was when he left the city. But the man sitting across from me was barely more than a stranger.

"Lethe is doomed," he murmured. "You're saying that you and I have to go down with it?"

"Maybe it's not doomed." My mind hunted for a path out of the mess, some way of solving this problem without more bloodshed and torture. Basil was always the problem solver, not me. I sucked in a deep breath. "Talk to Dorian."

"I saw he was here." Basil lifted his head, watching me. "You think he'll have ideas?"

"There are a hundred Renewables in the Iron Wood, at least." I spoke slowly, turning it over in my mind. "The city—our city, the architects—know where they are. They need a safe place. You need Renewables to keep this place safe. Maybe there's common ground there."

Basil sat up, brow furrowed. He didn't reply right away, but I could see him working it over in his thoughts, the same cautious excitement spreading over his features that he always had when designing a new fantastic machine in his sketchbook at home. "With that many, we wouldn't need full-time donors. They could go in shifts. Donating a little magic at a time. It would be hard—but not unbearable. They could volunteer."

I leaned back, grimacing as the movement triggered a new ache in my arm. Breaking it had been the easy part. This slow healing, clawing myself back bit by bit to fighting form—this was the hard part.

Basil's eyes flicked up, meeting mine. "And you say I'm the brilliant one."

I shook my head. "You spend enough time trying to outrun this darkness, you get better at finding alternatives."

Basil reached across the table for my good hand, cupping it in his. "I'm glad you're here, Lark. I can stay if you're with me. Maybe you're what I needed all along."

I fell silent. A few weeks ago all I'd wanted was to have my big brother hold my hand and tell me I could spend the rest of my life at his side. Now, though . . . now it was different.

"I can't stay," I whispered.

"What?" His hand tightened. "No. No, don't even joke about that."

"Something isn't right. Everything they told us in the

city, about the wars, about how the world came to be what it is; it doesn't make sense."

"What could that possibly matter to you now?"

"Everyone here—they believed the Renewables caused the world to be what it was, because that was convenient for you. If they feared the Renewables, then it'd be harder for them to hide. Easier for you to find and use them." I ran the fingers of my good hand through my hair, wishing I could straighten out my thoughts so easily. "Back home, we believed it was from a war, because it helped keep us in line, all working to run the city."

Basil shook his head. "And to find the truth you're willing to go back to a place where they torture children to power their lights?"

I thought of Oren and his secret, and of how we'd both wished we could unlearn it. The truth was never comfortable or easy. "The architects know something that no one else does. And if they know how this cursed world came to be, maybe they know how to heal it. At the very least, I have to know."

"But why you?" Basil's voice was fierce. "You've done enough. Stay with me, rebuild this place. Why does it have to be you that goes?"

Even as it all solidified into certainty, I felt a flicker of fear for what I knew I had to do. "I ran away, Basil." I swallowed. "I turned my back on our home the way you wanted to turn your back on Lethe. Our people are desperate, more desperate than you or Adjutant or anyone here in Lethe. I was the only hope they had, and I ran away from them."

He shook his head wordlessly, his eyes on mine.

"I have to go back."

. . .

320

I ate a quiet dinner in my room, alone but for Nix's company. At least this time my isolation was by choice—though the others didn't quite know what to do with me, they wouldn't have turned me away. Hero, villain—the lines blurred, and for now I was content to let the line stay blurry. Part of me knew that I ought to go out anyway, enjoy the company. I was never a social person back in my city, but my time alone in the wilderness had proven to me that even I got lonely. I felt almost as though I ought to store it up, like water collecting in a rainstorm, to last me through the drought to come. But I didn't want a drawn-out farewell.

I had my pack all set out. Basil knew I was leaving, and we'd made our farewells. When he realized he couldn't change my mind, he settled for telling me that we'd see each other again, when Lethe was safe. When our city was safe, too. There was my paper bird, crumpled, rescued from the depths of CeePo where I'd thrown it in Basil's face. Oren's knife in its sheath. Some cheese, some of the rebel-made grain bars that lasted for weeks, a packet of crackers. A water canteen. My running shoes, and my leather jacket with the tear in the shoulder neatly stitched up.

And the newest addition: a little metal flask of a clear, odorless liquid. Basil had given it to me, saying it was the way back through the Wall enclosing my city. When the Institute had sent him out, they did so intending him to come back and report on the location of the Iron Wood—it was Basil's defection from the plan that made them try again, lying this time, with me. I was never intended to return, but Basil—Basil had a way of getting back inside. When I asked him how he'd managed to keep track of it for all these years, he was quiet, and I realized the answer: he kept it because he'd always intended to come back for me.

"You're sure you want to go back there?" Nix was not a fan of

my decision and told me so at every possible juncture.

"I have to go," I said with a sigh. "I'm not trying to sacrifice myself or be a hero or something. But they're dying there, sooner or later. The Renewable they have will die, and then the city will have nothing."

"But they're the ones who did this to you."

"It was only a small group of people who did this to me. Gloriette. The other architects. Kris." My thoughts tangled as the image of the tousle-haired, handsome architect flashed before my eyes. "And even they were acting because they thought it was the only way to save the city."

"Trying to talk sense into you is like trying to fly into a headwind."

I tried to hide my smile. "And you love it. You're coming, after all, aren't you?"

Nix made an irritated grinding sound with its wings and then took off, headed for the ventilation shaft it used to go from room to room. I grinned, shaking my head. The little bug might be annoying and full of itself, but it was good company. And it was loyal.

I surveyed my supplies, trying to think if I'd missed anything. The people here would do just fine without me. They had Basil and Dorian, and Wesley too. If I slipped out in the night, there'd be no fuss, no pleas and no demands made.

There was just one problem: Oren.

I'd follow you anywhere, he'd told me in the Eagles' prison cell, back before everything had happened here. I didn't want to force him to put that promise to the test now that he'd found a home. He was different here, and even he had to realize that. He was quieter, calmer. Still just as strong and fierce as ever, but he was in control of himself. He was even in control of his shadow self—if only barely.

I couldn't ask him to leave, but if I told him I was going, I knew he'd follow. My only other option was to leave without telling him, and I couldn't bring myself to do that either. It was a betrayal nearly as bad as forcing him to leave this new home.

There was a tap on my door, and I jumped. "Oren?"

"Sorry to disappoint." It was Wesley, the door opening half a moment later so that he could slip inside. "I noticed you weren't at dinner and wanted to see how you were doing."

"I'm fine," I said quickly. I was standing in front of my bed, which was covered in supplies, but I couldn't be concealing much. "Just want to be alone tonight."

Wesley's eyes raked over everything arrayed on top of the blanket, then fell back on me. "Running away again," he said quietly, though there was no judgment in his voice. Just a mild comment on what he saw.

"Running back," I corrected him.

Wesley made a noncommittal sound. I waited for him to speak, to explain why he'd come to find me. Instead he just stood there, watching me, his expression difficult to read.

"Wesley," I found myself saying, "back in CeePo, when Adjutant called Basil Prometheus. You weren't surprised."

He inclined his head, conceding the point. "The possibility had crossed my mind."

"That the author of the journal was Prometheus himself?" He nodded, and I struggled to understand. "Why didn't you tell anyone?"

Wesley ran a hand across his scalp, not replying immediately. "Because when you're fighting an impossible enemy, your best weapon is hope."

"I thought I was your best weapon," I said dryly.

"Indeed," he said, although his tone was serious, not echoing the humor in my voice.

I swallowed, scanning Wesley's face. He was still a little

haggard, dark circles under his eyes. He looked wan in contrast with the brightness of his peacock coat, which no one had dared suggest he get rid of even though he was no longer posing as one of Prometheus's highest lackeys.

"I'm sorry I hurt you," I said softly.

He gazed back at me for a long moment, reminding me of the teachers I'd had back in my home city, pinning me to my chair and making me want to squirm. Then he nodded. "I know you are. But I knew what I was offering. And I *did* offer."

"I could've killed you."

Wesley smiled. "But you didn't."

"But I *could* have."

Wesley laughed. "We could be at this all night, Lark. Life is full of coulds and shoulds. Those things have no bearing on reality. You do what you do, you make the choices you make. I respect your choices. You should do the same."

When I had no answer for him he straightened, reaching for the handle of the door. "Goodbye, Lark. Be well."

I was left staring after him as the door swung loosely closed, thinking of all the exercises he'd made me do, learning how to recognize the point of death, how to automatically stop myself before I passed it.

Did he know? Could he have somehow suspected, all along, that it would come down to that moment—him offering his magic to me, me having no choice but to take it?

Before I could consider that idea any further, the door squeaked open again, shattering my thoughts. Oren was there, one palm pressed against the door, his expression locked down. His eyes were on the supplies strewn over my bed, and for a wild moment I considered using my reserves of magic to slam the door in his face and pray he hadn't seen.

But it was too late. I could see the betrayal in his gaze, the way they flicked from object to object, avoiding my face.

With a tiny whir, Nix darted out from behind Oren's head, and hovered over his shoulder.

"*Told you she was leaving.*" Though it was impossible, I could have sworn it sounded smug and petulant.

Traitor, I thought. When I turned my furious gaze on the pixie, it gave a startled screech and fled. So much for loyalty.

And so much for getting out of here without telling Oren.

"What is this?" he asked, stepping into the room and letting the door bang closed behind him.

"Oren, I wasn't going to—"

"No, you tell me now. What is this? Are you planning another scouting mission somewhere?"

He knew I wasn't. He was giving me a chance to lie, so we could both pretend. I lifted my chin. "I've been headed back there ever since I left, I just didn't realize it. I've got to go back. I'm done running away."

He closed the gap between us so he could speak in a low voice. "You're still healing. Your arm—"

"Is fine. The splint will stay on another week or two, and it'll be good as new. The healers have done what they can, now it's just time. There's no reason I can't travel."

"And the people here?" Oren's pale eyes were icy hot, jaw clenched. "You're just going to up and vanish on them?"

"They've got Basil and Dorian. They'll be fine."

Oren took a breath in and then let it out audibly—it was shaking. "And me? Were you going to leave without telling me?"

I stared at him, trying to catch my breath. "I don't know."

His throat moved convulsively as he swallowed. "What do you mean, you don't know?"

"Oren, you're happy here!" I burst out, suddenly angry—angry that he wouldn't just let me do this for him, angry that this wasn't just my choice to make. "You have friends here, you can do some good here. You're in control. You're living an actual life. You're safe here. How can I ask you to leave home behind?"

Oren was breathing hard, as though he'd just sprinted up a hill—as if standing in front of me now was some monumental feat of strength. "You think it's this place that's done all that?"

"Of course it is." I gazed back at him, the fury draining away.

"You still talk too much," he said wearily, taking another step forward so he could reach up, fingers tracing the line of a healing gash along my cheekbone. "And you don't pay any attention to what's really going on."

I wanted to shake my head and deny what he was saying, but his fingers were like fire tracing down from my cheek, across my jaw, down my neck.

"It's because of you, you stupid girl." Oren's brow was furrowed, his eyes not quite meeting mine—scanning my face. "This place is just a place. It's the place where you are. If I'm in control it's because I fought for it, to make sure I never lost it and hurt you. If I'm happy here, it's because I've gotten to see you become this warrior. It's you, Lark. It has nothing to do with where we are, except that it's the place where you are."

We were standing so close that I could smell his scent—here in civilization he was clean, with no traces of dirt or blood or sweat, but I could smell him all the same. Some fiery hint of the wilderness about him, that quality I could smell in the rain and the wind in the world outside.

"I should've told you before," he mumbled, wrapping an arm around my waist. "Before everything, before it could've been too late. But I meant it when I said I'd follow you anywhere, Lark."

"And if I'm going back to where this all started?" I asked.

"Then I'm going with you." He paused, breath catching.

"That is, if you want me. If you can see past what I am."

"You're Oren," I replied, dizzy. "That's all I care about."

"I'm a monster," he said gently, firmly.

"So am I." It came out in a whisper.

His mouth twitched again in that little smile, helpless, exhaling half of a laugh. Then, as if he couldn't stand it anymore, his mouth was on mine, and for the first time it was real, normal. He still had his darkness and I still had mine, and we were going to have to find a way to deal with them both. But for now it was just him and me, and our monsters would have to wait.

He learned harder against me—my good arm wrapped around him, pulling him close—I stumbled back a step until I hit the end of the bed. He gasped for a breath, then ducked his head, burying his face against my neck, lips finding my pulse.

Then something clanked, a whir of mechanisms interrupting us. We flew apart, Oren's preternatural reflexes sending him halfway across the room before Nix even popped out of the ventilation shaft.

"Are you done yet? Can we go?" The pixie affected boredom, sounding impatient. And, perhaps, just the tiniest bit smug.

I looked back up, meeting Oren's eyes. He inched back toward me, reaching for my hands again. His gaze was steady, calm, certain. And behind that all, I thought I caught a glimpse of excitement.

And I knew why, because I could feel it rising in myself. Maybe I wasn't the only one who had missed this. The journey, the danger, the sky overhead. Wind and stars and sunlight, and not knowing what lay over the next hill. A world so vast we could walk forever and never see everything there was to see.

Oren squeezed my hands.

"When do we leave?"

ACKNOWLEDGMENTS

Second books are hard. If there are any writers reading this, right now they're snickering and thinking, "Yeah, understatement of the century." The pressure is high, the glamour is low, and the novelty's worn off. (Well, for everyone else, that is. To me it's still pretty crazy that I get to do this!) But that just makes me even more grateful to the people around me who've cheered me on and supported me just as much, if not more, as on the first exciting day when I got to tell everyone I'd sold my trilogy. For those people who kept listening, even when I was in the depths of writerly despair, and considering changing my name and fleeing the country.

I'm so glad to have my family, my mom and dad and my big sister, all cheering for me—and commiserating with me when things aren't all sunshine and roses. And I couldn't do without my extended family of friends and relatives: the Miskes, Harry, Natalie and Rod; the aunts and uncles and cousins who ran out to buy the book as soon as they could; my strong Nana and my fearless Grandma—I feel so lucky to have all of you.

Thank you to my agent, Josh, and to Tracey as well, for being such awesome warriors. You make me glad you're on my team. And special thanks to Abby and Jessie too, for making me feel like part of the family!

I also want to thank my editor, Andrew Karre, for never flagging in his faith in me and my writing. To the rest of the team at Carolrhoda Lab, thank you for believing in my books!

To the other authors I've met and gotten to know over the past few years: I never would've gotten through this without you. Veronica, Beth, Kimberley, Megan, Kat, Sarah, Susan, Lindsay, Stephanie, Diana—having people to talk to who know what it's like on the other side of the manuscript has made all the difference.

All my friends are forever in my debt for being so understanding of my occasional crazy, especially my roommate, Caitlin, who's heard me run the gamut from shrieking about awesome news to throwing tantrums about feeling stuck and blocked. Also Kim and Frazier, for going out of their way to see me when otherwise, left to my own devices, I'd become a complete hermit and lock myself in my writer-cave for months on end. My Australian friends and family have been extra awesome—the day science invents a long-distance teleporter, I will be visiting you every day.

And finally, there's no one who deserves my gratitude more than Amie Kaufman, my critique partner, co-author, and all-around pillar of sanity. This book very simply wouldn't exist without her.

ABOUT THE AUTHOR

Meagan Spooner grew up reading and writing every spare moment of the day. She graduated from Hamilton College in New York with a degree in playwriting and spent several years living in Australia. She's traveled with her family all over the world to places like Egypt, South Africa, the Arctic, Greece, Antarctica, and the Galapagos, and there's a bit of every journey in the stories she writes. She currently lives and writes in Northern Virginia, but the siren call of travel is hard to resist, and there's no telling how long she'll stay there.

In addition to writing the Skylark trilogy, Meagan is the co-author of *These Broken Stars* with Amie Kaufman. You can visit Meagan online at www.meaganspooner.com.